Headturner

Headturner

Tanya Nicole Anderson

To order additional copies of this book, contact:
Xlibris Corporation
1-888-795-4274
www.Xlibris.com
Orders@Xlibris.com
68366

Contents

Dedication

Thank you to my family and friends and to everyone who has supported me and who has been a positive influence in my life. I appreciate you all so much more than you know.

I thank my mother Gwendolyn Johnson for her love and encouragement. My best friend Dora Williams for her love and emotional support and William Beverly for his encouragement and for making me feel unstoppable. Tiffany Piggott, Joy Anderson and George Anderson, I love being your sister. Deena and Steven Williams thanks for "adopting me". Thank you Dalayja Williams for always being so sweet and supportive.

Thank you Camille Renshaw for pushing me and giving me a listening ear. Thanks to Albert and Sharon Anderson for being just as excited for me as I was for myself. I'd also like to thank Aishah Hope and Delisha Scott for listening to and reading my stories as a teenager and for making me feel that I could write my own book someday. Thank you to Charisse Dennis for being there for me whenever I called. I'd also like to thank Michelle Watson for letting me vent when I needed to. A special thank you to the city of Cleveland for being my muse and last but not least, I thank you Lord for taking my fear away and for blessing my every endeavor.

I dedicate this book to my only son Robert Michel-Eden Anderson. Live to your limitless potential.

Introduction

Nicole was a fighter. She fought with her fists, her feet, her teeth and her nails and she would pick up anything that she could get her hands on. And she was a good fighter too. Ferocious like a pit bull. Kids that picked on her in junior highschool didn't tease her for long. Not after she did what Daddy Ray had told her to do. "Beat her ass!" He'd said "Get the one with da most mouth and take her down. Bust her in da mouth while she's still talkin' and do it when a buncha kids are around. If she can talk shit in front of 'um', then she can take dat ass whoopin in front of 'um too."

Shanique was the main one that always had something to say about Nicole. Nicole was quiet and stayed out the way, but Shanique would always stare at Nicole and make some sort of smart ass comment about her. Nicole wouldn't say anything back, and of course Shanique mistook, Nicole's silence for weakness and fear.

Shanique carried a heavy Louis Vuitton bag to school everyday. She claimed that it was so heavy because she carried a brick in it in case "any of these bitches wanted to step to her or got too fly at the mouth." Nicole ignored Shanique and her taunts until the day that Shanique tripped her as she was trying to walk down the aisle in homeroom to get to her seat.

Nicole had tripped and she had fallen into a desk in front of her, nearly hitting her mouth on the edge. Of course everyone laughed. It was hilarious that Nicole nearly knocked out her two front teeth trying to go and sit in her assigned seat. Wasn't it?

Anyway, Nicole didn't know what had come over her. All she saw was red. She picked up that heavy Louis Vuitton bag and raised it high over her head then came down with it over the top of Shanique's head, splitting her scalp. When Shanique attempted to stand, Nicole raised the heavy bag again and hit Shanique directly under the chin with it, causing her head to sling back and Shanique to bite her tongue. Shanique had cried out in pain and her mouth began to bleed. Nicole raised the bag again hitting Shanique on the side of her head as her head twisted violently with the blow. Nicole smacked that heavy bag across the other jaw as Shanique cried and begged her to stop. Blood was everywhere. Shanique was squealing in horror. Nicole imagined that she sounded like a slaughtered pig. Nicole wouldn't have stopped, had it not been for Dave the school security guard and Mr. Howard her homeroom teacher. Turns out Shanique really did have a brick in that bag.

Nicole was in big trouble and Mama couldn't make it to school. So Daddy Ray went instead. Nobody bothered to call Otis, Nicole's biological father.

When Nicole and Daddy Ray entered Mr. Todd's office they could hardly get in the door good before, Mr. Todd started in on them. He said that he was disturbed and appalled by Nicole's actions. Ray didn't say a word, but Mr. Todd seemed very intimidated by him, almost afraid. Mr. Todd spoke of Shanique's extensive injuries, but Daddy Ray seemed completely unphased by that. "We can't tolerate this type of behavior here at Wilbur Wright."

Daddy Ray had answered, "Nicole here is a good girl. She don't start nothin' wit nobody. But ya see she will finish it." Mr. Todd was in shock. Nicole couldn't believe that he'd said that either.

Nicole did as she was told and the teasing stopped. From that point on everyone knew that she wouldn't tolerate being picked on. Her reputation soon changed. She didn't have to fight anymore. At least not about that. They may not have accepted her dark skin or her coarse hair, but they shut up about it. Daddy Ray had taught Nicole lots of things. He'd also taught her the value of her "V". He told her that a woman's "V" would make a man do strange things and that her "V" belonged to her and that she should be careful who she gave it to. He told Nicole that her "V" was a very powerful thing. She learned a lot from Daddy Ray.

Nicole

She nearly tripped in her stilettos as he grasped her ankle with his huge clumsy hands.

"Get off me!" she said, as she shook her foot to release his grasp. His hand fell limp as it hit the pavement with a dull thud. She stood over him and stared down at him, disgusted by his weakness. She stared down at this big, strong man, face bloodied and lying on his side, whimpering like a bitch. She kept replaying their last night together in her head; she pictured him saying, "But I don't love her, I love you," as he cried, begged, and pleaded. And she thought to herself, "But I don't love you."

His body was lifeless now. She didn't know if he was dead or alive. She didn't care. It must have been the way his head hit the ground. It wasn't as if she'd shot or stabbed him. He did this to himself, she thought. Look at his punk ass. He was useless to her. What could she have possibly seen in him?

She stared down at him, left upper lip curled in contempt. "And you were supposed to beat my ass?" She spat at him and watched under the illumination of the streetlight as her saliva slowly sank into his dark curls. She laughed out loud as she recalled her initial conversation with him when he described himself as having "good hair." "Not a good-hair day for you, Darren."

She laughed the same sweet laugh that he claimed he loved most about her. Yea, right. It was the laugh that lured him out of his wife's bed and into hers. It couldn't possibly be the ample bosom or the booty. It was the laugh.

Darren didn't move. She laughed some more staring down at his lifeless body. She wondered what it would be like to pierce his temple with the pointed heel of her stilettos. She imagined it'd be like piercing a cantaloupe or a honeydew melon. She turned her right foot to the side and examined the thin, pointy heel of her shoe, then glanced at his temple, grinned, and then stumbled a few steps backward as she lowered her foot to the ground. She tasted blood at the corner of her mouth.

As her tongue moved across the small open area, it stung a little. She held her hand to her mouth, the place where the small cut was. She smiled and nodded. "It's all right. You got that one off." She took a few steps back, head cocked to the side, her long hair draped across one shoulder. She watched to see if he moved as she walked away. She didn't care if he ever moved again; she just didn't want him sneaking up on her as she tried to leave. But he didn't move, and she didn't notice the rise and fall of his chest.

She turned to walk away, and she took her time. It was dark, but she didn't care if it was broad daylight; there was a lesson to be taught. It was a night of discovery. Darren discovered the importance of keeping his hands to himself, and in a few short hours, Darren's wife would discover her husband.

Aniyah

She lay there staring at the back of his head wondering how she always ended up lying in the cold, wet spot on the bed, while he lay on his side away from her. He always told her not to be offended that he couldn't sleep without lying on his stomach, but he never actually slept on his stomach. It was always on his side. And it was always on the side away from her.

When they first got together and she spent the night at his place, she slept on the right side of the bed and he slept on the left. It was sort of an unspoken agreement. They'd have sex, make love, or whatever you want to call what they did, and he'd come, yawn, roll over, and go to sleep on his side away from her. She told him she didn't care when he'd tried to explain to her that he had always slept like this and that all his exes used to be offended by this turning-away thing that he did, but that she shouldn't be because he always slept on his stomach, which was really his side.

She told him that she didn't care, but she did care and she was very much offended by the way he turned away from her immediately after coming and yawning and then falling comfortably asleep as she lay on the cold, wet spot that, no matter what position they ended up in, always seemed to be on her side of the bed.

She sighed and tried to be very still so as not to wake him. It was so hard for her to sleep comfortably at his place. He always tried to make her feel at home, but she just didn't feel comfortable. Afterward, she'd lie there wide awake as still as possible, afraid that she'd fall asleep and inadvertently fart, snore, slobber, or sleep with her eyes wide open as her family said she was often known to do. She worked so hard to be pretty for him and to look sexy when in his presence, and she dreaded the thought of all that effort being destroyed overnight.

She stared at the back of his head. She wanted to go home. As a matter of fact, she wished that she could go home immediately afterward. Why not? It wasn't as if they cuddled. He wasn't going to spoon with her as she fell off to sleep. He tried to but it didn't feel like it was something that he wanted to do, so she'd told him that it was okay he could go back to lying on his side.

She wanted to gently stroke the back of his head but he was such a light sleeper, and she could tell that he didn't like when she did that. He didn't complain but she knew, so she stopped. It was difficult for her to lie next to him without touching him or staring at his body. She felt as if she had to literally hold her hands to keep from touching him. She'd watch him sleep, and he'd wake up to find her staring at him. She knew that he probably thought that she was crazy. She didn't know why she felt this way. Normally, she could care less if a lover stayed, cuddled, rolled over on his side, or went to sleep. But for some reason, with Nathan, she wanted to stay connected in some type of physical way after sex. She wanted her body to touch his body. She wanted her hands on him; she wanted to lay her palms across the soft skin off his smooth butt, her lips on his back, and her fingertips on his muscular thighs and to kiss him and feel the stubble on his face against her lips.

She thought about watching television, but he couldn't sleep with the TV on. He never told her that, but he would always ask her to turn it down so low that as far she was concerned, it might as well be off.

She got out of bed and waddled to the bathroom. She hated that wet, sticky, after-sex feeling.

"Where you goin'?" Nathan asked groggily.

"To the bathroom," she answered. She let the water run in the sink while she peed. When she was done, she soaped up her washcloth and cleaned herself up. She was going home to her own bed where she could sleep like a baby.

She saw him looking at her as she stepped out of the bathroom. She smiled and said, "Stop looking at me." She bent down and picked up her black lace panties off his bedroom floor. He watched her as she slid them on. She recalled how he'd told her that his ex wore nothing but thongs; he said it like he missed it. She'd replied to him, "I never wear thongs. They're too uncomfortable." She lied; she'd worn them, but she didn't particularly like them and after that comment, she'd thought if she wanted to wear them for him, she wouldn't do it now. He watched her as she put on her bra.

"What are you doin'?"

"Going home."

"Why?" he whined.

"I'm tired. I can't sleep over here."

"Why? I sleep just fine over your house. Don't go."

"I'm tired and if I stay over here, I'll stay awake all night trying not to wake you up, and then, I'll be tired in the morning and I won't be any good to nobody."

Nathan sat up on his side, reached over and pulled her on top of him, and kissed her on her lips. "Don't go." He nuzzled her neck sleepily. It gave her butterflies.

"I hafto. I'm tired. You're off tomorrow. Call me when you get up, and we'll get together and do something."

"It is tomorrow," he said glancing at his digital alarm clock.

"I'm leaving," she said, pulling away from him. "You know what I mean." She pulled her red sweater down over her head. He watched as she eased it down over her breasts. She pulled up her jeans. He eyed her butt as she fastened the belt around her waist.

"Ooh, I love your ass in those jeans," Nathan said. She could see him move his hands to his crotch from beneath the covers. She smiled and slid her shoes on. She grabbed her purse, cell phone, and car keys off his dresser.

"Okay, I'm gone." She leaned down and kissed Nathan good-bye. She could taste herself on his lips.

As she turned to leave his bedroom, he said. "Okay, I'll call you later, Tasha."

She turned to him slowly; her purse slid from her shoulder, down her arm, and into her right hand. Head cocked to the side, clutching the strap to her small black, Coach, she exclaimed, "My name is Ah-ni-yah!" she stressed every syllable. "How in the fuck do you forget that?"

"What?" Nathan said, as if totally oblivious to the fact that he'd just called her by some other woman's name.

"You know what! You just called me Tasha!"

"I didn't."

"Yes. You did, Nathan," Aniyah replied nodding her head.

"No. I didn't," Nathan answered, closing his eyes and shaking his head.

"I'm not going to argue with you. I know what I heard."

"You mad?"

"Naw, I'm not mad. As a matter of fact, I think you need to find Tasha since you can't seem to keep her name out cho mouth."

"Sort of like you can't seem to stop calling me Marcus."

"That was an accident." Aniyah smiled and was a little embarrassed recalling the last time she called Nathan by her ex's name.

"Three times?" he said sitting up in the bed and facing her. "Three times in the past week you've called me Marcus."

"No. I did not," Aniyah said shaking her head, with a slight smile on her face. Emphasizing every word as if that would change the fact that she did indeed call Nathan by some other man's name three times this past week.

"As a matter of fact, the last time you called me Marcus while we were having sex."

She gave him a half smile, shook her head emphatically, and said, "No, I didn't."

"Yes, you did. And every time I mention it, you smile. You think it's funny."

"I think it's funny that you think that I would call you Marcus while we were having sex," Aniyah said trying to hold back nervous laughter.

"You did. I was hittin' it from behind, and you said, 'Oooh Marcus,'" Nathan answered with a weak imitation of Aniyah's voice.

"No, I did not." She laughed. "I did not do that. You know I didn't do that. And if I did, why didn't you stop? I don't remember not one time this week or any other week that you stopped in the middle of sex because I called you by another man's name."

He laughed and said, "I am not a woman. You would have stopped if I called you by another woman's name during sex. Anyway, I didn't press the situation because you were here with me. And I had to handle my business." Nathan shrugged his shoulders. "That's all that mattered."

"Whatever, Nathan." Aniyah laughed. "I'll admit that I have accidentally called you Marcus before. By accident," Aniyah emphasized. "But you know that's not true."

Aniyah looked at Nathan and smiled. He smiled at her. She wanted to laugh.

"How about you stop calling me Marcus and I stop calling you Tasha."

"Agreed." Aniyah sighed and mumbled something under her breath.

"What was that?" Nathan asked.

"Nothin', I just don't understand why you had to go through all that."

"All of what?"

"You know what? Why couldn't you just say, 'Aniyah, it really bothers me when you call me Marcus.' Why do you hafto make a big scenario out of it?"

"What big scenario? I called you Tasha. And it pissed you off. And in pissing you off, it enabled you to feel how I feel when you call me by another man's name. Not just any man but your ex-man. You know. Somebody you've been intimate with that you shared three years of your life with. It bothers me that he's still on your mind," Nathan said, tapping his temple with his finger tip. "Sorta like it bothered you when I called you Tasha."

Aniyah looked at him and smiled. She didn't know why she kept calling him Marcus. It must have been some kind of subconscious thing. She absolutely did not want Marcus back; she didn't miss him; as a matter of fact, she couldn't stand him. It must have been the way they broke up. He was supposed to come and do a favor for her one day, and she never heard from him again. He just disappeared from her life abruptly, as if those three years meant nothing to him. She knew he wasn't dead because a mutual friend of theirs kept in contact with him. It was just strange to her that after a three-year exclusive relationship, he could call her and volunteer to do her a favor, one that she hadn't asked him to do, then never, ever called her again. And she never called him back to see why. Instead, she just moved on. Strange man, strange relationship. She was happy it was over; she met Nathan three weeks later, and the rest is history.

Nathan put on a pair of jeans and walked Aniyah to her car, trying to convince her to stay along the way. He was so tired, and she was wide awake. She would have liked it if he had offered to come along with her. But he didn't. He just gave her a passionate-kiss good-bye and watched her as she backed out of his long driveway and drove down the street. If he'd really wanted to be with her tonight, he'd have come home with her, she thought. But Aniyah didn't ask him to, afraid that his answer would be no.

Aniyah guarded her feelings in every relationship. They couldn't be trampled on, if she kept them to herself. Besides, her feelings didn't matter to anyone but her. If she didn't ask, then she wouldn't have to beg. And she could see herself asking Nathan to go home with her, him saying "No," and making up some lame excuse, and then, there she'd go begging him to come with her as if he was the last man on earth. Not Aniyah. If he wanted to be with her, then he would have to speak up. And he didn't. Instead, she was driving home alone with the remains of unprotected sex seeping out of her.

Aniyah tried to be hard and cold like she thought her big sister Nicole was, but it didn't come easy to her. She was very emotional, and it was almost painful for her to fight that part of her nature. She'd gotten a lot of practice though. Relationships had come and gone, and she had asked herself what she had learned to keep her from making the same painful mistakes over and over again. And the answer was unequivocally, "Not a damn thing."

Aniyah wondered how many men she'd have to go through before she'd be able to clearly identify "that one." She knew she was a lousy judge of character. She couldn't tell by how well a man treated her or by the sweet words they said to her or how they made her feel. Because they'd all treated her pretty well at first. She had to admit that they all came up with some damn good lines and if she wasn't careful, she'd fall for them every time. And each one of them at one time or another made her feel pretty good. But nothing seemed to last. And it seemed like men were coming and going in and out of her life, as if through a revolving door. This made Aniyah very unhappy, and it left her feeling very lonely and empty inside.

There was a void, and there was no denying that. And Aniyah filled it the only way she knew how—with empty meaningless relationships that ended almost as quickly as they'd begun. Her problem hadn't been finding a man; it was keeping him.

As Aniyah headed home, she'd decided she wasn't that sleepy after all. She drove down the street listening to Jill Scott's "The Way." And she immediately went into relax mode. She loved Jill Scott. Her music calmed her nerves and made her want to just chill. She sang the hook with Jill and smiled. She thought about Nathan. She really liked him. She wasn't sure if she liked him anymore than any of the others, but she was feeling something for him. Something strong that was indefinable at this time.

When "The Way" went off, she clicked around on her CD player until she found the song she wanted. "He Loves Me" is what she wanted to hear next. She sang and she drove. She harmonized with her as if she was her background singer. She was so into the song that she almost missed her cell phone ringing.

"Hello?" Aniyah answered, turning the stereo down.

"I miss you."

"Whatever," Aniyah said. "I just left you," she said, giggling a little.

"I know and I miss you. I miss you lying in the bed next to me."

"You'll be all right. Just turn over on your side like you always do, and you'll be snoring before you know it."

"I don't snore."

"The hell you don't," Aniyah answered, laughing.

Nathan laughed too. "If I snore, I only snore when you're around."

"Go to sleep," Aniyah answered.

She could hear the sleepiness in his voice. But she was glad that he called. She was glad that he was denying himself some much-needed rest for a little playful banter on her ride home.

"How far are you from home?"

"I'll be home in about fifteen minutes."

"Oh," Nathan answered.

"Why'd you ask me that?"

"No reason," Nathan said. Aniyah bobs her head to the music playing faintly on the stereo. "Can I come and lie in your bed with you?" Nathan asked as if he didn't already know the answer.

"Sure," Aniyah answered nonchalantly. "You want me to come back and get you? Or are you gonna meet me at my place?"

"Baby, I'm right behind you."

Aniyah heard a car horn beep behind her and she looked in her rearview mirror and she could see the shadow of a hand waving. It was Nathan; he was following her home. Aniyah saw that it was him, and a big smile spread across her face.

Fatimah

"Look Serena, it's late and I'm tired, don't come calling me about Nicole. I don't wanna hear about it."

"She's your sister too, Fatimah."

"Well, you can't choose your family."

"Nicole could be in trouble, and you don't even care?"

"Trouble always finds Nicole."

"That's not true, Fatimah, and you know it."

"I don't wanna hear about her, Serena, okay? So don't bring her up to me."

Serena sat on the line. She didn't say a word. It hurt her that Fatimah hated Nicole so badly. Neither of them would say why, but whatever it was had caused a huge chasm between those two that spanned seventeen years. Serena and her other sisters would try to speculate as to what happened to cause Nicole and Fatimah to become such bitter rivals. But nobody knew the truth.

Serena hated that Nicole and Fatimah didn't get along. Serena suspected that jealousy on Fatimah's part played a huge factor in the rift between her two elder sisters. Nicole was beautiful, successful, and wealthy. She didn't have a husband or children to tie her down, so she was able to experience life to the fullest. Unlike Fatimah who had married her high school sweetheart and had kids, and although she had her degree as a nurse practitioner, it wasn't of much use to her, seeing that she'd chosen family over much-needed clinical experience.

"I love you though," Fatimah said to Serena. But that wasn't any consolation. She felt that Fatimah hated Nicole as much as Serena loved her. How could that be possible?

"I'm not talking about me, I'm talking about Nicole."

"I told you, don't mention her to me."

Serena had an uneasy feeling about that Darren. From the moment she'd met him, she felt that something just wasn't right about him. She didn't mention anything to Nicole at first because she couldn't quite put a finger on it. Then, when everybody found out that he was still married, her suspicions were confirmed. Nicole left him alone as soon as she found out. No sobbing, or crying, or emotional good-byes. That was one of the things she admired most about her big sis—how she kept her emotions in check. But Darren wouldn't leave Nicole alone.

First, he responded with emotional apologies on her voice mail, texting her, e-mailing her, and sending her gifts and flowers. Then, he responded with anger, threatening her. The most recent thing he did that Serena was aware of was sending their mama an e-mail with a picture attachment that she couldn't pull up. The last she heard was that Mariah was supposed to stop over Mama's house to see if she could pull it up, that is if Mama didn't delete it. It was hard for her to keep up to speed on the Nicole-and-Darren saga with her being away at school. She felt like, next to Fatimah, she was the last to know everything.

Serena didn't mention Nicole again. Nicole was such a hot-button subject, and she didn't want Fatimah mad at her. So they talked about the kids, college, and the new man in Serena's life.

"His name is Eric. He is so smart, he's sweet and he's so sexy," Serena gushed.

"So how'd you meet?"

"We met in the cafeteria," Serena answered, including as little detail as possible.

She hated that she'd brought him up, but she was so excited about meeting him and he was an easy transition in her attempt to change the subject from Nicole to herself. Serena went on and on about Eric, totally oblivious to the fact that Fatimah could care less about her sister's escapades with some boy.

"Did you sleep with him?" Fatimah asked, bluntly.

"What?" she said slowly, dragging out the word.

"Have you slept with him yet?"

"Why you ask me dat?" Serena asked.

Fatimah sighed into the phone; she didn't have time for the back-and-forth. Serena didn't say anything. Fatimah didn't say anything. The pause was so long you could hear crickets in the background.

"What difference does that make, Fatimah?" Serena asked, breaking the silence.

"That's a yes then. I don't understand what it is about Turner women. Just can't seem to keep their legs closed."

"I can keep my legs closed."

"Well, then why don't chu? Where is your restraint little girl?"

"I am not a little girl" is all that Serena can bring herself to say.

"Well, act like it then. Close them legs and open them books."

"I'm doin' good in school, Teemah. Ask Momma. She'll tell you."

"Yea, I know you are, but you hafto maintain it."

"I don't believe this. You act like I just went to school to meet guys. I am doing very well here. Thank you very much." Serena was reminded why her phone calls to Fatimah were so few and far between. "I got this."

"Uh-huh. I want you to have it. You have so much potential little girl."

"I know."

"So don't screw it up," Fatimah said to Serena." I've gotta go, but I love you, baby doll."

"I love you too, Fatimah."

"And I can't wait to see you on Friday," Fatimah added.

"I can't wait to see you too," Serena replied.

When Fatimah hung up the phone, she couldn't help but wonder what was going on with Nicole. True she couldn't stand her, but she was still her sister. She wouldn't inquire about her though. It seemed she got more information by pretending she didn't care. But not tonight. Serena started talking about some silly boy she's dating, and she didn't get anything. Fatimah felt a little sorry for Nicole. She thought that Darren was the one. He seemed perfect. Almost too perfect, like the cherry on top of Nicole's all-too-perfect life. He seemed to slow Nicole down, and Lord knows Nicole needed to slow things down, before everything came grinding to a halt.

Mariah

Carl Jr. was knocking on the bedroom door as Carl Jr. always did when Mommy and Daddy were locked in the bedroom. Even though the children were instructed to never disturb Mommy and Daddy once the door was closed unless it was an emergency, i.e., bleeding or head trauma, Carl Jr. without fail would make his way to his parents' bedroom door. Unfortunately, Mommy was pleasuring Daddy at the moment, and he was just about to pop. Mariah tried to ignore Carl Jr.'s knocks. She looked up at her husband. His eyes were closed, and he was making sex faces at the ceiling.

Carl looked down at her and mouthed, "Not yet."

Mariah knew that her husband was begging her not to answer the door. She could ignore the knocks, but it was something about hearing her babies calling out her name from the other side of a locked door that was a deal breaker for her. And she knew her hubby was praying that Carl Jr. wouldn't say it.

Mariah enjoyed sex as much as the next gal, but at five months pregnant, it was becoming more and more uncomfortable. Less like lovemaking and more of a chore.

She could hear it in her husband's moans and she could tell by his body language, and she could see it in his face that he was right on the verge of climaxing, when Carl Jr. called her name from the other side of the locked bedroom door.

"Mommy!"

Mariah looked up at her husband, eyes bulging, jaws all sunk in like she was trying to suck a peanut through a straw. Carl looked down at her and shook his head. Another love session interrupted by his son.

"Mommy! PJ is dead!" Carl Jr. said, referring to their dog.

"Baby, did you hear that?" Mariah said, looking up at her husband. "Junior, baby, what did you say?"

"PJ is dead, he not movin'."

"Carl, how you know he ain't movin' when you're supposed to be in the bed?"

"I went to get a drink of water, and I saw PJ and he not movin'."

"Okay, baby, here we come."

Mariah hit her husband in the chest as she struggled to get off the bed.

"What?" Carl replied; he was used to the false alarms. Every single time Carl and Mariah made a date for some loving, something happened without fail. It was as if they sensed it.

"My baby found his dog dead, and you askin' him why ain't he in the bed. He might be traumatized," Mariah said to Carl. Carl noticed his wife struggling to get to the edge of the bed and helped his pregnant wife off the bed.

"Well, an obedient child wouldn't be traumatized, he'd be sleep."

They both headed to the bathroom to freshen themselves up a bit. Then, they put on their robes and headed into the hallway. Mariah put on her long red flannel robe and tied the belt just below her swollen breasts and right above her baby bump. She stepped out of the room to see her five-year-old son looking up at her with his big, dark eyes.

"Okay, baby. Where's PJ?" Mariah didn't ask where her ten-year-old daughter was. The daughter who was supposed to be watching a SpongeBob video with the little ones.

She wanted to know where in the house the dead dog was. She didn't smell anything, and she'd hoped he hadn't relieved himself right before he died. Cleaning up dead doggie doo was not a task you wanted to tackle at twelve o'clock in the morning.

"He's in there," Carl Jr. said, pointing into the living room.

"What's he doin' in there? Before we went to bed, he was locked up in the basement."

"How'd he get up here?" Carl said.

Mariah felt herself walking slower as she approached the dark entrance to the living room.

"Well, who turned off the light?"

"I did. I didn't want to see him anymore."

"Awww, my baby." Mariah hugged Carl Jr. to the side of her body and pressed him against her protruding belly; she gave his shoulder a squeeze as the baby inside kicks away.

"Well, if you took yo' little ass to bed, you wouldn't have seen PJ," Carl said under his breath. Mariah gently nudged him in his ribs.

"I can't see a thing, Junior where's the dog?"

As the child started to answer, Carl tripped over the dog's body.

"Dammit."

"What happened?"

"I tripped over the damn dog!" Mariah didn't chastise Carl for cursing in front of Junior. She thought that tripping over a deceased family pet was just cause for a curse word or two.

Carl clicked on the living room lamp. PJ was dead all right. Mouth open with his tongue hanging out, eyes slightly open. He looked scary. He looked big as hell too.

"Junior, go on upstairs, son." Carl looked at the dog. Actually, seeing this dead family pet made him a little more sensitive about the situation.

"Remember when I first got him Mariah?"

"Yea, Bay, I remember."

Carl shook his head. "Seems like just yesterday. I can't believe he's dead now. I wonder what happened. Hope the kids ain't kill 'um."

"Carl, don't say that.

"What? Our kids are bad as hell. Shit, we need to line their little bad asses up and interrogate 'um. Ask 'um, what the hell happened to this dog."

Mariah shook her head as she rubbed her stomach.

"Quiet as it's kept, we need to sleep with one eye open," Carl said staring at the dead dog in the middle of their living room floor.

"Stop it," Mariah said to her husband.

The couple crossed their arms and looked at their dead pet, unconsciously giving him a moment of silence. Both of them shook their heads, when Carl said, "Now, how we gon' get him outta here?"

"Ooh. You took the words right out of my mouth."

Serena

Serena laid on her back staring up at the ceiling. She turned toward Eric who was hugging an oversized pillow and gently stroked his hair and his cheek. Serena laid on her side and exhaled slowly. She had so much on her mind and she felt completely and utterly overwhelmed. She worried about Nicole and her crazy assed ex Darren, she thought about Hakeem her own cheating ex boyfriend and she prayed that she could keep him out of her thoughts. Serena thought about school and her studies as she stared at Eric and wondered how he could sleep so soundly, so peacefully.

Serena licked her lips, and rubbed her eyes. Things were moving too fast between her and Eric, they did seem really perfect for each other. But so had her and Hakeem.

Serena and Hakeem had had a crazy on again off again relationship. One minute they'd be at each other's throats and the next they'd be having mind blowing makeup sex, unable to keep their hands off of each other. Serena thought that they'd be together forever. She had never met a man like Hakeem. So stubborn, so bull headed. But it was his obstinance that had made him so attractive to her. Hakeem and Serena were officially broken up this time. She had said it was over and she had meant it. She hadn't called him and she wouldn't accept his calls. It was over. But she couldn't get him out of her head.

The natural scent of his skin was so hypnotic. She missed the feel of his warm muscular body pressed against hers. She missed the feeling of his lips teasingly kissing her inner thigh. And she missed the way he'd looked at her with such love in his eyes. Serena sighed and she touched

Eric's face again. Hakeem had really had a hold on her; Serena knew that she had to stay away from him or she'd lose control. She knew that she would. She still loved Hakeem so she had to keep her distance in order to stay firm and stand strong.

Chapter 1

AS HOT AS SHE CAN TAKE IT

Nicole stepped into her car and slammed the door behind her. "How did I get myself into this shit?" She said to herself, gripping the steering wheel. "I knew I should have left his ass alone the first day I laid eyes on him. Wasn't even my type."

She started the car and mashed the gas a few times; her tires spun wildly and kicked up dust and smoke as she smashed her foot down on the accelerator. The smell of burning rubber wafted through the night air and slowly dissipated. She stared at Darren's body as it lay in his driveway; he looked huge, like a beached whale, she thought to herself. She could have sworn she saw him move a little and a wave of disappointment washed over her. She wanted him dead. She felt like finishing him. She wanted to shift her Porsche into reverse and mash him into the pavement, leaving a crimson trail of blood and guts as she drove away; she smiled as she pictured his demise and then the smile faded.

"Yea, muthafucka, I dream in color," she said aloud as she recalled the day they met at the art showcase; he'd asked her if she dreamt in color, and she'd never answered him.

She looked to each side of her at the big beautiful homes and the well-manicured lawns. She watched as, one by one, porch lights clicked on and the fronts of houses were illuminated. She sat in her Porsche and let the top down, shook her hair, and let the long dark curls fall across her shoulders. The police would be there soon, she thought as she stared at each of the homes.

"Take a good damn look," she spoke as if speaking to each individual home owner. She knew that they couldn't hear her, but she'd hoped that they could read the "fuck you" tone as she sat alone in her car snapping her neck and muttering those words. She shifted the car into drive, slamming the gearshift hard. Her wheels screeched noisily as she drove away.

"Don't let your hatred consume you," a voice said in her head. But it was too late. It already had.

Nicole drove recalling the beginnings of the relationship gone bad, back when she thought that Darren would be the one to settle her down.

*   *   *

"I like it when you do that," Darren had said as he lay on the king-size bed in his apartment.

"You like it when I do what?" Nicole had looked at him puzzled, knowing that she hadn't done anything of any significance as far as she was concerned.

"I like the way you climb in the bed next to me."

She'd looked at him, brows furrowed and wrinkling her nose.

"They way you climb into bed one knee at a time. Like a jungle cat, a panther, or a jaguar. You're so sexy," he'd said before pulling her into bed on top of him and embracing her. She recalled how it felt to be in his arms. She couldn't adequately describe it, but it was close to feeling safe.

*   *   *

Nicole shook her head hard as if that was all it took to erase her memory. As if shaking her head would disperse those recollections like artificial snow in a snow globe. She thought about him as she drove away. She remembered how it used to feel to be near him. She remembered how—"Fuck 'um," she said interrupting her walk down memory lane. "I cannot believe this shit!" She wanted to kick herself. "What did I ever see in his sorry ass?"

She drove with the top down. The early-morning air was crisp and clean. She felt exhilarated, free. "I can go back to being me now," she thought to herself. "Because that shit wasn't me." Exclusivity and Nicole in the same sentence? Never. Or so she thought until she met Darren.

She never should have listened to everybody who claimed she needed to settle down. Why? Why did she need to settle down? She was just fine living her life. Hell, she was enjoying her life. She never envied the woman with the husbands or the steady men at home. Because Nicole knew their secret. Nothing was as good as it seemed or as good as people pretended it to be in most cases. Nicole knew many married couples, but no happily married ones, not a single one. They were either on the verge of divorce, trapped in a loveless marriage because of the kids or due to the bad economy, or one or both of them had another on the side.

She'd often see married couples that were in their eighties and married sixty years or more. She'd see their little aged faces grinning and watch their little arthritic fingers cling to the so-called love of their lives and instead of looking at them as a tribute to love gone right, she'd be thinking to herself, "How many outside babies did he bring home? Or how many nights did she stay up waiting for him to come home from his rendezvous with his women on the side? Or how many ass whoopin's did she take in the name of keeping her family together?" No, she didn't look at them and see wedded bliss. She saw sixty years of pure dee hell and waste. Because as far as Nicole knew, no man could be faithful. No way. No how.

No matter how hard they tried or how much they claimed they loved their woman, they still had the need to roam. It's in a man's nature to cheat. Who could blame them? Imagine being forced to drag around an insatiable creature with a mind of its own in your pants and see how you'd fare. She wasn't a man basher, and she wasn't mocking them, at least not intentionally. She just didn't think that as a whole, men had the stuff that it took to be faithful and stay faithful. Besides, a pair of tits and a nice ass couldn't be in the same neighborhood of the male genitalia without it reacting to it. It can't help it. That's the nature of the beast. Nicole accepted this as an undeniable fact of life; she dealt with it. End of story.

However, Nicole was well aware that women weren't blameless either. She knew plenty of women who stayed out in the streets and her mama, Tangie Turner was one of them. Or at least she use to be. Tangie had had a man at home and she flitted around as if she was a single woman. She'd always say, "I am not married to that man," referring to Ray. Daddy Ray was what Nicole and her sisters used to call him. He wasn't their step daddy, but he was as close to a step daddy as the girls were going to] get, and he was the man of the house or at least when Tangie allowed him to be. Tangie stayed with him from the time that she was sixteen up until the day he died. She spent their entire relationship chasing after a married man, who didn't love her enough to make her his wife, but could bring himself to screw her on the side all the while he was married, resulting in six children that didn't even carry his name. That was Otis, Daddy Otis.

*   *   *

Tangie had met Otis when she was fourteen and had had a huge crush on him. She used to light up when she talked about Otis—how fine she thought he was and how nice he used to dress. How he use to make her laugh and how he always played and joked with her. He'd ignored her advances though at first, without being harsh or embarrassing her. He knew that she was a young girl with a crush. He kept it clean and was as appropriate with her, as he knew how to be. But Tangie thought she was in love and she just knew that Otis was going to be hers some day and she'd wait.

Otis paid Tangie a lot of attention back then. Every man did. She was a pretty little red bone with thick hips and full breasts that bounced enticingly when she walked. She was a brick house. A fourteen year old brick house with the face of an angel and the body of a goddess. There wasn't too much that Tangie could do without bringing attention to herself. Whether it was jumping rope, playing jacks on the sidewalk just below her Mama's front steps or riding her bicycle around the corner to the store. She was a child who played as a child. She was somehow unaware of the stares and comments made by men and women alike. She couldn't help the way that God had made her. It wasn't her fault that men would stop and stare and drive slowly past her house as she jumped rope with her girlfriends. She couldn't help that men would drive slowly behind her watching her swollen buttocks mount the banana seat of her bicycle as she rode her bike through the neighborhood.

Tangie was a sight to see indeed. Her soft dark hair that her mother kept in huge spiral curls, draped across her soft shoulders as she walked. Her grandmother use to try to keep a tiny little bow in her hair with a bobby pin, to hold the hair away from her face, in an effort to remind grown men that they were gawking at a child, but it was to no avail. Tangie was turning heads wherever she would go, no matter how her Mama would dress her. If only they would have looked into her eyes, they would have seen the innocence of a child. But it wasn't her eyes they were looking at.

Otis had made an honest effort. He tried to be good at first. The attention that he had paid to Tangie had truly been quite innocent. But Tangie really liked Otis. He was kind to her and she looked forward to him coming by the house to see her older brother Kevin. She'd planted some seeds along the way. She had to make him curious. Her skirts started getting a little shorter, showing off her thick shapely legs and her shorts a little tighter, that accentuated her healthy curves as if they wouldn't have been already visible in more appropriate attire. After two years of temptation, he finally noticed her. But he wasn't the only one who noticed the blossoming sixteen year old beauty.

That was where Ray came in. Ray was Otis's best friend, and he lived with Otis and his family after a few undisclosed family problems. Ray was several years older than Otis. Dark brown skinned, dark features and a flawless smile. He looked like he could be a model. But there was something dark about his personality too. Tangie could sense it and as fine as he was, Tangie couldn't see past the uncomfortable way he made her feel. Ray had wanted Tangie at fourteen. He watched her as she ran behind Otis, giggling and grinning in his face. He watched as Otis thwarted the young girl's advances, and he imagined that she could be his. Ray didn't see any harm in it; after all, Otis didn't want her. Otis kept calling her a kid, but Ray saw her as fully grown and ripe for the . . . . plucking.

Anyway, as the story goes, Tangie had invited Otis to her sweet-sixteen party. Otis came, and Ray did too. Tangie snuck off with Otis in the middle of her birthday party and had her way with Otis, who at the time was engaged to be married. Thus, the start of Tangie's obsession and their very unhealthy relationship.

Tangie was well aware of Otis's impending marriage. But she didn't care. She thought she had him and that on her sixteenth birthday, everything would change. But it didn't. He wouldn't leave his fiancée. He'd told her it was a mistake—which was the worst thing he could have said to her. Tangie was hurt, and she thought she'd hurt Otis like he'd hurt her. She'd known that Ray wanted her. She'd seen it in his eyes for a long time. She just wasn't the slightest bit interested. He was very handsome. Actually, better looking than Otis. But she thought that Otis had more personality. She couldn't quite lay a finger on it, but Ray lacked something that Otis had.

On a whim, Tangie had decided to sleep with Ray. She knew that Ray would be eager. In fact, he took the extra effort to make it special. Not on the old mattress in Otis's basement, like on her sixteenth birthday, but in a nice hotel room. He'd even taken her out to dinner first and treated her like a lady. Tangie didn't care though; it was all a means to an end, to hurt Otis as he had hurt her.

Tangie had had sex with Ray, and it was much better than she'd expected. It felt better too. Ray was tender, and Otis was hasty. But Tangie didn't care. She loved Otis and that was who she wanted, and she wanted him to want her just as much as she wanted him.

Afterward, she thought she'd feel justified, but she didn't. Ray was in love and thought he had what he wanted, but Tangie was still unhappy and she'd felt that she'd made a terrible mistake. She wanted Otis to know at first. She more than hinted around that she wanted Ray to tell him what they had done. But she'd changed her mind and had cried and had begged Ray not to tell Otis. Ray was hurt discovering that he had been used and told Otis everything right away. This was something that Tangie would live to regret.

Sex had changed her somehow. Otis's forbidden fruit had opened her eyes, she'd become fully aware of how men looked at her and she could finally read what their eyes were saying as they stared and scanned her loveliness through the windows of their soul. Rejection had changed her from an innocent girl to a bitter and vengeful woman. Her love for Otis burned within her like an unquenchable fire every day and her hatred for Ray grew daily like a rabid weed, as she tried to make his life a living hell.

*   *   *

Nicole was a beautiful, confident woman, blessed with a fabulous body, and she exuded sex appeal. That wasn't arrogance. It was a fact. She had absolutely no trouble attracting a man, because she was an unmistakable beauty. She was a Headturner, just like her Mama. But she wouldn't let a man leave her broken and damaged like her Mama did. No one would ever say that she use to be fine as fuck like they did her Mama, because Nicole would never let a man drag her down like that. Especially not a man like Darren. Too many men out there to go around for her to allow that to happen. Too many men to go around.

It was miles between her house and Darren's house. She was angry, but she felt a combination of anger and euphoria. She felt jubilant. After months of holding her feelings inside and avoiding confrontation, she was finally able to release it all. Amazing what a stiff uppercut to the groin will do.

She'd replayed the events that led up to Darren's demise in her head; she knew she would have to hit him with enough force to drop him, because if she wasn't successful, he'd probably kill her. Nothing ever goes as planned, but she never imagined that he would drop like he did. She'd totally caught him off guard. He grabbed his crotch and let out a shrill scream, and he hit the ground like a ton of bricks. His head kind of bounced off the pavement. She looked around right after he fell, to see if something else had happened. But it was just the two of them in his driveway.

She'd parked her car in front of his house. She started to keep it running, figuring that it would only take a minute to say what she had to say to him and move on, then decided that it would probably be best to turn off the car because again, nothing ever goes as planned.

He was standing in the driveway, smoking a cigarette. She hated those things, and she hated him for lying about quitting. He was such a liar.

He flicked the cigarette out of his fingers as she approached. She sensed his nervousness. He pressed the cigarette into the ground with his plain black shoe. She smelled liquor in the air as she approached. "Good," she thought, "that'll slow his reflexes."

"Your rebound time is amazing," Darren said to Nicole.

"What are you talking about?"

"You know exactly what I'm talking about."

"Okay, whatever, that's not why I'm here," she replied and waved her hands as if erasing his words from an invisible blackboard.

"You see, that's your problem. You think that you can control every situation," Darren said as he pointed at her defensively with his thick stubby finger.

"Look, I don't even know what the fuck you're talking about! I didn't come here for this. I came here to look you in your face and tell you that it is over! Leave me the fuck alone! And leave my family out of this! Don't call me, don't write me, don't text me, and don't threaten me! It's over! I don't want chu anymore!"

He slapped her hard as if slapping those words out of her mouth. He reached for her and missed. She darted out of the way and punched him in his nose. He squinted as his nose stung and burned with pain. He grabbed her around her neck with one hand and squeezed hard. She gasped. His fingers nearly touched.

Her eyes bulged as she watched the blood trickle from his right nostril and into his slightly parted lips. He was enraged. He tried to pull her face into his. He tried to press his lips against hers as she struggled against him. He placed both hands around her neck squeezing harder. He pulled her face close to his, and she held his forearms and braced herself. She couldn't turn away, his grip was too tight.

Her eyes watered, and she felt him lifting her body from the ground. It hurt so badly, but she couldn't scream. She wanted to fight, but she knew that if she let his arms go, he'd probably take her head off. She was on the tips of her toes praying that he wouldn't lift her any higher. Her throat ached; she could barely swallow. She watched as he closed his eyes, leaned forward, and pulled her face close to his. He pressed his lips against hers; she could taste his blood on her lips and it turned her stomach; she felt nauseated. He lowered her to the ground and loosened his grip from her neck, and without letting go, he whispered into her ear, "I'll kill you first."

She squirmed and pried his thick fingers off of her neck. She pushed herself away from him. She knelt and poised herself like a character out of an anime cartoon. One punch, hard and fast to his groin. She felt like she had the power to hit him so hard that he'd do a back flip from his driveway to his front lawn. One punch, hard and fast to his groin. All that hatred and anger stored up in her fist and let loose on his most private of parts. She wanted to drive all night without stopping. She wanted to drive far away from Darren. She wished she could just drive forever and start over someplace where no one knew her and where she wouldn't be constantly reminded of all the stupid mistakes she had made within the past year. She didn't like how this relationship had changed who she was so drastically. She didn't recognize herself. She was lonely and unhappy. This mess with Darren had made her so bitter. She'd always been distrusting of men, but this just confirmed it. As far as she was concerned, all men were selfish liars. They were only good for two things, both of which she could handle just fine all by herself.

That confrontation solved nothing. She didn't want him back. She didn't want to talk it out, and she really didn't want closure. She wanted him to feel what she felt, and she knew that he never would. They never do. They hurt you, then they move on to the next. She swore to herself that she would never get emotionally involved. To invest so much of your time in someone just to end up hating them in the end was so painful, not to mention emotionally draining.

She could taste him. His kiss lingered in her mouth, and she couldn't stand it. She needed to get home to shower and brush her teeth. She debated as to whether she would take a long hot shower or soak under the pulsating jets of her whirlpool tub. Her neck was starting to throb, her head ached, and she felt like she needed an all-over-body massage.

Names and telephone numbers ran through her mind as she scrolled through her mental Rolodex to decide who would be the lucky man to give her one. Jermaine was the lucky man. Nicole decided she'd give him a try. Normally, on occasions such as these, Nicole would go for a young, experienced guy or at least someone she had fucked before. You can't go wrong with a guy who's made you come at least a thousand times in every room of the house. But tonight, she wanted to give Jermaine a try.

Jermaine was young about twenty-five years old and oh so sexy. He was tall, jet black, and fine as fuck. She liked his swag; he walked upright and with confidence, but he was shy as hell. He had been watching her for months and had finally got up the nerve to say something to her. They'd exchanged numbers, but she never called. He called her every day at first, but the phone calls became less frequent, because Nicole politely shot him down each time.

Nicole parked her car in the winding driveway in front of her house. She disabled the alarm and stepped inside. It was dark and quiet except for the tip-tapping sound her stilettos made on the ceramic-tile floor. She headed up the massive staircase and to her bedroom. She wanted to just climb on to her big king-size bed and sink into the plush comforter. But instead, she slid off her shoes, clicked on the light, and headed into her bathroom.

Her bathroom was huge: Jacuzzi tub on a platform in the center of the room, a glass-enclosed shower that seats four at the rear wall of the bathroom, a huge lighted vanity mirror that spanned the length and width of the wall adjacent to the shower and the Jacuzzi tub, cream-colored ceramic-tiled floor, brass lighting and fixtures throughout, and it's heated. Nicole set the timer on the wall and the heating mechanism was set.

She turned on the water in the whirlpool and adjusted the temperature of the water to as hot as she could take it. She ran her hand through the water in the tub and giggled, imagining the things she was going to get into tonight. She hoped he wasn't timid because she had every intention of giving it to him as hot as he could take it.

Nicole dried her hands off on one of the big, fluffy, oversized towels hanging on the towel rack in the bathroom. She walked into her bedroom to check her messages. Her answering machine was full. She fast-forwarded through voice after voice of men begging, men talking shit in high-pitched voices sounding like Alvin and the Chipmunks. She had to check her messages though because she was always open for calls from her family. But she didn't have time for those raggedy-ass men. She heard a high-pitched voice; it was Serena talking a mile a minute. She was asking Nicole if she was excited about her coming to visit next Friday. Nicole was excited; she missed her little sister, and she couldn't wait to see her. She wasn't sure if Serena was staying with her or if she was going to float from house to house that week, but she couldn't wait.

She stopped fast-forwarding when she heard his voice.

"Hey, it's Jermaine," he said nervously. "I've been trying to get with you for like a month now. Are you not interested in talking to me? I don't wanna keep buggin' you, but I really would like to take you out sometime. Give me a call if you're interested."

He left his number, and she thought to herself, "Aww, ain't he cute?"

Nicole jotted the number down on a notepad on her nightstand. "Good," she thought to herself, "he called me first, now it will look like I'm just returning his call."

Nicole never much cared how a situation looked or what others thought about her, but in this case, she didn't want it to appear as if he were her last resort or her only option for that matter. She simply wanted sex for sex's sake with the possibility of other encounters depending on how this session went. And she didn't intend for this initial encounter to be mucked up right from the start with this Young Buck thinking that he was getting over on her somehow.

She dialed his number. A sleepy male voice answered the line, "Hello?"

"Hello? May I speak with Jermaine?" she said in her naturally sultry voice.

"Speaking."

"Hello, Jermaine. This is Nicole."

"Pretty Nicole?" Nicole didn't comment. "Pretty Nicole. The one I always see at Ricos every other Wednesday night. Long black hair, pretty smile, bad-assed-body Nicole."

"There are a lot of Nicoles out there," she commented, trying to be modest.

"The stunna." Jermaine said. Nicole didn't say a word. She could tell that he was smiling, she could hear it in his voice.

"The one I've been trying to reach for about a month."

"That's the one." Nicole answered.

She could hear his voice perk up as if he was trying to mask the sleepiness in his voice. "What's happenin' lady? I'm so surprised you called me back. What time is it? One o'clock in the morning?"

"Yea, that's what I have. You feel like coming out?"

"Sure, what chu wanna get into tonight?"

She thought to herself, "You have no idea."

Arrangements were made for him to come to her house. He told her that he'd have to shower and he'd be right over; she knew he'd take a while. But she was patient; she'd wait. As if she had a choice.

Nicole undressed. She tossed her designer clothes on the floor and walked into her bathroom naked. She admired her nude body from all angles in her bathroom mirrors: her full, perfect breasts; flat, toned stomach; tiny waist; full, thick hips and thighs; and a perfectly full round booty. She knew she was blessed. She wasn't just easy on the eyes; she was beautiful to look at.

Nicole wasn't a petite woman. She was tall and shapely with a long dancer's torso. Her dark brown skin was flawless as if dipped from head to toe in the finest chocolate. Her large almond-shaped eyes were framed with thick perfectly arched brows and long dark lashes. Long, thick black hair that took hours of maintenance cascaded down her back and over her shoulders. She wasn't the glamour mag's idea of beautiful, but she was stunning, even with her hair tousled and dried blood on her face. She was still quite lovely.

Nicole laced her bathwater with her signature freesia-scented bubble bath and bath salts. She soaked under the pulsating jets of the Jacuzzi. She didn't light her scented candles; she didn't have much time, but she did dim the lights and she turned on the stereo that was built into her bathroom walls.

She listened to Tyrese's "Signs of Lovemaking" as she bathed. It pleased her to imagine turning this young man out. It excited her to imagine him climbing the walls. She touched herself as she pictured herself pleasuring him in the middle of her bed and watching him kick and scream his way to orgasm. She had big plans for this young man at nearly two in the morning. She hoped he was up for the task.

She rubbed her body down with her fragrant shea butter and sea-salt scrub as she listened to Eric Benet's "Pretty Baby." Her body would be smooth and soft, and she'd smell delicious when he arrived.

She dried herself and applied body oil. Then brushed her teeth and put on a sheer red laced bra and panty set. She inspected her face in her bedroom mirror. She couldn't see the cut at the corner of her mouth, but she could feel it. It stung. She put a dab of antibiotic ointment there and put a natural-looking shade of lip gloss on her lips. She rubbed her lips together and stared at herself in the mirror and debated as to whether she'd wear her hair up or down. Down was less fuss, so she kept it down. She inspected her body to make sure she looked as sexy as she felt and she did. She put on a short satin robe, tying the belt snuggly around her waist, which really accentuated her curves.

She stood in front of the mirror and stared at herself. She looked good, but something wasn't right. But what was it? Stilettos or no stilettos? Should she wear the robe or shouldn't she wear the robe. "Hmmm?" she thought as she further examined herself in the mirror. Aha! It was the underwear. She untied the robe, removed the bra, and slid the red-lace panties off. She then put on the robe, tied it snuggly around her waist as before, and stepped into her black, strappy Jimmy Choo stilettos. They made her feel so sexy as if she didn't feel sexy enough.

When the doorbell rang, she couldn't get down the stairs fast enough. The winding staircase was one of the biggest selling points when she bought the house, but it was a bitch trying to get down them quickly, wearing a pair of stilettos. When she made it to the bottom of the stairs, she tried not to look over eager; she stopped and caught her breath. She believed that women emitted some kind of scent that alerted men that they were horny, and she hoped that it was somehow camouflaged by her beauty regimen. She'd gotten herself all worked up just thinking about the endless possibilities.

Nicole opened the door for Jermaine. His eyes lit up when he saw her. He didn't notice the robe right away. He enjoyed looking into her face.

"You are so pretty."

She smiled.

"Were you surprised that I returned your call?" she asked.

He noticed the robe. He ran his hand over his mouth and beard and looked her over. He wasn't trying to be discreet. But he didn't want to stand there drooling either.

"I was surprised but happy," he answered.

Nicole led him through her foyer past the staircase and into a huge living area.

"Care for a drink?"

"No, thank you," he said, staring at her ass as she walked away. "You have a beautiful home."

"Thanks, you want a tour?"

"Sure."

"Let's start upstairs with my bedroom." She smiled seductively as she walked toward the staircase."

Jermaine grabbed Nicole by the hand. "Why not start here?" Jermaine pulled her close to him. He kissed her, his lips soft, his mouth so warm. "Good kisser," Nicole thought to herself and wondered what that warm mouth would feel like between her legs.

He smelled so good. She wanted to rip his clothes off and devour him.

Jermaine tugged at the belt of her robe like he was pulling a parachute's rip cord. Her robe fell to the floor. She loved the look on his face as he furrowed his brows. "So sexy." She thought to herself. He mouthed the word "Oooh" as her nakedness was revealed. Nicole wrestled with Jermaine's belt, and his pants dropped to the floor. His erection forming a tent underneath his boxers. Nicole reached inside. He liked the look on her face too.

She wanted him now. No foreplay, no formalities. But Jermaine had other plans for Nicole. Jermaine backed her into the chaise lounge and told her to turn over onto her stomach. He massaged her neck and back, leaving a trail of wet, hot kisses along her spine. Her body was so soft, and she smelled so good. Clean like a fresh shower.

Jermaine grabbed two heaping handfuls of her butt and massaged. He spread her legs and stuck his finger inside of her vagina.

"Ooh you're so wet." Jermaine licked her like an ice-cream cone. As he held her butt in each hand. His mouth so warm, so wet. He felt so good.

She moaned with pleasure. She closed her eyes as he licked her and pushed his finger in and out of her deeper and harder. With every thrust, he could feel her walls tightening around his fingers, and he could hardly wait to be inside her.

He enjoyed hearing her moan as he pleasured her. And as much as he wanted to hit it from behind, he told her to turn over. He wanted to see her face. He wanted to see her face when she came.

Nicole felt as if she needed this release. She felt she deserved to lie back and allow this young man to work on her. "Yea, work it out, baby," she whispered.

She oohed and aahed as if easing into the hottest bathwater. She let her walls clinch and tighten around his manhood as he dug deeper and deeper inside of her. She'd found a rhythm that he enjoyed. His eyes rolled up in his head, and she could tell he was fighting orgasm. Jermaine shook his head as if shaking that feeling away. Nicole made eye contact with him as she squeezed her breasts in her hands, her nipples hard and dark protruded between her curved fingers. She watched as beads of sweat ran down his brow, down his face, down his neck, and then down his chest. As good as he felt to her, she wanted to make him come. She wanted him to feel like she was too much for him. She prided herself in that. She looked at him and ran her tongue across her right nipple. He moaned and his body jerked from sheer excitement.

Nicole threw both legs up over his shoulders and arched her back a little. She continued her Kegel rhythm as she arched her back and grinded her body against his in concentric circles. She moved slower then faster, depending on his reaction to her movements. He held her butt in his hands, lifted her bottom off the chaise lounge, and pounded away.

"Oooh you feel so good," she moaned as she ran her fingertips down his chest and rested on his tight abs. She watched as he moved in and out of her. She listened to her own wet and slippery sound. His eyes were closed, and she watched the sweat run down his face. His body glistened. He jerked again and bit his bottom lip.

Then he lowered her bottom on the chaise and pulled out, breathing heavily.

"Are you finished?" she asked, concerned that he hadn't come. She'd come several times, but she hadn't reached the Big O. She wasn't done.

"Nope," he said, beckoning her to sit up. When she did, he lifted her over his shoulder. "Take me to your bedroom. I'm ready for the rest of the tour."

Jermaine carried her up the staircase over his shoulder effortlessly. She was impressed. She liked the way their reflection looked in the huge hallway mirror. There was something primal about it, and it turned her on even more. He stood there in front of the huge wooden mirror and waited for Nicole to tell him which room to go in. As he walked down the hallway toward her room, the intermittent light made shadows of their naked bodies. They literally looked like one person. Their shadow was grossly distorted but beautiful like contemporary art.

He walked into her bedroom past the clothes strewn on the floor. He laid her down on the bed, next to the red underwear. He picked up the laced panties, held them to his face, and inhaled her sweetness.

"You smell so delicious." He said to her as he gave her what she thought was the sexiest look in the world, along with a devilish smile

Nicole spread her legs invitingly. Jermaine buried his face there. Nicole writhed and moaned with pleasure. Jermaine teased her clit with the tip of his tongue as Nicole tried to fight orgasm. He darted his tongue in and out of her then slowly ran it back up to meet her clit. She thought she was about to explode.

Nicole was impressed. But Jermaine didn't know her. He didn't know that she'd been here before, at this place called ecstasy. She wasn't just a visitor; she lived there, and she'd had many traveling companions. She looked at Jermaine's sweat-covered body glistening like a slowly melting bar of chocolate. They enjoyed each other in every way imaginable. Yes, this young man was worth the phone call, and if he didn't get too hooked like the others, then she'd call him again for a repeat performance.

Spent and exhausted, Jermaine stared into her eyes as they lay there on their stomachs facing each other. He moved a long dark curl away from her eyes and said, "You okay?"

"Oh, I'm fine."

"I know you're fine, but are you okay?"

She smiled. "Yes. I'm okay," she answered as she nuzzled her face into the crook of her left arm and faced him.

"I'm just askin' 'cuz I know I put it on you."

Nicole laughed and answered, "Yea, you put it on me." He didn't notice her patronizing tone.

Jermaine went on to tell Nicole how much he enjoyed her. He couldn't keep his hands off her as he spoke. He stroked her butt, her back, and her hair. He wanted to kiss her, but he didn't. He knew she wouldn't ignore his phone calls after this. He knew he had her climbing the walls. And Nicole was hands down the best lover he'd ever had. This night was so much better than he could have imagined. She was so uninhibited. Tantric.

Nicole had a great time too. She thoroughly enjoyed Jermaine. But wasn't she supposed to? Wasn't that the whole purpose of inviting him over in the first place? Jermaine was an excellent lover. But so was Marcus, Bill, Benjamin, Tim, and so on. Sex for sex's sake. Nothing more and nothing less. She wouldn't make the mistake of feeling otherwise again.

Chapter 2

SHE'LL NEVER TELL

The children were hysterical when Carl Jr. told them that PJ was dead. Tamia bounded down the stairs, screaming uncontrollably and ran right into her mother's stomach, sobbing. Mariah flinched as the baby kicked.

"My dog! What happened to my dog?!"

"I don't know, baby. Come on, let's go in the kitchen." Before Mariah could lead her into the kitchen, the rest of the crew came down, all but three-year-old Tyler. Tyler could sleep through anything. Mariah sat her crying children at the kitchen table and heated a pot of water for cocoa.

"Mommy, what happened?"

"I don't know, baby." The last time Mariah saw PJ, he was in the basement in his cage, alive. "I don't even know how he got out of his cage," Mariah said, eyeing the children at the table. "Does anyone know how PJ got out of his cage?"

No one said anything.

"Maybe he bit through the bars," seven-year-old Zenobia said quietly.

"No, my dog didn't chew through his cage. It's metal, stupid!" Tamia said to her younger sister.

"Tamia!" Mariah exclaimed, scoldingly. "Don't talk to your sister like that."

"Mommy, that was stupid. PJ didn't chew through his cage, crawl upstairs, and kill himself!"

"Tamia! Don't be mean. I don't like that. PJ was not just your dog, he was everybody's dog. We all loved PJ."

Mariah made the cups of cocoa and added mini marshmallows, being careful to add equal amounts to each mug. She sat at the table with her children. Mariah cooled the three little ones' cocoa off with a small piece of ice. She wiped tears off faces and tried to comfort them as best she could. They sat and talked about PJ as they drank their cocoa, each one adding a story. The tears flowed.

Mariah cried a little, too, remembering when Carl bought PJ home. Tamia had just turned two. Mariah didn't want a dog. She didn't want her baby around a dog. She didn't want a dog in her house. Plus, she had a hard-enough time keeping up with Tamia. She knew that she'd be the dog's primary caregiver because Carl was way too busy with his contracting business to even help her at home with their daughter. Carl insisted that she'd love the dog; he'd even said that if she didn't fall in love with him, then she could just say no and he'd never mention that dog or any other dog again. But when she met PJ, he was the cutest little thing and he kept nipping at her heels as if begging her not to leave, and she just couldn't say no. Tamia really loved him too. Little did she know that she was pregnant with Shant`e, at the time. Had she known, she probably would have answered differently.

Carl called her into the living room and told her to take the children upstairs. His brothers were coming over to help him dispose of the dog. Mariah took the children to Tamia's room and went in to check on Tyler; he was sound asleep. They watched the SpongeBob movie that they were supposed to be watching earlier until they all fell asleep on the bedroom floor like a litter of kittens.

Mariah ran some warm bathwater and joined her husband downstairs in the living room. PJ was gone. Carl didn't tell her how they disposed of the dog, and Mariah didn't ask. She kissed her husband and told him, "Come on upstairs."

She loved PJ, but there was no getting in her bed without bathing after handling a dead dog.

That morning, Mariah was the first to wake up. She couldn't sleep and her little Ukulele kept moving around inside her belly, and if baby wasn't comfortable, then Mariah wasn't going to be comfortable. Mariah eased her legs over the side of the bed and let them dangle a bit. She held on to the edge of the bed and hung her head as she watched her legs swing listlessly over the side. She sighed and grunted a little as she scooted off the edge of the bed. Easing her feet down to the floor, first the tips of her toes, then the balls of her feet, and then her heels until finally she was standing teetering on weary legs. She waddled to the bathroom on tender, swollen feet. Mariah preferred to soak in the tub, but she knew she'd never get up without help and she didn't want to disturb her sleeping husband. She yawned, stretched, and started to scratch a particularly itchy spot on her mid-upper back but couldn't reach it.

Frustrated, she gave up and turned on the shower.

The rest of her family slept in, including Carl. Carl owned a contracting business with his three brothers. For twelve years, he had been on the grind, trying to get his business off the ground, and finally, it was happening. Life was good. This was the first time that Mariah had gotten pregnant without Carl going into panic mode. He felt like he could finally afford to take care of his family.

Carl was a workaholic, but not today. Today, he'd spend with his family. He didn't know what to say to his kids to make them feel better, but he knew he wasn't going to ignore the fact that they had suffered a loss. He was raised by a distant, inattentive father who was always present, but he was never available emotionally. Carl swore that he wouldn't be the same way.

Carl's dad was a hardworking man and a good provider. Carl was like his father in that respect. But Carl's dad didn't know how to be a father to his children. He was firm and strict, and somehow, his children knew that he loved them, but he didn't quite know how to show it. Carl's dad had never been a very good communicator. Now at seventy-two years old, his dad loved everybody. Every loved one that came by the house, his dad said "I love you" to them. That's how he ends his conversations now. Carl wasn't going to wait until he was seventy-two.

Mariah made a big breakfast with everyone's favorites. Her family would be awakened to the fragrant aroma of french toast, bacon, eggs, sausage, pancakes, and flaky buttered biscuits. Tyler would have grits and bacon. Those were his favorites.

Tyler and Mariah were the only two up. Tyler was trapped in a high chair while his mommy finished cooking. Tyler whined and begged to get down, and he begged for juice from his special sippy cup. Unlike her husband, Mariah had mastered the art of ignoring whiny babies as she called it. Periodically, Mariah would walk past her son and kiss him on his forehead as he reached for her face.

"Does my baby want some bacon?" Mariah asked as she handed him a strip of bacon. Tyler could eat bacon for breakfast, lunch, and dinner. On bad days, she was tempted to feed him just that to keep him quiet and out of trouble. She reasoned that his pediatrician, Dr. Lewis, said it would be okay.

The phone rang, and Mariah answered on the first ring.

"You awake?"

"Yea," Mariah answered hesitantly. She didn't recognize the voice. "Who is this?"

"It's yo' sister, fool!" Mariah instantly recognized Aniyah.

"Good Lord. Clear your throat or somethin'. Take that bass out cho your voice."

"I just woke up," Aniyah said, clearing her throat. "How's my babies?"

"They're okay, I guess. Considering that PJ died last night."

"Oh my god. What happened?"

"We don't know. Junior found him dead early this morning at about midnight."

"Oh my god, Mariah. I'm so sorry to hear that. How's he handling it?"

"Actually, he took it pretty good. He didn't start cryin' till Tamia started up, as a matter of fact, once Tamia started, everybody started."

By now, the entire Daley clan started filing down the stairs eyes red and swollen. Each one kissing their mother as they took their seat. Carl was not far behind.

"I bet nobody bothered to brush their teeth," Mariah said to her children as she covered the phone's mouthpiece.

"It makes more sense to brush your teeth after you eat mother," Tamia said sarcastically with a smile.

"You are always trying to find some way to get smart with me on the sly."

Tamia giggled and smiled at her mother.

Carl grabbed his wife around the waist and kissed her full on the mouth.

"Daddy, did you brush your teeth?" Tamia asked.

"Don't worry if my baby brushed his teeth. He knows not to get in people's face with morning breath. Hmmm." Mariah said to her daughter and kissed Carl again.

"Hmmm," Tamia responded and smiled at her mother.

"Let me speak to them," Aniyah yelled into the receiver, feeling ignored. She recognized the muffled sound in the phone, and she knew Mariah's ear wasn't to the phone.

"No, no," Mariah whispered into the phone, "they're okay now. I don't want you getting them started."

"Okay, well, tell everybody I said 'Hi.'"

"Auntie Niyah said 'Hi.'"

"Hey, Auntie Niyah!" the kids said in unison.

"Let me speak to her!" Tamia said.

"About what?" Mariah asked.

"Mommy!"

Mariah glared at her.

"Put her on the phone." Aniyah yelled.

"Here, Tamia, and no beggin'."

"All right, Mommy. Gosh," Tamia whined. Carl started preparing plates of food. Grits and bacon for Tyler. Tamia tried to get up from the table, and her father directed her to sit back down. "Auntie, I'mo call you back so we can talk in private, okay?" Aniyah agreed, and they got off the phone.

"A closed mouth don't get fed. Right son?" Carl said to the crying toddler as he placed the bowl of grits and two slices of crumbled bacon on his high-chair tray. Carl leaned down and kissed the toddler on his forehead. Youngest to oldest fed first. Carl got his plate last.

Mariah sat in front of her plate, rubbing her belly. She was not very hungry, and her legs felt tired. She felt like lying down.

"You okay, Mommy?" Junior asked.

"I'm okay, baby." Mariah smiled at her son. She appreciated how much he paid attention to her. He was always very concerned about his mommy.

"I think I cooked too much food."

"You always cook too much food," Carl answered, smacking on his eggs and bacon.

"I think I need to call my sisters," Mariah said, with that melancholy look in her eye. Carl started to eat faster. "Honey, slow down." Mariah laughed.

"I just want to hurry up and eat and get out of y'all way."

"Stop acting like you don't like my sisters."

"Baby, I love yo' sisters," he said, smiling and talking with his mouth full. "But if you plan on inviting Fatimah and Nicole, you'd better move the furniture out the way, because that last time they got together over here, Nicole nearly broke Fatimah's back on the old cocktail table."

"Nicci paid for it. And why you gotta bring that up? Stop focusing on the negative." Mariah said as she glanced over at the children.

"I'm not focusing on the negative. I'm just keepin' it real. Keep 'um away from the big screen," Carl said, laughing.

"Carl, stop it." She waved her hand at him.

"I'm serious."

Carl told the children that he had something special planned for them and that they should get washed up and dressed. The children were so excited that they quickly finished up their meal. The weatherman forecasted rain for today, so they packed up raincoats and umbrellas. It was a beautiful, sunny Saturday morning and Carl wanted to get out and enjoy it with his kids while it lasted.

Carl knew that his wife's family had their share of problems, but it was very difficult for him to get used to it. His mother-in-law didn't like her oldest daughter Nicole, and no one knew why. Mariah's two oldest sisters Nicole and Fatimah couldn't be in the same room without arguing or coming to blows, and again, no one knew why. But what was so strange about it all was that no one would ever ask, because no one ever wanted to talk about it. Everyone was quite comfortable with ignoring the situation as if nothing was wrong or as if the problem would solve itself eventually.

It was so confusing to the point that Carl thought he was crazy. He wanted to talk to somebody about it, but the only other brother-in-law was Jason, Fatimah's husband, and he definitely had his own issues.

Mariah called her sisters and invited them over for brunch. Nicole and Fatimah declined, and she didn't ask why. Aniyah was over in fifteen minutes. She hugged her sister and rubbed her belly saying, "Hi, Ukulele," which was the nickname Mariah had given the baby. Carl hated the nickname. "What if it's a boy?" he'd say. "It's not," Mariah would always answer as if she already knew for sure that they were having a baby girl.

The sisters laughed and talked. Aniyah kept her updated on her and Nathan. She told Mariah what Nathan accused her of doing. The sisters talked under their breaths as Mariah's family got ready for their outing.

"Well, did you?"

"No!"

"You probably did."

"No, I didn't."

"You've even called him Marcus to me."

"That was an accident."

"Okay, so maybe you accidentally called him Marcus." She laughed. "While he was banging you from behind."

"You are so not funny."

"Well, you are hilarious," Mariah said, pointing at her sister and giggling.

Mariah's children were dressed and ready to go. Each one kissed Aniyah and were excited to see her. Zenobia wanted to be the first to tell Aniyah about PJ, stuttering every other word. Aniyah listened to four different versions of the same story. Junior didn't say a word; he'd had enough. Aniyah scooped up Tyler kissing him all over his face and commented on how fat he was getting. Carl gave his sister-in-law a big hug before loading his five children in the minivan as Mariah stood at the door waving good-bye to them.

"Well, I start my vacation Tuesday. I've got one last double shift to do on Monday night, then I'm on vacation for two whole weeks."

"So how's it going at twenty-four seven?" Mariah asked.

"Everyone misses you, Juicy."

"I miss everybody too and stop calling me that."

"I'm sorry. I keep forgetting." Juicy was the nickname their dad gave Mariah when they were kids, sort of an homage to Mariah being the thickest of the sisters.

"I miss you too. I've been having a hard time finding anyone to pick up those night shifts."

"What about Fatimah?"

"Fatimah doesn't want to work. Anyway, she's over qualified. She likes managing the cases. She doesn't want to get her hands dirty, and Mama's too busy tryin' to move to care."

"Well, why should Mama care? She's turned everything over to you. The only thing she has to worry about is her and Cleo and the move to Baltimore."

"She didn't hand this over to me. She handed it over to us. Twenty-four seven is ours now. I have a full-time job. I can't do it all by myself."

"Yea, well, I'm not excited about it. It's a lot of work." Mariah answered. Mariah didn't want any part of Twenty-four seven. It belonged to Mama and it would always belong to Mama. She didn't care what her mother said. Mariah knew that her mother would always have her hands in it and that she would want full control of it even though she'd be all the way in Baltimore. Aniyah on the other hand was very excited. She had always wanted Twenty-four seven and she looked forward to running it after Mama moved to Baltimore.

Twenty-four seven was a nursing agency that Mama started when she was thirty-five years old. It was Mama's baby. In the beginning, the agency was staffed by most of Mama's old coworkers, the ones she called the best of the best. These usually consisted of a group of old complaining ass women nearing the end of their nursing careers. They worked their asses off. They were trustworthy and reliable, and they gave quality care. Despite a few minor customer complaints, usually due to personality differences, Mama had the best reputation in the state. She never ran out of business. And now at fifty-one, she was moving to Baltimore to retire with Cleo, her thirty-five-year-old boyfriend.

Neither of them liked Cleo, but he made Mama very happy and she wasn't chasing after their dad for a change. Their "stepdaddy" or rather their mama's live-in boyfriend Ray had been dead for years, and Mama didn't waste much time with grieving.

First, there was David, the chocolate brother with the "S" curl. David was a handsome man with pretty white teeth, with one gold tooth in the front of his mouth. He used to wink and smile, flashing that lone gold tooth. It used to make Mama giggle, but only when he did it to her. But he winked and smiled at every woman. That was the problem and thus the end of her relationship with David, with the "S" curl.

Next, there was Calvin. They all liked Calvin. Calvin was an insurance salesman, and he was very well to do. Calvin and Mama seemed like the perfect match. He was nice, smart, and funny, and he treated Mama like a lady. But Mama didn't like him. She said he acted too old. It took her five years to figure that out. Calvin was devastated, and Mama was single.

There were many men in between. Her children hadn't met them all. They didn't care to. Mama's taste in men left a lot to be desired. Calvin tried to keep in contact with Mama. But Mama wouldn't have it. She'd say, "Why is this man stalking me?" But he wasn't stalking her; he just loved her. They felt sorry for Calvin. Aniyah felt sorry for Mama; she felt it was sad that she could confuse true love with harassment. She felt it said that Mama didn't recognize love.

"I know you said you talked to Nicole this morning. What did she say?" Aniyah wanted to blurt out, "Tell me what happened, tell me everything!" But she couldn't with Mariah; she'd have to take it slow because Mariah would clam up in a minute.

"She didn't say much of anything. I think she had company."

"So she didn't say anything to you about that crazy-assed Darren?"

"No, did he do something else?" Mariah sat up in her seat and rubbed her belly. She placed her steaming cup of coffee down, afraid that she was going to hear something that would make her spill hot coffee on herself. "She has me so stressed out about his crazy ass. She needs to call the police, that's what she needs to do. He's crazy! You know he sent Mama another e-mail last week? She couldn't pull it up at the time, but I did. The text read, 'Do you really know your daughter?' This picture was supposed to pop up. Thank God, it didn't."

Aniyah put her coffee on the table and stared at Mariah. Mariah didn't say anything.

"Juicy!" Aniyah yelled.

"Stop calling me that!"

"Finish! A picture of what? What was the picture of?"

"Just pictures." Mariah shook her head in disgust.

"Mariah, I'm a grown-up! I can handle it." Aniyah hated how Mariah protected her from things as if she were a little child.

"If Nicole didn't tell you about it, then I don't think I should."

"I hate when you do that, Juicy. Then why would you bring that up!"

"You're right. I shouldn't have said anything." Mariah sipped her coffee. "And stop calling me that." Mariah hated the nickname Juicy. She hated that her father had burdened her with that particular term of endearment and she hated that she would answer to it anytime anyone called her that.

"You shouldn't be drinking that."

"Thank you, Aniyah. But this is decaffeinated coffee," Mariah said, looking at her sister as she took a larger gulp, nearly burning the inside of her mouth.

"That's what you get," Aniyah retorted.

Mariah shrugged her shoulders and turned her back to Aniyah and watched the news on the small kitchen TV.

"Mariah, what was it?" Aniyah begged, as Mariah ignored her and continued sipping her coffee. She had tuned Aniyah out. She didn't even hear the door slam when Aniyah walked out the door.

Chapter 3

I LOVE YOU

Aniyah hopped in her car, turned on her radio, and drove away. She hated when her sister did that. It was so annoying. To start telling someone something and stop right at the good part was like starting a joke without ending with the punch line. It irritated Aniyah to no end, and Mariah did this all the time. Aniyah promised herself that she'd give her some of her own medicine, but she could never bring herself to do it. She shared most everything with Mariah, her secrets as well as others'; Aniyah was the only one she knew who would keep it.

She wasn't going to ask Mama about it because she didn't want Mama snapping her head off. Besides, Mama couldn't stand Nicole, and she didn't want to get anything started. She couldn't talk to Fatimah about it, because Fatimah hated Nicole and she probably didn't know or care for that matter. Serena might know a little something, but she was away at college and too hard to reach. She'd have to wait for Serena to call her.

Aniyah ran her fingers through her hair, and her hair fell back into place. She blew up to move the hair from her eyes and down it fell, back into her face. She ruffled her bangs with her left hand as she held on to the steering wheel with her right. But again, the hair fell back over her eyes.

She was having a hard time getting used to the new haircut and color. Despite the selling point of the hairstyle staying in place, she couldn't stand the bangs falling in her face. Everyone commented on how the cut brought out her features. They said it made her look like a teenager, but she wasn't so sure that she wanted to look like a teenager. They said the color really went well with her caramel complexion, but she couldn't tell. It wasn't quite conservative enough for her, and she'd considered dyeing it back to her natural color, dark brown.

Aniyah kept playing with her bangs as she drove down the avenue. She didn't notice the men stopping to stare. She didn't realize the double takes she was getting as she caught their eyes. She was beautiful, but she couldn't see it. Aniyah's hand was sweating, she slid her hand down her thigh, then grasped the steering wheel again. As she thought about how her older sister made her sick. She wanted to call Mariah back and cuss her out. She was part of the family too and she had every right to know what was going on with Nicole. She wasn't being nosey, she was showing concern, after all Nicole is their sister not just somebody off the street.

Aniyah glanced in her rearview mirror at the gym bag in the backseat. She made a right at the light and headed down Northfield Road to Let's Get Physical, a local fitness chain. She stopped at the stoplight, and a silver Suburban pulled up next to her. Its shiny chrome rims spinning and glistening in the noonday sun, music blaring from every possible crevice, and the bass loud and booming. She'd never heard the song before, but the melody was beautiful; it was mellow like something Will Downing would sing, and the man's voice stirred something in her soul. She bobbed her head and moved her hips in her seat as the music from the silver Suburban bounced off the walls of her car. The music was loud, too loud, Aniyah thought, for such a smooth, sensual beat. She wanted to ask the name of the song, and she wanted to inquire about the artist. But she didn't. She didn't like the way the passenger was looking at her.

The passenger of the silver Suburban stared at her profile, waiting for her to turn in his direction. She stopped dancing in her seat. The traffic light was too long. She knew he was waiting. The driver turned the music down. Still she didn't turn around. The light turned green, and she smiled at the man in the passenger seat of the silver Suburban and then drove away.

Aniyah loved music, all kinds of music. She loved to sing, she loved to dance, and she could do both very well. Marcus hadn't been much of a dancer, but Nate loved to dance. He would dance with her at clubs, cabarets, block parties, and street fairs, and sometimes, he'd dance with her with no music at all; he'd just hold her and sway. He appreciated all types of music too. He had an impressive collection of CDs and vintage albums. He even owned some old eight-track tapes. She thought it was so funny that he had an old copy of Michael Jackson's "Destiny" on eight-track cassette. She'd told him that that was what Nicole made her and her sisters listen to the entire ride during trips to visit their dad on the weekends. Her phone rang, and she started not to answer it thinking it was Mariah. But when she noticed it was Nathan, she answered on the next ring.

"Good morning, love." Nathan's voice was cheerful. She'd left him sleeping in her condo.

"It's noon." Aniyah answered, correcting him.

"Good afternoon, my love."

"Good afternoon, baby." Aniyah smiled; he could hear it in her voice, and it made him smile too.

"So what have you got planned for today?"

"Well, right now I'm headed for the gym. But I can meet you afterward. I'm gonna work on my upper body today and do some cardio."

Nathan laughed and said, "Cardio huh? I got some cardio for you."

"Yea," she said, noting the sarcasm in his voice.

Nathan laughed at his own joke, "How far are you from the gym?"

"I'm right around the corner."

"You up for a game of racquet ball?"

"Sure, are you ready to play this time?" Aniyah said, referring to Nathan's crushing defeat at the last game. Nathan laughed sarcastically as if she'd said the funniest thing in the world, then stopped abruptly, and said, "I can be there in twenty minutes."

Aniyah couldn't wait. She was very competitive, and she could not wait to blow him out of the water. Aniyah's phone rang again. It was Nate.

"Hey, are you wearing those red shorts?"

"No, why?"

"Good, they're too distracting," Nate said as if that was the real reason that he lost the last game.

"Whatever, you just bring your A game or prepare to get spanked."

Aniyah smiled. Everything about Nathan made her smile. She couldn't believe how well their relationship was going. She hadn't had this much fun in a long time. She liked that he was so attentive and that he made time for her. Wet spot and sleeping arrangements aside, she really adored him, but she wasn't sure if she wanted him to know it yet. Aniyah was trying to take it easy. She didn't want to get burned this time. She was making quite the effort to pay attention to the signs. It seemed that just when she would get comfortable with a man or think that he was 'the one', then he would go and do some stupid shit and reveal that he was nothing but a big jerk.

Aniyah pulled into the parking lot. It was packed. She parked in between a black Toyota Corolla and a green LeSabre. She grabbed her hot, pink gym bag and her purse. She locked her car, and after hearing the chirp of the alarm, she headed for the door.

The front of Let's Get Physical was mostly tinted glass. You couldn't see inside from the street, but you could see figures moving behind the glass, and as you neared the front doors, you could see people working out on various exercise equipment. As she approached the desk, she was greeted by Kali, one of the trainers. Aniyah handed Kali her membership card, and she scanned it and handed it back to Aniyah with a smile. Aniyah liked Kali's short, black, polished fingernails and the silver rings on Kali's tiny fingers.

Kali was short with a small round head, smooth olive skin, and small, dark eyes. Aniyah thought her smile was very beautiful, but when she smiled, it seemed her teeth were too big for her mouth. She wore her hair short and wispy; it was cute on her, but Aniyah thought she'd look crazy with that style. Kali was Japanese, and even though she didn't speak with an accent, she'd sometimes use an accent with new clients just for kicks. For some reason, Kali thought it was funny; Aniyah did too.

"Hey, Kali."

"Hey, Aniyah." Kali said as she flashed a wide smile. "Ooh I'm lovin' that new cut, and the color is really funky. Looks great on you."

"Thanks," Aniyah said and moved her bangs away from her eyes.

"Oh, I like that mysterious eye thing you got goin' there." Kali pointed a ringed finger at Aniyah's eyes.

"Yea, I know," Aniyah said, moving a big clump of her bangs and throwing it to the back. "This is so annoying," Aniyah said pointing to the bangs as they slowly fell back into place. "I think I'm gonna go back and have her do something about these bangs. I can't stand it."

"Oh no, leave 'um alone. They look sexy."

Kali smiled, and it looked as if she closed her eyes. This happened every time she smiled. She'd smile, and her high cheekbones seemed to force her small eyes shut. Kali was every bit of ninety-eight pounds and probably four percent body fat. She was lean and toned with tiny little breasts, a tiny little waist, and a tiny little butt. The guys were crazy about her.

Before Aniyah went into the locker room, she reserved a racquetball court. Kali asked about the "tall cutie," and Aniyah smiled and told her he'd be coming by in a little while. As Aniyah changed into her salmon-colored, Under Armor workout short set and matching tank, she thought about her oldest sister Nicole and her crazy ex, Darren. She remembered how impressed everybody was when she brought him home for Mariah's birthday party. He was the first serious boyfriend Nicole had had since Darius. She seemed so happy with Darren. Who knew he was a nut?

Aniyah clipped her cell phone to her hip and put her earphones in her ear. She liked listening to music as she worked out and every now and then, the earphones would keep the less-determined guys away. She worked out as a group of men watched. It annoyed her but she closed her eyes and continued. She pretended that she didn't see them standing there. Every now and then, she'd glance up and get a glimpse of some eye candy. But she never stared long enough for them to catch her. She didn't want any one trying to approach her. It made her really uncomfortable.

She looked up and saw a young man in an old, tight, Superman T-shirt. The shirt looked as if it was once a light blue, but was now dingy and gray. The "S" on the chest was worn. It was tattered, the cotton fabric ripped in strategic places, revealing areas of his pecs and his abs. There was one long rip across the back, which revealed his sexy muscular back.

He wore a pair of cargo shorts and a pair of new wheat-colored Timberlands with the laces untied. "Not proper workout attire," Aniyah thought to herself. He worked out a bit, grunting as he lifted the heavy weights. He knew he was fine. But she could tell he was obnoxious. He talked very loud and brought a lot of undue attention to himself as if his bulging muscles weren't enough. He paraded around the gym, flexing and walking as if in slow motion, making eye contact with women as he passed by. She wondered if he was arrogant or just really insecure.

When Superman's cell phone rang, he stood in front of Aniyah and answered it. He laughed loudly and stood there talking to whomever, as Aniyah worked on her curls. Aniyah ignored him. She was totally oblivious to the fact that he was trying to get her attention. She mouthed the words to the music playing in her ear, being careful not to sing loud enough for anyone to hear. She closed her eyes with each set of ten and breathed as her trainer had instructed her to do until she felt a tap on her shoulder.

It was Superman. She could see him moving his mouth, but she couldn't hear what he was saying. She sat the weight down on its base, and you could hear the heavy clink of metal on metal. She squinted at him, as if he was speaking in a foreign tongue, then she pulled an earphone out of her ear and listened.

"Huh?" Aniyah said, staring at Superman with a look of confusion on her face.

"Oh, I was just saying hello."

"Oh, hi," Aniyah said and smiled. He was standing in front of her with his feet apart. Aniyah tried picturing him with his hands on his hips and a red cape blowing behind him.

She wasn't sure if he was done, and she didn't know whether or not she should be putting her earphone back in her ear or not. She looked at him to see if he was going to say anything more. "I've seen you around here a lot. And I just wanted to come around and say hi and introduce myself. My name is Derrick." Derrick held out his hand. Aniyah wiped her sweaty palm on her shorts and shook his hand. She smiled. "It's nice to meet you, Derrick." She wanted to blurt out "I have a boyfriend," but she didn't. She didn't give him her name at first because it was an invitation to talk if they met again, and she wasn't there to talk; she was there to work out. But he asked for her name, and she told him, "Aniyah." He tried to make small talk, and she thought about how he was messing with her workout time. She wanted to scream, "Please leave me alone!" But instead, she smiled and nodded and pretended to be interested. Eye candy was nice to look at but not much fun to talk to.

Eventually, Aniyah made her way downstairs. She bought a way-too-expensive bottle of water, then went back up the stairs, and stared out the tinted glass window into the parking lot below. She could see clearly outside. She sipped her water and watched as couples walked in together and as other couples left. She waited for Nate and wondered what could have been taking him so long. She had enough time to get on the elliptical machine, but she didn't because she figured racquetball with Nathan would be enough of a workout.

She watched as a familiar figure approached the building She smiled as she saw him walking up. She wanted to run down the stairs and greet him, but she didn't. She just stared down at Nate as some woman ran up behind him, grabbed him around his waist, and buried her face in his back. Her heart sank as she watched. She couldn't hear them, but she knew there was laughter. He looked from side to side as if trying to see who held him as the woman darted back and forth trying to hide from him. He reached from behind and pulled her to him and gave her a big hug. It looked like he kissed her forehead, but Aniyah couldn't tell; his back was to the window now. Her eyes burned, and she was jealous and angry. She remembered what her oldest sister always said, "Don't let them see you sweat. But don't ignore disrespect, address it!"

Aniyah didn't meet Nate downstairs; she didn't want it to appear that she was waiting for him. She didn't want to question him in front of her either. She thought about how she'd approach him without making a scene. She was probably the least confrontational of her sisters. Aniyah stretched her muscles, preparing for their racquetball game and biting into her bottom lip as a means of trying to control her anger. She could hear Nicole's voice in her head, telling her, "Calm yourself, Aniyah. You can't get your point across if you lose control." Aniyah thought it was strange that the voice in her head was that of her sister's instead of her own. Aniyah's music was off. She pulled her earphones out of her ears, tucked them away, and watched as Nathan approached her, walking with this woman alongside him. Nathan embraced Aniyah and kissed her on her neck. Aniyah smiled. "He's mine," she thought to herself, and she smiled at the woman. He introduced Aniyah to her. "Sheila, this is my girl Aniyah. Aniyah, this is Sheila."

Sheila was very pretty up close. She was fair skinned with hazel eyes. She wore her curly hair au naturel and poofy. She smiled and held out her hand to shake Aniyah's hand. Aniyah shook her hand and smiled. She noticed a small gold band on Sheila's ring finger. That didn't matter to her; married women cheat too. "This is the one I've been telling you about," Nate said to Sheila as he embraced Aniyah and kissed her again. Aniyah smiled and wondered why she'd never heard of Sheila.

"It's so nice to put a face with the name," Sheila said and smiled again. Aniyah wanted to say, "Well, I've heard absolutely nothing about you. Who the hell are you?" But she didn't say a word. He was holding her in front of this woman. He'd kissed her several times as Sheila stood there watching, and he let Sheila know that Aniyah was his girl. So what was the problem? "So, Nathan," Aniyah rubbed Nate's stomach as she pushed the other arm around his waist and gave him a squeeze, "how do you two know each other?" Nate smiled and explained that Sheila was the wife of an ex-coworker and a close friend of his. Aniyah thought to herself, "Yea right, does her husband know that she likes to play tag out in the parking lot with other men." "Oh, okay," Aniyah said with a smile, hoping that her skepticism wasn't showing on her face.

"Well, I've gotta get this workout started. So nice to meet you, Aniyah."

"Oh, nice meeting you too, Sheila." The two shook hands again.

"G'bye, Nathan," Sheila said as she winked, smiled, and gave him a nudge with her elbow.

"Now what the hell does that mean?" Aniyah thought, suspiciously.

"Good seeing you, Sheila. Tell Rich I said 'Hi.' Maybe we can all get together sometime. Tell him to call me."

"I will," Sheila said, flashing a smile. "Take care."

Nate and Aniyah had missed their racquetball reservation. But there was a court available and the time was free, so they got their equipment and headed to the court. They laughed and trash-talked. But Aniyah couldn't help but feel as if something was amiss. She wasn't very trusting of the opposite sex. Given time and opportunity, every man was going to cheat. It was how they were made. At least, that was what Mama always said. Aniyah tended to believe it.

Aniyah was very competitive. She loved the excitement she felt playing this game with him. She enjoyed the anticipation of smacking the ball with the racket. She loved the pace of the game, and she liked watching Nate go for the ball and hearing him grunt with each serve. They had so much fun together. Nate was new to the game, but he was a fast learner. He was so funny to watch, and he made her laugh without even trying.

Aniyah won, and the game ended with the both of them covered in sweat and with Nate making excuses for losing the game this time too. Aniyah thought to herself, "I really like this one," as she looked at Nate's sweat-drenched face. She placed her hand on his cheek and kissed his lips, and she wondered if it would be so easy for her to let him go if she had to.

The two headed to the locker rooms for a much-needed shower. They met in the lobby when they were done. Nate's face was still wet, but from water from the shower this time. Aniyah's hair was flat, but it still looked very nice and the cut still stayed in place. When he saw Aniyah in the lobby, his face lit up. Aniyah noticed that expression, and she liked it. There was something in his eyes that told her that that look was reserved for her. She told herself that she stirred something in him that caused him to look at her in that way.

"Why do you look at me like that?" she asked.

"'Cuz you're my baby."

Nate leaned in and kissed her. He looked down at her and smiled. She liked how he closed his eyes when he kissed her. Her eyes were open, and she could see the curl of his long, thick lashes. She liked how his thick, dark brows framed his beautiful brown eyes. Nathan was a cutey. She saw how other women looked at him. She could see how they got all giddy when he smiled at them or when he looked their way. He had dimples, not deep dimples like Aniyah's but creases in both cheeks. He had a movie-star smile and a laugh that made others want to laugh with him. "Ooh you smell so good," Aniyah said, as she inhaled and took in a big whiff of the air around him. "Thanks, it's the cologne my girlfriend bought for me on my birthday," Nate said, winking at her. She loved when he did that.

"Well, your girlfriend has great taste," Aniyah said with a smile.

Nathan and Aniyah walked to the door, and they noticed the storm clouds. The sky was dark and menacing. "So what are your plans for the rest of the day?" Aniyah asked, looking at the sky.

"I'm with you, boo. I'm going wherever you're going."

"Okay, well, follow me home."

It was about three in the afternoon, and it was dark. She knew the rain was coming soon. And she was looking forward to it. It was good sleeping weather. The air was cold, too cold as far as Aniyah was concerned. She hated how the weather changed so quickly in Cleveland. Aniyah missed summer rains. Not just any rain. Warm, country, southern summer rain. Cleveland rain never got warm enough to walk around in like she did when she was a kid, when she and her sisters visited down south. Aniyah recalled the way the water felt so warm on her skin back then. She'd never experienced anything like it. Before then, all she knew was cold rains. The kind of rain that you run away from, trying not to get a drop of it on your skin as you run for shelter. Those southern summer rains were different though. They felt like a warm shower. You wanted every drop to touch your body. Afterward, their hair would be all drawn up and soaked, but it was worth it. It was remarkable how something as simple as rain could let you know that you were so far from home.

Nathan followed Aniyah to her lake-view condo. He parked beside her in the underground parking garage. Nathan walked over to her car, opened her door for her, and walked with her hand in his as she unlocked the door to the building and entered the hallway. "She's so beautiful," he thought to himself, as he looked at her without her noticing. But she didn't know it though; he didn't like her lack of self-esteem in that respect, but he was well aware that being overconfident was not a good thing, especially not for him. He noticed how men looked at her even if she didn't.

Aniyah just wanted to relax. She was a homebody, and she couldn't wait to slip into something more comfortable and just chill. They walked down the mirrored hallway to the elevators. They stepped inside, and she pressed the number 15 on the wall panel inside the elevator. Aniyah backed herself against the mirrored wall, and Nate approached her, pressing his body against hers. Nate was big and tall enough that if someone else stepped into the elevator, they wouldn't be able to see her.

He leaned down and kissed Aniyah on the neck and whispered to her, "Have you ever done it on an elevator?" Aniyah smiled. He'd asked her that many times before, and she'd always answered him in the same way.

"No, I haven't."

"Want to?

"Not today, I don't," Aniyah said, answering as she always did.

"Well, you'll let me know when you change your mind, won't chu?"

"I promise you, Nathan, you'll be the first to know."

Nathan kissed her again on her neck, then again on her lips. "So what are we doing tonight," Nathan asked. "This is it. We're going to spend a rainy night together. We're going to order out, watch a good movie, listen to some good music, then lie in each other's arms until the morning," she answered and stepped off the elevator.

"Okay, so what are we really going to do?"

Nathan and Aniyah walked down the corridor toward her apartment. Her apartment was her pride and joy. She didn't have any children. She didn't have any pets. It was just her and her beautiful lakefront condo. She didn't have to fight over bathroom time and what to watch on the television or argue about who ate the last of the cereal. She didn't have to share, and she liked it like that.

Aniyah was the middle child, and although she never cared much for that title, she felt she was the embodiment of the expression. Very insecure and having had trouble maintaining any long-term romantic relationships, she'd always attributed that to middle-child syndrome. She was sweet in some ways and very selfish in others, especially when sharing made her vulnerable. And for those reasons, she felt she'd be a better lover than a mother, a better girlfriend than a wife. So it didn't matter much if a relationship didn't last, because they inevitably led to marriage and motherhood. Neither of which she felt she was suited for. But she really liked Nate, and for the first time, she wanted this to really work and she wanted it to last. And she was curious as to where this relationship would take her. Nathan and Aniyah sat on the balcony and looked over the water as the rain fell. Nathan jumped as the lightning flashed over the water.

"This is dangerous," Nathan said, as he sat bouncing in the rocking patio chair.

"Are you afraid?" Aniyah asked, as she sipped her sweet tea from her bendy straw.

"This just isn't safe is all I'm saying," he said, as the thunder cracked, and he nearly jumped out of his skin.

It wasn't safe. Aniyah knew that it wasn't, but she felt safe and she felt comfortable. She bounced in her patio chair a few times with her legs crossed and took a few more sips of her sweet tea before heading inside with Nate.

"Scaredy-cat," she said, as she shut the patio screen door.

"Call it whatever you want," he answered. She plopped down on the couch next to him. She threw her legs across his lap, leaned against one of her large couch pillows, and sipped her sweet tea. He pulled her legs closer to him in his lap and held them there. The heat from his large, warm hands seemed to radiate through her entire body.

They listened to Marvin Gaye and made out on the couch like a couple of teenagers. She lied and told him she wasn't in the mood, because she liked the way he encouraged her to change her mind. He knew her body so well. He really paid attention to what felt good to her. He was such an unselfish lover. She hoped he felt the same way about her, but she dared not ask. She didn't want him to know that it mattered. He told her, "You mean so much to me," in between kisses.

"You mean a lot to me too," she said, as she unbuckled his pants and kissed him passionately. He stopped her busy hands and held them in his own. He looked deep into her eyes and said, "I'm serious." He'd stopped her mid pucker. She leaned forward and kissed him and answered, "I know." Nathan moved his face and said to her, "Aniyah, I love you." Aniyah moved her head back and looked at him as if he'd just said something horribly wrong. He was embarrassed. "What made you say that?" she asked.

"Because it's true. I've been wanting to say it for a long time. I don't want you and me to be some casual thing. You're special to me. I don't want nobody else, and I don't want you with anybody else. We're good together, and I felt like if I didn't tell you how I feel that I might lose you and I don't want to risk that."

Aniyah rubbed her eyes as if she had just woken up. She looked at him and smiled uneasily, and he smiled back. "What made you say that to me now?"

"I just felt compelled," he said and smiled that sexy smile of his.

Aniyah wondered to herself if it was the expectation of sex that compelled him to confess his love for her. Sex and the anticipation of it had been known to make people blurt out all sorts of things.

"No, whatever you're thinking, no," he said, smiling and shaking his head as if reading her mind. "What?" she laughed. "I didn't say a word."

"I told you because I have felt overwhelmed with this, and I had to get it off my chest. It's hard for me to keep my feelings inside. I'm not like you."

"I don't keep stuff inside."

"Yea, you do. There are things that you don't like, but you won't mention it. I usually have to guess, which I'm not good at by the way. I guess wrong because I'm not a mind reader, and instead of you coming right out and telling me what it is, you just say, 'Forget it, it doesn't matter,' when it really does and then you move on. Just listening to you talk about your exes, I see that there's a pattern of that with you, and I don't want our relationship to fall victim to that. You know?"

"I don't know where all of this has come from. I'm happy with how our relationship is going. I am very happy."

"Why are you acting like I just told you something bad? You act like you've never had a man say I love you before."

She'd heard it before. Many men had told her that in the heat of passion or during so-called serious conversations. She'd heard it said right before bogus marriage proposals, and she'd be grinning with stars in her eyes like some naive child. But she had yet to meet the man who truly meant it.

Aniyah felt something for Nathan too, but she didn't want to call it love. It was something like that though. Up until now, it wasn't enough to make her faithful. She'd learned a long time ago to be careful with her feelings, and if she was faithful, he had to be worth it. She had to be sure that it was real because she knew that she could never trust her feelings. She was well aware that she couldn't distinguish love from like for the life of her. She had loved so hard and misjudged one good time, and that was enough to make her very wary.

*   *   *

She was careful of the men who said I love you too quickly or said it as if it were a payment for services rendered. She'd believed her first love Matt, when he told her he loved her. She was fourteen, and he was sixteen when she'd given her virginity to him. He was the cutest little black thing on the block, with his brush waves and his black and gold mountain bike.

Matt use to ride his bike back and forth in front of her house, wearing his blue jeans cut off at the knees, sometimes shirtless or with a throwback jersey on. She ignored him for most of the summer. She wouldn't even smile at him as he popped wheelies in front of her house as she sat on the porch steps. He was tall and bowlegged, and he had the smoothest dark skin. She ignored him as he did his little bike tricks to entertain and impress her. He'd thought she wasn't really paying attention until she reacted the time he fell off of his bike and nearly got hit by a neighbor's car.

Matt was so sweet. He tried to get Aniyah, all that summer. Buying her ice cream, whenever the ice-cream truck came strolling by. Telling her how pretty she was. "You are so fine," he used to say, "the finest girl on the whole street, the finest girl at the whole school." If only she was a little older, she could have read that look he used to give her a little better; she'd be able to see through all that flattery.

It all started with the day that Matt had asked her to go to the park with him. Aniyah went, but she went with three of her closest girlfriends. It might have made a difference if these three little girls weren't so fast and if Aniyah wasn't so impressionable, but they were fast and she was impressionable. Aniyah went from going to the park to meet him with some friends to going all by herself, to lying and sneaking away to be with him.

Aniyah liked the way he looked at her. She liked the sweet things he said to her. She liked the way he'd whisper in her ear even when no one else was around. It gave her butterflies. She had never felt this way before. She enjoyed being around him, and every morning, she looked forward to the possibility of spending a new day with him.

Their first kiss was awkward. She was embarrassed, but he was very understanding. After all, he could teach her how to kiss; it only required more kissing for practice. And practice they did. They kissed at the park, behind the bleachers at the school at dusk, right before the streetlights came on. They kissed on his back porch when no one was home, only because Aniyah was too afraid to go inside.

He'd invited her to dinner so that she could meet his mom. Aniyah thought Matt's mom was so nice, and Matt's mom really liked Aniyah. She thought Aniyah was sweet, well mannered, and very pretty. Matt's elder brothers kept nudging Matt and embarrassed him as they ate dinner, but other than that, it seemed to go pretty well. Aniyah never invited Matt over to her house for dinner; she thought it was enough that her mama said that it was okay for her to go over to his house.

That summer, as Aniyah and Matt's relationship progressed, Matt began to ask Aniyah a bunch of different questions and approach her with what-if scenarios, just to see what her responses would be. He asked his questions until he felt her answers were acceptable. He tried to feel her out so that he could make his move.

One day, as Aniyah sat on his back porch, Matt acted out a movie he'd seen that past Friday, the movie that Mama wouldn't allow her to go see with him. Matt loved to entertain her; he liked the way she laughed and the way she hung on his every word. She couldn't remember the movie, but she could vividly recall him acting out the movie, changing his voice for the different characters and moving all around with the different action sequences of the movie.

She remembered him stopping in the middle to kiss her and to tell her how much he loved her. She believed him. She had no reason to believe otherwise. Why else would he want to spend so much time with her? Why else would he buy her gifts and announce to everyone that she was his girlfriend? Why else would he introduce her to his mother?

Matt invited her inside that day. His mother was at work, and his older brothers were working too, and they weren't expected to be back home until much later on. Matt had convinced her to come inside and she was so scared, but Matt made her feel comfortable. He made her feel as if everything was all right. They sat on the couch. It was beige with a floral print. Matt's mom liked flowers, and there were flowers and pictures of flowers all throughout the room. There was a huge family portrait of Matt, his three brothers, and of his late father. Matt looked more like his mom. She was a pretty woman. Aniyah liked the way she wore her hair feathered with a short bang to her brow. She was too nervous to look around. She couldn't bring herself to look at the family portrait; she felt as if guilt was filling up her insides. "You wanna see my room?" Matt had asked. "No," Aniyah had answered and shook her head.

"Come on," Matt said as he'd extended his hand.

If only Aniyah could have turned back the hands of time, she would have walked out of his house right then. If she knew how that day thirteen years ago would have affected her life today, she would have turned around and told him she never wanted to see him again.

But Aniyah followed him up to his room. She followed that smile to the part of the house that was forbidden to her. Aniyah remembered that his bedroom was exceptionally neat, and it smelled good, as if he had expected company, as if he knew that that would be the day that Aniyah would cave in and would come into his room with him. She noticed that his window shade was down and that the curtains were drawn, but that hot summer sun seemed to fight its way through. She was flattered when she saw the picture that he'd taken of her, framed and sitting on his dresser. It made her smile.

Aniyah didn't see it coming when he had begun kissing her and backing her up on the bed. She didn't resist his hands underneath her halter top, and she didn't stop him from pulling it over her head. He kissed her neck, and it sent shock waves through her body. She had never felt anything like it. Aniyah didn't stop him when he kissed her bare breasts, and when his mouth trailed to her nipples, she couldn't believe how good it felt. She was so nervous and afraid, and she held her breath so long that she had hardly noticed the long, high-pitched sigh coming from her when she exhaled. She didn't answer him when he asked her if it felt good to her. But he knew that it did.

When Matt pulled down her shorts and her pink cotton panties, she didn't say a word. Instead, she'd looked him in his eyes and helped him by kicking them off as she'd propped herself up on her elbows staring at him. He'd promised her that he wouldn't hurt her, and he didn't. Magic is how she'd later describe it to her young friends. Sex with Matt was nothing like she'd imagined it would be. It was wonderful, she thought. "I love you," he'd said, just above a whisper. "I love you too," Aniyah had answered.

Aniyah fell to sleep next to her young lover, as he held her in his arms. She had thought to herself, "So this is what it feels like to be a woman?" He had made her feel like she had never ever felt before. She knew it would feel special with Matt, because he'd made everything else between them so special. They had had such an extraordinary connection prior to that day that she knew sex with him would be fantastic. The closest that her young mind knew to describe it was like being on a rollercoaster and she wanted that feeling over and over again.

Aniyah hadn't realized that she wasn't ready for a relationship at that level. She had no idea of the flurry of emotions that a sexual relationship would bring. She didn't know that she was only Matt's young conquest and that he'd soon become bored with her. She didn't know that Matt would make her cry.

All in the course of one summer, Aniyah found herself stalking the boy who had said she was the finest girl around. The same boy who said he loved her so tenderly that she knew it had to be sincere. No one ever could have told her that she'd hear him call her a bitch and say, "Stop calling my house." Or that he'd avoid her calls, telling his friends to answer the phone and say he wasn't around as he laughed in the background. She'd felt she was in love with him, and she was sure he loved her too. How could his feelings for her not be genuine? How could deceit be masked with such sincerity?

Her self-esteem shriveled that summer. Her embarrassment knew no bounds when Matt's mom called her mama to talk to her about Aniyah's incessant phone calls. Aniyah had wished she could just disappear.

Aniyah knew that Matt's mother was a nice person, and though she couldn't hear the conversation between Matt's mother and hers, she knew that it was as respectful as could be, considering the circumstances.

Matt's mother was very uncomfortable talking to Aniyah's mother. Aniyah's mom was not a warm person. Aniyah's mother could sense Matt's mom's uneasiness, and she wouldn't go out of her way to make her feel at ease.

Matt's mom began by telling Aniyah's mother how much she loved Aniyah. She told her that she had always been well mannered and respectful of her, but that her concern was for Aniyah's well-being due to the fact that she couldn't let her son Matt go. She told Aniyah's mother about Aniyah and the phone calls. The messages left on the voice mail with Aniyah crying and begging Matt to talk to her and of seeing Aniyah sitting outside of their house on her bike watching the house. She told Aniyah's mother that she tried to talk to her, but that it didn't help and that as a parent she felt the need to call Aniyah's mom so that she could "get her some help," as Matt's mom politely put it.

Aniyah's mother had sat quietly as Matt's mom spoke. The entire conversation had angered Aniyah's mother. It had made her very angry with Aniyah too. She could deal with the lying and sneaking around. That's what teenagers do was what she thought. But she couldn't deal with the fact that Aniyah would let this little nothing-ass boy get her all turned around like that. Aniyah was better than that. And she didn't like the way this woman made it seem as though the phone call was for Aniyah's well-being when she knew that the call was this woman's way of saying that she needed to address the situation, and in Aniyah's mother's eyes, it was this woman criticizing her as a parent. The phone fell silent after Matt's mother was done. "Hello?" Matt's mother had said.

"Oh, are you done?" Aniyah's mother had asked.

"Yes," she had answered, and she was dismayed by Tangie's tone.

"First of all, there is nothing wrong with my daughter. So I don't need to seek any help for her. Okay? Let's get that straight."

"Oh, no, I wasn't implying," Matt's mother had tried to explain.

"I am not finished. Second of all, you or your son don't ever hafto worry about my daughter calling your phone or coming to your house ever again and I mean no trying to get in touch with your son or going to you for your so-called counseling. Furthermore, your son is not to see or call my daughter."

"My Matthew has not been—"

"Please," Aniyah's mother had interrupted. "I have a little girl here whose feelings are hurt by her first love, and you have the little boy over there that hurt her. They had sex and they shouldn't have, but he's not completely innocent in this either."

"Oh I know. I'm not saying—"

Aniyah's mother didn't let Matt's mom continue talking. She'd allowed her to talk when it was her turn, and she wouldn't let Matt's mom prevent her from having her say. When she was done, she hung up the phone without so much as an apology or a good-bye. She didn't apologize for her daughter's behavior because she felt that that would be just as absurd as Matt's mom apologizing for her son sticking his dick in her daughter. She felt that Matt's mother's tone was very judgmental, and she didn't like it, not one bit. She did agree on one thing though and that was that the matter needed to be addressed, and so she addressed it.

Aniyah recalled her mother coming into her room and turning the music off. She walked over to her and held Aniyah's jaw in her hand and looked her daughter straight in the eyes. Aniyah's cheeks hurt as her mother forced her to look into her face. Aniyah's eyes were red from crying. But her mother didn't pity her red eyes or her heartache. She felt like she should have punished her as soon as she found out she was messing around with that boy, before it had gotten so far.

"Are you crying over that boy?"

Aniyah didn't answer her.

"Do you hear me talking to you?" her mother had said as she shook her face by the jaw.

"Ooow," Aniyah had whimpered, as she tried to avoid her mother's gaze.

"Look at me, little girl."

Aniyah looked at her mother. "He may be the first to hurt you, but he won't be the last. Get over it! I mean it! And if I ever get another phone call like the one I just received again, I will beat yo' ass. Do you hear me Aniyah? It will be me and you. I better not ever hear of you chasing after no boy like that again. I am so serious, you are not to call that boy. You are not to go to his house. I better not hear of you speakin' to him or his mama or I will hurt chu. You hear me?"

Aniyah had nodded as tears streamed down her cheeks and onto her mother's hands.

"Aniyah, I said, 'Do you hear me?'"

"Yes, ma'am," Aniyah had answered.

Her mother let go of her face, wiped her hands on her shorts, and left the room.

"Get it together, Aniyah" were the last words she heard her mother say on the subject.

She was such a hypocrite, Aniyah had thought to herself. "Get over it like you got over Daddy?" She wouldn't dare say it, but she thought it. She didn't want to be like her mother and spend her life pining over someone who clearly didn't want her, and she didn't want to feel her mama's wrath if she had disobeyed her. So she left Matt alone. She never called his home again, and she never went by his house again. She saw his mother at the grocery store, and she hid from her so she wouldn't have to speak. She did just as her mother instructed her to do.

She recalled Mama telling folks about her and Matt, and even though Mama used the words, "that boy" and "that heffa," Aniyah knew she was referring to him and her and if that wasn't embarrassing enough, her mother would call her Hot Mama when family came around, and they'd all look at her as if they could actually visualize every act of fornication performed by her and Matt before their very eyes. She didn't know if Mama was trying to shame her or if she was trying to hurt her feelings, but she'd sometimes wished that she'd have gotten that whoopin'.

"Your heart will heal someday, baby," Grandma said to her, "you just wait an' see. When you're grown and the right man comes along." Aniyah remembered her granny saying that to her as if it were yesterday; she remembered her grandmother hugging her, and as she squeezed, what was supposed to be a comforting hug sent chills of shame through Aniyah right to the bone. Nope, she vowed in that moment that that would never happen to her again.

Reflecting on that summer, she was amazed that her mama didn't strangle her. Clearly, Aniyah had plumb lost her mind. But instead, Mama just kept her cool and let nature take its course. One of two things would happen: Either Aniyah would inevitably come to her senses and see the error of her ways or she would end up older and bitter, longing for someone she couldn't have and looking for love in all the wrong places, just like Mama.

*   *   *

Aniyah was sure not to mention any of this to Nathan. She made a promise that she wouldn't allow anyone to get to her like that again. She learned early, too early not to give all of yourself so freely and not to love so deeply.

She cuddled up to Nathan after he'd given her that rollercoaster feeling multiple times and he had worked his magic on her as the storm raged outside. She made sure that he slept on his own wet spot as she lay on his chest reflecting on those three treacherous words and what they meant to her.

Chapter 4

MIGRAINES AND HEAD GAMES

"My eyes! My eyes!" Fatimah's daughter cried, as she washed her hair.

"Your eyes are fine, Lana. Now be still."

"Oh, oh. It hurts," Lana cried.

"I'm almost done, Lana. Just let me rinse it."

Fatimah rinsed her daughter's hair as they sat in the bathtub. Lana's hair was long and thick, and Fatimah hated washing it just as much as Lana hated having it washed. She didn't have to braid it though, thank God. Fatimah found someone that Lana was crazy about to braid it, and that was where they were headed as soon as she was done in the tub.

"Oh, Mommy!" Lana cried, as she held the sides of her head.

"Lana, I'm not even combing it. It's only water."

"It hurts."

Lana played with her doll, dunking her head in and out of the water as her mother finished rinsing conditioner out of her hair. Fatimah dried herself off and wrapped herself up in a towel as her daughter played in the tub. She then dried off six-year-old Lana's hair, wrapped it in a towel, then dried the rest of her off, and wrapped her little body in a towel. Lana liked the way she looked with the towel wrapped around her head like a turban. She admired herself in the bathroom mirror as she posed in front of it talking to herself in her high-pitched voice.

"I look cute," she said, as she looked at herself in the mirror.

Fatimah grabbed a bottle of baby lotion and put lotion on her daughter as Lana said, "Oh, oh Mommy, it hurts."

"Cut it out, Lana," Fatimah replied, as she continued applying lotion to her daughter's damp skin.

The house was pretty quiet despite the fact that it was full of children. Fatimah had five—her oldest Leah was twelve; Jordan, eleven; Joshua, nine; Lana, age six; and Tori, three years old. The rain was coming, and it had a way of keeping things calm. Everyone was in their rooms doing whatever. But they were keeping quiet, and that was what was most important, because Fatimah had been battling some awful headaches lately and she welcomed the peace and quiet. When the phone rang, everyone came out of their prospective hiding places. They sounded like a stampede. Even the baby, Tori, ran for the phone saying, "I got it, I got it!"

"Mommeee, it's for you," the oldest yelled up the stairs.

"I'll get it for you, Mommy," Lana said as she shot out the bathroom and ran into her parents' room for the telephone.

"Who answered the phone?" Fatimah yelled down the stairs.

"Me," Leah answered.

"Come here, Leah."

Leah headed up the stairs. Something in her mother's tone let her know that she was in trouble.

"Leah, did you check the caller ID?"

"Yes."

"Who was it?"

"It said private."

"What have I told you all about those private and restricted numbers?"

"You said don't answer them."

"Then why did you?" Fatimah asked as Lana handed her the phone.

"I wasn't thinking."

"That's not good, Leah. Don't ever stop thinking. Because that's not a good thing. It doesn't even sound right, does it? To stop thinking."

"No, ma'am," Leah answered.

"You can go now," Fatimah said sternly. Leah left the bathroom and went into her room.

Fatimah ran a tight ship. She was very firm and a strict disciplinarian. And she was rewarded with some of the best, most well-behaved children a parent could ask for. They did their chores without being asked. They all played a role at their local church. Their teachers praised them endlessly. Never an unkind word was said about her kids. They were perfect.

Bright, talented, and beautiful were words often used to describe Fatimah's babies. They each took classes in some creative form of expression. She allowed them to choose, and she told them to choose carefully, because whatever path they chose, they would have to stick with it because she was going to enforce it. She wouldn't be like Mama and introduce them to fine arts and force them to do it, then when they were old enough to appreciate it and enjoy it, snatch it away from them and force them into sticking with something that she thought was more practical.

Fatimah was a stickler for education, discipline, and respect of authority, because she said she was raising children who would one day be viable members of society, who would make fine contributions someday. She didn't hit her children, but each of them thought that she would. All she had to do was give them a look, and they'd fall right in line.

That Lana was a challenge though. She had a mind of her own, and she used it. Lana asked all kinds of questions, and she was very opinionated. While Fatimah's other children were wallflowers, Lana was a butterfly, and as much as she wanted to stifle her, she couldn't bring herself to do it. Lana was very entertaining, and Fatimah liked that she was independent of the others. Fatimah wouldn't be the one to clip her wings.

Fatimah was never the type to run from phone calls. She was responsible. If she didn't pay her bills in full, she at least paid them on time. Creditors didn't call her home; they didn't have to. She didn't need any reminders. She rarely even looked at the caller ID, let alone ignored her ringing phone because of a number that appeared on the screen. Now, she wouldn't answer the phone without looking at the caller ID first, and she admonished her children to do the same.

Fatimah answered the phone and heard a familiar voice on the other line.

"Hi, Mrs. Thomas, it's Nina."

"Hi, Nina. We'll be over in a minute. I just want to let her hair air-dry a little more."

"No, I was just calling to tell you that I can come over to your house if you don't mind. I know how hard it is to get Lana's hair done, and I don't want it to get wet."

"Nina, that is so sweet of you. You're such a lifesaver. Are you at your grandmother's house?"

"Yep," Nina answered.

"Well, you can come on down now if you want, so you can get here before the rain starts."

"Okay. I'm coming."

Fatimah wanted to tell Nina that her little brother Tye wouldn't be over today. She knew that Nina had a crush on Tye. Nina could hardly concentrate on her daughter's hair for staring at him. She didn't expect Nina to ask her anything about Tye, but she expected that Nina would be grilling her kids once Fatimah was out of sight.

Nina tried to portray herself as a quiet little bookworm. She was sweet and conscientious enough, but she had a sneaky way about her. Nina would watch as Fatimah's husband would kiss or embrace her as if imagining that she was in Fatimah's place. Nina had offered to babysit for her numerous times, and even though her children really seemed to like Nina, Fatimah always declined. For some reason, Fatimah couldn't help but imagine that one day, she'd come home early and find her in her bed with Tye or some other male. She had a sneaky kind of flirtatious way about her that Fatimah didn't like, and she hoped that it was limited to teenaged boys and not to other women's husbands.

Leah was in the living room reading a book that had been approved of by her mother. Fatimah screened her children's music, their reading material, and their friends. She watched their association closely so as not to add anyone in the mix that would taint or ruin them. They were so precious to her, and positive association was vital to their well-being. Her sisters said that she was creating monsters. But she said she was nurturing soon-to-be responsible adults.

Nina came over with her lips covered in a shimmering, pink lip gloss. She wore huge pink and black bangle bracelets, matching pink hoop earrings, a pair of Baby Phat shorts and a Baby Phat halter. "Yea," Fatimah thought to herself as she eyed the teenaged girl.

"She's looking for Tye." Fatimah shook her head. She had to keep reminding herself that the only reason why she allowed Nina to come over was because she did such a beautiful job with her daughter's hair. That and the fact that she'd known Nina's grandmother, Mrs. Watkins, for well over ten years. She'd heard things about Nina in the neighborhood, and against her better judgment, she'd allowed Nina to come over, but only under her close supervision and never when she wasn't at home.

She invited Nina in, and the children came down to greet her. The girls admired her jewelry and her glossy lips. Fatimah stopped her from sharing her lip gloss with her girls, telling Nina that they had their own. She didn't want to offend Nina, but she didn't want her sharing lip gloss with her girls either; she didn't know if the rumors about her were true, and she wasn't about to take any chances.

Nina set herself up at Fatimah's dining room table. Fatimah covered her cherrywood table with a large vinyl tablecloth, and she covered the floor with a huge sheet of plastic. Hair would be everywhere, and this would save on cleanup time.

Nina put what seemed like excessive amounts of moisturizer in Lana's long, thick hair. Her hair seemed to suck it up like a sponge. She combed it through gently to the ends, and Lana didn't say a word. She just sat there combing Vaseline through her doll's matted, synthetic hair. Fatimah knew that if she had been anywhere near Lana's head, that her daughter would be screaming bloody murder. She wanted to say to Lana, "I can't believe you!" But she didn't say a word. She just let her daughter sit there as Nina blew-dry her long, thick hair with absolutely no resistance at all from Lana.

Lana had long, curly hair. It was so thick that it didn't lather when it was shampooed, and it had a tendency to be very dry. As beautiful as it looked when it was styled, you'd never realize how much work went into the care of it. It was so exhausting for Fatimah to fight with Lana and to spend hour upon hour in Lana's head, just for the style to look good for a mere week before the process needed to be repeated again.

On the other hand, it took no time at all for Nina to finish Lana's hair. She was really good with her. She'd sing, laugh, and play with Lana to distract her when she'd get to an especially difficult comb-out. She'd talk to Lana about school and comment with interest as Lana discussed "important" school events, and she'd laugh at Lana's made-up knock-knock jokes as if they were the funniest thing she'd ever heard. Yep, she was good, and Lana ate it up.

It was Saturday afternoon, and everybody was responsible for getting themselves prepared for church in the morning. Everyone except Tori had a job to do. Suits, dresses, and shoes had to be picked out by 7:30 p.m. Bibles, notepads, and pens had to be out and either in the girl's church bags or on top of the dresser for the boys. On Sunday mornings, each child had an allotted bathroom time—fifteen minutes each. Church was early, and each of them got their baths at night, so there were no excuses.

The phone rang, and after yelling, "I've got it," to her stampeding children, she checked the caller ID and saw that it was Mama and answered it. Fatimah sighed, and her head was really pounding now. The ibuprofen that she'd taken one hour earlier wasn't touching the constant, throbbing pain. Fatimah braced herself; she loved her Mama, but Mama somehow had a way of making that headache pain worse.

"Hi, Mama," Fatimah said as she answered the phone.

"Hey, baby. How are my grandbabies doing?"

"They're fine. Lana's getting her hair done."

"Oh no." Mama laughed into the phone receiver. "So who's the brave one this week?"

"Nina. You know, Mrs. Watkins's granddaughter."

"Yea, I know," Mama said, and her tone was suspicious and the laughter left her voice.

"What have I told you about that girl? You'd better listen to your Mama. I wouldn't tell you wrong. You had better be careful invitin' that girl over your house. Where's your husband?"

Fatimah didn't comment. She didn't know where he was. She hadn't even thought about it. Having him home was sometimes as bad as having an additional child in the house. Sometimes, she just relished the peace and quiet that came from his absence.

"Hello? You there?"

"Yea, Mama. I'm here."

"Yea, you're there, but are you listening?"

Fatimah and Jason had had their share of problems, but she didn't like what her mother was insinuating. But she had no intention of getting into that with her mother because all she could think about was getting in her bed, resting her eyes, and trying to stop the pain in her head that seemed to be worsening by the minute. Fatimah stood in the doorway of her kitchen and leaned against the doorjamb. She closed her eyes and rested her palm on her weary forehead.

Fatimah sighed into the phone and said, "Mama, I am exhausted," which translated into "Make your point so I can get off this phone."

"I just called to tell you that your brother is on his way over your house. I told him to wait till later, but he insisted on coming. I swear I don't know what's wrong with that boy. Did you have something that you wanted him to do over there?"

"Nope. Nothing," Fatimah said as her head throbbed. "Is he bringing the baby?"

"No, he doesn't have the baby this weekend. Did he know that little hussy was coming over there?"

"No. I haven't talked to Tye since Wednesday."

"Well, I'll tell you what. You'd better keep that girl away from my baby."

Fatimah wanted to say to her mother that if she couldn't control her son what would make her think that she could. But Fatimah didn't say a word.

"Fatimah! Girl, what's wrong with you?" Her mother snapped.

"I've got a headache, Mama, a really bad headache."

"Well, did you take something for it?"

"Yea, about an hour ago, I took some Motrin. And it hasn't done a thing for this headache. As a matter of fact, I think I'm going to send Nina home just as soon as she's done with Lana's head and try to lie down and take a nap."

Fatimah got off the phone with her mother and did just that. She thanked Nina and sent her home right after Lana's hair was done. Then Fatimah climbed into bed. It was so dark outside, and the rain was coming down in sheets. She closed her eyes in her dark bedroom and tried to rest, but her mind kept going a mile a minute and it literally hurt just to think. She was getting a migraine. She was glad to be in the dark room.

The children were doing pretty good with keeping quiet. Her three-year-old was napping, which was a blessing in itself. Their uncle Tye would be over soon. The kids loved him. They had so much fun with Tye. Fatimah thought he'd have his little boy this weekend. He was such a cute little fat thing. She still couldn't believe her seventeen-year-old brother had a son of his own. He looked just like Tye when he was a baby, just juicier.

When Lana's hair was done, she had a head full of long twists flowing down her back and shoulders. Her head was full of colorful hair bows and barrettes. Lana loved it as always, and she stood in front of the mirror in the living room, admiring her hair and saying how cute she was. Lana stood there with her hands on her hips and a little purple purse on her shoulder, shaking the twists in her hair being very careful so as not to hit herself in the face with the barrettes.

Fatimah paid Nina fifty dollars every two weeks but would have gladly paid her one hundred if she had to. Three girls, all with long, thick hair, and none of them behaved like Lana. Not even the baby girl, Tori.

Fatimah's head pounded. She usually offered Nina a snack, which she always accepted. Nina would try to stick around as long as she could—waiting for anybody to stop by. But not today. Fatimah's head hurt, and she didn't have time to supervise two little horny teenagers, so Nina had to go and she did, reluctantly, right after neatly cleaning up after herself, folding the white vinyl tablecloth and clearing the hair-covered plastic from the floor.

Fatimah lay there exhausted. She knew the headaches were directly related to the phone calls. The first of which she'd received two weeks ago this Friday. The initial call seemed to be that of a woman genuinely concerned about her well-being. She had asked for her by name, and she introduced herself as her husband's friend, Danny's girlfriend. Fatimah was bathing Tori at the time, so she wasn't as focused as she would have been if the caller would have reached her under different circumstances. The woman went on to tell her about how she had heard that she was a good woman, sweet and kind. Fatimah thought that maybe this stranger was in some sort of trouble and had thought that somehow Fatimah could help her. So Fatimah stayed on the line.

The woman went on to ask her if she had a husband named Jason Thomas.

Now that was what made her ears perk up. At that moment, she'd taken the phone away from her ear and checked the caller ID. It read private. She put the phone back to her ear and didn't say a word, curious as to what this woman would say next. She asked Fatimah if she knew a woman by the name of Terry. Fatimah answered, "Yes."

"Well, this woman Terry has been spending an awful lot of time with your husband, and having heard what the two of you have gone through, I felt I oughta let you know."

Fatimah didn't say a word and neither did the woman. She'd said all that she had to say, and then she was gone, leaving Fatimah holding the phone to her ear with her shoulder as she held the limp washcloth in her hand. Fatimah wondered why she thought that she ought to let her know. Why did she think that it was her place? Had she thought that it was her duty as one woman to another? Or was she just trying to be cruel and hurtful? Fatimah ignored that call, but she couldn't ignore the others.

It seemed a different woman called each time. She knew they were mocking her. How could they be so cruel? Fatimah never hung up though. She would not give them the satisfaction, and she would not act like the wounded victim. No, not this time. They played, so she played, and not once in those two weeks did she let her husband know about the phone calls. If what these women were saying were true, he'd come to her. He'd tell on himself somehow as he always did whenever he did anything wrong.

Once a woman called to ask her if she knew where her husband was. Fatimah sighed into the phone knowing that that had to be a rhetorical question because, of course, whoever was on the other line was going to tell her exactly where her husband was. Or at least where she wanted Fatimah to think he was. This woman had said, "He's right here with me." Fatimah had said to her, "Well, when he's done, tell him that his wife said to pick up some milk and a loaf of bread for his family. Because wherever he is, he will come home." The woman hung up on her, but not before calling her a bitch.

Those calls were eating her up inside, but Fatimah wouldn't give these woman the satisfaction of knowing that it hurt. When they came at her, she would come right back at them with whatever she thought would cause the most pain. Her words were like daggers to those home wreckers. She knew that if it was true that Jason was cheating, that these women would go back to him all hurt and hysterical, and she'd be able to see it in his behavior when he got home. What does a woman in love with a married man want more than anything else in the world? She thought she knew the answer to that, and she'd use it as her ammunition.

Fatimah replayed the calls in her head, strategizing the what-ifs. What if they said, well then she would say, and so on. She wouldn't become the hysterical Why-Me woman that she was the last time her husband had cheated. This time she'd play it calm, cool, and collected. But in order to do that, she had to gather her thoughts.

At first, Fatimah thought to herself, "Not this shit again." She instantly wanted to toss Jason out on his ass. He had promised after the last time that it would never happen again. He swore before God and man that he would keep his dick in his pants and at least pretend to love, honor, and cherish his faithful wife. He'd promised.

Fatimah didn't need him. Hell, half the time, she didn't want him. He was a sorry lazy ass, who thought he was too cute to be the man that Fatimah thought he should be. At this point, the only endearing quality he had was that he was great with the kids. Sure, he worked every day, but every man should. He did his share around the house with much coaching and prodding from Fatimah, but Jason had never been a go-getter or a self-motivated man. Most, if not all, the accomplishments in his life had been because he had a good woman by his side to push him, encourage him, and bring out all the hidden potential that he had that only Fatimah could see. He would never leave her; she knew that. He needed her.

There hadn't been any obvious indicators that he'd been cheating. They'd make love on a regular basis. He would always come home on time. While the children were tucked away in their beds at night, her husband would always be in bed next to her. When and how he got the time to form these intimate bonds with other women, she didn't know. Nor did she care.

For all intents and purposes, they were good together. They looked good together. No, they looked perfect. On the Christmas cards with their beautiful family, they looked exquisite. They were the model couple. The ideal family as far as their fellow church members were concerned. On the surface, they were what other couples wanted to be.

No one knew the work or the time Fatimah had invested in that marriage. They didn't know about the bitter arguments. Or the fervent prayers that she sent up into the heavens that her husband would be faithful and remain faithful only to see the prayers go unanswered. No one knew about the incessant headaches.

Fatimah tossed and turned in her bed. She was becoming nauseated; her saliva was thick in her mouth, and she looked for the wastebasket next to her bed just in case she needed to vomit. She could hear the rain coming down, tip tapping against her window pane, and she just wanted to sleep. Flashes of light intermittently lit up her bedroom and gave it an eerie glow, as lightening glowed in the dark evening sky, making shadow puppets out of various inanimate objects in Fatimah's bedroom.

She could hear the commotion downstairs as her little brother Tye came in from the rain. Tye was so loud, and his voice really carried. He was loud every time he was around, and her children were loud when they were with him. She hoped that they would go in the basement and play video games or shoot some pool or something. Anything but sit in the living room, loudly talking and laughing.

Fatimah heard the heavy footsteps coming up the stairs, and she moaned out loud. She knew it was Tye coming up to mess with her, and she wasn't in the mood. She turned away from the bedroom door trying to avoid the light from the hallway when he opened the door.

Tye slowly pushed the door open, then pounded on the door really hard with his palm. Fatimah jumped, squeezed her eyes shut, and groaned.

"Fatimah!" he said with his loud voice. "Wake up, it's your brother!"

Tye jumped in the bed next to her. He was tall and thick for a seventeen-year-old, voice deep like a grown man.

"Wake up!" he said as he gave her a big wet kiss on her cheek.

"Get off my bed, Tye! You're soaked," Fatimah said.

"No, I'm not. It's just a little moisture," Tye answered. He played too much, Fatimah thought to herself, just like a little kid.

"Do you have your shoes on in my bed?"

"What I look like havin' my wet shoes on in yo' bed? I have home trainin'."

"I can't tell. You came in my room, and you didn't even knock," Fatimah said snatching her covers from up under him and covering herself. "Get outta here."

"What's the matter? You don't feel good?"

"No, I don't, so go down stairs wit cho loud butt. All the way downstairs. I don't wanna hear you."

"Why you so mean?" he said, squeezing her in a too-tight hug.

Fatimah elbowed him and yelled, "Go on now, Tye! I told you I'm sick!"

"Okay, okay," Tye said as he got off the bed. Fatimah bounced as the mattress rebounded from his weight. "I'm leavin'. But I wanted to ask you. What's up wit shawty down the street?"

"Boy, I know you didn't come all the way over here in the rain for Mrs. Watkins's granddaughter." Fatimah turned toward Tye, squinting at her brother.

Tye winked at Fatimah, flashed a dimpled smile, and said, "Naw, but since I'm over here."

"Boy, if you don't go 'n get outta here!"

Tye left her bedroom and bounded down the stairs like an oversized puppy. And of course, he didn't bother to close her bedroom door. The light from the hallway burned her eyes, and her head hurt so badly that her teeth started to ache. "Oh boy," Fatimah thought to herself, "not another one of these."

Fatimah gritted her teeth. It hurt. She slowly turned on her opposite side, away from the light, but the reflection of the light bounced off her bedroom walls. The least Tye could have done was turned off the hallway light, especially if he wasn't going to close the bedroom door. Fatimah couldn't yell to ask somebody to turn off the light. Her head hurt so badly that she couldn't bear to hear herself scream. She waited in the hope of someone turning off the light in an effort to conserve energy, but she could tell by the peace and quiet that they had all gone downstairs as she had asked. Fatimah sighed, grunted, and started to get out of bed to close the bedroom door when the phone rang. She reached over to pick the cordless phone up off the base. Private flashed across the caller ID's digital display.

Fatimah answered, "Hello?"

"Yes, may I speak to a Jason Thomas?" a young woman asked, her voice soft and nervous. Obviously not a professional call.

"He's not here right now. May I ask who's calling?" Fatimah answered.

Fatimah sat up in bed, her ears perking up like a hound, a slight smile on her face. The pounding in her head seemed to cease for just a split second as if allowing her to hear clearly enough to catch the woman's name. Yes, the games had begun.

The woman answered, "I'd rather not say. It's personal."

"Personal? Did she just say personal?" Fatimah thought to herself. No, this heffa didn't just call her house, ask to speak to her husband, and then have the nerve to tell her that it was personal. Fatimah reminded herself to keep her cool. The head games didn't work if she got frazzled or lost control. So she calmly stated, "Well, this is his wife, Mrs. Thomas." Fatimah said, emphasizing the Mrs. she continued, "May I ask what this is regarding?" The woman sighed long and deep into the phone. Fatimah recognized that sigh. It was the sigh you hear right before someone was getting up the nerve to say something they'd been rehearsing for a long time. Fatimah braced herself for the blow, but wasn't prepared for what she was about to hear.

"Well," she said, with a boldness that Fatimah was totally unprepared for. "I'm Natalie. The mother of his one-month-old daughter."

Fatimah's jaw dropped; it felt as if it was completely unhinged. The phone hit the floor. Fatimah thought she let out a yelp, but she couldn't quite recall. She felt paralyzed. She stared straight ahead, unable to close her mouth, unable to pick up the telephone, as lightening flashed and thunder cracked in the distance. Her eyes filled with water. Plump, salty tears rolled down her cheeks. She felt a knot in her throat, and she thought she might suffocate. It seemed as though her autonomic nervous system was shutting down. Maybe her body was attempting to put her out of her misery, to spare her from the shock and devastation of what this woman had just said.

Her hands were clenched into tight fists. She couldn't move. She didn't want to cry, but the tears continued to fall. Her throat ached, her head throbbed, and her heart was broken. She wouldn't be going to anymore counseling. At that moment, she decided that she wouldn't keep praying to sustain a marriage that both parties weren't willing to work hard to maintain. And she wouldn't welcome child upon outside child every weekend and grin and bear it as her stepmother had done for so many years. Nor would she continue to try and prove that she was woman enough to stay. Instead, she'd be woman enough to walk away.

Chapter 5

NEGATIVE EXPOSURE

Serena really missed Hakeem, but he was extremely jealous and he was too controlling. But she had to let him go, and she was glad that she broke away from him when she did. He had her doing all kinds of crazy stuff. If Mama knew half the stuff she'd been getting into while she was away at school, she'd come all the way out there to beat her butt.

Serena pulled the plastic bag filled with used condoms, empty beer bottles, and snack food wrappers out of the trash can next to the bed and tied the open end into a tight knot. She'd have Eric take it to the dumpster when she left. She walked around the small apartment with a garbage bag, straightening up the small space. She piled the bag up with newspapers and empty Chinese-food containers. She stuffed an old extra-large pizza box in the bag, being careful not to let the corners of the box rip the bag.

She thought Eric was so lucky not to have to live at the dorms. She wanted her own apartment off campus too, but Mama didn't think it was a good idea and since Mama was paying for it, then Mama had the last say. It wasn't worth the argument that she was nearly twenty-one years old, a grown woman. So she never used that on Mama. She just went to class every day and stayed in her books, and she let her extracurricular activities revolve around campus.

Sure, Serena partied, but she didn't get too out of hand. She drank a little too but not as much as Eric. She use to be amazed at how well Eric could hold his liquor. An entire six-pack and he wouldn't even appear to be drunk. She had attributed his high tolerance to alcohol to his height and weight. Eric was big and tall, Serena thought that that had to be why he could hold his liquor so well. That was until the other night

"Eric!" Serena had screamed as she pressed her palms against the dashboard and braced herself for impact. She'd wanted to close her eyes, but she didn't, she couldn't. She made eye contact with the child who stood frozen in the street like a deer in headlights. Serena's heart pounded in her chest. Eric had been drinking, he wouldn't be quick enough to avoid hitting the child.

Eric slammed on the brakes. The tires screeched and their backs slammed hard against the car seats.

God's Grace had saved this boy, because the car came to a halt as if it had hit some sort of an invisible barrier.

Serena covered her heart with her hand. Eric clutched the steering wheel with both hands, eyes wide as if he had just been splashed with ice water. Eric turned to Serena and let out a deep breath. A long deep sigh of relief. "What had just happened?" Eric wondered to himself.

Serena had known the answer to that. Eric's drunk ass had nearly struck a child.

Serena had wanted to yell at him. She'd told him before they'd left that he had been drinking too much to drive, but Eric had insisted on getting behind the wheel. But Serena didn't remind him of that, instead she got out of the car to see if the boy was alright. As soon as Serena had stepped out of the car, the startled boy had ran out into the darkness. Serena had started running after him when she heard Eric yell out to her. "Serena! Get back in the car!"

Serena had turned to look at Eric. "We have to see if he's okay."

"Get in the car!" Eric had said firmly.

Serena got back into the car and slammed the door.

"I've been drinking. I don't need no police coming by questioning me while I got liquor on my breath."

"I told you you had been drinking too much to drive."

Eric had looked at her and said, "If I'd been drinking too much I wouldn't have had the reflexes to stop the car."

"If you hadn't have been drinking too much, then maybe you would have seen the boy in the first place."

Serena sat back in the passenger seat with her arms crossed and stared at Eric. She pictured the boy's face in her head and she thought about her little nephews. She wondered if he was afraid, he likely thought that he was at fault.

"His young ass shouldn't have been in the street this late at night anyway."

"I'll drive." Serena had said as she snatched his keys out of the ignition and stepped out of the car. Serena walked over to the driver's side and beckoned for Eric to step out of his car. Eric reluctantly got out of the car and walked over to the passenger side. He slid the seat all the way back. Serena was much shorter than him, she had been sitting too close to the dash.

Eric had grumbled a little. He hadn't seen what had just happened as a warning. He hadn't seen it as his fault. Serena didn't say a word as she drove him back to his apartment. Eric was quiet because he had slept the rest of the way home. Eric had slept soundly. Serena was a nervous wreck, she saw this as the first of many drunken incidents and she wondered if she'd still be with him for the next one.

*　　*　　*

Eric didn't get loud and belligerent like Mama when she'd been drinking. And Eric never got plastered. Serena had seen Mama plastered, and it wasn't a pretty sight. She'd be pissy drunk, lying on the floor crying and talking about how much she loved Otis, their biological father. She'd do this right in front of Ray, their "stepfather," and Ray would clean her up and put her to bed every time.

Serena wondered if Ray was ever really hurt by that. Imagine, the woman you love lying flat out drunk in your home, with you, pining and crying over another man. Mama had done so many things to hurt Ray, but he never left her. For years, Mama stayed with Ray and went out and made babies with Daddy as if Ray didn't mean a thing. And Ray would just stand back and take it. He never laid a hand on Mama. Of course, they would fight, but every argument ended up with Ray forgiving her, and Mama would be out doing her own thing, as if Ray didn't really matter. Mama didn't respect him. Serena didn't want him to, but she wondered if Mama would have respected him more if he had put his foot down or if he had hit her. Serena reminisced as she continued gathering up garbage and pushing it down into the bag.

Serena thought about going home to visit on Friday for her birthday; she could hardly wait. Her birthday was on Saturday, and she was so excited.

Eric came up behind Serena and grabbed her around the waist; it startled her. She was so deep in thought. He laid his face on her neck and kissed her there.

"You don't hafto do that," Eric said as he took the trash bag out of her hand, tossed it aside, and led her back to the bed.

"This place is a mess," Serena said. Eric took Serena by the hand and led her as he walked backward toward his bed.

"I'll get it later. Don't worry about it," Eric said as he landed on the bed pulling her on top of him.

Serena smiled at Eric. He loved her dimples. He examined her body as she sat on top of him, straddling him in her white bra and panties.

"Take that off," Eric said smiling as he loosened the strap to her bra, pulling it down slightly over her right shoulder.

Serena smiled and shook her head "No."

"I hafto get going. I have a lot of studying to do," Serena answered.

Serena was so homesick. She missed her mother and her sisters. She missed Daddy and her little brother Tye. And she missed all her nicccs, nephews, and grandparents. She couldn't wait to be back home with her family and friends. They had so much to catch up on, and she couldn't seem to fit it all in during her visits.

She'd really miss Eric though. Her rebound boyfriend. She never did too well with long-distance relationships though. He was sweet, outgoing, and intelligent. He wasn't pushy or arrogant, like the other guys she'd gone out with. He wasn't cruel like Hakeem.

Her eyes brightened as she looked down at Eric as he admired her half-nude body. He put his hands around her tiny waist and ran his fingers down her flat stomach. Why was she thinking about Hakeem's sorry ass when she was here with this fine specimen of a man? Serena smiled, leaned down, and kissed Eric. His eyes were closed. She let her tongue explore his mouth, and she nibbled on his full, perfect lips. She moaned as she kissed him. She gyrated on his already-erect dick. She knew she was a tease. She hadn't planned on doing anything with him this morning. She had to get back. But she'd let him enjoy the show. She slipped her bra down around her waist, but she didn't unhook it. She let him nibble on her nipples and kiss her firm breasts as his hands explored the rest of her body.

"You are perfect," he whispered, as he slipped his hand into her white cotton panties and massaged her butt. He moaned. "Come on, baby, take it off," he said without even opening his eyes.

Serena didn't answer. But she didn't remove her underwear either. With her bra still around her waist, she scooted her body down, leaned forward, and ran her tongue across his nipples. She could feel them getting harder with each stroke of her tongue. She sucked them; she knew he was very sensitive there. She knew what he liked.

"Come on, Serena," he begged as he tugged on her panties. Serena laid her hand over his hand and gently removed his grip from her underwear.

She kissed his neck. He didn't even feel it when she left her mark there. It was her mark, because it would let other women know that he was taken. Not that they cared.

"Baby, I've gotta go. I'm serious. I've got so much work to do."

"I'll help you," Eric said as he stroked her breast.

"I can't concentrate with you," Serena said as she climbed down off of Eric and pulled her bra back over her shoulders. "If I'm gonna stay on schedule, then I've gotta leave now."

Eric stopped trying to convince her to stay. He had important things that he needed to do too, but he wanted to be with her. He wanted to be able to look over at her as he studied; he wanted her with him as he ran his errands and continued with his day. But he wasn't going to share that with her, not yet. It was too early for that.

Serena showered and changed her clothes, and she kissed Eric good-bye. She headed back to her dorm, and the first thing she did was pull out her journal. She reached into her overnight bag, removed a slip of paper from her pants' pocket, and copied it from the paper and into her journal. It was Friday's journal entry.

It wasn't that she couldn't remember what had happened on Friday. She just had to write it down just as it hit her, while she was feeling it. It wouldn't be the same to try to recall it a day later. It wouldn't feel right. So she wrote her journal entry on a slip of paper and buried it in the pocket of her jeans.

Serena had kept a journal for years, but had become more diligent about writing in it daily since she entered college. She wrote in poetry or prose about the day's events. Some days, only a few lines, on other days, a page or two, but she never missed a day. She had to write something that summed up the essence of her day.

Sometimes, her writings were bitter and pained like after a breakup. And other times, they were beautiful and vividly descriptive. She wished she could get up enough nerve to perform her poetry to music in front of an audience. She'd love to recite her poetry at an open mic night at Rico's or something, but she was too afraid.

Serena lay on her stomach across her twin-size bed with pen in hand and her face in her journal. She wrote with her pretty pink pen—the one with the colorful fuzzy puff on the end that moved ever so slightly with each pen stroke. The journal was a hardbound book, and Serena thought it was so pretty with its bright purple, electric blue, and hot pink designs. It had big flecks of gold throughout, which to Serena made it look elegant. It also had a heavy lock on it, as if the lock could really keep anyone out. She kept the key on her car-key ring. It was a pretty little gold key.

This was Serena's addiction. Not a day went by without a journal entry. Each day would find something written under that day's date, even if Serena had to write it on the back of a cocktail napkin. All of her friends thought she was nuts, jotting things done here and there. They thought she was super-obsessed with studying, but they were wrong. She was super-obsessed with her journal, the journal that nobody knew anything about, not even Mariah, who could keep a secret like nobody's business.

Serena hid the journal underneath her mattress. She was pretty cool with her roommate Tiffany, but she didn't trust anyone with her journal. It was her baby. Not to mention that it had some very incriminating entries in it—things that she'd never be able to live down if it got out and things that may be pretty hurtful to others if they found out about it. Serena knew this, but her journal allowed her to be brutally honest, in a way that she could never be in real life. So she never held back. She felt compelled to write in it, and she wrote exactly as she felt.

Serena was the baby girl. Baby doll was the nickname her daddy gave her. He said when she was born, she looked like a little white baby doll and that she sounded like one when she cried. Her skin was smooth and creamy. She was lighter than the rest of her siblings. But she had all the characteristic Turner features: the high cheekbones, the large, dark eyes, and the famous dimpled Turner smile. She was sweet and bubbly, but a bit naive.

Serena was also the shortest of her sisters: five foot, four inches tall, slightly bowlegged, which made her look a little hippier than she actually was. She had thick, wavy, wash-and-wear hair that she kept short and in cute funky styles. She loved designer clothes, but could pull off a T-shirt and a pair of old jogging pants and still look sexy. Her voice was high pitched, and most times, Fatimah found it to be irritating. Her other sisters thought it was cute and would mock her lovingly. But Serena didn't like it.

Their dad had given all his children nicknames. None of them were really original, but his children answered to them. Nicole was Nicci. Fatimah was Teemah. Mariah was Juicy, Otis's rather indelicate tribute to Mariah's struggle with her weight. Aniyah was Niyah. And Tye's nickname was baby boy.

Tye was Daddy's pride and joy. The only boy out of their mama's six children and daddy's four with his wife, Barbara. Mama made six children with Otis while he was married to his current wife. Nicole was born the day Daddy got married, and Daddy was right there in the hospital waiting for her to come out. While his wife waited in the waiting area on her wedding day.

Serena really liked her stepmother. She thought she was classy. She wasn't argumentative or confrontational like Mama, and she was good to all of Otis's children. She'd make them feel at home whenever they visited. She hugged and kissed them like they were her own babies, and she never discriminated against them. But what impressed Serena the most is that Serena never saw her take a drink, and she liked that.

Barbara, their stepmother, was a clean woman. She kept a meticulous home and didn't complain about how the girls played. She cleaned for a living. She worked for rich folks all of her life, and they loved her and were very good to her and her girls. She didn't have much education, but Serena found her to be quite intellectual in her own way. She knew a lot about the world around her. She was very intuitive and knowledgeable, but Serena thought she was too weak.

How could a woman with so much to offer settle for a man that repeatedly cheats and cheats right in her face, and not only does he cheat, but he makes babies on you, babies that you watch every other weekend or more. Serena wondered if Barbara secretly hated them. She wondered if she'd just mastered being phony. She had years and years of practice pretending to love Otis's illegitimate babies. Nicole, Fatimah, and Mariah were the first group of kids. When Mariah turned eighteen years old, she stopped visiting every other weekend just like the two oldest girls. It was just Aniyah and Serena and Tye visiting every other weekend.

Serena wondered how Barbara must have felt when Tye was born. Barbara was unable to have children after her youngest daughter Lacey was born. She'd had really bad fibroid tumors, and she had to have a total hysterectomy. She couldn't give Otis a son, but Mama could and she did.

Serena wondered why Barbara wasn't mean and bitter. She wondered why she didn't have tantrums. She wondered why she didn't leave. Serena loved her daddy, but she couldn't understand why Mama was so obsessed with Daddy and why Barbara didn't just let Mama have him. Hell, she was "having" him anyway.

Serena continued to write, oblivious to the world around her, because she was off in her own world. She heard a rustle at the door but ignored it. It was probably someone playing around outside in the hallway. She heard it again, and she shifted around in her bed to see where it was coming from. Serena watched as a manila envelope was slid underneath her door. She waited for it to come all the way to her side of the door, as her heart raced.

Serena watched all types of scary movies, and she knew that it was never a good thing for someone to slide anything up under the door. Sure, every now and then, she would get some unimportant school correspondence in that manner. But most information of any importance would be posted on the bulletin board. Serena wasn't the type to leap to the door and swing it open in an effort to see who the deliverer was. Besides, whoever it was hadn't knocked, and they hadn't bothered to call.

Serena waited. She waited until the rustling had stopped and most of the envelope was on her side of the door. She listened for footsteps trailing off and away from the door before she got off the bed. As she approached the envelope, she noticed words across the entire front of it written in a bold black marker. She tried to read it upside down, afraid to touch it, but when she read the name Hakeem, she picked it right up.

The envelope read as follows: I have been trying to get you to talk to me but, you won't answer my calls. You ignore me all over campus. Maybe you'll talk to me now. Hakeem.

Serena opened the envelope; it was sealed and reinforced with scotch tape. Inside were three smaller envelopes. She opened the envelope marked with number one. It was filled with old cards and old love letters and poetry that she had sent to Hakeem. Some of the letters she hadn't even remembered writing. "See," she thought to herself, "that's why it's a good thing I keep a journal. I'd never remember any of this stuff." She wondered why Hakeem had sent her all of this. Maybe he'd finally come to the realization that it was over. She started to go through all the old cards and letters, but she decided she'd do that later and she stuffed everything back in the envelope and put it in the original larger envelope.

Next, she opened the envelope marked number two. In it, she found tons of pictures of her and Hakeem in various stages of their relationship. "Aww," she said to herself. "We did look cute together." She couldn't help herself. She flipped through all of the pictures and recalled a pleasant memory with each one. She liked how Hakeem used to make her feel. She missed him, but she was glad that she'd ended their relationship; she wasn't going to tolerate an unfaithful boyfriend. It was too damaging to her self-esteem. And she didn't want to be like so many women that she loved, who allowed their men to tear them down and change them at every turn. Hakeem was cute enough and boy, was he sexy, but cute and sexy wasn't worth it.

Serena stuffed the pictures back in the envelope marked number two, being careful not to bend the pictures. She'd hold on to these; after all, they did bring back some good memories. She'd hide them in the bottom of her trunk because she didn't want Eric to come across them and get the wrong idea.

She opened up the next envelope and noticed a big black X across the front. "Hmm," she said, this envelope really peaked her curiosity.

She opened it, and before she could pull out its contents, she noticed there were pictures in this envelope too. Serena's heart raced. She was afraid to look. She dropped the envelope on her bed as if Hakeem had contaminated it with something. She sat there on the bed with her legs crossed; she pulled both ankles in close to her, crossing her legs tighter. She pressed a tightly clenched fist to her mouth as if she was going to cough into her hand and said out loud. "Okay, let me think."

Her mind raced to every possible scenario, none of them good. She'd taken some very suggestive photographs after hours in several bizarre locations around the school. It was sort of a dare, and she'd accepted the challenge. Serena was by no means ashamed of her body. But she wasn't an exhibitionist either. She'd wondered every now and then what Hakeem would do with those photos if their relationship ended. She wondered if he would ever try to use the photographs against her.

If these were the photographs that she thought they were, they could get her in a world of trouble. Not only were the poses very racy, but the locations were off limits. She could be expelled from school if they were ever exposed. She thought about the different locations. It seemed like so much fun at the time to strip or change into different costumes and race to the other sites before the deadline. Hakeem had only had access to the keys for a limited amount of time, and he had to get them back before anyone had noticed.

She thought about the most incriminating of all the pictures. The one with her lying on her back in the nude across the dean's desk. It was a silhouette shot, and you couldn't see her face. Her back was arched, and she posed just as Hakeem had instructed. It came out beautifully. The arch of her back was perfect. Her head was thrown back over the edge of the desk, and she covered her face with her hands just as Hakeem had posed her—hands flat, with fingers spread over her face, pinkies together, touching side by side, forearms together with elbows up, as if covering her face in shame. She was lying lengthwise, and her toes were pointed toward the opposite end of the huge mahogany desk. She remembered how hard it was to hold the pose without sliding off the side of the desk headfirst.

It was beautiful. It was an awkward pose and a bit uncomfortable for Serena, but it turned out very tastefully. That is, if you can call lying butt naked across the dean's desk tasteful. The room was so dark when the photo was taken. The only illumination was the outdoor lighting on the grounds and the flash from Hakeem's camera; it was a black-and-white photograph. She remembered how impressed she'd been with his photography, how much she loved being his subject. Now she just felt like a puppet.

She picked the envelope up. It was exactly what she suspected. She wasn't angry, and it wasn't as scary as she thought it would be, seeing the pictures after such a long time. She was sort of happy to be able to see the photos again. She flipped through each of them one by one. She found herself a little embarrassed, but not by the pictures. She couldn't believe she let anyone talk her into being so foolish. Serena looked at each of the pictures, without realizing how beautiful each one of them were. They could easily be in any magazine or art gallery. She was an excellent model, and her body was the perfect canvas and Hakeem knew it. She reflected on how fun and exciting it was at the time. Serena turned the photos over and began to stuff them in the envelope when she noticed a note attached to the photograph of her on the dean's desk. It read as follows: You see me. Or everyone sees you. Hakeem.

Serena called Hakeem immediately. He answered on the first ring.

"Hello?"

"What is it that you want?" she asked Hakeem.

"I want to see you."

"See me about what?"

"We have a lot to talk about."

"So what are you saying, Hakeem. If I don't see you anymore, then you'll do what?"

"Come, see me, and find out."

"Hakeem, you're not making any sense. I don't have time for these games."

"If you have time to go over to what's his name's dump of an apartment and fuck him, then you have time to see the man that holds your future in his hands. So I advise you to make time."

Serena told him that she'd call him back. She didn't trust Hakeem; she knew he wanted her back, but she didn't know why. He had cheated on her with Stephanie, and she wanted no parts of him. As far as she was concerned, Stephanie could have him. What was the problem now? It wasn't as if either of them were single. He had Stephanie, and she had Eric.

Serena tried to reach Eric, but she couldn't reach him. She tried to reach her friend Stacey, but she couldn't reach her either. She knew she didn't want to meet with Hakeem by herself. She didn't want him trying to touch and kiss on her. But she didn't want to ignore the fact that he had the negatives of the pictures that lay in front of her.

Her phone rang. She hoped it was Eric or Stacey. It was Hakeem.

"Hakeem, where's your girlfriend."

"I'm talking to her."

Serena sighed into the phone; she was becoming very irritated. She knew this was what he wanted. "Where is Stephanie?"

"How the hell am I supposed to know? She ain't here." Hakeem was becoming irritated with her too. Serena wondered if that was the answer he'd given when the women that he cheated on her with had asked about her. "So what's it gonna be, Serena?" Hakeem asked.

"It's over, Hakeem. Do what you want to do with the pictures."

Serena hung up the phone and smiled. She was proud of herself. The phone rang again, and it was Eric. He told her how much he missed her, and she told him she missed him too. She invited him over to spend the rest of the day with her. He gladly accepted her invitation.

When Eric came over, she decided to go back to his place. She packed an overnight bag, and she gathered her books. She prepared a portion of the day's journal entry and stuffed it in the pocket of her jeans as Eric grabbed her overnight bag and her book bag, and they headed out the door together.

Serena was a little nervous. She kept looking at her surroundings suspiciously as if Hakeem could be lurking in the shadows, watching her. She gripped Eric's hand tightly. Eric looked down at Serena and smiled.

"You've got a good grip on my hand." Eric said.

"Am I hurting you?"

"No," Eric said and smiled.

Serena loosened her grip on Eric's hand, but she didn't want to. She was nervous, but she didn't know why she felt this way. He had never put his hands on her. She knew that Hakeem had a real mean streak though. She had seen it in action, and it wasn't pretty. Serena wondered why she should even be thinking about him right now. He was unfaithful to her. She wasn't the one running around on him. Why couldn't he just let her go?

Eric opened the passenger door to his '98 Ford Escort and let Serena in. Then he closed the door behind her. Eric tossed Serena's bags in the trunk of his car. Serena rolled down the passenger side window as Eric got into the car. She looked around outside. Why did she feel so uneasy? She felt as if she was being watched.

"You okay?" Eric asked, genuinely concerned as he leaned over to give Serena a kiss.

"Yea, I'm fine," She said and smiled.

She liked that Eric was concerned about her. Eric made her feel protected and secure, the way she used to feel with Hakeem. Serena kissed him again at the next stoplight. The stubble from his light beard pressed into her face and left it a little reddened. She didn't mind. She liked the way it felt on her skin.

Once they got to Eric's place, they studied a little, ordered pizza, made love, and tried to watch a rented movie, but both of them ended up falling asleep on the couch. Serena and Eric had both deviated from their plan for the day, but to them it was well worth it. To spend quality time with each other seemed more important than what was written in their day planners.

That night, Serena couldn't sleep very well. She had a very uneasy feeling. Eric was sleeping on his side spooning Serena; he had her body pulled in close to his, and he held her with his entire body as if shielding her and protecting her. His body was always so hot that sometimes, she'd wake up drenched in sweat and sometimes, she felt smothered. But she always felt safe.

Serena gently moved Eric's arm and rolled her body out from underneath him. It was hot, and his small apartment seemed to hold heat. The air conditioner wasn't strong enough to cool the efficiency effectively, and the fans just recycled the hot air throughout the room. Serena's wavy hair was soaked, and her thick, dark curls were pasted to her head. Eric was soaked too, and his naked body glistened under the glow of the moonlight.

Serena was miserable. She pulled the wet camisole off her body and threw it on the chair next to the bed. She slipped out of her panties, tossed them on top of the camisole on the chair, and headed into the bathroom, closing the door behind her. Serena stood in front of the bathroom mirror and ran her fingers through her hair.

"It's so hot," she said to herself as she pulled back the shower curtain, leaned over the tub, and turned on the bathwater. She stood and wiped the sweat off her brow with the back of her hand. She felt so tired. It was as if the summer heat had drained her of every bit of energy.

As she soaked in the too-hot bathwater, she asked herself if she should be afraid of what Hakeem might do with the photographs. All of the possibilities went through her mind as if her life was flashing before her very eyes. Her sweating body sank into the steaming bathwater. Serena used the toes of her right foot to add cold water to the hot bath. She was so confused that she hadn't realized that she hadn't made the bathwater cool enough. After all, that was why she was getting in the bath in the first place, to cool her sweating body off. She closed her eyes and considered waking Eric and telling him everything that she'd eventually wind up telling him later.

That was the one thing that she was not afraid of. She wasn't afraid of telling Eric that she'd posed for pictures for a man that she believed that she was in a loving, trusting, relationship with. She'd be a bit embarrassed about revealing to him the risky places and the crazy position she'd put herself in. She felt really stupid allowing Hakeem to photograph her on the desk of her dean's office, but because of the lighting and the angle, no one would ever be able to tell that it was her. That was true of all the photographs. Hakeem had been clever enough to pose Serena and to add lighting to each pic in such a way that it would make it very difficult to guess the true identity of the featured model.

Serena wanted to call her sisters. She wanted to have a group meeting with them to ask them what she should do. She secretly wished that she could have done that right after she received the envelope, but she didn't have time for that, Hakeem wanted an answer quickly. Besides, she didn't feel like hearing her older sisters tell her how stupid she was for posing for those photos in the first place. Fatimah would embarrass her and make her feel like a fool, Mariah would keep asking her, "Why would she do that?"

No one could ever tell how Aniyah really felt about a situation because she was always torn between fussing at her baby sister and not expressing herself at all. But not in this case; she suspected that she'd tell her how stupid and irresponsible she was too. Especially since everybody didn't think she could handle going to school out of state and away from them.

Nicole was something different though. Of course, she agreed with everyone else that Serena should have attended her freshman year of college at home, but she didn't put the pressure on like everyone else. Serena was curious about what Nicole would say, but not curious enough to call her. Serena decided she'd handle this herself and she wouldn't call anyone unless she absolutely had to. They already thought she was naive and foolish, and she didn't have any intention of proving anybody right.

Serena used her hands to splash the cool water over her body. She slid herself down in the deep bathtub and closed her eyes. She remembered her baths in Gramma's old white bathtub with the feet. She remembered how deep it seemed and how difficult it was for her to get out of it by herself. She remembered how easy life used to be back then. Back when none of the major life decisions were made by her. She remembered a time when the scariest thing was going to sleep with the lights off.

Serena slid herself in the water so that it totally covered her head; then she slid herself back up and shook her head. She held the sides of the tub with one hand and smoothed her curly hair back with the other hand. "Too much to consider. There is entirely too much to think about right now," she thought as she stood and stepped out of the tub.

She let the water run out of the tub, and she exited the bathroom without drying off. It was hot, and she liked the way the fans felt on her damp skin. She glanced over at Eric. He was fast asleep as always. Serena walked into the kitchen and grabbed a cold bottled water out of the refrigerator. She sipped the cold water as she stood in front of the kitchen sink. The water from her hair ran down her face and neck. She looked out the kitchen window at the streetlights as they shone down on the cars. The quiet street seemed completely deserted now, as if everyone but her had fallen asleep. Serena turned away from the sink and continued drinking her water. It didn't take long for her body to dry. At least, she felt a little cooler now.

She was very tired, but too anxious to go to sleep. She felt as if her heart was racing, but she couldn't for the life of her understand why. She wanted to wake Eric up to talk, but she knew he'd be too incoherent to have any type of quality conversation with her, and she needed to talk to somebody.

Serena paced with the empty water bottle in her hand. She walked back into the kitchen and looked out the window again into the still darkness. The street was clear, and it was eerily quiet outside.

Her skin was hot again. She was miserable. Her short hair gave her a little relief. She thought about calling La Maya. But she had two little girls, and she didn't want to wake them. She missed La Maya. She was fun to talk to, but she didn't think she'd be much help with the Hakeem situation. She had to call somebody though.

Serena put on a pair of panties, walked over to the nightstand, and grabbed her cell phone. She walked into the living room area and sat on the big green velour couch with her legs crossed and dialed.

"Hello?" La Maya answered groggily.

"Hey, La Maya," Serena whispered into the phone.

"Serena?"

"Yea, it's me."

"What's goin' on. What time is it?" La Maya asked, eyes still closed with her head on her pillow.

"It's two o'clock here," Serena answered without actually looking at the time. It was one fifty-nine. when she dialed her number.

"Mmm?" La Maya moaned into the phone, her voice full of sleep. "So what's going on that would make you call me at two o'clock in the morning?"

"One o'clock Cleveland time."

"Okay. One o'clock Cleveland time," La Maya said, her voice dry and sleepy. "Why are you whispering?"

"Maya, you've got to wake up for this. I need you to be fully awake and focused," Serena answered, totally ignoring La Maya's question.

La Maya laughed, but not her usual laugh; she seemed really exhausted. "Okay, baby doll."

La Maya opened her eyes, looked up at her ceiling, then slid her legs over the side of the bed. "Let me get my bearings." She sighed. "I was in a pretty deep sleep."

La Maya got up and walked into the bathroom. She turned on the cold water and let it run a bit; then she splashed a little onto her face, then she dried it with a hand towel.

"Okay, I'm awake. What's up?"

Serena gave La Maya the back story of the Hakeem/picture situation. But the background info was so vague and rushed that La Maya kept interrupting Serena to get a clearer picture of what was going on.

"La Maya, pay attention! You keep interrupting me."

"Serena, I hafto ask questions so that I can understand what's going on. I can't help you if I don't have a clear picture of what you're saying."

"All right, all right. But you keep asking me about stuff that I've told you about already."

"I'm sorry, but it is one thirty in the morning. I was sound asleep when you called, and it's a little difficult for me to get it together."

"Well, maybe I should have called you in the morning."

"Helloo? It is the morning," La Maya said.

"You know what I mean. Later on in the morning, when you're fully awake."

"Yea. That would have been great," La Maya said sarcastically. "But I'm up now, so go on with the story."

"It is not a story."

"Whatever, just get on with it."

Serena continued to explain her situation to her cousin. This time La Maya yeahed, and uh-huhed in all the right places indicating to Serena that she understood what she was saying. When Serena was done, there was a noticeable silence. Serena was unsure if La Maya had gone to sleep or if her phone had dropped the call.

"You there?"

"Yea, I'm here."

"Well?"

"I'm thinking."

"And your advice is?"

"Did you call yo' mama?"

"No, I didn't call my mama. I called you. Tell me that's not the best advice you have."

"Serena, I don't know what to say. The only thing that I can think to tell you is to talk to Hakeem."

"I am not talking to him. I did that already."

"All I'm saying is that maybe you can meet with him and talk and maybe you can talk him out of doing whatever he plans on doing with those pictures." La Maya sighed. She was not sure if it was the best advice, but that was the only advice that she could think of.

"I'm not going to meet with Hakeem. There was a reason that I broke up with him in the first place."

"Yea, because he cheated, right?"

"Yep."

"Then what are you afraid of? You can meet him at a public place. A fast food place or something."

"I'm not meeting with him Maya."

"Fine, Serena. I don't know what to tell you. I mean this was your boyfriend. You know him better than I do. I am in no way tryin' to get you to put yourself in an uncomfortable or dangerous situation. It's just that I'm the type of person that has to talk about things of any importance face-to-face. I'd need him to look into my face to see that I'm serious, and I'd need to look into his face to see that he's serious. This is a serious situation. I'm just sayin' you can't properly gauge emotion over the phone. People tell all kinds of lies in their voices. You hafto be able to look a person in the eyes."

Serena didn't have to look Hakeem in the eyes to know that he was serious. And she didn't need to meet with him face-to-face to tell if he was lying. He was a liar and a cheater, and he couldn't be trusted. She knew that if he intended to use the pictures against her, then there was nothing that she could say or do to stop him. Yes, Serena knew that meeting him was not an option, and unless she was willing to succumb to his wishes, Hakeem wouldn't even consider changing his mind.

"La Maya, I know that I really am in a bind right now. Actually, I didn't really think that you would be able to come up with a quick fix. I just need to know if this is fixable. Do you think it's fixable. I mean, without calling my mama, without calling my sisters, do you think that I can fix this myself?"

La Maya sighed and paused as if she needed some time to think. She didn't want to be insensitive; after all, her little cousin called her for her help.

"Yes, I think it's fixable." La Maya answered.

"Okay." Serena said with a sigh of relief.

"But no, I don't think you can fix this yourself."

"And why not?"

"It doesn't matter why. I just think that you'd be making matters worse if you tried to fix it yourself. Things have obviously gotten out of hand.

You're about to graduate from college, and your focus should not be on this. You should be focusing on your studies, not this shit."

"And how would my mama and my sisters help me?"

"First of all, you may not need their help right away. But it would be nice to keep them informed so that they'd know what to expect in case something happens. Who knows, Hakeem may be bluffing. You might be getting yourself all worked up over nothing."

"Yea, you're right. I'm just getting worked up over nothing." Serena said as she thought to herself, "Was La Maya even listening to me?"

It took Serena a little over two hours on the phone with her cousin to realize that she wasn't going to be any help at all—at least not with this situation. But sitting and talking with La Maya helped that panicky feeling subside, and Serena was grateful for that. La Maya had come to the conclusion that Serena's problem was fixable, which was a good thing, but she didn't have any really good solutions as to how.

When Serena got off the phone with La Maya, she wondered what her cousin was thinking about her. She wondered if she thought that she was just a stupid little girl. She didn't bother telling La Maya to keep her secret to herself. That was a given. She hadn't told her that she agreed with her suggestion to call her mother and sisters because that would be a boldface lie. Serena had no intention of calling them. She'd decided that she was perfectly capable of handling the situation herself. She'd called Hakeem's bluff' now it was time to sit and wait for his next move.

Chapter 6

MELANCHOLY SUMMER RAIN

Nicole sent Jermaine away early. He said it was okay because he had to be at work early anyway, but he'd called her several times since he'd left her home. She could tell that he didn't want to leave her. Her face and neck were sore and she thought that she was going to bruise, and she wasn't about to explain that to Jermaine. Plus she wasn't in the mood for his ego-boosting questions like was it good to you? did you like it when I . . . ? and did you come? She sent him home before he could get the impression that he was anything more than a late-night hookup.

She didn't sleep after he left; she thought about the one thing that should be furthest from her mind—that sorry, stankin'-ass Darren. She sat up in bed and wondered how it could have come to this. How, after being so careful, could she let herself fall in love with that asshole Darren?

Things were great the way they were before she met him. Her business was booming, which was a great feat in this economy. She wasn't lacking at all, not financially, physically, or emotionally. Her sister Fatimah would disagree with her; she thought that Nicole most definitely was lacking spiritually, but Nicole would always remind her that her spirituality was her business and that her relationship with God was just that hers and that she should mind her own business. She wasn't lonely before Darren, nor was she unhappy. There was absolutely no void in her life that needed to be filled, at least not by Darren's sorry behind.

Nicole lay in bed and thought about her last night with Darren. Their last night together as a couple. The night of the silk scarf. It had felt like a noose tightening around her throat. Nicole had slept so soundly that she hadn't felt Darren wrapping the silk scarf around her delicate neck. She awakened to feel the squeeze of the scarf against her windpipe. She awakened to find Darren straddling her as he held the loose ends of the scarf in his tightly clenched fist.

Nicole didn't have to ask him what the fuck he was doing, because he could read it in her eyes.

"This will make our love making more intense." Darren had said as he pulled the scarf tighter around her neck.

Intense? She'd thought. Intense? She'd allowed this man to do whatever he wanted with her. She had contorted her agile body into every conceivable position. She had performed acts with him that should have been reserved for the man that she intended on spending the rest of her life with. And he wanted intense?

Nicole's eyes watered. She ignored the pain and focused on her anger. She raised her hand and smacked him hard across his face. She watched as the print of her hand rose up on his cheek and as his skin turned bright red from the slap. Darren turned his head slightly. It stung. He turned to her and smiled. He released the scarf. And after coughing to clear her throat Nicole had said to Darren, "How's that for intense?"

Darren dismounted her as Nicole sat up in the bed and pulled the scarf from around her neck. She could feel the friction burn that the scarf had made on her skin. Such an ungrateful bastard, she'd thought to herself.

"I thought you'd try anything for me."

"I have you thankless bastard."

"I was trying something a little different." He'd uttered as he smiled furtively.

"What? To kill me in my sleep?"

"No." He'd laughed. "It's called scarfing." He had tried to explain what scarfing was when Nicole had interrupted him.

"I know what scarfing is!" She stared at Darren as if he had lost his mind. "What you did was not scarfing! We were not having sex! I was asleep. I was sound asleep, because I thought I was sleeping with a man I could trust."

"Don't take this overboard."

"Muthafucka are you crazy? You just tied a fuckin' scarf around my neck while I was asleep." The shrillness of her own voice had even annoyed her.

Nicole could smell the stench of the loud perfume soaked scarf. It smelled like perfume and body odor.

"Ugh." She'd said as she held the scarf away from her and tossed it to the floor. "Who does that belong to?" Nicole had said to Darren with a raised brow. "Please don't tell me that you tied some random bitch's scarf around my neck." Nicole shook her head and squeezed her eyes shut, then looked up at Darren again. "Answer me!" Nicole had yelled at him as she sat there with her arms crossed and with her lips pressed firmly together. She had pictured another woman wearing that scarf, the material soaking up the sweat and grime from her neck, she pictured the same scarf being used by Darren during sex as he and some unnamed woman engaged in erotic asphyxiation.

"No, the scarf doesn't belong to some random bitch."

"Well then whose scarf is it?" Nicole had asked, she knew that it wasn't a new scarf, it wasn't even clean.

"It belongs to my wife."

"Come again?"

For an entire year Darren and Nicole had dated and he had always referred to his wife as his ex wife. Now all of a sudden she's his wife?

Needless to say she had wanted an explanation as to why the sudden change. And the explanation she'd received was that he was currently married and still living with his wife. Nicole thought it was a joke at first, but quickly dismissed that thought, because it wasn't at all funny. It didn't take much convincing for Nicole to see that it was true. And that the man she was dating exclusively for an entire year had belonged to someone else and had been making a fool out of her all along.

Nicole had calmly slipped off of Darren's king sized bed and had gotten herself dressed. Darren didn't try to stop her. She shook her head and mumbled something to herself as she buttoned her blouse. You can't please anybody, she'd thought to herself. That was why she had always focused on pleasing herself. Darren had shared with her that day, that he was a married man and that he had been married for many, many years. And on that day Nicole had ended what she thought would be a beautiful and lasting relationship with the man whom she had mistakenly thought had been her soul mate.

Last night's sweat had dried in Nicole's hair and had left it matted to her head. She had a standing appointment with her cousin La Maya to get her hair done, but she'd received a voice-mail message from her asking if it would be okay if she'd come later. It was about six in the morning, and Nicole was in no position to answer her call. She still hadn't called her back, but La Maya knew it was cool and that Nicole would see her whatever time she decided to come. She appreciated that La Maya was willing to drive out to her home and do her hair on one of her busiest days of the week. Nicole paid her well though, and she was sure that La Maya appreciated that too.

She didn't have much planned today. She knew rain was in the forecast, and she'd decided that she'd just sit at home and chill. Nicole had given her house staff the day off, and she didn't have any plans to entertain today.

Nicole thought about Darren's little boy, Kamar. Darren's son loved her. Kamar was a cute little boy. Big, almond-shaped eyes, with lashes long enough to touch his eyebrows, he had Darren's round head, but other than that he looked nothing like Darren. He looked every bit like his mother, the woman who Nicole then thought was Darren's ex-wife.

*   *   *

Kamar was four years old when Nicole was first introduced to him; he was tall for his age, and Nicole was amazed at how well he spoke. She was so impressed with the child's grammar and of his vocabulary. She could tell that someone spent a lot of time with this little boy.

It was a beautiful day, and Darren had planned to meet Nicole at a local delicatessen. She'd asked Darren, "Why the deli?" and he'd answered, "It's my son's favorite spot." She didn't believe Darren. Nicole knew early on that Darren stretched the truth, but she'd convinced herself that his little white lies were harmless, little did she know.

It was hot, the day she met Kamar. A scorcher. She wore the halter sundress with the big, colorful flowers because it was so cool and pretty. She wore her wedged-heeled flip-flops and a pair of sunglasses. She'd briefly considered dressing to impress and then thought how do you dress to impress a four-year-old. She was showing a lot of cleavage, but Nicole didn't care; it was hot as hell that day. The less material the better.

Darren didn't stop by to pick Nicole up, because he claimed that he had to pick up his son from his ex's house, and it would be more convenient for Nicole to meet them at Damon's deli on Rockside Road.

Nicole arrived there first, and it was packed. She preferred to sit at a booth, but there was none available. As a matter of fact, all the seats were filled, and Nicole had to wait near the cash register by the door for an available seat. A little elderly woman with a big toothy grin offered Nicole a seat at the counter; she just smiled and told her that she was waiting for two other people and that she'd wait for an open booth. She tried calling Darren, but she couldn't reach him. He wouldn't answer his phone, which always used to piss her off royally. She hated the thought of him looking down at his phone's caller ID, seeing her number, and ignoring her call.

The wall at both sides of the hallway that led to the entrance was lined with benches for those waiting for seats, and they were all filled. Nicole just stood over to the side, with her purse hanging on her shoulder, holding her hands in front of her. A few people brushed past her, trying to get to the seats at the counter. Nicole caught a tall, slim, balding man looking down her dress at her ample cleavage. He didn't even turn his head when they made eye contact. His companion cut her eyes at Nicole as she pulled him by the arm away from her.

She saw the stares, but it didn't phase her. A few polite men had offered her their seats as she stood waiting. But Nicole smiled politely and declined. She didn't want to sit as men walked in and looked directly down her dress. Nicole was striking and was used to that kind of attention. She wasn't dressed immodestly, and as a matter of fact, she'd received quite a few compliments on her halter sundress with the colorful flowers, that day, right there in the deli. Nicole stood in the doorway of the deli, shifting her weight from hip to hip for about fifteen minutes before she decided to call Darren and tell him that she was leaving. She'd arrived on time, and he should have arrived on time also or at least have the decency to call.

Nicole had dialed Darren's number for one last time, and she told herself that if he didn't answer that time she was going to leave and she'd have to meet Kamar some other day. But before she could hang up on his voice-mail recording, there they were, walking up behind her.

Darren came up behind her, grabbed her around her waist, and planted a moist kiss on the side of her neck. She knew it was him; she recognized his kisses, and it still gave her butterflies. Just the recollection of his lips on her skin made her tingle. She remembered looking down into little Kamar's face as he held tightly to his father's hand. He stared up at Nicole with his large, dark eyes.

"Hello, handsome," Nicole said to Kamar and smiled. The little boy didn't return the smile, and he hid behind his dad, still holding on to his hand.

Darren laughed and said, "Boy, stop acting bashful." He pulled Kamar from behind him and said, "Say hello to Ms. Turner."

Kamar looked down at the floor and raised his hand in a little wave. Nicole smiled at him again.

"So how long have you been waiting?" Darren asked.

"What time did you ask me to be here?" Nicole answered, looking at Darren with raised eyebrows.

Darren looked down at his watch. He knew that Nicole had arrived on time.

"I apologize for keeping you waiting."

"Uh-huh," Nicole answered. Darren knew he would have gotten an earful if his son wasn't with him. A greeting, a kiss, and an apology was what Nicole thought she should have gotten as soon as Darren stepped through the door, and not necessarily in that order.

Nicole looked at Kamar; he was a tall thin boy, too tall to be four, Nicole thought. Darren had mentioned that he was pretty tall for his age, but tall was an understatement. The child looked as if he was about six years old.

The three of them were seated shortly after Darren and Kamar had arrived. Nicole thought it strange that the four year old didn't need a booster seat. Kamar sat in the booth next to his dad and across from Nicole. A friendly, but weary-looking young woman had come over to the table to take their order.

"Hello, my name is Marcy, and I'll be taking your order this afternoon." Marcy recited the specials and then asked if they were ready to place their order. Darren looked over at Nicole to see if she was ready and she shook her head no.

"Give us a minute," Darren answered and smiled back at the waitress.

As Nicole flipped through the big stiff pages of the menu, she could feel the remnants of sticky fingers and dried food, and she told herself that she'd have to wash her hands again before she ate. She could feel a pair of little eyes staring at her, so she looked over at Kamar and said, "So what's good here, Kamar? I heard this was your favorite restaurant."

Kamar's eyes widened, and he looked up at his dad. Nicole laughed and Darren smiled down at his son and said, "Answer the lady. She asked you a question." Kamar let out a long, soft sigh and tried to avoid eye contact with Nicole. Nicole caught Kamar stealing glances at her, but he stopped when Nicole winked at him.

Marcy returned as promised with pad and pen in hand. Nicole ordered a grilled chicken cobb salad with a tall glass of ice water. Darren ordered a grilled Rueben with mustard instead of the standard, thousand-island dressing, with a side of french fries. And Kamar ordered a grilled cheese sandwich with a side of sweet potato fries. His absolute favorite meal. Darren ordered a large glass of orange soda, and Kamar had a glass of water like Nicole.

Nicole watched Marcy hustle from table to table as sweat rolled down her brow. It was a hot day, but it was pleasantly cool inside the diner, but you wouldn't have been able to tell that by Marcy. Nicole watched Marcy wipe her forehead with the back of her hand. And Nicole watched as loose strands of Marcy's unkempt hair fell into her face, and she saw the look of pained frustration as she constantly batted it away from her eyes.

"Did you hear what I just said?" Darren asked, a little annoyed.

"No, I apologize. What did you say?"

"What were you looking at?"

Nicole shook her head and said, "Nothing. Just looking around. Is that what you had to ask me?"

"No, I was saying that I wanted you to try their ice cream, it's some of the best ice cream I've ever had."

"Darren, I'm not really in the mood for ice cream."

"Who doesn't like ice cream?"

"I didn't say I didn't like ice cream. I said I'm really not in the mood for ice cream. Anyway, who offers ice cream to a woman ordering a salad? That kinda throws off the whole 'I'm watching my diet' thing."

"You don't need to watch your diet. You're perfect. But you hafto try this ice cream. This ice cream is da bomb."

Nicole laughed and said, "Does anyone even say that anymore, 'da bomb.'"

"Whatever," Darren said and laughed. "I don't know what the kids say nowadays. What is it? This ice cream is da sshh." Nicole and Darren both laughed; then Darren looked over at Kamar and said, "They have some good ice cream here. Don't they, son? Tell her."

"They have some good ice cream," Kamar said and smiled at Nicole.

"Oooh, wee. He speaks, and look at the pretty smile." Nicole had said to Kamar with a smile.

Kamar frowned and said, "I'm not pretty. I'm a boy."

"You are absolutely right, Kamar, I apologize, you are very handsome, and you have a very handsome smile." She smiled and winked at Kamar again, and he blushed and put his head down on the table. Darren patted his back and said, "Look at him blushing. Are you tryin' to take my woman? Smiling and grinnin' at her, showin' all those teeth." Kamar looked over at Nicole and smiled again.

Nicole hadn't seen Kamar's mother, but she'd imagined that she was very beautiful, judging by Kamar. Of course assuming that the child was the spitting image of his mother. He looked nothing like Darren as far as Nicole could see. She'd imagined that Kamar's mother was an exotic-looking woman with large, dark eyes, long, dark straight hair, and olive-colored skin. But that was as far as her imagination took her. She didn't envy the woman, and she didn't imagine what her life had been like with Darren. Nicole wasn't threatened by what she thought was Darren and his wife's previous relationship. Nicole wasn't that type of woman. What was in the past was in the past. After all, she didn't need anyone holding her past against her.

Nicole laughed and chitchatted with Darren while they waited for their food to arrive. Kamar looked bored, so Nicole flipped his paper placemat over and handed him a pencil from her purse and told him to draw her something on the back of the placemat. Kamar wrote his name all over it in big letters. He drew a picture of a house, a car, and what looked like a dog. Nicole was impressed. She pointed at the dog and asked Kamar its name.

"Trevor," Kamar answered. Darren laughed.

"What's so funny?" Nicole asked.

"That's his older brother's name," Darren answered.

"You must really love your brother. Is that why you named your dog after him?"

"Trevor calls me Kmart, and I don't like it, so his name is Trevor," Kamar said, tapping the picture of the dog with the pencil.

"Oh, okay," Nicole said as she nodded and smiled.

Nicole looked down at her watch and said to Darren, "This food betta be da bomb because it's taking forever to get here."

But Darren didn't hear her; instead, he had turned his attention to a table full of young men staring over at Nicole. Nicole turned her head to see what Darren was looking at, and they smiled at her. Darren looked at Nicole. She was beautiful; her long neck was so sexy to him, and he liked the way she was wearing her hair that day. It was upswept and secured with a tortoise shell hair clip that matched her sunglasses. Darren thought the wisps of dark hair that fell to her face and neck were so sexy. And he loved the way her deep dimples would pop up unexpectedly, with the slightest change of her facial expression. She was so fine, Darren thought to himself, and whenever he'd get upset about the gawkers, he'd remind himself that Nicole was all his and she'd be leaving on his arm.

*   *   *

Nicole reminisced as the rain fell. She wanted to open the two big doors to her balcony so that the breeze could rush through her bedroom, but she didn't want to let the rain inside with it. She'd remade her bed and washed all of her bed linens. She could still smell Jermaine's cologne in the air, and even though it was faint, she had no intention of smelling it all day and she was so relieved that his scent hadn't sunk into her mattress.

She called La Maya to cancel their appointment, but La Maya wouldn't hear of it. She told Nicole not to worry about the rain and she'd be there soon. Nicole asked her if she was bringing the girls, but she said, "No, Donte` picked them up earlier, and he was keeping them for the rest of the weekend." The house was big and empty, and Nicole looked forward to La Maya and her daughters coming over. She enjoyed being around children every now and then. She couldn't have any children of her own, due to complications resulting from an untreated miscarriage when she was 13.

Nicole went through the house, turning on lights so that the house didn't seem so dark and empty. La Maya said that she was really tired, so Nicole decided she'd put on a pot of coffee. La Maya was a coffee drinker, and she'd appreciate that.

It was late afternoon and her voice mail was full. Her personal assistant, Aaliyah, had phoned her on her blackberry several times about a few upcoming appointments. She loved Aaliyah. She was bright and efficient. Aaliyah was arguably the best decision she'd made this year. She was well tuned to all of her responsibilities. She was very well informed, and she went above and beyond what was expected of her, anticipating Nicole's needs before she was even asked. And she was loyal, which was a very valuable quality in an assistant.

Thunder clapped in the distance as the rain fell hard against the shudders. It was a cold rain, and Nicole felt a chill that went deep into her bones. She imagined that Darren was still outside lying in his driveway, being pelted by icy-cold raindrops. She'd imagined that he was still alive, even though a dead Darren seemed more appealing to her right now. She imagined that Darren was still lying outside in his driveway, paralyzed by pain, and that the rain was like tiny icy daggers piercing his flesh.

"My god!" Nicole yelled and shook those wicked images out of her head. She never let any man occupy this much of her thoughts. "Married men are devils," she exclaimed. Men were men and would always be men. But there was something about those married men. They preyed on what was left of a woman's self-esteem like vultures over picked-upon carcasses. Habitual liars, all of them.

She sat at the kitchen counter and poured herself a cup of coffee. She added a lot of Irish creamer and didn't add any sugar; it was sweet enough. Nicole wasn't a big coffee drinker, so it was more like having a little coffee with her cream. She clicked on the television and watched the news, waiting to hear about the suburbanite found dead in his driveway. Instead, she got the weatherman reporting everything that she could have gotten just by looking out her own windows. The phone rang, and it was La Maya telling Nicole to look out for her; she'd be coming up the road in a few minutes.

Nicole ran to the front of the house and looked out of the big bay windows. She touched the side of her face and her neck; the skin was tight and a bit swollen, but she'd camouflaged it perfectly with a little concealer and some foundation. La Maya would be none the wiser. It was dark outside, and Nicole could see the headlights of La Maya's car as she drove up the driveway. Nicole used the garage-door opener to raise the garage door as La Maya drove around the side of the house and into the garage. Nicole waited for La Maya to step out of her car, and then she held the side door open for her.

"Girl, it is wicked out there! Whoo!" La Maya said as she slammed her car door. She walked around to the other side of the car, opened her passenger door, and started unloading bags.

"What's all that?" Nicole inquired. Everything La Maya needed was already there.

"Just stuff."

Nicole held the door for La Maya, and La Maya walked past her and into the mudroom. She stepped out of her shoes, hung up her jacket on one of the brass hooks on the wall, and followed Nicole into the kitchen.

"Mmmm. It smells so good in here."

"Have a seat," Nicole said, pointing at a stool at the kitchen counter. Nicole grabbed a mug and sat it in front of La Maya. She filled the mug with the fragrant black coffee. La Maya sat her bags down at her feet and took a sip before any cream and sugar was added.

"Girl, this is some good coffee." La Maya said to Nicole.

"I thought you'd like it."

"It smells so good, and it has a great taste."

"What kind of cream do you want? I have Irish cream, vanilla, amaretto."

"This coffee is so good, I could drink it black. But I won't. Pass me the amaretto," La Maya said and laughed.

Nicole took the amaretto cream out of the cupboard and sat it in front of La Maya. "Want some sugar?"

"No, this'll be fine." La Maya smiled, closed her eyes, and took another sip of the black coffee before adding the amaretto cream.

"Whoo. Girl, I am so tired. I've been rippin' and runnin' all morning long. I didn't get much sleep last night." La Maya started to mention Serena's early-morning phone call, but stopped herself remembering the content of their conversation.

"Well, I told you we could reschedule," Nicole said to La Maya.

Nicole didn't inquire as to what kept La Maya from getting sleep last night. She'd assumed that it involved her ex, and she didn't want to hear anymore about him than what La Maya wanted to share. Besides, as far as

Nicole was concerned, that on-again, off-again thing they had going on was ridiculous, and hearing about it over and over again made Nicole's head hurt. She wanted to tell her cousin to leave his sorry, stankin' ass alone and move on, but she decided she'd save that line for when La Maya was ready to hear it.

"No, that wouldn't be a good idea. Honestly, with our schedules, when would we find the time to get this done? Besides, I look forward to this each week."

Nicole looked at her cousin and smiled. She looked forward to these Saturdays too. Usually, La Maya wouldn't come so late in the day. Their appointments are usually early enough for them to have the rest of the day to themselves.

La Maya drank two mugs of coffee as they talked and laughed about their past week and the events there of; then they headed to Nicole's own personal salon. This consisted of a large room with three shampoo bowls, three hair dryers, and three stations. La Maya liked to refer to it as her home away from home; it was like a miniature version of her salon, Anew You. La Maya lugged her bags with her to the mini salon. She dropped a heavy bag onto one of the stations, unzipped it, and pulled out a jar. She sat the jar on the counter and untied her hair. Her hair fell to her shoulders, and she shook her head off hair as if she was in a shampoo commercial, to show her cousin its bounce and body.

Nicole nodded and said, "Yea, it's pretty?" Nicole hunched her shoulders and looked at her cousin, unsure of what La Maya wanted her to say. She didn't know what she was getting at but, whatever.

"Feel it," La Maya said as she grabbed Nicole's wrist and put her hand in her hair. Her hair was very light and soft.

"It feels good."

"Yea, it does." She nodded. "And guess what I put in it?"

Nicole shook her head. She was not in the mood for guessing games. "Your hair is always soft and pretty." Nicole shrugged her shoulders without acknowledging that there was obviously something different about her hair.

"This." La Maya held up a jar of Nicole's Tamani Almond Body Butter. "Huh?" she said, running her fingers through her hair and looking at Nicole. "Did you know it does this for hair?"

"Yea, I had been using a variation of it on Mariah's hair for years."

"Nicole, you could start an entire line of hair care products without changing anything but the name."

"Not interested."

"Are you serious? Nicole, the fact that it does this for hair," La Maya said, shaking her head again, "can be an excellent marketing tool. Girl, you think you're makin' money now, imagine what this could do for all those unruly heads out there."

Tamani had been an extremely successful business venture, but Nicole had no intention of expanding her skin-care product line to include hair-care products, at least not at this time. It had taken Nicole a lot of time, effort, and money to ensure that the Tamani skin-care line was safe enough for the public. It was a clean, natural, hypoallergenic product that, she was proud to say, had not been tested on animals. As a matter of fact, it was something that Nicole had been experimenting with on her younger sisters and herself since she was a teenager. Back then, she used a special combination of moisturizers and essential oils to soften their dry skin. She'd grown tired of bathing and moisturizing her younger sisters' skin only for their skin to be dry and ashy looking only moments later. Her sisters were the inspiration for the Tamani skin-care product line.

"Nicole, this stuff is amazing," La Maya said to her cousin. Nicole was well aware of what Tamani could do for the hair. Nicole was flattered, but a hair-care product line wasn't her focus right now.

Nicole smiled as if beaming with pride over a child. Tamani was her baby, and she couldn't ask for anything better. But she had enough on her plate right now, so La Maya's suggestion wasn't even a consideration at the moment. It wasn't as simple as La Maya was suggesting that it was. And though La Maya realized this, she couldn't resist the chance of bringing this discovery to Nicole's attention.

La Maya protected Nicole's neck with a neck strip before draping the vinyl shampoo cape around her neck. She adjusted the cape's Velcro straps so that it wouldn't be too tight and so that it wouldn't allow the water to run beneath it, and she was sure not to let the Velcro catch Nicole's hair.

La Maya ran her fingers through Nicole's long, thick hair. She parted it with her fingers and examined her hair and scalp to determine which of the hair products available would meet her needs. She eyed her hair ends to see if they need clipping, before sending Nicole to the shampoo bowl.

"Did you sweat it out, girl?" La Maya said with a laugh as Nicole scooted her body down into the seat and lowered her head into the bowl.

Nicole didn't respond; she just shut her eyes and smiled slightly. Deep dimples appeared in both cheeks. Nicole didn't kiss and tell. She didn't think that many people would be able to handle hearing the details of her sexual escapades, and even though she wasn't ashamed of them, she had no intention of sharing.

La Maya had to be hands down the best at giving shampoos, but she'd love to talk through them. She'd talk and laugh and share stories about her girls, but Nicole would just ignore her as her magic hands went to work on her head. She didn't have to tell La Maya where her scalp itched, because La Maya hit every spot. She just talked too much. It used to be hard for Nicole to relax during La Maya's wonderful shampoo sessions, because Nicole was trying so hard to focus on La Maya's conversation. But Nicole learned to relax and totally block La Maya's voice out of her head as she shampooed away. She knew that La Maya would inevitably repeat herself, and everything that she had missed during the shampoo would come up again later in their conversation.

"Nicole?" Nicole didn't answer her. "Nicole?" Nicole still didn't answer. "Nicole!"

La Maya stopped massaging Nicole's scalp, and Nicole opened her eyes. "Did you hear what I just said?"

"No," Nicole said as she closed her eyes again.

"Stop ignoring me."

"Stop talking through my shampoos. I keep telling you that I can't hear you while you're shampooing my hair."

"So you just ignore me?"

"Yes, ma'am. I ignore you each and every time you talk while you're shampooing my hair. I have absolutely no idea what you're talking about. In fact, I think I have mastered blocking your voice out completely as soon as the water hits my head."

"Nicole."

"La Maya," Nicole said as she lay there with her eyes closed, waiting for her cousin to continue shampooing her hair. "Don't act surprised, La Maya. I've told you to shut up all that yackin' while I'm getting my shampoos. This is therapeutic for me."

"Nicole, I can't believe you!"

"Believe it."

"I don't appreciate your honesty," La Maya said as she began to massage Nicole's scalp.

"Appreciate it. Embrace it." Nicole smiled, showing her pearly whites. La Maya laughed and rinsed the sweet-smelling lather out of Nicole's hair.

The room that the two women were in didn't have any windows, and it was very well insulated. Nicole and La Maya talked as La Maya did Nicole's hair. Both of them totally oblivious to the raging storm outside. The crackles of thunder were muffled by the old school R&B and the laughter of two women catching up with each other and winding down after a rough week. As much as they shared this evening, neither of them mentioned to each other the highlights of their week. Nicole didn't mention her run-in with Darren and the fact that she thought she might have left him for dead in his driveway, and La Maya didn't mention her latest baby-daddy drama or the fact that Nicole's little sister might have gotten herself in enough trouble to get herself kicked out of school. These Saturdays or at least these little blocks of time each Saturday were occasions to relax and unwind. No drama allowed. It was clear and just as plain as if it were posted on the door.

Nicole and La Maya shared a special connection, a connection far beyond blood. La Maya had shared some things with Nicole. Some very private and sensitive things that she hadn't shared with anyone else. Nicole didn't feel compelled to share her deepest secrets with her though, and she had some doozies. But the fact that La Maya had entrusted her with hers gave them a connectivity far beyond that of just a mere friendship. She trusted Nicole not to be judgmental, and she appreciated that Nicole didn't offer unwelcome advice. She merely listened and gave her an outlet. She allowed her to ramble on until she came to her own conclusions, solutions, self-realizations, or whatever. She allowed La Maya to be La Maya when she couldn't be La Maya around anyone else.

La Maya admired Nicole. Nicole was confident and very self-aware. She was savvy and intelligent. And she was a force to be reckoned with. She radiated power, poise, and beauty. She had a sort of presence about her that made everyone take notice when she walked into the room. And although Nicole appeared to be very hard and cold at times, she had a smile that lit up her face and made you want to smile too, no matter what mood you were in. La Maya's daddy called her black diamond, because she was just as hard as she was beautiful.

Nicole was tired, and she sat under the dryer and slept, as she often did on these Saturdays. She slept and she dreamed. She dreamt about Darren and the way he clamped his hand around her neck, they way he looked at her as if he couldn't have cared less if she died by his hands that night. She could see it in his eyes, she could hear it in his voice, and she could feel it in the grip he had on her throat. It didn't bother her that he didn't really love her, at least not in the way she wanted to be loved. She got over that almost as quickly as she'd gotten over the fact that he had a wife and a family that he had lied about being separated from. She supposed he loved her as much as he knew how. The giving of his precious time and his attention was most certainly an act of love as he'd often reminded her.

As Nicole drifted off to sleep, she dreamt of clowns and of amusement parks. Darren was there with clown makeup on as if sloppily applied by a child, dried blood on his nose and lips, with fresh blood trickling from a wound to his forehead. He looked horrendous. The white-clown makeup made his teeth appear beige. He wore a big, tattered top hat and an old, black, pin-striped tuxedo with a tail that was worn, and the spilt was ripped. He wasn't the dapper Darren that Nicole was used to. In fact, he looked like he stank; he didn't look like a clown either, but more like the corpse of a clown. As if he was reanimated for the sole purpose of acting as ringmaster or carny.

There was no sign on the outside of the dingy, purple, and white-striped tent. Nothing to warn of what awaited inside. Darren stood at the tent's entrance with a big toothy grin, beckoning passersby to the main attraction inside.

"Ladies and gentlemen, step right up!" Darren announced, voice booming through the bullhorn that he held too close to his lips. "Somethin' here you really don't want to miss!"

She didn't want to go there. She didn't want to see what was inside the big purple and white-striped tent. But in her dream state, she could feel herself being drawn inside. She looked around outside the tent at the pink sky and the blue clouds. She could smell fresh buttered popcorn, cotton candy, and hot funnel cakes frying in vats of boiling oil.

Nicole was afraid now. Her heart pounded in her chest. She watched as people piled into the tent in droves like cattle. They seemed all too eager to see what was inside. Darren called the amusement-park goers by name. She recognized some of their faces too. Some were friends of his. Some were clients that she'd met at the business dinner parties, which he was so bold enough to invite her to. Mama was there with Fatimah. They were both dressed in their Sunday's best, with big, fancy, Sunday-service hats adorned with lace veils, artificial silk flowers, and big flashy bows. They were sharp. Nicole watched as they all disappeared through other side of the tent's entrance.

She prayed to wake up. She wished that La Maya would nudge her and shake her awake. She felt like she'd been dreaming forever. Nicole could feel the hair on the back of her neck, standing on end as if she were paralyzed, and someone was standing behind her talking too close to her back. She felt warm breath on her neck.

Darren laughed heavily and heartily. She could hear murmuring and gasping coming from the other side of the tent, but she still wasn't the slightest bit curious about what was going on inside. Nicole hoped that La Maya would wake her up; she hoped that she appeared to be in distress as she slept under the hair dryer and that La Maya would try to wake her. Nicole tried to wake herself, but was unsuccessful. Instead, she felt herself being drawn inside.

Nicole could smell the faint scent of freesia as she approached the tent's entrance. Freesia, the same scent that she used in her bedroom. It was comforting to her. She inhaled deeply. The light inside the tent was blinding. She could actually feel her eyes stinging from the overpowering white light. She'd hoped the bright light would prevent her from seeing the inside. As she went further into the tent, the aroma of freesia was stronger, not subtle like in her bedroom.

She still couldn't see anything, but the rest of her senses were more acute now. She felt as if goose bumps were forming on her skin. She still felt the annoying sensation of someone standing behind her, breathing on her neck.

"Oh god," she prayed. "Please get me out of here."

She could see Fatimah's face clearly now, glaring at her as if she'd heard her prayer and disapproved. She could see Mama's face too. She wasn't sure if Mama could see her or if she was there just standing on the outside looking in like she did in most of her dreams as an unwilling participant. She recognized the hate in Mama's eyes; she thought she was used to it by now, but somehow it hurt Nicole and she wanted to turn her head away from her hate-filled gaze.

Nicole felt as if her eyes were being forced to open. She still couldn't see clearly though. She couldn't identify faces due to the fog that seemed to fill the tent. She heard music—an acoustic guitar and classical piano. She didn't recognize the song, but it was beautiful. She heard snickering and gasps of disgust. She'd gone from being an onlooker to feeling as though she was actually in the tent being pushed by people whose faces she couldn't see.

"Please wake me up. Please wake me up," Nicole repeated to herself.

She hated not being in control of her environment. She hoped that it was time for her conditioner to be rinsed out and that La Maya would be waking her right away.

The thunder cracked and boomed so loudly that it began to penetrate the walls of the mini salon.

"Ooh girrrl! Did you hear that?" La Maya said to the sleeping Nicole. La Maya turned the music down and attempted to listen to the storm through the walls of the room. The low rumble of thunder could still be heard through the room's insulated walls. The lights flickered off and then on again.

La Maya hurried over to the dryer and lifted the lid, waking Nicole before her nightmare could reach its climactic ending.

"It's really coming down out there. Let me get your hair rinsed." Nicole followed La Maya to the shampoo bowl.

As Nicole slid down in the chair and rested her head on the neck rest of the shampoo bowl, she breathed a sigh of relief. She had had nightmares before, almost every day for several years when she was a little girl. Nobody to wake her up back then and nobody's arms to run into for comfort back then either. The circumstances of the dream kept her from revealing its contents. She predicted that the contents of this dream would be the same even though she didn't stay asleep long enough to see the conclusion of it.

"I hate that I am so afraid of thunder and lightning. I know it's a childhood thing. But ooh, it is so disturbing," La Maya said with a hand over her heart, as she walked over to the door, closing it and locking it securely. Nicole's big house made La Maya nervous at times like this. Too many rooms and too many corners for something to jump out at her from. La Maya hadn't gotten over the fact that the previous owner had died in this house. Nicole's step mother's former employer had died in the master bedroom and Nicole was able to purchase this home at below market value. In other words it was a steal, the family wanted out, but they wanted someone who they trusted to have the house. Someone that would take good care of their old family home and treasure it. Barbara couldn't afford it so she suggested it to Nicole. La Maya turned on the music and turned it up a little. Nicole didn't say a word. She closed her eyes and waited for the warm water on her head.

"Yea, I know, nothing scares you," La Maya said as she tested the water with her hand.

Nicole didn't open her eyes. She smiled as if what her cousin was saying was true. She sighed as the warm water washed over her scalp. She was relieved but a little curious as to how the nightmare was going to end. She wondered what was so fascinating and astonishing in that tent. She gathered that it would be something humiliating to her. At least, that's what her subconscious led her to believe. She was dwelling on this nightmare so heavily that she was sort of afraid to open her eyes while La Maya was rinsing her hair, but she did and she saw her cousin smiling down at her.

"Close your eyes. I promise not to talk while I rinse your hair," La Maya said, and her smile was comforting.

Nicole smiled back at La Maya. She wouldn't have cared if she did talk to her now. Anything to keep her mind off Darren and that nightmare. She didn't want to think about him or it anymore. She just wanted to relax.

Nicole imagined that it was warm outside. Even though it was actually unseasonably cold. She imagined that the rain was warm and that she was standing out in it, on her granny's land on the old dirt road where the summer air smelled fresh and clean. Oh, how she wanted to go back there. She wasn't getting that "anywhere but here" feeling that she used to get when she was a kid. No, she had a specific place in mind—Statesville,

North Carolina, where she didn't have a care in the world; everyone was happy to see her, and all the problems in the world didn't matter. Nothing could touch her there, nothing could hurt her. At least, that was what she felt when she was a little girl.

But things were so different back then. It had been many years since she'd been to North Carolina. She wondered if she'd even recognize anybody now or if they'd recognize her. She'd changed so much from the tall, gangly, awkward little girl with the nappy hair. "She'd change color in the summer, like ripe fruit," is what uncle Marvin used to say.

Nicole hadn't grown into her features back then. Her eyes seemed too large for her small, oval face. Her teeth seemed too big for her mouth. She had adult-sized features on a baby face. "Don't worry, you'll grow into your look," Daddy Ray would always say, when Nicole would come home from school crying about some new mean remark that an insensitive child would say. Or some new cruel label they'd give her. "They don't know nothin' 'bout this beauty you got. Just wait till it comes all the way out. You'll see." Nicole didn't know what "all the way out" meant, until the summer that she turned fourteen.

Nicole knew that her cousin had used Tamani on her hair as if the result would convince Nicole to change her mind about marketing her skin-care line as hair-care products too. Nicole loved her hair almost as much as La Maya did. La Maya styled it straight and was amazed at the body it had.

Nicole thanked her and paid her what she owed along with a generous tip. The women cleaned up behind themselves; then La Maya loaded her bags on her shoulders, and they headed upstairs. La Maya stopped in front of the window and stared into the night sky. "Michael and I are supposed to grab something to eat, but I don't know. It's pretty bad out there."

La Maya stared outside as if staring at the storm would make the rain go away. Nicole knew that La Maya was afraid to drive home in this weather, and although she was welcome to stay, she made a suggestion to her.

"Why don't you have him pick you up here? You can pick your car up tonight or later tomorrow."

La Maya turned her head, looked at Nicole, and smiled. "I'm a scaredy-cat, aren't I?"

"Yea." Nicole nodded and smiled. "You are."

La Maya smoothed her hands down her blue jean miniskirt and walked over to the island in the kitchen and sat next to Nicole. La Maya looked really cute in her blue jean mini. She was tiny, and the skirt showed off her shapely legs.

"What's the matter? What's that look for?" Nicole said as La Maya sat at the stool next to her.

La Maya smiled at her and tears began to well up in her eyes. "I have so much on me right now." La Maya closed her eyes and shook her head, and tears began to slowly stream down her cheeks. "I try to keep it together, but I am so overwhelmed."

Nicole put her arm around her cousin and rubbed her back. "What's wrong La Maya?"

"Just shit. Same ole same ole, but on top of that, Daddy's sick. We don't know what's wrong. He won't go to the doctor. His feet keep swelling up really bad, and he gets short of breath a lot lately. He's been having this terrible cough for a while now. Coughing up shit. He had the girls over the other day, and Summer said he was coughing so badly that he had to hold on to the wall." La Maya cried, and the tears fell uncontrollably. "I'm just scared. I don't want to lose him. He's all I've got."

Nicole grabbed a wad of tissue out of the nearest bathroom, brought it back into the kitchen, and handed it to La Maya. She didn't know how to console her. La Maya lost her mother in a terrible car accident when she was twelve, and she had clung to her father ever since. He is her everything. La Maya blew her nose and shook her head. "It's just so hard because my brothers are no help. I don't think they're taking it as seriously as I am. I'm not getting any real support from them." La Maya shook her head and sighed. She dabbed at her eyes with the tissue and then blew her nose. "I don't know. I'm just stressed I guess. Donte` and his games. And my daddy being sick and—" La Maya sighed and rolled her eyes up in the air.

"I'm sorry. I'm just." La Maya shrugged her shoulders and smiled.

Nicole hugged La Maya. She didn't know what to say. How do you convince someone to do something they don't want to do? If it was that easy, she'd tell her cousin that she could eliminate one of her problems by leaving Donte`'s sorry ass alone. He was nothing but drama. He enjoyed the negative effect he had on La Maya's life because he thought it gave him control. He liked the power he had over her emotions and her mental state. Nicole knew that as much as La Maya respected her opinion, that she wouldn't leave him alone. She wouldn't stop inviting him to her bed, and she wouldn't stop crawling into his.

"I don't know, Maya. You've got a bunch of health-care professionals in the family. Why don't you get my mother or one of my sisters to talk to him? Fatimah would love to get all in your business. Ask her."

La Maya chuckled and said, "Yea, Fatimah loves to get all up in your business, don't she?"

Nicole nodded and smiled. "Maybe you could have a family meeting and invite all of your brothers over. Sort of like an intervention. You really need to talk to your daddy, La Maya, tell him how you feel. Say it just like you said to me, he's all you got left and you don't want to lose him."

"I know, but I get so emotional when I talk like that. I start crying, and he doesn't like to see me cry."

"Hello? That may be just what he needs. Maybe seeing you cry will show him just how serious you are."

"I don't want Daddy to be mad at me."

"Well, what's more important? His health or him being mad at you? I mean what's the alternative?" A healthy mad daddy or a sick dead one? Nicole didn't say it, but she was thinking it and it was as if La Maya read her mind.

La Maya felt badly about bring up her problems to Nicole especially knowing how close Nicole was to her daddy Ray. But Nicole didn't seem to mind.

The tears dried, and eventually, they stopped falling. La Maya stayed and talked to Nicole for a while about lighter, happier subjects, before calling Mike to pick her up. Nicole would have loved to shake some sense into her cousin's head. She felt that if she could take over La Maya's problems for just one day, she could solve her problems overnight. She'd get Donte' told and break it off with him once and for all; she'd get her daddy the medical attention that he needed, even if she had to drag him there herself, and she'd tell Mike that she loved him just as much as he loved her instead of selfishly stringing him along like she did. The latter didn't bother Nicole as much. It was refreshing for Nicole to see a man in pursuit of a woman being strung along for a change. Lord knows she'd seen it the other way around far too many times. But the idea of La Maya with Michael made Nicole happy because she knew that he really loved her cousin; he was the best choice for her, and if Mike was La Maya's man, then Donte' would most certainly be out of the picture.

But she supposed that everybody felt the same way about everybody else's problems. How easy it is to think you can fix what you think is wrong with someone else's life when you aren't emotionally invested. Nicole wondered how many people felt this way about her. Not counting Fatimah, of course. How many people on the outside looking in felt that they knew how to manage her life better than her?

Mike arrived, and La Maya gave Nicole hugs and kisses before saying good-bye. Mike met her at the door with an umbrella and carried her bags to the car. She watched as Mike covered La Maya's head with the umbrella, opened the passenger-side door for her, closed the door behind her, and then put her bags in the trunk. He waved good-bye to Nicole before climbing into the car, and La Maya waved as they drove away.

Nicole shut the heavy mahogany doors. The house was so quiet and still. The rain sounded like coffee percolating or chicken frying. Nicole realized she hadn't eaten anything at all today, and she was starving. She was alone now as she rarely had occasion to be. She just wanted to sleep, but she knew if she went to sleep this early in the evening, she would either sleep too long and wake up even more exhausted or wouldn't sleep long enough and she'd find herself wide awake at two or three o'clock in the morning.

Nicole caught a glimpse of herself in the mirror in her vestibule. The straight hair gave her an exotic look. She liked her hair straight, but she preferred it fuller and with a little more curl. This made her look like Pocahontas, she thought. It disguised the natural coarseness of her thick, dark hair. It was attractive, but she knew it wouldn't stay that way in today's humidity.

The phone rang, and it startled her. It was her little brother Tye.

"I'm on my way over there."

"What? In this storm?"

"I got your nieces and nephews."

"What? Who?"

"I just left Fatimah's house," Tye said.

"Tye, why would you bring the kids out in a storm like this? And where is Fatimah?"

Nicole couldn't imagine that Fatimah would let Tye take her children out in this storm, especially not to bring them to her.

"Fatimah's not feelin' good. She said she got a bad headache, so I figured I'd take the kids off her hands to give her a break."

"Tye, does she know that you have her children?"

"I didn't tell her."

"Tye?"

"What? I'm doin' her a favor."

Nicole knew that she couldn't convince Tye that he was wrong, so to avoid the back-and-forth, she asked, "Tye, how far are you from here?"

"Not far. What chu got to eat? We hungry."

She didn't argue with Tye; she had learned a long time ago not to. She had practiced the art of allowing him to believe that he was right. In fact, she had gotten it down to a science. She had actually honed the ability so well that she even amazed herself. She'd found it was easier that way. An argument would go on for hours, and Tye would inevitably chose to do what he felt was best anyway, no matter how illogical it was. Just to prove that he was right.

She loved her little brother, but he was the only boy and the youngest boy; that gave him two strikes against him. Mothers have the tendency to spoil and cater to these types of sons, babying them. Which inevitably ruins them as grown men. Nicole had dated these types of men. They were selfish and totally insensitive to the needs of others, because they never had to be. Tye was a prime example of this. Mama didn't raise Tye; in fact, they never stayed in the same home together. Granny raised him. But Mama gave him everything he wanted, and he was repeatedly rewarded for doing nothing. Now because he had a child, he thought that made him a man. Nicole had to admit she was guilty too. She'd spoiled him and babied him until one day he grew up to be this big-ass, grown-ass boy with his hand out and thinking that the women of the world would treat him the same way.

"Is it really bad out there?"

"Not too bad, but it's really coming down though."

"Oh," Nicole said as she nodded.

"What are you driving?"

"The van."

"Uh-huh." Nicole paused to collect her thoughts. "The van with the bad brakes?"

"Granny's van," Tye said, correcting his sister.

"The van that Granny says needs new breaks?"

"The van does not need new brakes, Nicole."

"I'm just sayin' when I talked to Granny, she said she needed to get her brakes fixed. As a matter of fact, she said she was parking it until she could put it in the shop."

"Nicole, the brakes are fine," Tye replied raising his voice.

"Look Tye, watch your tone. All I'm saying is you have your five nieces and nephews in a car with bad brakes in the rain. Are the little ones in car seats?"

"No," Tye answered under his breath.

"Okay. You have your nieces and nephews in a car with bad brakes in the rain with no car seats. Tye, these are your sister's kids."

"She's not feeling well," Tye interrupted.

"You have your sick sister's kids, and she has no idea where they are."

"You're making me sound like I'm stupid or something."

"Tye, I haven't called you anything. I have only stated the facts from the information that you're giving me. You're coming to your own conclusions." Tye tried to argue, and Nicole nipped it in the bud. She could hear a female voice in the background, and she knew that it wasn't any of her nieces. "Tye, who was that?"

"A friend."

"What friend?"

"What does it matter?"

"Boy, if you don't stop playin' with me! Who is the girl?"

"Nina."

Nicole shook her head. She wanted to shake him. He could be so completely and utterly irresponsible at times. This angered and scared Nicole because he'd be eighteen years old soon. He had a nine-month-old son, and he hadn't seemed to mature.

"Where are you now, Tye?"

"I gotta stop home for a minute."

Home was Granny's house, where he had lived since he came into the world. Mama never brought him to the home that she and her sisters were raised in. Mama said she had her reasons. One of them being that Tye was not Ray's son.

"Do me a favor. Stay at Granny's with the kids. I will pick up Nina and the kids and drop them off at home later. Tell Granny to call me when you get there."

Tye agreed and didn't give his sister any lip about it. She tossed her cell phone in her purse. Then she went into the kitchen, leaving the small TV on the kitchen counter on. It was either that or turning her radio on. She didn't want to come in to a totally quiet house tonight, not during a storm.

She picked a jacket and an umbrella before heading out the door. She armed the home alarm system and wondered how much damage an intruder would do before the police could get there. The alarm company assured her that the authorities would get there very quickly, but she wondered. They'd have to be parked right on the street to really be able to stop anything or help her if she really needed help.

Nicole stepped into her truck and raised her garage door. The storm seemed to be worse than it was earlier, and the wind was blowing small broken branches and debris. She couldn't believe Tye would do something so stupid. But they would be safe at Granny's for the time being.

Nicole drove through the wind and rain. She turned on the CD player; Layla Hathaway's song "Breathe" played, and Nicole turned it up and drove. Her mind drifted to a place she didn't want to go. Her mind wandered to the time she first met Darren.

*   *   *

Darren was big and tall. He had a looming presence because of his size, but he had the prettiest smile. She knew that he was very arrogant. He was handsome, but Nicole wasn't attracted to him or his smile. He wasn't her type. She could tell that he pretended to be having a good time, but secretly, he felt that everyone around him was beneath him. Nicole could sense that he had an air of superiority about him, and she didn't want to be a part of his inner circle. But Darren was very attracted to her.

She'd met him last summer, at an art show in a luxurious penthouse suite downtown. It was a hot and humid night, but it was breezy. Nicole remembered how good those cool breezes felt on her back. She recalled looking at the sun setting on the horizon. The rich orange, yellow and reddish hue against a back drop of evening blue, had made the sky look as if it were on fire. A talented young musician played, Teena Marie's "Portugese Love" on acoustic guitar as pampered and prestigious guests snacked on hors d'oeuvres and admired an eclectic collection of art. In other areas of the penthouse, smooth jazz played softly in the background. Aniyah had planned to attend the event with Nicole, but for some reason or another, she had cancelled at the last minute. Nicole had been disappointed at first, she knew that Aniyah would have loved that experience. But there would be other art shows and other opportunities for Aniyah.

Nicole's presence attracted a lot of attention. She was among the Cleveland elite and the hostess made it a point to introduce her to as many of her guests as possible.

The featured artist's name was Jeremy Clarke, and he was truly a gifted artist. His art had captivated Nicole. The paintings had seemed to jump off of the canvas. Nicole was amazed by this man's raw talent. Jeremy had evoked an array of emotions through his artistry as varied as the paintings he had on display. Nicole had walked among the diverse group of guests, admiring the artist's work. She could honestly say that she loved every piece of his art, but one painting in particular had fascinated her and as she walked around and stopped to view Jeremy's work, she kept finding herself standing in front of this particular piece. It was a painting of a mother holding a child. The woman had appeared to be very young, her skin was very light almost white and she had curly brown hair, the child she was holding was a little girl who looked to be about two or three years old, The child's skin was very dark and she had beautiful, large dark eyes and course, kinky black hair. Nicole wasn't quite sure if the child she was holding in her arms was her own, but the woman had held onto the child as if claiming her as her own and she had such love in her eyes. Jeremy watched Nicole as she walked along admiring his artwork piece by piece. She could tell that Jeremy had wanted to talk to her further after the host had introduced her to him. But Darren wouldn't allow that to happen. Darren had followed her the entire evening, making the male guests feel intimidated, and it made her appear unapproachable. Finally after Nicole's last stop at the painting, Jeremy had stood next to Nicole and said to her, "I see you like this one."

Nicole was standing in front of the painting with her arms crossed as if pondering something deep and personal.

"Yes, I like this one." Nicole had said without looking at Jeremy, "I like this one a lot."

"Yea that's Myra and her daughter Tatiana." Nicole had looked at Jeremy and smiled, she had been interested in hearing the back story of these two subjects. "Myra and Tatiana live in New York. She's seventeen and Tatiana is two."

"Well it's beautiful," Nicole had said with a nod. "You did a wonderful job."

"Thank you," Jeremy answered.

"You are incredibly talented." Nicole had said as she looked at the painting.

The painting had reminded her of her own mother. She had remembered when her mother had loved her like that. But it had been so long ago, that her memory of that kind of love had become faint. This painting had made her remember.

Nicole didn't mention any of that to Jeremy. She didn't tell him that her mother had been quite young when she'd had her and that her mother was so light skinned that when she was a young girl some people didn't believe that Nicole belonged to her. But Nicole did indeed remember that her mother had had that same look of love in her eyes and that she had held her in her arms long ago claiming her as her own.

"I think a lot of people like this. I've gotten a lot of feedback on this one. I met Myra and Tatiana at a woman's shelter. She didn't have anyone but herself and her baby. Myra has a very interesting story." Jeremy could tell that Nicole wanted to hear more even though she wasn't making eye contact with him. He could tell by the way his painting had repeatedly drawn Nicole to it. "Nicole is it?" Jeremy had said as if he really couldn't recall her name.

"Yes?" She'd said turning to him. Jeremy wore blue jeans, brown suede shoes and a white button down shirt. He was neat but had dressed far too casually for this type of an event, Nicole had thought. "I've enjoyed talking to you."

Nicole smiled. Then Jeremy handed his card to her and asked her if he could see her again.

Nicole smiled at him. She had no intention of calling him. She had thought that he was very attractive and he seemed to be a nice guy, but she hadn't intended to collect phone numbers that night. Though events such as that were great for networking, she had known that that was not what Jeremy had in mind. She took Jeremy's card and had given him hers and she'd noticed Darren staring at her from across the room. But it didn't frighten her, it annoyed her.

Nicole remembered how Darren stood behind her as she admired an oil painting of an elderly couple sitting on a park bench. He stood too closely behind her, invading her space. He flirted with her as he stood behind her. He didn't even have the decency to make small talk first. She was polite as possible to him, seeing that she was a guest in someone's home. But she had absolutely no attraction to Darren. Absolutely none. She knew that other women there did. She could see why they were attracted. He had a nice body, he dressed well, and he was very handsome. But there was something about him that had rubbed her the wrong way, and she just wasn't interested. Darren had appeared to be very pretentious, but she could see that he still had a lot of hood in him. She could see it in his walk, she could see it in his stance, and she could read it in his eyes.

"Why are you standing so closely behind me?" She had asked him as she turned to face him. Darren had enjoyed staring at Nicole from the back, but the view of her from the front was just as alluring. She hadn't said it loudly and Darren was surprised by how completely unintimidated she was by his bravado.

"What do you mean?" Darren had answered as he slowly looked Nicole up and down, as if soaking in her beauty.

"I think you know what I mean. You keep following me around and walking up on me like you're my man. You don't even know me." No one could tell that Nicole was speaking to Darren this way. She hadn't seemed a bit annoyed and she spoke to him loud enough for only the two of them to hear.

"Are you afraid of me?"

"No, I'm annoyed. Very annoyed. So please back up off me." Nicole had not intended on being confrontational, but she wouldn't tolerate this type of behavior from her boyfriend, and she certainly was not going to take it from a complete stranger. She knew that Darren had understood every word that she had said. Even though her irritation wasn't reflected in her demeanor it was quite evident in her tone.

Nicole was sure that Darren's behavior could be very unsettling to most women, but not to her. She could handle herself and she had no problem addressing the things that she thought needed to be addressed.

Darren had apologized to Nicole, but he'd become even more attracted to her after she'd confronted him.

*　　*　　*

As she reflected on that day she thought to herself that of the two men, Jeremy and Darren, she'd never would have thought that she would have hooked up with Darren. If anyone would have told her that she would have chosen the nut that she met at the art showcase over the talented young artist she would have told them they were crazy.

"Do you dream in color?" She huffed as those words ran through her mind. She hadn't known what he was talking about when he had asked that question so she ignored it and didn't give him an answer. But whenever she reflected on those words and imagined herself causing Darren bodily harm she'd have to answer a resounding, "Yes. Yes I dream in color."

Nicole had her windshield wipers on high as she entered the freeway. It would take her about half hour to get to her sister's place. Her grandmother's house wasn't far from Fatimah's. She knew something was wrong. Even though the two didn't get along very well, Fatimah was still Nicole's sister, and she cared about her. Nicole knew that something had to be wrong with Fatimah for her to be completely unaware of her children's whereabouts.

As she drove, she thought about Darren. She thought about him because she didn't talk about him. Everybody thought Nicole was so cold because of how she didn't show any emotion when she found out that Darren was a married man. She didn't cry, she didn't ask why, and she didn't even bring up his name. Darren was here today gone tomorrow, and she didn't even put up a fight. It was as if she never really loved him at all.

You would think that everyone would have been proud of her reaction to finding out that the man that she loved and had been dating for the past year was married. She didn't try to fight or argue; she just told him it was over. She told him not to bother trying to keep in touch. She told him she didn't want him anymore. It was as if any love that she had was gone just as soon as the truth escaped his lips. It was over as far as she was concerned. No ifs, ands, or buts. Wasn't that the right thing to do?

The rain was coming down in sheets. Nicole could barely see in front of her. She could hear her cell phone ringing in her purse. But she didn't think that she could answer it safely, so she let it ring. She took her time, with headlights beaming and windshield wipers ineffectively sweeping the rain off the windshield. She thought about pulling over to answer the phone, but didn't think that to be too wise seeing that visibility was so low.

Thunder crackled in the distance, and lightning illuminated the highway. Nicole thought the road was exceptionally crowded this evening. She watched as people drove much too fast, and she prayed silently that none of them went hydroplaning into her vehicle.

Nicole checked her rearview mirrors to see if she could pass a big freighter that was splashing water onto her truck. It seemed to be clear enough to pass. But it was hard to tell though. There was too much traffic on the road. She hated those big trucks; they always splashed extra water on her vehicle, and if she drove behind them, they blocked the freeway signs.

"Damn," Nicole said out loud as she wondered what was going on tonight to make the roads so cramped and busy.

Nicole signaled and got over in the right lane as soon as she was able. She sped up to get past the large freighter because now it was splashing water all on the side of her truck. Her phone rang again and again, and she ignored it. It would have to wait until she was on a safe road and could pull over to answer it. She hit the repeat button on her CD player and listened to "Breathe" again. She liked that song, and she couldn't really get into it the first time it played because she was too busy thinking about Darren's old sorry behind and trying to pay attention to the road.

Nicole took a deep breath and exhaled hard and slow. She had to admit she was having a hard time getting over how Darren had abused their relationship. She'd loved him. Did a woman always have to be crazed and distraught after a breakup? Or was it okay to just pick up the pieces and walk away? She caught herself thinking about what she could do differently to prevent this from happening the next time. Then she told herself, "There won't be a next time."

Chapter 7

UKULELE

Mariah didn't bother calling Aniyah back. Whatever Aniyah was mad about, she'd get over it eventually. Mariah didn't think twice about it. It was dark now, and she worried about Carl and the kids. Carl was a good driver, but Mariah never felt really comfortable until all of her family was at home and safe under one roof. She couldn't really rest until then. She attempted to though. It was dark and rainy, the best sleeping weather. The baby was kicking all over the place earlier, but was resting now.

Mariah went up to her room to get into her comfy, cozy bed to try and take a nap. Thunder and lightning didn't frighten her, and she'd never had a problem with it keeping her up before. But somehow, now it was disturbing to her, and she imagined her family out on the road trying to make it home. She knew how frightened her seven-year-old and her three-year-old were of storms, and she figured her hubby probably had his hands full right about now. She thought about calling Carl to ask if everybody was okay, but decided not to. Besides, what could she do?

Mariah lay on her left side facing the bedroom door, with a pillow in between her knees and two beneath her head. She rubbed her belly and sang to her little Ukulele. The baby moved a little. Mariah smiled.

"I'm worried about Daddy and your siblings," Mariah said, talking to the baby. "Zenobia and Tyler are afraid of the storm."

Mariah lay on her side, quietly singing to her belly. Her mind wandered off every now and then, but she continued singing to her unborn child. She thought about the events of the early morning. She wondered how the children were dealing with PJ's death. She didn't want to take it too lightly and then have her children scarred for life. She thought that maybe they should have had a burial service for PJ, but where would she have stored the body while they made plans? Mariah quickly dismissed that thought from her head. Carl had done the right thing by getting the dog's body out of the house and disposing of it quickly. She'd never had a pet die before, and she didn't have time to look up how to handle the death of a pet on the internet; they just had to handle it.

Carl was such a good father she thought to herself. He was a keeper; she smiled as that thought went through her mind. Mariah felt a little nauseated, and she got up and went to the bathroom. She leaned against the vanity and stared at herself in the mirror. She took a deep breath and splashed a little cold water on her face. She felt a little dizzy, so she held on to the bathroom counter with both hands, stared down into the sink, and took a deep breath. She stretched her neck from side to side and exhaled again. Sharing that body with Ukulele was rough. She always felt so achy.

Mariah stood up straight and leaned backward stretching her back and rubbed her belly. She didn't feel too well, but she wasn't alarmed by that because she'd felt that way with her pregnancies before. No big deal, she just needed to lie down and get some rest.

Mariah walked over to the bed, holding her stomach as if it would fall to the floor if she let go. She crawled onto the bed and lay on her left side again, but before adjusting her pillows, she turned on the radio. Luther Vandross sang, "Love Won't Let Me Wait", and Mariah smiled and hoped it would lull her off to sleep and it did.

As Mariah drifted off to sleep, she didn't dream; her body was stiff and still. She was sleeping in one spot like she used to when trying to protect a new hairdo. She was a little chilly, so she woke up long enough to pull an afghan over herself as she lay on top of her satiny, burgundy comforter. The comforter was cool on her skin and she would prefer to cover up with that, but it would be too much trouble and would require more energy than she is willing to exert right now.

The phone didn't ring and the family wasn't home yet, but Mariah didn't have to worry about this because she was sleeping soundly. The house was still except for soft music playing and thunder intermittently reverberating through the walls of the two-story home. Mariah slept, guarding her huge belly with her right arm.

Mariah knew that Aniyah was upset with her, but she didn't think Aniyah or anyone else had any right to see or even know what was on those pictures on Mama's computer. She didn't even tell Mama what they were. But Mariah had seen them, and it was very disturbing to her.

Darren had sent Mama pictures of Nicole going in and out of different hotels rooms with different men and a few pictures of different men entering her home. The faces of the men were not clearly seen in the photos, but Nicole's face was as plain as day in all of them. Mariah had lied to her mother and said that there was something wrong with her computer and had offered to get it fixed, then pretended to fix it after deleting all of the photos. She did tell Nicole though. She told her to warn her, not to embarrass her. She knew if Darren was watching her that closely, then she had to let her sister know.

When Mariah told Nicole about it, she wasn't a bit embarrassed. She told Mariah that she didn't know what Mariah was so disturbed about it for. He hadn't sent Mama any nude or sexually explicit pictures. Nicole told her that Darren was just trying to get a rise out of everybody. Just trying to get some attention, because she wasn't seeing him anymore.

Mariah sat up abruptly as if awakened by an alarm clock, heart thumping violently in her chest. She felt something warm and wet on her inner thighs, and she knew that something was terribly wrong. She wasn't cramping, and she didn't feel nauseated anymore. But this much wetness at anytime during a pregnancy was never a good sign.

She placed her hand between her legs and touched her damp thighs. She examined her fingers, but it was too dark to see. She sat on the side of the bed and eased herself off it, and when she stood, more wetness came. Mariah began to cry; she knew this was bad.

"Please, please, no," she cried as she scrambled to get to the bathroom to see what she feared to be true. She was bleeding. Bright red blood and she was only twenty weeks pregnant.

Her hands trembled, and she cried harder. She reached for a towel off the towel rack in the bathroom and placed it between her legs. She held her legs tightly together as if trying to hold her unborn child inside of her. She cried harder as she ran warm water over her hands and watched her own diluted blood run down the drain. She waddled, with the towel still in between her legs, as fast as she could to the phone. With wet hands, she picked up the receiver and dialed her husband's cell phone, only to hear it ringing beneath a pair of pants on their bedroom chair. She had told her husband time and time again to make sure he kept his cell phone on him at all times. He had a family and that was what it was for, she'd told him. Carl always agreed to do it, but would often forget his phone and would have to come back home to pick it up. "Anything could happen to us, any type of emergency, and we may not have the time to call all over the place looking for you" is what Mariah would often say to him. She hated to be proven right this time.

Mariah cried and prayed under her breath. She didn't have time to be mad at Carl. She felt like dropping to her knees and begging the Lord to save her baby. But instead, she kept saying, "Please, please, please," as she scrambled frantically to dial her sister Nicole.

First, she tried Nicole at home and got no answer. She tried several times to reach her there, leaving messages that would have scared the life out of Nicole if she had gotten them.

"Nicole, please help me," she cried. "I'm bleeding. Please come get meee. I'm bleeding. I'm bleeding." No other details. Nicole wouldn't have known what had occurred.

Next, Mariah dialed Nicole's cell phone. It rang and rang, and the voice mail came on and again a series of disturbing messages. "Nicole, please help me. Something is wrong. I won't stop bleeding," She said as she cried hysterically, trying not to hyperventilate.

As a registered nurse, Mariah knew exactly what to do. She was well aware of every action she should be taking, but she couldn't think straight. All she could think about was losing her baby. What could she have possibly done wrong to hurt her child? What could have caused this? Why was this happening to her?

It never occurred to her to call her mother or her sisters Fatimah and Aniyah, all of whom were registered nurses too. Fatimah was a nurse practitioner, and it never even entered her mind to call Fatimah and to try and get in touch with her. Nicole was the first person she thought of, her big sister, her protector. Nicole was more of a mother to her than her mother ever was. And that was who she wanted with her.

After several attempts to locate Nicole, Mariah gave up and did what she should have done in the first place and that was to call 911. She tried to calm herself. She knew how annoying 911 dispatchers could be, and she didn't want to get overly excited. A woman answered the phone.

"9-1-1. What's your emergency?"

Mariah wanted to blurt out, "I'm bleeding!" But instead, she answered the dispatcher as if she was making the call for a patient of hers and not herself. The dispatcher was very kind and sympathetic. She asked Mariah if she was able to get to the door to unlock it for the EMS. Mariah answered, "Yes." The dispatcher assured her that they would be at her residence shortly.

Mariah had checked. She hadn't soiled her gown, but she put on her big pine green robe over it and zipped it all the way up to her neck.

Mariah slowly eased herself down the stairs still squeezing the towel tightly between her legs. She didn't dare check to see how bloody it was; she knew that if it was too bloody, she would panic so she didn't check. She just eased herself down the steps, holding onto the railing with her right hand and guarding her belly with her left.

When she made it to the bottom of the stairs, she was calmer; help was on the way. She wasn't in any pain, and she would soon be at the nearest emergency room, which in this case was South Pointe Hospital. Mariah tried to go over the questions that she knew they would ask her at the hospital. Any pain or cramping? How long have you been bleeding? Any nausea, vomiting, fever or chills? Any elevated temp? etc. But when she thought about the most important question, she panicked. Because she wasn't quite sure of the answer. When was the last time you felt the baby move? She thought hard. When did she last feel the baby move? It was before she fell asleep, but how long before?

She unlocked both the front door and the security door. She remembered her purse was upstairs and wondered should she try to go back up to her room to get it. She remembered that her cell phone was charging on her dresser. She could also remember what time she heard Aniyah's car start up when she left her home. But she couldn't remember when she'd last felt her little Ukulele move.

Tears streamed down her face as she stood looking out the window in her foyer, as the rain tip-tapped on her windowpane. Her baby moved all the time. She had a very active baby. Somehow, she'd taken for granted the little kicks, stretches, and waves of baby movement. She had had five healthy pregnancies and five healthy babies. Never a complication. Easy pregnancies and easy deliveries. Folks would always say that was why she had so many babies because it all came a little too easy for her. Why was this pregnancy different?

Mariah stroked and rubbed her belly. Gentle strokes and pushes turned into more forceful movement. She poked and pushed her belly trying to get her little Ukulele to move, but there was no movement.

"Come on, baby," Mariah said gently through her tears. "Move for Mama." Ukulele didn't move. She sang softly to her child, but still, Ukulele did not move.

Mariah saw the ambulance as it came rolling down the street with lights flashing, splashing through sheets of rain. She met them on the front porch. She was ready to go; she hadn't even grabbed her keys. Two men dressed in rain gear got out of the ambulance and motioned for her to go back inside. As she stepped back inside, she heard the phone ringing. She went into the kitchen to answer the phone. It was her neighbor Jean. She had seen the flashing lights and called over to see what was wrong.

"Mariah, you okay over there?" Jean asked.

"Jean, I'm okay," she lied. "I'm glad you called. Could you get a message to my husband for me when he and the kids get home?" Mariah had been so concerned about her current predicament that she hadn't even thought about leaving a note for her family.

"Of course," Jean answered. "Do you need me to come over there?"

"No, no, Jean. I just need you to get a message to Carl for me." Mariah could hear the EMS coming in through her front door. "Will I be going to South Pointe?" Mariah asked.

"Yes ma'am," the tall one answered. "Tell him I'll be at South Pointe," Mariah said into the phone.

"I sure will. Listen, call me if you need anything."

"Okay."

"God bless you, baby, and I've got you and the little one in my prayers."

"Thank you, Jean."

Under normal circumstances, she would have told Jean about PJ and how Carl took the kids out to spend time with them and console them about the loss of their pet. Jean would have expressed her condolences and probably told Mariah a related story about the loss of a dear pet. Their conversation could have ranged from a few short minutes to a few long hours, depending on the subject matter on a day other than today.

Mariah walked into her foyer. The two men stood dripping water on her hardwood floors. She looked at the gurney and wondered if it was too late. The short, round one asked, "What seems to be the problem ma'am?"

"I'm bleeding," she answered. She almost didn't recognize her voice. It was softer than she'd expected.

The taller man dropped the gurney so that it was low enough for Mariah to get on to it; he held it firmly as the other man helped her up. She answered all the necessary questions as they strapped her onto the gurney. When they raised the gurney up, it startled her a little and her stomach sank. But little Ukulele didn't move.

The men covered her with loads and loads of blankets, before taking her out in the cold rain. The tall one looked so familiar, but she couldn't place his face. She probably could have recalled where she knew him from if she'd tried hard enough, but she didn't care. All she could think about was saving her baby. The short, round one's name was Dave; he was kind, and he tried to be reassuring to Mariah. He told Mariah that his wife was pregnant too.

Mariah was so afraid. She began shaking, and Dave asked her if she was warm enough. She told him that she was. The tall one drove, while

Dave hooked her up to the monitors. She held her lips together tightly, because she could feel them begin to tremble and she knew the waterworks were soon to follow. Her heart raced. She closed her eyes and wrung her hands tightly and tears escaped her closed eyelids. Then she felt it, and she lay very still with her eyes opened wide.

"Oh boy," Dave said with a laugh. "That was a strong one. They never like these monitors."

Mariah smiled, and the tears fell. Ukulele was moving all over the place. She closed her eyes, and she couldn't stop the tears from flowing. She wrung her hands tighter, and she kept repeating to herself, "Thank you, Lord. Thank you."

Chapter 8

TOO MUCH STIMULI

Mariah knew that it wasn't over, but she felt like her baby was communicating with her somehow, as if to say, "Don't worry, Mommy, I'm okay." She didn't live too far from South Pointe Hospital, and she arrived at the emergency room in no time. Everything was moving so fast, and she wished somebody was there with her.

Nurses came in and took blood, started an IV, and tried to make her as comfortable as possible. She hadn't bled as much as she'd thought she had. She thought her little flowered hand towel would be soaked by now. There was only a small stain on the towel about the size of the base of a twelve-ounce Styrofoam cup.

One of the nurses informed her that the doctor would be in to perform a pelvic exam. She was a kind nurse, with a calm demeanor, very personable. She made small talk with Mariah as she worked, rarely looking up at Mariah as she spoke.

"Hello. My name is Gwendolyn, but you can call me Linda." Mariah must have had a strange look on her face because Linda said, "Yea, I know. Everybody always asks me, 'Linda, how did you get Linda out of Gwendolyn,' and I always say, 'I dunno.'" Linda hunched her shoulders. She talked as she worked, and she worked fast, setting up the room for Mariah's pelvic exam. "How far along did you say you are?"

"Twenty weeks."

"Boy, you're huge, no offense."

"None taken. I always get really big with my pregnancies."

"Yea, you look like you have half a huge watermelon in there."

Mariah smiled. Mariah lay back on the hospital bed and stared at the ceiling. The baby's heart rate was fine. Ukulele was moving around as if trying to kick the monitors off her belly.

"Feisty little thing," Linda said as she stopped for a second, looked at the fetal monitor, then winked at Mariah.

Mariah wasn't crying anymore, but she was still very anxious and afraid. She was still spotting, and she didn't know what was going on with her body and why. Mariah asked Linda to call her husband. Linda tried and was still unable to reach him. She started to have her call Jean, but she didn't really feel like talking to her. Besides, she hadn't been completely evaluated yet, and she didn't want to fill Jean in on the details that brought her there.

Mariah tried to sit up when the doctor walked into the room. But he just smiled at her, waved his hand, and motioned for her to lie back down. He was a small middle-aged man, with a large pink face. He wore his thin, blond hair short on the sides with a few sparse strands combed over the top of his shiny pink scalp. His lab jacket was stained with what she hoped was coffee, and it was too small for his stout body.

He was an emergency-room doctor, so she knew he kept long hours; she wished he was a little less slovenly though. He hit the soap dispenser hard with his palm about three times and liquid soap squirted into his open hand; he rubbed his hands together vigorously before running them under the warm water. He sniffed a few times and cleared his throat as he snatched several paper towels from its dispenser, and he walked over to the bed as he dried his hands.

"Ms. Daley, I presume? It is Ms. Daley, isn't it?"

"Mrs," she answered, as if it mattered; she didn't care what he called her at this point.

"See," he answered, "it's a good thing that I asked."

Mariah nodded.

"So I hear you've been experiencing some bleeding?"

Mariah answered his question as well as a series of other questions she had answered numerous times before. He made her feel at ease.

"You know, Mrs. Daley, there are a number of reason's you could be experiencing this vaginal bleeding. Not all of them serious, okay?" He gestured for Mariah to scoot to the edge of the table and place her feet in the stirrups as he snapped a pair of gloves on.

The doctor palpated her stomach and nodded. Mariah observed the serious look on his face. He smiled when Ukulele kicked at his hands though.

"Now that's what I like to see, kiddo," the doc said talking to Ukulele. Mariah liked that he talked to her baby. The doctor beckoned for Mariah to scoot down closer to the edge of the table, making a come-here motion to her with his pointer finger. She did as he requested. "Anyway," he said with a grunt as he eased himself down on the stool right in front of her widely spread legs. "As I was saying, there are a number of potential causes for this vaginal bleeding that you're having. The more serious causes, I don't think apply to you."

Mariah was happy to hear that. "The baby's heart rate is nice and strong," he said as he lubricated two of his fingers. "Okay, deep breath now, you're gonna feel a little pressure here."

Mariah always thought that was an understatement. She felt more than a little pressure as he examined her, one hand on her belly the other in her vagina. She grimaced a little. She looked into his eyes as he examined her. She was good at reading facial expressions. His expression was serious. His brows were furrowed as if deep in thought.

He readied her for the speculum. She knew that people assumed that she'd be used to it after having so many children, but she wasn't. She absolutely hated it. She despised that feel of metal inside of her. This speculum was plastic, and she thought that maybe she could tolerate this one better, but it wasn't any different.

The doctor looked puzzled.

"What's wrong?" Mariah asked.

"We need to get an ultrasound," he said, turning to Linda, who stood quietly in the front of the room. She acted as Mariah's chaperone.

"What's wrong?"

"These are routine diagnostic tests, Mrs. Daley. Okay? The baby's fine, we just hafto look a little further to try and determine what may have caused the bleeding." The doctor stood and snapped off his gloves, then discarded them in a nearby trash can. "All right?" the doctor said, looking into Mariah's eyes. Mariah nodded.

Mariah was drowsy, and she was mad at Carl now. He'd been gone all day and not once did he call home to check on her. She'd been in that emergency room for an entire hour, and Carl was nowhere to be found. Things were calmer now, and she was really embarrassed about the voice-mail messages she'd left for Nicole. Her voice was anxious and panic stricken, and she hated when she felt that way.

Mariah had been prone to panic attacks when she was a child. But after her mother's reaction to the first one, she'd decided that she'd keep it under control ever since. It made her feel like a freak. She had them quite often, but no one knew. She'd developed her own coping mechanisms, and they worked quite well. Tonight was the first instance of her losing her grip, and she told herself she wouldn't let that happen again.

Mariah had dosed off for a bit, but couldn't sleep long before the ultrasound tech came along to whisk her away. She wasn't fully awake, but she could hear the tech introduce himself. His name was Stan. Mariah's eyes were closed when Stan rolled her bed out of the triage room and into the hallway. It was a very busy night, but Mariah suspected that the triage staff always moved this quickly, out of habit.

"You okay," Stan asked.

"Yes," Mariah answered.

"Wait a minute! That's my sister!"

Mariah recognized Nicole's voice, and she was relieved immediately. It was as if everything was going to be all right, as if Nicole could make it all better. Mariah opened up her eyes and looked for Nicole. Stan stopped rolling the bed. Nicole had been standing in the hallway, sipping ice water from a paper cup. She sat the cup down at the nurse's station and ran over to try to stop Stan from going any further.

Mariah couldn't turn her head around enough to see her because of the direction the bed was facing. But Nicole leaned over and looked Mariah in the face; her eyes were full of fear and concern. Nicole leaned forward and kissed her sister on the forehead, and Mariah began to cry.

"What's the matter, boo?" Nicole looked over at Stan as if he could answer her. Then she looked back at her sister.

"Didn't you get my messages?"

"No, I'm here with Teemah."

"What's wrong with Teemah?"

"She's been having those migraines again."

Nicole sighed and wiped the tears from her sister's face. "Hold on a minute," Nicole held up one finger and looked at Stan. "I'm going with her."

Nicole didn't know where Mariah was going; all she knew was that she was going too. Nicole stepped into a triage room that was two doors down from Mariah's. Then she came out and jogged over to Mariah's bed.

"Okay, so where are we going?"

Mariah held her sister's hand as Stan rolled the hospital bed along the cramped hallways. It was hard for Mariah to hang on due to the awkward maneuvering of the bed, but Mariah held on to her sister's hand as if her very life depended on it, bending her sister's wrist every which a way. Nicole didn't complain. She knew that Mariah was scared and that she needed her.

The room was dark and cold. The lighting was very dim. Mariah felt like she was in a bad dream. She was so afraid of what the ultrasound would reveal. Nicole didn't tell her to calm herself down. Even though Mariah didn't appear to be too anxious, Nicole knew that her sister was scared out of her mind.

Ukulele was kicking like crazy; Mariah didn't mind though. Nicole could see the movement through Mariah's gown.

"I see Ukulele's cutting up in there."

"Who's Ukulele?" Stan asked.

"That's my baby's nickname," Mariah answered.

"Oh, so you know it's a girl."

"No, this is my first ultrasound."

"Great," Stan said with a smile. "So I'll have the honor of introducing you to Ukulele for the first time."

Mariah smiled and for the first time, she felt a little embarrassed about giving her unborn child the nickname Ukulele. It sounded funny when Stan said it, but she liked that he referred to her baby by name and she thought what he'd said was very sweet. She knew the potential seriousness of her situation, and she appreciated the kindness of their staff and the efforts on behalf of her and her child. She also appreciated all of their attempts to allay her fears no matter how fruitless they were.

The ultrasound gel was warmer than Mariah expected. Stanley glided the ultrasound's transducer across her stomach as she saw Ukulele for the first time on the monitor's screen. Ukulele kicked and stretched as if fighting an invisible force from inside her wound. Mariah smiled, and more tears fell. She looked up at her sister, but her sister was focused on Stanley, more specifically the expression on Stanley's face.

Stanley looked bewildered.

"What's wrong, Stanley?" Mariah asked.

"Yea, what's wrong, Stanley?" Nicole said, and her tone was protective. Mariah squeezed Nicole's hand harder, and she placed her other hand on the side of her protruding belly. Mariah stared at the monitor's screen, and she had no idea what she was looking at.

Nicole stared at the picture on the screen also. She squinted at it and moved forward toward it, leaning her face into it.

"So, Stanley," Nicole asked, with her head turned in his direction. "Which one is Ukulele?"

"Huh?" Stanley said. He was caught off guard by the question.

"This one?" Nicole said, pointing to what looked like a blob to Mariah on the screen. "Or this one?" She then pointed to what looked like the top of the baby's head.

Mariah sat up a bit and looked over to her left at the screen. She wanted to see what Nicole saw. Mariah stared at the screen as if looking at it long enough would make the image magically appear.

Stanley smiled and said, "The doctor reads the results to the patients. I only take the pictures."

"But you can read it though, can't you? And I'm right, aren't I?"

Stanley sighed and pointed at the screen. "This is baby A," he said pointing to the area that Nicole had pointed out. "And this is baby B. Baby B is Ukulele. Because this," he said, pointing to the picture of the top of the baby's head, "is a baby girl."

Mariah didn't smile. Her mouth dropped. She didn't get it right away. When it did sink in, she looked at her sister as if to say, "How did this happen?" Her emotions went from shock back to worry. After all, this wasn't a routine visit at her physician's office; she was in an emergency room. Mariah was overcome with emotion. She was at first concerned about losing one baby; now she was worried about losing two, and she began to cry again.

Nicole could sense what was wrong. "You see two healthy babies there, don't you, Stan?"

"Yes, I do," he said reassuringly.

Since Nicole had gotten him started and he figured he had already said too much, he pointed out more things on the screen. He told the ladies that baby A, the boy was slightly larger than baby B and that both appeared to be the normal size for twenty-gestational-week-old twins. Stanley talked until he felt Mariah seemed less anxious; then he rolled Mariah back to her triage room. Nicole told her she'd be back, but she wanted to check on Fatimah.

Mariah had hoped that her husband would be in the room waiting for her, but he wasn't there. She worried about them now, and she couldn't wait for this night to be over with. She knew in the morning she'd have to hear Aniyah and Mama's mouth for not calling them sooner. She would have called Aniyah sooner but with the phone call came the update, and she wasn't in the mood. Mariah rang the call light and asked the nurse to turn the lights off for her. She thought she'd fall asleep easier that way.

Mariah loved Carl. She thought about him as she drifted off to sleep. He wasn't perfect, but he was absolutely perfect for her. They had the same corny sense of humor, their own secret looks and glances. She could read him like a book. Mariah could honestly say that she didn't desire anyone else. She believed that he felt the same way about her. But she knew better than to just take that for granted.

Mariah wasn't sure if Carl knew exactly how much she loved him, only because she let him know that she wouldn't be taking any shit. She had to make him fully aware of the fact that although she loved him dearly, she had no qualms about leaving him at the drop of a hat if she suddenly felt that it wasn't working out. Mariah had to let him know that with five children or not, she wasn't having it. She wasn't one of those neck-snappin', finger-poppin' women, but she had a way of getting him told in a classy no-nonsense kind of way and Carl knew that she meant every word.

What Carl didn't know was that Mariah had a secret stash of cash just in case she and her babies had to up and leave. Mariah wasn't paranoid; she just knew that shit happens sometimes and she had to be prepared. She knew enough to learn from other's mistakes; she didn't always have to make her own.

Carl genuinely loved her though. Mariah wasn't like any other woman. He knew Mariah was his soul mate, and he wouldn't let another woman come between him and his family. He loved his wife and his children without a doubt.

Mariah had tested him before, claimed she'd found another woman's number in his pants' pocket. He begged and pleaded for Mariah to believe him, that he'd never do anything to ruin what they had. She had the poor man thinking that she was on her way out the door. He was almost in tears. It might have been cruel, but she had invested a lot in this man—her time, her money, her emotions. She had to be sure that he knew that she was not playing with him. She had to let him know that she wasn't trapped in that marriage, no matter how trapped she sometimes felt; she had to let him know she was there because she wanted to be.

Mariah didn't want to be cynical and promiscuous like Nicole, stupid like Fatimah, putting up with senseless bullshit, and she didn't want to be afraid of commitment like her sister Aniyah. She had put a lot into her marriage, and she expected to get a lot out of it. And so far, she was blessed. She had a good, hardworking man who loved her and their children, a man who loved being a husband and a father and was pretty good at both.

Nobody looked at their relationship with envy. They were a young couple with too many kids as far as everyone else was concerned. People felt they worked too hard and spent too much time away from their kids. People wondered how they could keep a marriage together when they spent so much time apart. But Mariah didn't care what anybody said or what anybody thought. It worked well for them, and their family was just fine.

Carl startled her when he kissed her lips. She jumped, and for a few seconds, she had forgotten where she was. She was so happy to see him. She hugged him around his neck hard, pushing him into her bosom.

"Honey, I'm so glad to see you. I was so worried about you and the kids. Is it still bad out there?"

Carl didn't answer Mariah's question; he was concerned about her. "What's happening, Mariah? Are you okay? How's the baby?" He pulled a chair next to the bed, but didn't sit down, realizing he couldn't get a good look at his wife in a seated position. "Baby, are you okay?"

"I was taking a nap, and I started bleeding. I was a little dizzy and nauseated right before I laid down for my nap, but it was no big deal. I wasn't cramping or anything, so I didn't worry about it. But I started bleeding and I panicked."

Carl nodded as she talked, trying to soak everything in. She could see the fear and concern in her husband's eyes.

"I'm not bleeding anymore," Mariah said, trying to allay her husband's fears. She started to say to her husband that Ukulele is moving all over the place, and then she got a sinking feeling in her stomach as she remembered that she had two babies in her belly.

She held her husband's face in her hands and began kissing him lightly on his lips. His eyes were closed, he held his head low, and his face felt heavy in her hands. Carl's eyes watered, and Mariah wiped tears from his face and continued kissing him, but he still couldn't look at her because then he'd really break down. Carl had no idea what was going on, but he was glad to be there with her. He had feared the worse. And as calm as Jean was when she'd informed him of Mariah going to the ER, he was scared as hell.

Carl held Mariah's hand, his face wet with tears. He buried his face in her chest, and he didn't make a sound. He sighed and Mariah knew it was a sigh of relief. He didn't know much, but he knew his wife was okay. Carl couldn't imagine being without Mariah. He wasn't thinking about having to raise the kids alone. He just didn't see how he could be without her. She was all he ever really knew. Carl had been with other women before Mariah. But Mariah was something special. He knew it the moment he met her. It was something in her laugh and that deep-dimpled smile of hers. He knew she was going to be his. And he knew that he was going to be with her forever.

Carl was relieved and worried at the same time. He wasn't sure what he was going to walk into when he made it to the hospital. He had no idea what condition or what state of mind he'd find his wife in when he got there. He'd imagined the worse. He'd imagined that he'd come in to her crying hysterically and trembling, and he wouldn't know what to do to comfort her. But now she was comforting him. Carl didn't say a word because he wasn't sure how his voice would sound when the words came out. He'd cried in front of his wife before at his mom's funeral last year and at his elder brother's funeral the year before. He didn't like the way it looked or made him feel, especially around his wife. Crying made him feel weak and vulnerable.

Mariah placed her hand on the back of her husband's head and stroked his hair, fingering the tiny waves of hair with her fingertips. She had stopped crying now, but her eyes were red and puffy. The anxiety was gone, and her babies were okay. Carl gripped Mariah's left hand tighter as she stroked his head with her right.

She didn't mention baby number two. She knew her husband well enough to know that now wasn't the time. Too much stimuli for now. So Mariah rubbed her belly with one hand and held her husband close to her with the other.

Chapter 9

SO ADDICTED

Aniyah couldn't sleep, no matter how hard she tried. She tossed and turned for a short while, before deciding to get up and go to her PC. She loved that thing. She'd become so addicted to it that she had to move it out of her bedroom. She couldn't take it. The glow of the computer screen seemed to be calling her, and she couldn't resist the lure of the illuminated screen. Even turning off the monitor didn't work. So it had to go, but not too far though, just down the hall and around the corner, to her den.

Aniyah got out of bed trying not to rouse Nathan. He woke up briefly but went right back to sleep. She slid on her mint green satin nightie and her matching robe and headed to her computer.

It was waiting for her. She entered the room and sat in front of it with a smile as if meeting with an old friend. She clicked on to the internet and scanned some of the current events on her homepage before checking her e-mails. She had one hundred messages, most of them spam. Aniyah scrolled down to view her mail, deleting the unwanted messages along the way.

Delete. Delete. Delete. She deleted so many e-mails that her hand was getting tired. She shook her right hand and opened and closed her fingers, but just as she prepared to delete another message, she recognized a name.

Her mouth dropped a little, and she looked puzzled. "How did he get my e-mail address?" she said to herself. "And what would make him think I'd respond to his ass?" Aniyah had an itchy trigger finger, and she knew how to use it. She'd delete spam, personal e-mails, and a friend or two on one of her many social-networking sites. She contemplated deleting this one too. She stared at the name on the screen. Her cursor centered on the delete button. Aniyah rested her hand over the mouse, gently tapping the left side of it without clicking it. "He has got a lot of nerve. Trying to contact me after all these years."

Aniyah moved the mouse on the mouse pad, and the cursor stopped at the message. She clicked on it. It was a message from Matthew Davis Tullamore, the first person to ever break her heart. There was no message, only a link to her high school networking site. She'd have to go to the site if she wanted to see the message.

Aniyah turned abruptly toward the door. She'd thought she heard keys jingling. She sat perfectly still and listened. She sat so still that all she could hear was a faint humming in her ears.

Aniyah closed her eyes and took a deep cleansing breath, inhaling through her nose and exhaling through her mouth. Why couldn't she be the type of woman that could let go of things easily? Aniyah had heard of women like that, but she didn't know any personally. She had heard that there were woman out there who would have seen that message in their inbox, deleted it, and quickly emptied their trash bin so that the message would be gone forever, never to be seen again. She'd imagined that whomever these women were, they were a lot stronger than she was.

Aniyah had clicked on the link because she was curious. She wondered what Matt could have possibly had to say after all these years. She had to admit that she wanted to know what he looked like now, this boy who had hurt her so many years ago. What sort of man had he turned out to be? Was he married? Did he have any kids? She wondered, "Is his wife better looking than me." She didn't know why it mattered. She hadn't a clue why she cared. But she did.

Aniyah entered her password and waited for her profile pic to appear on the screen. Then she slowly scrolled down to see the comment that Matt had left.

The first thing she noticed was that the message was all in capital letters. As if he was making an important announcement. The next thing that she noticed was the tiny profile picture, next to his comment. She could barely see him; it was so small. She started to click on the picture to go directly to his profile before even reading his message. But she thought that she might change her mind about wanting to see his picture after having read his comment. So she read his comment first.

It read, HELLO ANIYAH. SO GOOD TO SEE YOU ARE DOING WELL. I HAVE WAITED SO LONG TO GET UP THE NERVE TO APOLOGIZE TO YOU FOR MY ACTIONS SO LONG AGO. I WAS NOT RAISED THAT WAY AND I AM SO ASHAMED OF MYSELF. PLEASE ACCEPT MY APOLOGY.

Aniyah sat there staring at the screen as the lights from her computer's modem flickered and danced. She couldn't believe what she was reading. Could it be that this man was actually trying to give her some closure after all these years? Or was he just trying to ease his guilty conscience? Either way, she was shocked. She'd imagined this day for a long time, but she'd seen it playing out so differently. She'd day dreamed that she was out at a concert or at a movie with somebody that she was truly in love with. She'd be walking hand in hand with her beau, looking her very best, and then she'd run into Matt and she'd act like she didn't even know who he was.

She never imagined this though. Not in her wildest dreams. She never ever really thought that he'd ever apologize and so publicly. Especially when it was so much easier to pretend that nothing ever really happened.

Aniyah moved the mouse, stopped the cursor over Matt's picture, then clicked. Matt's photograph appeared in the upper left-hand corner of the screen. Matt looked so different to her. Recognizable, but different. His skin was darker than she'd remembered—flawless, not like the skin of a teenaged boy. It looked so smooth. She stared into his dark eyes, and she couldn't look away. That was him all right. She sighed again and remembered the way she used to feel about him. The way her stomach used to flutter when he looked at her and smiled that smile of his. The one he was smiling at her now. She knew she was entering dangerous territory. But she couldn't look away. She remembered how those feelings had caused her to act, back then, when she was fourteen and how they had her thinking she'd lost her mind.

She thought about the man in the other room, sleeping in her bed. The man who'd said he loved her hours earlier. The one she hadn't said "I love you" back to, because of how this man had treated her when her heart was young and fragile.

Aniyah reminded herself that the man whose picture she was admiring had damaged her somehow, and she hadn't been the same since, but she couldn't look away. Aniyah looked at his mouth and remembered how it felt to kiss him. She liked his beard; it was short and neatly trimmed. His moustache was neatly trimmed also. Without realizing it, Aniyah licked her lips. She wondered what his hands looked like now. And she wondered if they would make her feel the way they used to, touching her skin.

Aniyah lightly rubbed the back of her neck and glanced over her shoulder. She felt guilty about the way she was thinking. She felt silly, reminiscing about how some young boy had made her feel. She remembered overhearing her grown cousins talking about young girls having sex saying, "These old fast-ass girls don't know nothin' about sex. Hell these little boys don't know the half. Huh! Think they doin' somethin'." Aniyah had known those comments were directed at her because of Mama and her big mouth. And she'd thought to herself that *they* didn't know what *they* were talking about. Because the truth was no one had made her feel the way Matt had made her feel before or since.

Aniyah stopped staring long enough to view his profile info. He was single with two children, nine-year-old twins, a boy and a girl. He had earned a master's degree in business and owned his own web-based marketing firm. Impressive, Aniyah thought to herself.

Aniyah viewed his photo album; there were only two pictures in it. There was his profile pic, one professional-looking picture with him posed by himself and one picture with him and his two children.

They were cute kids. The little boy was dark like his father. He wore a short haircut, shorter than his dad's. He smiled in the picture, a wide, forced smile as if it were rehearsed, but he had happy eyes. His daughter wore two pigtails, and she smiled as wide as her dad; her eyes were bright and happy, and she squinted as she smiled. She had her father's smooth dark skin also.

The caption beneath that picture read, The Loves of My Life. Aniyah wondered where their mother was or who she was, for that matter. She was curious about the woman he chose to start a family with. Were they still together? Had he ever called *her* a bitch?

Aniyah was thirsty, so she got up and went into the kitchen. She opened the refrigerator and pulled out her pitcher and poured herself a tall glass of cold water. She drank the first glass down quickly, gulping as if she were parched. She could hear herself breathing deeply into the glass as she threw her head back and drank. She poured herself another glass, but before heading back in the den, she stopped in her room to peek in on Nate.

Nathan had taken up the entire bed now. Unlike Aniyah who couldn't sleep on the other side of her own bed even if Nathan wasn't there. It was weird, but it was as though she was saving his side for him. Nathan was lying naked on the bed, flat on his stomach, with one leg bent and the other leg extended. He looked like he was climbing up the side of a cliff. His body was perfect, Aniyah thought to herself. She loved his lean muscular frame. She looked at his butt and smiled. He had such a cute butt; it was firm, with just the right amount of roundness to fill out his jeans. She sighed as she held on to her glass and looked at him.

Aniyah leaned against the doorjamb and stared at him in her bed. He was such an attractive man; he was sexy for sure. But that wasn't what she liked most about him. She liked Nathan so much because she had so much fun with him, and she really enjoyed his company.

When she first met Nathan, they hit it off immediately. She liked his sense of humor. She liked his boyish smile; it had a mischievous air about it that she thought was appealing. They had an instant chemistry as if they'd known each other in another lifetime. She liked that he was a quiet man; she appreciated his silence. Aniyah was used to abrasive, mouthy, know-it-all men. So Nathan was a refreshing change.

Aniyah didn't mind that people thought it strange that he didn't talk much. She felt special in that she was able to get him to share so much with her. He wasn't quiet when he was in her presence. Besides, what did he need to talk about with her family and friends anyhow? Nathan was a man who quietly observed the world, not quick to voice his opinions to strangers, mild mannered, and slow to anger. He thought before he spoke; he tried to choose his words wisely, and that was all that mattered to Aniyah.

Nathan would always tell Aniyah how beautiful he thought she was; sometimes, he'd stare into her eyes and say to her, "You so pretty," in his playful tone, and she'd smile bashfully and say, "Stop it" or "Shut up." Aniyah thought he may have meant it when he'd said he loved her last night. But she could never be too sure; she thought as she sipped her water and stared at his naked body.

Aniyah slowly closed her bedroom door, turning the doorknob all the way to the right as she pulled the door shut. She slowly released the doorknob once the door was completely closed and returned to her den.

Aniyah sat in front of the dark computer screen and downed the rest of the cold water. She moved the mouse and the computer screen lit up, and there was Matt's page again. She glanced at the bottom of the screen where it read "online friends," and she was surprised at how many people were on line at this hour. "I guess I'm not the only one addicted," Aniyah said quietly.

The condo was still except for the occasional clicking of the mouse, as Aniyah studied every detail of Matthew's page. His profile's format was standard, so she assumed that was because he was new to the site and he hadn't had time to personalize it, but she wondered what he'd come up with, having a web-based business in all. He hadn't created a badge for his profile or joined any groups yet. She wondered if he would be posting anymore pictures of himself and his family anytime soon.

Aniyah twirled the hair at her temples around her fingers as had been a nervous habit of her since she was a small child. Mama used to hate it when she did this and would tell her, "You're gonna tear a patch of hair out, and then you'll be runnin' around her lookin' crazy," but that never happened. Aniyah had been twirling her hair for years, and her hair was as full and thick as ever. Aniyah coiled long strands of red hair around her fingers as she focused on the profile. She rubbed her eyes as if that would allow her to see things clearer. She wasn't a bit sleepy. But she grew tired of sitting in front of the computer screen and her butt was getting sore.

All of a sudden, a chat box popped up at the bottom right corner of the screen. It startled Aniyah when she saw who it was. It was Matthew and her stomach dropped as if he knew somehow that she was examining his page. She calmed herself, knowing full well that that wasn't possible.

His chat message read as follows:

Matthew: Hello, Aniyah.

Aniyah was unsure if she should answer. But she did without thinking it through.

Aniyah: Hello, Matthew.
Matthew: How have you been?

Matthew asked without inquiring if Aniyah had actually accepted his apology.

Aniyah: Fine and you?
Matthew: I've been doing great.

There was a long pause before his next message.

I'm so sorry for waiting so long to apologize to you. I've wanted to for a long time. I never knew how to get in touch with you.

Aniyah thought to herself, "Whatever," but answered.

Aniyah: Why so public?
Matthew: I hurt you publicly, so I apologized publicly.

Aniyah didn't respond to that.

So how have you been? Married? Any kids?

Aniyah: No husband, no kids, but I'm in a relationship though.

Matthew: Oh, that's nice, I'm not married, but I have a son
and a daughter that I'm raising. I'm not currently in
a relationship. But I hope to get married someday. I
guess.

"I guess?" Aniyah thought to herself, "Either you do or you don't." Aniyah didn't type in anything. After all, they weren't old friends reminiscing. He was someone who had been unnecessarily cruel to her, and she really shouldn't be continuing their chat but she stayed on just to see where it would lead. Matthew asked if he could call her because his hands were getting tired. She told him that she could call him. She didn't want the phone to wake up Nathan. Matthew typed in his phone number, and Aniyah called him right away.

"Hi," Matthew said. She could hear the smile in his voice.

"Hi," Aniyah answered.

"You still sound the same. The same sweet voice."

Aniyah didn't reply to his compliment. But she wanted to tell him that he didn't sound the same. His voice was deeper now, and she tried to imagine him using those same harsh words that he'd used long ago in this deeper, more mature voice.

"I never thought I'd see this day coming. I didn't think that I'd ever talk to you again."

"Neither did I," Aniyah said.

"I'm curious. Why are you talking to me?"

She didn't know why, but that question angered her. Hadn't she been cordial? Wasn't it nice enough of her that she'd responded? Why did it matter?

"I was curious too," Aniyah replied, with anger in her tone. "I wanted to know why, after all these years, would you want to apologize. I was curious to find out what you had to say. I mean, enlighten me? Because I sure would have appreciated that grand apology back when I was crying and begging you to talk to me. Back when I was nothing but a bitch and a ho to you. Back when you told me in front of your brothers, my friends, and your friends, to get the fuck away from you, you don't want my ass no mo. Where was my public apology back then?" Aniyah wasn't going to get into how it made her feel. How she used to lay awake at night crying, wondering what she had done wrong. She didn't share with him that her drop in self-esteem could be traced back to that very relationship, and she couldn't tell him that because of him, she'd somehow sabotage the few relationships she had had that were worth keeping.

Matthew sighed into the phone. He'd thought he'd gotten off easily. He sent her a typed apology. He didn't have to speak to her and look into her eyes. It was basically a take-it-or-leave-it message, as far as Aniyah was concerned. The words meant nothing; the delivery was cold. Because there was no face-to-face contact, Matthew didn't have to relive anything, nor did he have to face anything. He just put it out there. It didn't matter if she accepted it or not.

"Look," Aniyah said. "What's done is done. I'm not trying to rehash hurtful memories. That was so long ago. But I hafto tell you. That apology was for you, not for me. It was to help you soothe your guilty conscience and apparently you did. So whatever. I am so over that," Aniyah lied.

"Yeah, you are I can tell," Matthew said with an uneasy sarcasm.

Matt sighed into the phone and said, "Look, you are absolutely right. I have been carrying this guilt around for years, and I wanted to get it off me any way that I knew how. I just want you to know that I am truly, truly sorry for my behavior. My mother didn't raise me like that, and she wasn't aware of my actions toward you, she had no idea that I was disrespecting you in that way, and I am truly, truly sorry. I'm not making excuses for my actions. I take full responsibility for them. But in my defense, I was young. I had older brothers that I was trying to impress. I was getting teased by my friends and my brothers about how serious I was getting over you, and I let peer pressure win out and I'm sorry. I wish I'd never done that to you. I was so in love and everybody made me feel weak and corny for feeling that way, and they said things about me that I won't repeat and I just got beside myself." Matthew sighed, then continued, "Years later, I talked to my mom about my behavior, and she was appalled, she went off on me and my brothers about it. She told me she was so ashamed of me and that I should apologize."

"Thank God for mothers," Aniyah said.

There was a brief but heavy silence. Then Matthew said, "I have children now. I want my son to be respectful of women, and I want my daughter to know she is worthy of respect. I have to set the example and plant the seed deep enough so that peer pressure won't cause them to do things that they know aren't right no matter how much they're pressured."

Aniyah liked what he said about his kids. She hoped that the "worthy of respect thing" wasn't a dig at her, but she told herself not to be so defensive. She told Matthew that she accepted his apology, and he seemed pleased.

Matthew wasn't anything like Nathan. He could talk for hours. There was never any need to ask him any questions about himself, because he'd give you the rundown in the first five minutes. Aniyah thought it was overwhelming at first. But at least, she didn't have to ask him any questions. She knew that he was getting more comfortable the longer they talked. Matthew was enjoying getting to know her again.

To him, it was as if nothing had ever happened. But Aniyah felt she hadn't really forgiven him, not that easily. She was still hurt, and she wanted him to be hurt too. She briefly considered leading him on so that he would fall in love with her, and then she'd crush him by breaking his heart. But she knew she wasn't capable of pulling that off; she lacked the self-confidence, and she figured she couldn't get him to fall in love the first time around. She could see it backfiring, and then she'd be somewhere curled up in a ball crying, with him calling her a bunch of bitches again. It would be de`ja`vu all over the place.

Matthew didn't mention his mom or his brothers anymore, and Aniyah didn't ask about them. However, he did mention to her that the mother of his children left him and their kids to pursue an acting career. Matthew said that she wanted them to come too, but that she wasn't financially stable, and he didn't feel comfortable uprooting his kids when she had absolutely no prospects, no agent, no manager, and no money. Aniyah asked if she had talent.

Matthew answered, "Yea, I guess."

"You never know she might be the next Halle Berry or Taraji P. Henson." Aniyah loved them.

"Maybe," he replied.

"Then you'll be sorry that you ever let her get away," she said jokingly. Aniyah was very supportive of the arts, but thought it odd that a woman would leave her small children to pursue a dream that she hadn't even adequately prepared for.

"Nah, it's over between us. That ship has sailed. I wish her the best though."

Matthew asked about Nathan. Aniyah told him that she had been dating Nathan for about a year and that things were going really great. He seemed glad to hear that she was happy. He told her he was dating, but nothing serious. He also told her that his kids didn't like anybody. She laughed for the first time their entire conversation. He liked that, and he wished he could make her laugh again.

"You know I'd love to see you."

"I post pictures all the time," Aniyah answered.

"You know what I mean, Aniyah."

"I don't think that's a good idea."

"Why? Nothing's gonna happen."

"Oh, I know that. I just don't think it's appropriate. I'm seeing someone."

What Aniyah wanted to say was, "I got a man." But she knew that didn't matter to him. It was just an excuse.

"Bring 'um. I'd like to meet him."

"Yea, right. What would I look like, inviting my boyfriend to meet you?"

"Well, it's innocent. I don't see where that would be a problem. I'm not particularly fond of the idea of socializing with someone that you're in a relationship with."

"It was your suggestion."

"Well, I'd do it to be able to see you."

"Not a good idea."

"I think it's a great idea."

"Okay, where would you like us to meet you?"

"You bringing your man along?"

"Isn't that what you said?" Aniyah laughed.

"I said it so that you could see how harmless I am and then decide to go out with me, but naw, I don't really wanna meet your man."

Aniyah laughed and said, "So you grew up to be sneaky."

Matthew laughed too and said, "I just wanna see you. Take you out. Consider it part two of my apology."

Aniyah pictured his face. She pictured him saying these very words with his grown-up face. His grown-up lips. "I don't know."

"Pleeease. I really wanna see you." Matthew went on to say that at the very least, he could take her out to dinner. Aniyah reiterated that it just wasn't appropriate.

Aniyah let him beg. She liked to hear him beg. She already knew what her answer was going to be, because she wanted to see him too. Just out of curiosity. She was happy with Nate; he was good to her, and she had absolutely no intention of doing anything that would ruin their relationship. Even though she had difficulty committing herself to him, she knew she didn't want him going anywhere. And she was most certainly not going to lose him over Matthew Davis Tullamore.

Aniyah was careful not to let him beg too long. She didn't want him to take back his offer. Aniyah said, "Yes," and Matthew seemed to be so happy. So they arranged a time and place to meet. Before getting off the phone, Aniyah said to him, "I'll call you later to make sure plans haven't changed."

"Believe me. Plans won't change."

"You have children. Anything can happen."

"You're right," he said. "Tell you what, if plans change, I'll send a message to your inbox. Do you get an alert on your cell phone?"

"Yea," she answered.

"Okay then I'll see you tomorrow at seven o'clock."

"All right."

Aniyah was still sitting in front of the computer screen. With her legs crossed in a classic yoga pose. Her butt was sore. She logged off and turned off the computer, then she walked into her bedroom. Nathan had changed positions now. He was lying curled up on his right side, and he was lying on his side of the bed now. Aniyah covered him with the comforter, and his body relaxed a bit. He was cold. Aniyah took off her mint green satiny robe, draped it over the vanity chair, stripped off her gown, and laid it on top of the robe and lay in her bed. It was warm as if Nathan warmed it up just for her, anticipating her return. Aniyah lay on her side away from him and faced her bedroom window. She watched as the sun creeped in through her partially closed blinds. It was dawn, and she'd talked to Matthew all night long. She couldn't sleep, but it wasn't because she felt guilty, instead she scanned her wardrobe in her mind, trying to decide what to wear for her meeting with Matthew tonight.

Chapter 10

LIFE IS BEAUTIFUL

Aniyah got the news at eight o'clock Sunday morning, and she was pissed.

"Why would you wait until now to call me?" Aniyah yelled.

"What? I'm calling you now."

"My sister is in the hospital, and nobody called to tell me?"

"Sisters. Plural," Mariah said, stressing the "s" at the end.

"What?! This is ridiculous. We're family. Why does everyone always exclude me?"

Aniyah always took everything as a personal assault against her. Mariah wanted to tell her sister, "Look, it's not always about you." But Mariah didn't say a word, because she knew that her sister was genuinely concerned about her well-being and that she loved her. Instead, she said to her, "Aniyah, I am very sorry. I was scared. I had a lot going on, and I really didn't have the time or the energy to call. There was so much excitement and again I am sorry."

Mariah felt really silly apologizing to her sister; after all, she'd been the one who was rushed to the ER. But Aniyah was satisfied to hear it. She felt she deserved an apology for not being kept in the loop.

Mariah had recapped the events of the previous night, being sure to include every detail. She told Aniyah how she just happened to see Nicole in the emergency room. And that Fatimah was in the emergency room also, just two doors down from her, with one of her bad migraines. There were several surprises that night, but Mariah only shared hers. She didn't feel right telling Fatimah's business. She'd let Fatimah tell her when she wanted to.

Mariah told Aniyah that she found out that she was having twins, a boy and a girl, and that they were healthy as far as they could see. Aniyah was ecstatic, and she kept telling her, "I told you there were two in there." She told Aniyah that the doctor had observed some vaginal tearing during her pelvic exam and that he thought that the bleeding may have come from sexual intercourse.

"Wow." Aniyah laughed. "Go head Carl. He must have been tearing it up."

"We haven't been doing anything any differently. No more differently than with my other pregnancies."

"Well," Aniyah said with all seriousness. "That diagnosis is better than any other."

"Yea, you're right." Mariah had to agree.

Mariah told her sister that she was still in the hospital for observation, but would be leaving as soon as the discharge paperwork was complete and that Fatimah would be leaving the hospital shortly too. Aniyah told her that she loved her and that she was so glad that everything was okay. She told her how excited she was about the babies and repeated how she had told her so.

And Mariah said, "Okay, then be excited about helping with them when they get here."

The two sisters talked until the nurses came in, then Mariah said, "Love you. I gotta go."

Aniyah told her sister, "I love you too." She tried to tell Mariah to call her if she needed her, but Mariah had hung up the phone before she could complete her sentence.

Aniyah hadn't wondered why Fatimah hadn't called. She knew how bad Fatimah's migraines could get. Sometimes, they would get so bad that Fatimah couldn't even function. Aniyah remembered that her sister used to get migraines so badly during her menstrual cycle that Aniyah was afraid to get hers. She'd thought that she'd be in agony just like her older sister.

Aniyah called the hospital and was transferred to her sister's room. Fatimah sounded awful when she answered the phone. Aniyah hardly recognized her voice.

"Hello?" Fatimah answered.

"Hello? Fatimah is that you?"

"Yea, it's me. Hey, Aniyah."

"Hi, Teemah. How are you feeling? My God, you sound awful."

"Girl, I feel awful. My head is killing me," Fatimah talked softly, and she sounded like she was drowsy or drugged.

"Is the medication not working?"

"What medication? All I'm getting is Tylenol."

"What? I don't understand. Why are they treating your migraine with Tylenol?" Aniyah was confused; surely, they knew better than to treat a migraine with that. Aniyah ran through a list of possible alternative medications in her mind. At the very least, they could have given her ibuprofen. Aniyah couldn't comprehend it. What in the hell was going on there? It wasn't as if she was pregnant.

"Fatimah, is there something you're not telling me?" Aniyah asked, waiting to see if she was going to get another shocker this morning.

"Yes, I'm pregnant," Fatimah said rather unenthusiastically as a wave of disgust hit her all over again. Fatimah didn't want this baby. She wanted that pregnancy ended as well as her marriage.

Aniyah didn't say anything at first. She could tell that she had to approach the subject very carefully. She didn't want to anger or offend her sister. She didn't want to be the cause of making her migraine any worse than what it was, and she didn't feel like hearing her sister scream and yell at her. Not this morning.

She wondered why Fatimah sounded so unhappy. She never seemed to get overwhelmed. She handled home, work, and the kids just fine. She didn't even work that much. Maybe three to four days a week. And it wasn't as if her job was difficult. She got plenty of help.

"I don't know what to say," Aniyah said to her sister.

"There's nothing to say."

"I mean I want to be excited for you. But you don't seem excited at all."

"I don't want this baby," Fatimah said abruptly as if the words were forced out of her mouth. That was the first time she'd said it out loud, since she'd gotten the news last night. It sounded so heartless and cold. She never ever thought she'd hear herself saying those words. Her voice and those words sounded so mismatched. But it fell out of her mouth before she could stop it. Fatimah sighed, and Aniyah could hear the frustration in her sister's voice. She had no idea what was going on, and she didn't dare ask.

"Is there anything I can do?" Aniyah asked.

Fatimah thought Aniyah sounded like she did when she was a child. Sweet and innocent. Of course, there was nothing she could do. Unless she knew of a way of getting rid of her piece of shit husband or performing an emergency abortion.

"No. Thanks. There's nothing you can do."

"Is Jason taking you home?"

Fatimah sighed as if hearing his name made her head pound harder, "Yea, he'll be here shortly. Mama just left. I couldn't wait for her to get out of here. I mean she was really workin' my nerves. I know she was only trying to help, but you know how Mama can get."

"Yea, I know."

"Man, I couldn't wait for Mama to leave. She just kept going on and on and on. I was like, what is she trying to do, see if she can make my head explode?"

Aniyah laughed a little. She knew how Mama could get. She'd make you feel that way even without a migraine. Aniyah and Fatimah said their "I love yous" and good-byes. And Aniyah got off the phone with Fatimah wondering what was really going on.

Fatimah wasn't going to church this morning. She didn't feel like it, and she didn't feel like calling anyone to let them know that she wouldn't be there. She wasn't due to sing her solo until first Sunday, and that was another week away. She didn't speak to the Lord as she had a habit of doing every morning. She didn't ask the Lord to watch over her husband and children or the rest of her family, and she didn't ask him for forgiveness for her wicked thoughts. She hadn't mentioned anything to her husband yet. She didn't mention the phone call she had received the other evening or the baby growing in her belly.

As a matter of fact, she didn't remember much from the other evening except Tye's visit, peace and quiet, then discombobulation. She barely remembered her sister, Nicole, coming over to take her to the hospital. Thank God for Nicole, because Fatimah was sitting in an unlocked house; her kids and her husband were nowhere to be found, and she had a debilitating migraine.

Nicole had come over, found her upstairs, got her dressed, and nearly carried her out to her truck and then drove her to the ER. When Fatimah asked her how she knew, she told her that Tye had had her kids. Nicole stayed with her throughout the night until her husband Jason came. Nicole had been there when the doctor had told Fatimah that she was pregnant. Fatimah was too sick to visit Mariah, but they talked on the phone. Fatimah told Mariah that she was pregnant too.

Mariah was so excited. This was the second time that they were pregnant together. Mariah thought it would be fun to do this again with her sister. They were so much closer the last time. It seemed like going through that experience together changed their relationship somehow or at least for as long as they were pregnant. It was so hard for her to get close to Fatimah. Lord knows she tried. Fatimah had this holier-than-thou air about her that just rubbed Mariah the wrong way. They'd start off just fine and then Fatimah would go and say some insensitive shit, and they'd be at each other's throats.

Mariah noticed that Fatimah didn't sound happy about the news at all, but she could understand that. They both already had five children each, and another child to raise could seem a very daunting task. Mariah didn't let Fatimah's gloom take away from her excitement though. She felt for Fatimah and whatever problems she was having, but she had to face what was in front of her. So until Fatimah was willing to talk about it, she wouldn't poke and prod. She'd place Fatimah conveniently on the back burner along with all the other problems she couldn't solve and the things that were out of her control.

Mariah rode home with her husband and with her babies in her belly kicking wildly. She was so happy, not to mention grateful. She smiled at her husband as he drove them home. "I really love this man," she thought to herself. She really didn't think she could be happier. She had a career that she loved, a loving husband, beautiful children, and she was content. Mariah rubbed her belly and hummed a lullaby to them. Carl couldn't hear her humming over the music that played over the radio, but she knew that her babies could hear her.

Mariah wasn't a religious person. She wasn't even sure that she could call herself spiritual per se. But she prayed and talked to God more in these last twenty-four hours than she'd prayed in her whole lifetime. She thanked him constantly. She could have imagined things going so much differently than it was going now. There could have been tears and depression on this ride home, instead of the happiness and joy she was feeling at this moment.

It was a beautiful Sunday afternoon. The sky was a bright and clear blue with patches of fluffy white clouds, which to Mariah looked like cotton candy. The sun beamed down, and it glinted off parked cars and windshields and made them sparkle like diamonds. Michael Jackson's "Butterflies" played on the radio. Carl turned it up, looked at his wife and smiled, bobbed his head, and mouthed the words to her as they stopped at a traffic light. Mariah blushed like a schoolgirl. They sang the refrain and she got goose bumps. That was their song. Mariah danced in her seat and snapped her fingers as she and her husband sang.

It looked hotter than it actually was. The cool breezes balanced the heat from the sunshine so that it was neither too hot nor too cold. Carl put his hand on Mariah's inner thigh and rubbed it as he held the steering wheel with his other hand. He rocked to the music and turned to Mariah and mouthed, "I love you," to her. Mariah liked that look in his eye. She thought it was so sexy. She was glad that he could still turn her on after all these years. She secretly feared she'd have grown tired of him by now. But she still loved him as much as she ever did. She just loved him carefully.

Before Mariah and Carl could get to their house, their children ran on the sidewalk alongside the car, screaming and laughing excitedly, glad that their mommy was home. The hot sun had dried up most of the rain, but there were still small puddles on the streets and the sidewalks. The pitted cement held rainwater like little bowls, and her children splashed through as many of them as their little feet could find. But, Mariah didn't fuss. She was so happy to see them running, happy and healthy, and smiling.

"Hold on, you guys. Don't run so close to the car," Mariah warned. She couldn't get out of the car fast enough. Her children climbed into her lap bombarding her with hugs and kisses. Junior accidentally kneed her in the stomach trying to get to her before his sisters could.

Her neighbor, Jean, walked over to the car as Mariah was getting out of it. Mariah held Carl by his hands as he kind of pulled her up from her seated position. It was getting harder and harder for Mariah to stand upright these days. Jean was holding Mariah's three-year-old in her arms, and as she hugged her, her child wrapped his arms around his mother's neck.

"Hold on, boo. You don't want to hurt Mommy." Mariah held her youngest in her arms, squeezed him tight, and covered his face with tiny kisses, before passing him to Carl.

"Come on, guys," Carl said as he waved the children into the house. Junior tugged at the bottom of his mommy's blouse and said, "Jeffrey's mommy is having two babies too."

Mariah nodded and smiled at her son. She had no idea who Jeffrey was, but it was important enough for CJ to stop and share it with her before running into the house. Mariah stayed outside for a minute to talk to Jean. She thanked Jean for keeping an eye on her children.

"I know they can be a handful."

"Oh no," Jean said, waving her hand and shaking her head. "Those babies are never a problem."

Mariah didn't know if she was lying or just being kind. Jean seemed to really adore her children, and they loved her too. Jean was a retired schoolteacher with two grown kids of her own. She didn't have grandchildren. Her daughter, her oldest, was thirty-three years old, unmarried and working on her PhD. She'd told her mom that she didn't have the time it took to put into a marriage and that she didn't see any children in her future. Her son, an architect, was twenty-eight years old, married, and he'd told his mother that he didn't want any children and neither did his wife. So Jean relished the time spent with Mariah's children.

"That Carl Jr. is as smart as a whip. You know he is really very good in math. I was astounded."

"Thank you, I know. He likes reading too." Junior wasn't even six years old yet, and he could read simple books and do basic addition and subtraction problems.

"You should get him tested. I'm sure that he's well advanced for his age. Normally, I wouldn't recommend it, but I can see him skipping second and going right into the third grade."

"Yea, Carl and I haven't really discussed it yet, but we know that something has to be done, especially while he's so interested in learning."

"Yes," Jean agreed. "So, my dear, how do you feel about your exciting news? Huh? Not one but two, healthy, beautiful babies."

"I know. Right? It was a shocker. But I am happy that everything's okay. I was so afraid. That was just an awful experience." Mariah started to pull the ultrasound pictures out of her purse, but changed her mind. She wanted to show them to her children first.

"I'm sure it was. I'm so glad that everything turned out okay."

Jean and Mariah waved to neighbors that passed by in their cars. Some waved and smiled. Others smiled and honked at them. Mariah liked Jean because she was kind, and she wasn't a gossip like some of the other neighbors were. Mariah knew they had plenty to say about the young couple with all the kids, but she didn't pay it any mind. She loved her life, and she appreciated it even more now. When Mariah went inside to Carl and the kids, she could hear her eight-year-old Shant`e saying, "She's coming, she's coming!"

Mariah didn't know what was going on until she went into the kitchen, where Carl and the kids were, and the kids yelled, "Surprise!" Mariah walked over to the table with a big smile spread across her face. There was a big lopsided cake with goo gobs of chocolate frostings on it. Big crooked letters spelled out: We love you Mommy! across the top, as if the children had been fighting over who would write on the cake.

"Do you like it Mommy?" Shant`e asked.

Mariah nodded and smiled as tears streamed down her face.

"No, Mommy loves it," Carl answered.

Mariah showed the children the ultrasound pictures; there were three. She was surprised at how well the children could see them, pointing out head, feet, and hands. Mariah looked over at Carl. She never really asked him how he felt about an additional baby. But he seemed okay; besides, not much he could do about it now.

The phone was ringing off the hook. Word of the twins had spread fast. Two of Mariah's closest friends Deena and Delisha called to check on her. Everybody called to congratulate her and to see how she was doing. Her stomach was huge, so nobody was really that surprised. Nicole and Aniyah came over to visit and to see how she was doing. Nicole couldn't stay long because she had a date. Aniyah didn't stay long either. Nicole never mentioned the voice-mail messages to Mariah. She didn't want to embarrass her. Mama came by shortly after her daughters had gone. Mama was concerned, but she didn't irritate Mariah like she thought she was going to.

Mama had a way of getting on your last nerve and stomping on like she was wearing a pair of football cleats. But she was calm today. Mariah hugged her, kissed her, and told her she was glad that she stopped by. Her mother spent a little time with her grand kids, and then she was on her way. Perhaps to harass Fatimah, who nobody had heard from all day.

Mariah tried to get in touch with Fatimah on her home and cell phone, but there was no answer. Nicole had stopped by her house and so did Aniyah, but there was no one home. Mariah thought that that was very inconsiderate of Fatimah. But she'd get that way sometimes. Everybody knew that Fatimah could be funny acting, but it was still nerve racking.

Mariah had talked to Serena shortly after she'd gotten home from the hospital. She'd tried calling her earlier, but couldn't reach her. She'd said she was over her boyfriend's house and was sleeping in because she didn't get much sleep last night. Too much information, Mariah thought, but she didn't tell her baby sister that though. Serena seemed a little distant, maybe even a little homesick. But, she was excited about Mariah's big news and was very happy to hear from her sister. Serena told Mariah that she'd call her back again later after she was fully awake and that she'd call Fatimah when they got off the phone to check on her. Mariah wasn't sure if she did because she didn't hear from her again.

That evening, Mariah sat on her patio and stared off into the backyard. The radio played old school R&B as Carl cooked hamburgers and hotdogs on the grill. There was an ice-cold beer waiting for Carl on the table. Mariah watched as beads of water ran down the long neck of the bottle and down its sides.

"This turned out to be a beautiful day," Mariah said, looking over at her husband.

Mariah pulled a chair out in front of her, put her feet up on it, and crossed her legs. She ran her fingers across her hairy legs. She hadn't shaved them in a while. It was too difficult to bend down to do it. Carl would do it for her, but he liked her legs hairy. He said it was sexy, and it really turned him on.

Carl walked up the deck steps, reached over on the table, and grabbed his beer. Mariah watched his Adam's apple move up and down as he swallowed. "So sexy," she thought as she eyed her husband.

"Aaah," he said as he sat the beer, almost exactly on the same spot where it had made a ring of water on the table. Carl stepped over Mariah's legs and stood in front of her, straddling her legs. He leaned over, holding on to each of her chair's armrests, and kissed his wife full on the mouth, a deep French kiss. She could taste the beer on his lips and tongue. Mariah held on to his muscular arms, tracing them with her fingertips. Her eyes were still closed when he stopped and said, "I'll be back. Let me go check on the kids."

The house was curiously quiet, which usually meant the kids were up to no good. But when Carl checked on the children, the baby was still sleep. The girls were watching a cartoon, and Carl Jr. was in the living room with his sisters, sitting in the big recliner chair, flipping through a book.

"That boy is a trip," Carl said when he came back outside. He described how CJ was sitting in the recliner reading.

"Yea, he's an old soul," Mariah said.

Mariah and Carl fed their children outdoors. They ate hamburgers, hotdogs, and their daddy's homemade coleslaw. Everybody's favorite. Afterward, each child had a generous slice of the massive chocolate cake they'd made for their mommy. Mariah laughed at her children's little chocolate hands and mouths. The children had wanted sweet tea with their dinner, but Mariah told them they could have some after dinner if they weren't too full. Nobody had sweet tea after dinner.

Mariah sent the children inside to wash their hands and faces. She went in behind them to make sure they did a thorough-enough job. She didn't want chocolate-hand prints all over the house. Carl cleaned up the deck and put leftover food away and made hot, soapy dishwater.

Mariah liked how they tag teamed. No matter how tired either of them were, they always helped each other out around the house. Carl vacuumed, washed dishes, mopped floors, and bathed his children. He did whatever was needed of him.

Mama would always tell Mariah that Carl was keeping her barefoot and pregnant, because he wanted to keep her under his thumb. Mariah knew that there wasn't any truth to that, but it angered her that Mama would even think that way, let alone have it come out of her mouth.

Mariah couldn't believe that a woman who went outside her household and made six babies could ever judge her or her husband. But she did; that was Mama's way and she knew she couldn't change it, so she wasn't going to try. She knew how to let her Mama talk, and she knew when to stop her when she'd gone too far. And Mariah had become quite skilled at blocking her mother out. She didn't let it stress her like Fatimah, and she didn't blow up like Aniyah. Serena hadn't mastered it yet, 'cuz Mama always made her cry. Nicole didn't care what Mama had to say 'cuz she knew Mama didn't like her anyway.

Later that night, Mariah and Carl met back up on the patio. It was late, and the sun was slowly fading on the horizon. The sky had the gray, dusky hue of twilight. Carl lit Citronella candles in anticipation of the mosquitoes that were to come, and he sat in one of the deck chairs facing Mariah, with her feet in his lap. "Chocolate High" played in the background. Mariah listened as India Arie and Musiq Soulchild sang melodically, comparing love to an addiction to chocolate.

Carl rubbed Mariah legs. Gently stroking them, he said, "I don't know why I love you so much. I think you're trying to trap me." Carl was joking; he knew the things Mariah's mother was saying to her. Her mother didn't keep it a secret; she'd say it to his face, around family and friends, and she'd say it behind his back if she wanted to. That was how she was.

Mariah countered, "Naw, you just tryin' to keep me barefoot an' pregnant. I know yo' game." She said pointing at him with a long slender finger. "Ma mama tol' me 'bout chu." They laughed, which was the only thing they could do. If love and a good, strong marriage hadn't been enough proof to her mother, then nothing would.

Carl lifted one of her barefeet and kissed the tip of her big toe. "Carl, stop it. That's nasty. My feet have been sweatin' all day. Yuk." Mariah tried to pull her foot away, but Carl held on to it firmly.

"Come on now. A toe?" Mariah blushed. She knew what Carl was insinuating. She got butterflies just thinking about it.

Carl ran his tongue around the tip of her toe, and then he slid her big toe in his mouth. He kept eye contact with her to see her reaction. Ooh, Carl knew what turned her on. Mariah held on to both armrests and pushed her body into the back of the deck chair. And just as it was getting good to her, Carl turned his head to the side, frowned, and pretended to spit; then he started laughing. Mariah pulled her foot away from him and frowned. Carl was laughing so hard that his eyes were starting to water.

"Stop it, Carl. Dat's nasty," Carl said, mocking his wife playfully. "Started getting good to ya, didn't it girl?"

"No," she said, lying, and she laughed along with her husband. "You play too much."

Carl sat up and leaned forward to kiss his wife on the lips. But she frowned and put her hand over her mouth and turned her face away. Carl laughed and grabbed his beer and took a big swig and said, "Aaah," as if that was the most refreshing swallow he'd ever tasted. Then he said,

"I needed something to wash that toe jam down with." Carl smacked his lips as if he tasted something foul, and Mariah pushed at him with the tip of her foot. And they laughed. They laughed and talked and enjoyed that summer night together as if it were the last night of the summer.

Chapter 11

TEMPTATION

"Nicole, you hafto help me. I need something really nice tonight. I mean I really hafto look good."

"Aniyah, I don't have anything in my closet that you can fit." Nicole wanted to help Aniyah, but she was a bit annoyed.

"You've gotta have something."

"Aniyah, you know that you can not fit any of my clothes. Why didn't you say anything sooner? I could've taken you out and bought you something nice."

"I don't need you to buy me anything, Nicole. I've got money."

"Listen, I wasn't talking about your money, the emphasis was on something nice."

Nicole didn't like Aniyah's wardrobe. And she didn't care for Aniyah's style of dress. Aniyah worked so hard at eating well, working out, and taking care of her body, but she worked even harder at covering her body up. Aniyah knew that Nicole wasn't her size, but she needed help and she knew who to come to.

"Aniyah, how soon can you be here?"

"I'm on my way over there now."

Nicole laughed. Nicole did have a huge wardrobe, because she didn't repeat her outfits too often. But she knew how to mix and match her wardrobe to make things seem fresh and new. It wasn't as if she had to though; she could afford to be very lavish when it came to her clothing.

"Aniyah, I have something for you. So don't worry about coming over here right now. Just come over in enough time for me to get you ready, and you can leave from over here."

"Isn't that cutting it too close?"

"Trust me. All you need to worry about is you. I got everything else."

That was all that Aniyah needed to hear. She left it all in her big sister's hands and trusted that she had her back. Aniyah wanted to get her hair done, but on a Sunday, the only person she knew to ask was her cousin La Maya, and she didn't feel comfortable using her family influence on her. Besides, her new do was only a few days old, and she'd kept it up pretty well, seeing that she hadn't wrapped it up as she was instructed to.

Nathan had plans today. He'd promised his mom that he'd take her shopping after Sunday service. It wasn't a task he'd looked forward to carrying out, but it was for his mom so what could he say? Aniyah had gone with them a few times, but shopping with Nathan's mother was an all-day thing, and if Aniyah didn't have any shopping to do, she couldn't see spending an entire day off at various shopping malls and wholesale clubs.

Aniyah cooked Nathan breakfast early that morning, kissed him, and sent him on his way. She knew they wouldn't be seeing each other for a while because she had to pull a double shift on Monday a three-to-eleven and a eleven-to-seven. Nathan had a long day on Monday too. No biggie. They both knew their schedules left a lot to be desired. But they knew how to work around their hectic schedules and still have a good time. She'd gotten Mariah's call before getting out of the bed, and when she woke up she had almost forgotten all about Matthew.

Aniyah tried not to be, but she was so excited about meeting Matthew. All the questions that she'd secretly had about him would be answered. She wasn't above admitting to herself that he'd run across her mind many times.

Aniyah walked over to her dresser and looked through her jewelry box. She looked at a few pieces of jewelry that were gifts from old lovers and a few pieces that were gifts to herself. She picked up an old butterfly pendant that she'd made when she was in kindergarten. She'd given it to her mother as a gift. She didn't know how she ended up with it. Aniyah examined her fingernails. They were neat and short and unpolished. She'd considered polishing them, but she knew she'd have to remove the polish before going to work in the morning. She worked in a nursing home when she wasn't helping out at the agency, and they had very strict policies about appearance. All nurses were to wear white and absolutely no colored nail polish. Aniyah didn't know if she wanted to wear any rings without polished nails. She didn't like her hands, and she didn't want to bring any undue attention to them.

Aniyah ran her hand across her neck to the chain that she wore faithfully. She moved her fingers down to the heart-shaped pendant that dangled gracefully between her breasts. She looked down at it as she held the delicate gold heart in her hand. Nathan had given it to her; he said it was his heart, and she sighed as she reminisced about how she felt when he gave it to her. It was a small three-toned heart, with two stripes of diamond cut etching diagonally across the front of it. She'd never seen anything like it. Neither had anyone else. She'd received so many compliments on it wherever she went.

Aniyah felt a little guilty, but she quickly dismissed it. She needed to focus on other things. Guilt not being on the top of that list. Aniyah asked herself what she had planned on getting out of this night. Meaning, after the date or meeting was over, what was the single most important thing that she wanted to see happen? She wasn't sure what the answer to that question was, but she knew she wanted to be the baddest chick in that restaurant. And she knew that if there was anyone who could help her accomplish this, it was her sister Nicole.

Aniyah closed her jewelry box. She'd decided simple was best. So she'd wear the diamond ring that her daddy purchased for her when she graduated from college and the necklace that her beau had given to her as a gift, along with a pair of gold-hoop earrings. Aniyah stared at the diamond ring; it was beautiful, and it sparkled endlessly. Daddy Otis had given it to her as part of a deal he'd made with her. He told her that if she finished college, he'd give her whatever she wanted. She didn't believe him, so she tried to be as extravagant as possible. She'd already had the car she wanted, so she didn't mention a vehicle. Instead, she'd asked him for a one-carat diamond ring. She'd even brought him a picture of it. And when she graduated from college with honors, he'd awarded her with that very ring. She was elated. Aniyah never imagined that her daddy could afford to be so generous, or that he even would be.

Aniyah beamed when he gave it to her, and she used to wear it everyday, without fail, until the day she'd almost lost it. Now it sat regally in its very own spot in her beautiful antique jewelry box. The one she inherited from Grandma May when she died. Aniyah was very particular about this ring because it was so exquisite and because it was the only thing of any real worth that her daddy had ever given to her.

Aniyah remembered the look in Mama's eyes when he'd handed her the little velvet box as he said, "You won, baby girl." Aniyah had cried and hugged him around the neck so hard. Mama was staring at the ring as if she could melt a hole right through that diamond. Aniyah could imagine what she was thinking. Wishing he'd given a ring like that to her.

Aniyah slid the ring on the ring finger of her left hand and remembered her daddy saying to her, "If a man can't match this or top this, then you don't want 'um." Aniyah remembered that and thought those words and that ring were the grandest gestures of love she'd ever received from that man, and it pleased her till this day.

Aniyah had received several phone calls from Nate, just checking on her. But she'd imagined that he was trying to escape his mom. She laughed as he told her about the wild-goose chases she was taking him on, as they tracked down sales that didn't exist.

"I don't know what Sunday paper she saw these sales in. But it definitely wasn't this Sunday's paper."

"It was this Sunday's paper," Nate's mother said in the background.

"Okay, well, where da paper at, Mama?" Nathan asked.

"It's at da house," his mother answered.

"Maybe you shoulda brought it wit chu. Because we been in an' out of these stores and don't nobody know what chu talkin' about," Nate said to his mother.

Aniyah laughed and said, "Tell your mama I said 'Hi.'"

"Aniyah said 'Hi,' Mama."

"Hi, baby!" Nathan's mama yelled. "I thought I was gonna get to see you today too."

"You hear that, Aniyah?"

"Yea, I heard. Tell her, maybe next time," Aniyah answered and prayed Nate didn't put her on the phone.

"She said 'Maybe, next time,' Mama."

"Okay," Nate's mother answered. "Tell her I hope to see her soon."

"Hear that?"

"Yea, I heard it."

*   *   *

Mrs. Reynolds was such a cutup. She had a way of saying whatever she felt whenever she felt it. What came up, came out, and it was always entertaining to Aniyah, because she never found herself on the other end of her criticisms. Mrs. Reynolds liked her and Aniyah didn't know it, but she always told Nathan that Aniyah was the one. She'd tell him that he never had a girl as sweet and as smart as her and he'd better snatch Aniyah up before someone else did.

Nathan would argue with his mother about it, but he had to agree that he hadn't met anyone that he'd clicked with like he did with Aniyah. Sure, he'd been with some beautiful and intelligent women. But to him, Aniyah was the total package. She was beautiful, intelligent, well—educated, and had a great sense of humor. She was a commitment phobe though, but hell, he was too. They had been dating for a while now, and it wasn't until about six months ago that he'd stopped seeing other women, his ex Tasha being one of them. Though he'd never accidentally called Aniyah by her name, he could just as easily have slipped up and done it.

Neither Aniyah nor Tasha knew it, but Tasha wasn't a threat to Aniyah at all. He didn't know why that, up until six months ago, he couldn't leave Tasha alone. Leading her on for the hell of it. Secretly getting upset about the possible men she was sleeping with, having sex with, in the bed that he'd bought for her while they were a couple. It was a man thing. It wasn't that he actually cared for her or wanted her back; he just needed to see that he could come back anytime he wanted to.

But that was over now. He was all Aniyah's. He didn't want anybody else. He'd actually had the self-control to tell a beautiful woman that he was taken and not look back or care about what he could possibly be missing out on when she walked away. Aniyah was all he wanted, and he didn't want her with any other man.

*   *   *

Aniyah packed a little bag with everything she thought she needed for her meeting with Matthew. But she wasn't really sure what to take. She'd shower over her sister's so she'd be fresh before her meeting. She was excited. She wondered what her sister had for her. She imagined the color and the style. She was hoping that it wouldn't be too risqué, but she knew that it would be classy. Nicole was a very classy woman. She'd know how to transform Aniyah into a seductress for the night. Aniyah smiled at that thought. Her, a seductress?

Aniyah drove through miles and miles of light Sunday traffic. It was about five o'clock in the evening, but Aniyah was too excited to wait. She drove with her sunroof open, music blasting, and with a big smile on her face. The long drive seemed to be cut in half by the light traffic. She made it to Nicole's house in no time flat. She had worked herself up from excitement to anticipation, and she felt as giddy as a schoolgirl on prom night.

"Aniyah!"

"What?" Aniyah said as she stepped into the threshold and through the door that Nicole held open for her.

"Girl, why are you here so early?"

"I was excited. I wanted to see what you had for me."

Nicole shook her head at her sister and smiled. She showed her upstairs to her bedroom and pointed to her massive closet. "It's in there."

Aniyah didn't know how she'd find anything in that big ole closet, but she stepped right in. Once inside, she saw a big flat box with a huge ribbon on top and several other smaller boxes and bags. She knew they were for her, and she couldn't wait to tear them open and see what was inside.

"I got those when Charisse and I went shopping the other week. I bought it for your birthday, so consider it an early birthday gift."

Aniyah lifted the lid from the big flat box. She carefully opened the pale-pink-and-white tissue paper to reveal a beautiful wine-colored dress. Aniyah lifted the dress out of the box and held it to her body. She tilted her head to the side as she looked at the dress, as she draped it across herself, and hugged it to her chest. It was beautiful and formfitting and sexy. Much too sexy for her, Aniyah thought to herself.

"Nicole, all my breasts are going to be showing, and it's too short. Look, it barely comes to my knees. When I sit down, it's gonna rise up."

"First of all, it's called cleavage. There's nothing wrong with showing a little cleavage. You don't plan on wearing it to church, do you? Secondly, you don't even have the dress on. You can't really tell how the dress looks until you have it on." Aniyah shook her head. She wanted to be sexy, but not this sexy. "Aniyah, put the dress down and looked in the other boxes." Nicole looked at her sister and shook her head. Aniyah opened the smaller box and saw the cutest little pair of strappy shoes.

"Ooh, Nicci! These are so cute!" The straps were thin and embellished with little rhinestones, and they went across the foot around the ankle and they buckled on the side. Aniyah slipped out of her sandals and slipped on the sparkly shoes and walked around in front of the mirror as if she were a supermodel.

"That's how confident I want you to be in that dress. That's the only way you're going to pull it off," Nicole said.

Aniyah stepped out of the strappy shoes and walked over to the other bag. She liked the way Nicole's plush carpet felt on her toes. She removed the tissue paper from the bags and pulled out a stylish, but simple, clutch purse that complimented the strappy high-heeled shoes perfectly.

Aniyah felt nervous inside. She felt like calling Matthew and canceling. She wasn't excited at all anymore. She was scared. She opened another small flat box, and there was a shrug inside that matched the burgundy dress to a tee. Aniyah went into the last bag. It was a Victoria secret bag, and in it was one lone pair of black lacey thongs. Aniyah looked at Nicole and her sister said, "No panty lines." Now, Aniyah really felt uncomfortable. She was about to go out and meet a man that she hadn't seen in years with practically no underwear on. So much for putting everything in her sister's hands.

"Stop over thinking everything, Aniyah, you'll be just fine."

Aniyah didn't argue with her sister. Instead, she turned to her sister and said, "Thank you, Nicole."

"You're welcome, Aniyah. Now let's get you ready."

It was like a spa day. Aniyah was primped and pampered by her sister as if she were a client. She got a relaxing facial, and she soaked in the whirlpool bath, hoping to ease her fears away. After her bath, she moisturized her skin in one of Nicole's popular Tamani fragrant body silks. Afterward, she wrapped herself in a towel and sat in front of Nicole's mirrored vanity. She looked at her hair. She hated it.

"Help me with this," Aniyah said as she flung a piece of her bang to the back of her head. Down it came back over her right eye.

"Aniyah, it looks beautiful on you. What don't you like about it?"

"I don't like these long bangs, and I can't get used to the color."

"Girl, please. She did a beautiful job. You needed a change. Believe me. I was sick of that tired old ponytail."

"I miss my ponytail," Aniyah said, stoking the shortest part of her hair in the back.

"I'm sure you do," Nicole said and smiled at her sister. She loved the cut and color. She liked the way it brightened Aniyah's face and the haircut were so alluring.

"Come on, let's get you dressed."

Aniyah got up out of the chair and walked sluggishly over to the closet like a listless teenager.

"Aniyah! Stand up straight." Nicole was annoyed by the lack of confidence her posture displayed. Nicole waved her sister over to the full-length mirror at the rear of the closet/dressing room. Nicole stood behind her sister and held the sexy minidress in front of her.

"Nicole, this is really not me," Aniyah said unable to look at herself in the mirror.

"Why isn't it you? It's perfect for you. You have the legs for it." Aniyah looked up at herself in the mirror, then dropped her head again." Nicole was clearly irritated. She stood behind her sister, and lifted Aniyah's head gently by placing the back of her hand under her chin. "Aniyah, look at yourself." Aniyah looked at herself in the tall mirror. "Girl, you are beautiful."

Aniyah pushed her bangs away from her right eye and took a good look at herself. She saw her posture left a lot to be desired and straightened up and stood upright. "Better," Nicole said. Aniyah could see the reflection of her sister nodding and smiling in the mirror. "Now get dressed, and I'll help you with your hair and your makeup."

Aniyah slipped on the thongs. They weren't too uncomfortable, but she hoped that by the end of the evening, she'd forget they were there. She dropped her towel and put on the burgundy halter dress. It was formfitting, but the pleating and the drape of the fabric in the front of the dress disguised how formfitting it was in the front. But there was no hiding it on the sides and in the back of the dress. The dress was without a doubt sexy, but it wasn't trashy at all and Aniyah looked drop-dead gorgeous in it.

Aniyah admired herself in the dress. Turning from side to side, smoothing her hand down the front and sides of the dress. It showed off her fit hourglass figure, her long shapely legs, and every sexy curve of her body. The dress was gorgeous; she liked the deep burgundy color against her caramel-colored skin. The cut of the dress and the spaghetti straps that tied around her neck lifted her bosom, so she didn't need a bra. And there was ample material in that area, so she didn't have to worry about her nipples showing through the dress. The pleating in the front billowed and flowed as she walked, and now that she was in it, she felt like this dress was made for her.

Nicole did Aniyah's makeup and styled her hair for her just like she used to when Aniyah was a kid. Aniyah looked drop-dead gorgeous.

"I don't even look like myself," Aniyah said, as she admired herself in the three-way mirror.

"Yes, you do."

"I mean I look beautiful."

"You are beautiful. It's not the makeup that made you beautiful. It's just a little eye makeup and lipstick."

Aniyah's beauty was so understated. She hid it under workout clothes and ponytails and such, but it still came shining through. Her self-esteem was nearly nonexistent. And no matter how much Nicole tried to convince her of her beauty, Aniyah wasn't trying to hear it. But tonight was different though.

Aniyah stood in front of the mirror, admiring herself. She practiced standing up straight and walking toward herself in the mirror. She couldn't stop the big, wide, dimpled smile from spreading across her face.

"I look good, don't I?" Aniyah turned toward her sister and giggled.

"Drop-dead gojus!" Nicole answered as she winked and smiled at her sister.

It was almost six thirty, and Aniyah had to go. She kissed her sister, hugged her, and thanked her for everything.

"I don't know where you're going or what you plan on doing, but you have fun." Nicole waved good-bye to Aniyah as she hopped in her car and headed off to meet Matthew. Aniyah didn't know if her sister suspected anything, but if she did, she didn't say.

Nicole had plans for a late-night dinner with a close acquaintance of hers. She'd met Don about two years ago through some mutual friends. Don lived in Chicago, but he visited Cleveland quite often. They'd run into each other at a few events around town, and they'd had lunch together, but always in the company of their other friends. This would be the first time that Nicole and Don had ever gone out together on an actual date.

Don had gotten up the nerve to ask, and she'd accepted. She liked Don. He was sweet and funny, and he was sort of cute in a out-of-shape, pale-and-balding sort of way. Nicole looked forward to meeting with him. He was very intelligent. He had a great sense of humor, and he made her laugh, which was a difficult feat for most. She found him to be very attractive, and she was really excited about going out with him tonight.

He let her pick the restaurant, and she chose Rustik's on Landerbrook Drive. She loved the ambiance and the dim mood lighting was superb. She was crazy about their fresh, hot-baked bread too and she could hardly wait to taste it.

Don couldn't believe that Nicole had said yes. He couldn't believe how nervous he was about his date with her. Sure, they'd been out with friends quite a few times, and he'd spoken with her on the phone, but he wouldn't exactly call them friends. He would love to be her friend though. He thought she was so lovely and fascinating, and he was so attracted to her beautiful smile. Nicole Turner. He was actually going out with every man's dream.

Matthew had arrived before Aniyah did. She hated that because it meant she had to make an entrance. She had had it all planned out; she intended to sit at a table by the window and facing the door so that she could see him as soon as he arrived. Then she would stare pensively out the window until he made his way over to the table and stood in front of her, at which time she'd act as if she didn't even know he'd arrived.

But things rarely go as planned, and this occasion was no exception. Aniyah didn't think he had seen her yet. At least, she had hoped he hadn't. She took a deep breath and smoothed her damp hands down the front and sides of her dress over the curves of her hips and thighs. She contemplated how she would walk into the dining area, but tried not to think about it too hard. She sighed again and went for it. She walked in with one arm to her side and her clutch purse underneath the opposite arm. Her posture was perfect and her dress accentuated every curve of her body. She looked confident as her hips rocked sensuously from side to side as she approached Matt's table, looking him directly in the eyes. Heads turned as she walked past tables, men stopped talking to their wives in midsentence, and people stopped to stare. A hush seemed to blanket the room. She could tell she made a successful entrance. She was sure of it by the look on Matt's face when he stood to greet her. Matt pulled out her chair for her and helped her scoot her seat in again. He sat down across from her and smiled. She smiled back at him but didn't say a word. He continued smiling, then he crossed his arms, and looked at her. He shook his head and said to Aniyah, "So what made you decide to come?"

"I don't know," she answered and wished that she'd said something a little more sophisticated.

"Well, it doesn't matter," he said with a smile, showing his pretty white teeth.

"I'm just glad you came." The server came over to the table and introduced himself and asked if they needed more time to make their selections. They said they did, and the server nodded and walked away.

Aniyah thought that she'd feel very uncomfortable, but they made easy conversation as if they'd never lost touch.

"So how' your mother?" Aniyah asked. She liked his mother; she was such a pleasant person.

"I lost my mother about a year ago," Matt answered solemnly.

"Oh, I'm so sorry to hear that." Aniyah was fond of Mrs. Tullamore, and she was sincerely saddened by the news. She remembered what she'd said during their last conversation, and she felt even worse.

"Yea, she was diagnosed with ovarian cancer and died six months after she was diagnosed."

"I am really sorry to hear that Matthew." There was a momentary silence; then Matt smiled and asked about her mother.

"She's okay. She's moving to Baltimore with her boyfriend in a few months."

"Oh," Matt nodded. "Why Baltimore?"

"I have no idea. She just woke up one morning, decided that she wanted to leave Cleveland, and told my sisters and I that she was moving to Baltimore."

"Just like that?" Matthew asked.

"Just like that."

"So you're okay with your mother living that far away from you?" Aniyah gave Matt a look, and he laughed. "What? I thought women would like to live close to their moms. I dunno."

"My mama will be just fine. We don't particularly care for her choice in a man, but he treats her good and he doesn't hurt her, so what else could we ask for?" Aniyah hunched her shoulders, and Matt smiled at her again.

They placed their orders with Stewart, the server, when he came back around to their table. Matt ordered a medium porterhouse steak with a side of seasoned rice and creamed spinach. Aniyah ordered grilled Salmon and a green salad with a tangy vinaigrette dressing. When Stewart asked what they'd like to drink, Aniyah answered, "A glass of ice water please."

Matt looked at Aniyah with a puzzled expression on his face. "I'm not much of a drinker," she answered as Stewart waited patiently for them to place their orders. Matt answered, "I'd like a glass of your house wine please."

"Yes, sir," Stewart answered and went off to place their orders, taking their menus along with him.

"So, Aniyah, what's been up?"

"Let see, what have I missed since we last spoke. Hmm?" Aniyah said, thinking about her response. "I think that I can honestly say that I've told you everything."

"So I'm completely updated on the goings on of the Turner clan."

"Oh, no. Not the entire clan. Just me. I have nothing to add about my life."

"So if you could sum it all up in one word. What would that word be?"

Aniyah was a bit perturbed by the question, but she knew the answer.

"Happy," she said with a smile. "If I could sum it all up in one word, I'd say happy."

"Well, that's great," Matthew said with a smile, showing his pearly whites. "Not many can say that they're truly happy. In fact, that's a blessing. Hmmph. Truly happy." Matthew repeated it as if pondering what she just said. "That's somethin' else."

Matthew never added if he was truly happy too. He just kept smiling at Aniyah. Aniyah smiled back, but her stomach was growling like crazy and she hoped it wasn't loud enough for Matt to hear. "I should have ordered an appetizer," she thought to herself as she sipped her ice water. She jabbed at the lemon slice in the glass with her straw and sipped her water again. "Aaah, this is so good," she thought to herself.

"I am starving,'" she said out loud without thinking about it. "I've had so much going on today, and I haven't eaten anything since breakfast."

"You want to order an appetizer?" Matt asked and raised his hand to wave over the server.

"No, no. I'm okay. I don't want to get too full, then I won't be able to finish my dinner."

"You can always take it home."

"I'd never eat it. I don't eat leftover restaurant food. It never tastes as good reheated," she said, wrinkling her nose. "I know wasteful, huh?"

Matthew stared at her. "Aniyah, you are beautiful." Matthew leaned back in his chair with his arms crossed and stared across the table at Aniyah. His eyes were squinted as if he was studying her.

"Thank you," she said and took another sip of water. She was nervous, and she made a conscious effort to swallow without making a loud gulp.

"So what about you, Matthew?" Aniyah said, changing the subject. "Do I know all there is to know about Matthew Davis Tullamore. Or is there some hidden agenda that I'm not aware of?" Aniyah couldn't believe that she had asked him that, but it was in the back of her mind.

Matthew laughed. His eyes roamed about her body as if he could see right through her clothes. He stared into her eyes; then his eyes scanned her neck, her shoulders, her breasts, and he caught a glimpse of a crossed leg and a dainty sandaled foot beneath the table. "Are you asking me if I plan to seduce you, take you to a hotel room, remove that sexy dress you have on, and have my way with you?"

"The shoes. What about the shoes?" Aniyah said as she extended a sexy brown leg from beneath the table and flexed and arched her foot. The rhinestones on her shoes sparkled as she moved.

"No, I like the shoes," he answered. "You can keep the shoes on."

Aniyah smiled naughtily and wondered how far to take this playful banter.

"Didn't you say you have a man at home?"

"I have a man, but he's not at home."

Matthew smiled.

"He doesn't live with me," Aniyah added.

"Is that an invitation?"

"No," she said lowering her leg. "Just stating a fact."

"What would you say if I said 'let's skip dinner and go some place quiet, where we can talk'?"

Aniyah tilted her head and said, "I'd say I am not a cheap date, and I'm very hungry. So, no, I'm not interested."

Matthew stared at her as if trying to read behind her words. As if trying to see if her no really meant yes.

Don was quite impressed by Nicole's home. Nicole told him she'd offer to give him a tour if they hadn't had such a late dinner date planned.

Don said it was okay, maybe next time but wondered if Nicole thought it presumptuous of him to assume that there would even be a next time. Nicole just smiled and said, "Alright."

Nicole enjoyed the music he played on his radio. She wasn't too sure of the type of music he listened to, but she pictured him being more of a light rock type of guy. Deborah Cox's song "Saying Goodbye" played on his car stereo. She looked at him as the music played, and she smiled.

"So you're a Deborah Cox fan?" Nicole asked. She was impressed with his choice of music.

"So you're not?"

"No, I love her."

"So what's the problem?" Don glanced over at her and smiled.

"No, there's no problem." Nicole answered. They laughed as Don sang the refrain to Nicole.

"So did you practice this song for our date?"

"No." Don said, shaking his head and furrowing his brow. Nicole thought that he looked cute when he did that.

"What type of music did you think that I listened to." Don asked.

"I don't know Don. What type of music do you like to listen to?" Nicole adjusted herself in her seat and turned to Don.

"I like all kinds of music. Jazz, pop, rock, R&B, neo soul. I even like a little hip hop every now and then."

"Oh no, please don't start rapping." Nicole said with a little laugh. Don laughed along with her.

"I wasn't going to start rapping." Don looked at her and smiled. Nicole smiled back at him.

They were an odd pair. Don was a handsome man but not in a rugged sort of way. He was not someone you'd take a second glance at, really. Other than his clear blue eyes, there was nothing eye catching about him. But Nicole thought he was such a nice, sweet, fun guy who was easy to talk to and not easily offended, and she enjoyed being in his company. She didn't care what they looked like together or what anyone thought about it. She felt very comfortable around him like she hadn't felt around any other man in a very long time.

Nicole and Don were seated, and they ordered right away. Nicole picked up a piece of hot bread from the basket, buttered it with that luscious honey butter, and took a bite.

"My. Hungry, aren't we?"

"Say whatever you want. I've been waiting to get my hands on this bread all day." Nicole slathered more butter on the bread, closed her eyes, and took a bite.

"Mmmm. Yea, bite that bread."

They both laughed. She loved Don's sense of humor. He always made her laugh. Nicole caught stares, but she didn't feel a bit uncomfortable. Don could see it too, but he didn't mention anything and he didn't seem to be the slightest bit uncomfortable either.

"They're looking at us," Nicole said as she nibbled her bread.

"No, they're looking at you," Don said with a smile.

"Well, let's give them something to look at, shall we?"

Nicole picked a roll from the basket. She tore a piece off, buttered it, and offered it to Don; he opened his mouth, and she put the bread inside along with a sweet buttered finger. Don followed her lead and closed his mouth around her finger and licked it, and she slowly pulled it out of his mouth. Nicole couldn't believe how much his soft lips on her finger had turned her on. Don chewed the small piece of bread and swallowed. Then he took a sip of water to clear his palate as Nicole dipped her finger in the honey butter and offered it to him again. This time, he gently licked the sweet butter off her fingertip and sucked her finger into his mouth. He worked his tongue seductively around her finger, sucking off its sweetness. Nicole was getting so turned on; she smiled at him, and he winked at her and released her finger.

Nicole tilted her head and looked to the left of her and then to the right. All eyes were on them, and the onlookers appeared to be as turned on as she was. Nicole looked at Don with her bedroom eyes and said as she rubbed a bare leg against his. "No, Don, I think they're looking at us."

Don looked around but not as subtly as Nicole did. He was proud to be there with her. She was a Headturner indeed, and he loved being in her presence.

Aniyah and Matthew's portions were huge. But Aniyah was so hungry she knew she'd finish all of it.

"Your steak looks good," Aniyah said to Matthew.

"It is. Wanna try a piece?" Matthew said, cutting a corner of his steak for her.

"Oh, no, thank you. I can't."

"You can't?"

"No, I don't do red meat. It doesn't digest well." Aniyah wished she hadn't said that. She wanted Matthew to see her as sexy, not picturing her and her bowels. She added, "I don't get sick or anything. I just prefer fish and chicken. It's healthier."

"So you're health conscious. It looks like it. You look like you take very good care of yourself."

"I try."

"Do you still dance?'

"You remember that?"

"Yea, I remember you use to dance and sing. You were in all sorts of talent shows and programs in school."

"Yea, they use to make me do that." Aniyah laughed before taking a bite of her salad.

"But you were good. Really talented."

"Thank you." Aniyah blushed.

"You know all the guys were after you."

"No, I don't remember that." Aniyah shook her head and smiled bashfully, looking down at her salad.

"Do you remember Lucas Farber," Matthew asked.

"Yea, I remember Lou." Aniyah squinted a little and smiled as she pictured Lucas's face.

"He had a huge crush on you. Went around telling everybody you were his girlfriend."

"Not Lucas," Aniyah said, shaking her head. "That was my buddy. We were good friends back in high school. I wonder what he's doing now."

"He's married, he's got four boys, and he's a delivery man. He works part time, delivering medications to different nursing facilities. I'm surprised you haven't run into him."

"Well, it depends on what pharmacy he works for. Do you know who he works for?"

"No, I don't know who he works for." The two ate a few bites of their food; then Matthew said, "So are you and Nathan planning on getting married?"

"How did we go from talking about a Lucas delivering meds to, am I getting married?"

"Well, actually our conversation took a natural progression. We went from talking about a high school crush to talking about the current man in your life. You were the one who changed the subject when you asked what Lucas was doing with his life. I answered you and we sort of veered off. But now I'm getting us back on track. So?" Matthew said as he took a bite of his steak. "Answer the question."

"Why is it that a man and a woman can't enjoy a healthy, fun, enjoyable relationship without being asked that question?"

"So that's a 'No.'"

"No, it's not a 'No.' We just haven't talked about it."

"How long have you been dating him?"

"A year."

"So you've been dating him a year, and the two of you haven't discussed marriage?" Aniyah didn't say anything, and she didn't make eye contact with Matt.

"Aniyah, do you love him?"

"Why are you asking me that?"

"Oh, so it's just a casual thing between the two of you," Matthew said, without answering Aniyah's question.

"No, he's my boyfriend."

"So was Lucas."

"No, he wasn't."

"He was a boy friend. Sounds no different than what you've got goin' on with Nathan."

"Look, Nathan is my boyfriend, he's how I spend my free time whenever I have any, he's who I enjoy being with."

"Hmmm, sounds lovely," Matthew said sarcastically with a grin. "But you didn't say that's who you love."

"Love is such an overrated emotion. Loved you, didn't I?"

Matthew nodded and smiled. "Okay, I deserved that." Matthew ran his hand down his tie.

"I'm not trying to make you mad at me. It's just that if you were my woman, I wouldn't let you out of my sight."

"Nathan trusts me."

Matthew nodded and said, "But does he trust me?"

Aniyah didn't say a word. She didn't like where this conversation was going, and she hadn't prepared herself for these types of questions. She should've known that Matthew would try to take her there, but she never thought she'd be forced to justify her relationship with her man. It would have been easier if she just would have said that she loved Nathan. But Matthew had taught her well. Love was not a word that she could claim so easily. She was very selective how she used it, and she usually reserved that emotion for family and dear friends.

"Look at you. This man has sent you out here naked."

Aniyah gasped, she was embarrassed; she dropped her fork on her plate and placed her napkin to her chest.

"No no no. I'm not talking about what you have on. You look beautiful, lovely, sexy, perfect. What I'm saying is that love covers you. It tells a man that you're taken, off limits, that you belong to someone else. When a woman is in love, she announces it. When you ask her about it, she'll say something like 'Yea, that's my boo. I love him. I love that man.' She loves him, and she'll claim it."

"And what does a man do?"

"Aaah, baby, we're a different breed. It all depends on the man."
Matthew stared at her and smiled. He looked so sexy. "I have to tell
you, Aniyah, until you're in love you're free game. Because that man,
that man, and that man," Matthew said, pointing to different men in
the restaurant, "any one of them may be able to show you a good time,
make you want to spend your free time with them. That's not what
keeps a relationship strong. That's not what keeps a relationship going.
That's where love comes in, that's what's gonna take your relationship
to another level. And frankly, you don't seem too enthusiastic about
that."

"Matthew you are such a hater. Is this why you invited me here? To
break up Nathan and me?"

"No."

"And since when did you become this love guru?" Aniyah replied. She
was becoming very irritated by all of this. She had told him earlier that
she was truly happy, and Matthew had seemed hell-bent on proving her
wrong. "You are still a huge asshole. Why did you invite me here? I love
my life, and I love my relationship just as it is."

Aniyah looked down at her hand at the ring her father had given her.
Why hadn't Matthew assumed that that was an engagement ring? Why did
he have to go on asking all those stupid-ass questions? She wanted this
to be over. She was tired of pretending to be this sexy, super-confident
vixen. She wanted to go back to being Aniyah with her comfortable, casual
clothes and her tired, old ponytail.

"I apologize. I'm not trying to make you angry or uncomfortable. I'm
happy that you came."

Matthew had made his agenda clear, and Aniyah wanted to make sure
that things would not go as he had planned. She couldn't believe how
bold he was. But she couldn't help but wonder how far he was willing
to go. Aniyah wondered if that meant that something was lacking in her
relationship with Nathan. Was it true that if she loved him, really loved
him, that she would have professed her love for him to Matthew when
he had asked?

"Look, thanks for dinner. But I've gotta go."

Matthew gently grabbed Aniyah's arm. She felt those butterflies again.
"Please don't go."

"Really, I've gotta go. It was nice seeing you after all these years."

"Aniyah, please, sit," Matthew said, urging Aniyah to stay. "I promise.
I'll back off." He sighed and smiled. "I assume you know why I invited
you here." Aniyah raised an eyebrow and looked at Matthew. "I knew this
would probably be the last opportunity for me to tell you how I've felt
about you all these years. I've regretted everything I've ever said or done

to hurt you. You didn't deserve it, and I wish there was some way that I could make it up to you."

Aniyah smiled and said to Matthew. "There's nothing that you can do. The damage has already been done. But," she said as she stood and grabbed her clutch. "I've accepted your apology, and I wish you a happy life."

Aniyah turned to walk away with the same swagger as when she entered the room.

"Aniyah, wait." Matthew stood, reached into his back pocket, grabbed a few bills out of his wallet, and tossed them on the table. He headed after Aniyah, and she ignored him calling her name. Restaurant goers and other onlookers watched as Matthew went after Aniyah. She didn't look back; she just continued walking into the dark parking lot. "Please, Aniyah. Wait!" Matthew followed her out the doors of the restaurant and to her car. When he caught up with her, he grabbed her by the arm. Her skin was so soft, and she smelled so good.

"What is it?" she said startled and annoyed.

Aniyah turned to him, her back against the car. Matthew looked her in her eyes, leaned in, and kissed her. His body against her body, his lips on her lips, his tongue exploring the inside of her mouth. Aniyah closed her eyes. She didn't know why she didn't push him away. He held her face in his hands as he kissed her. He pressed his hips against hers and kissed her. He held her and kissed her and wouldn't let her go.

Aniyah couldn't believe that this man could still make her feel the same way that he'd made her feel so many years ago. A kiss and the slightest touch of his hand on her skin made her body tingle all over, and she could feel her toes curling and digging into the soles of the pretty, strappy shoes. It was so passionate, so sensual, so raw.

Matthew lifted Aniyah up and held her against the car and kissed her passionately. Aniyah could hardly catch her breath as Matthew's strong, muscular arms embraced her. He had swooped her up with such ease, as if she was weightless, and held her there. She sighed deeply in his ear and held her eyes shut as if closing her eyes made this moment seem less real. It was hard for Matthew to keep his composure. He had to remember that they were on the street, that they were in public, but he wanted to touch her, to caress her, and to feel her body with both of his hands. He wanted to make love to her. He wanted to take her somewhere private and secluded and work her body into a frenzy of erotic pleasure like she'd never felt before.

Aniyah kissed him passionately too. She didn't kiss him like she loved another man. She kissed him as if there was nowhere else she'd rather be, or nothing else she'd rather be doing. Matthew wanted to tell her that he loved her. That he had always loved her and that he'd never loved anyone the way he loved her. But that required him to speak, and he didn't want to speak; he wanted to continue kissing Aniyah, feeling her sweet soft lips on his, tasting her mouth, smelling her fragrant skin, and holding her in his arms, never wanting to let go.

Aniyah couldn't believe what she was allowing him to do. She couldn't believe that she was letting him kiss her this way, or that she was even kissing him back. All of a sudden, Matthew stopped kissing her. He still held her up in his arms. He looked her in her eyes; she didn't look away from his gaze. He slowly released her and let her down until her feet were firmly planted on the ground. She looked into his face. His lips were moist from their feverish kissing. He didn't say a word; he just softly ran his hands down her arms and to her hands and held her hands in his.

"I have loved you for such a long time. I have loved you since I was a boy and didn't know what it was that I was feeling, and I love you still, I know you feel something too."

Aniyah felt something, but it wasn't love. It was a mixture of emotions, confusion being the only one she could readily identify.

"I can't do this."

"Do what?"

"Whatever this is."

Aniyah pressed her back against her car and stared at him. She licked her lips; his mouth was so soft. Matthew didn't want to let her go. He felt that when she left this time, she'd be leaving for good. He wanted to ask her to give him tonight, but he knew that if he loved her as he said he did, one night would never be enough. So instead, Matthew said to her, "Spend the night with me. And if you're sure, you don't feel anything for me when the night ends, then I'll leave you alone. I won't ever bother you again. I promise."

Aniyah just wanted to go home and act as if none of this had ever happened; she wanted to get into her cozy bed, watch the shows that she'd recorded on her DVR, and go to sleep. That was why she was so surprised when she heard herself say "Okay."

Nicole and Don talked and ate and laughed. They had been conversing for about a half an hour when Nicole had asked, "Are you married?"

"What?" Don said as he laughed. "Why do you keep asking me that?" He asked. Nicole laughed as she nibbled on a piece of bread. "You and that damned bread," Don said.

"This is my absolute favorite," Nicole said, holding up a piece of bread. "Now answer the question."

"Nope, not married. Divorced. Been divorced for eight years. I was married for twenty-one."

"What happened?" Nicole asked without realizing she was prying a bit too much.

"She wasn't what I wanted." Don answered. Nicole thought that was cold, but she appreciated his honesty. "I couldn't have who I wanted, so I settled for someone I wasn't in love with."

"That's awful," Nicole said. She stopped eating the bread and looked at Don.

"I know. I wasted twenty-one years of my ex-wife's time and made two people very unhappy."

Don reached into his wallet and pulled out a picture of a beautiful white woman, tall, blonde, thin, and tanned—an all-American girl. Nicole could picture her waving two fingers in a peace sign and wearing a headband of wildflowers. She looked like that type. Next to her in the picture was a handsome young man with a head full of thick, wavy, sandy brown hair. They looked like a happy couple.

"She's beautiful," Nicole said as she laughed.

"What are you laughing at." Nicole pointed to Don's head in the picture.

"Yea, those were the days. I was young and free, with a head full of hair. That was right before we got married."

"You two look good together."

"Looks can be deceiving," Don said as he took the picture from her and stuck it back into his wallet. Don dug into his wallet and pulled out another picture. It was old and worn. He handed this picture to Nicole.

"The blonde was my wife. Now this was the love of my life."

Nicole looked down at the picture; then she looked at Don. The picture was of a beautiful black woman. Don called her Olivia. She had rich, beautiful, dark brown skin. She was sitting at a table in a restaurant, holding a young Don by the arm, and she looked so in love. Don did too. There was a distinct difference in the way he looked in each picture. In this one, there was a definite feeling of love. The woman held Don by the arm and smiled as if claiming him as her man. She was a gorgeous black woman. She didn't look mixed; she wasn't light-skinned. There was no mistaking that she was a black woman, and she clearly loved this man and he loved her. You could see it in their eyes and in their smiles.

Nicole didn't ask what happened; she was sure it hadn't ended well. Nicole wondered if he had any children, and it was as if he had read her mind when he told her that he and his wife had none and that he had a twenty-year-old daughter that he hadn't seen since she was born. He'd somehow gotten a picture of her when she was ten. He didn't have that picture with him, but he said she looked just like her mother.

Real life changed the tone of their date. There was a lot less smiles and laughter. As if an invisible storm cloud had settled over their table.

"How's your dinner?"

"It's wonderful. Just what I wanted."

"Never thought you enjoyed food this much."

"Is that your way of calling me a pig?"

"No, I'm just saying that looking at you, I'd never guess that you enjoyed food the way you do. No offense."

"None taken."

Don watched her as she ate. Everything she did was attractive to him. Even the way she chewed her food. Don liked the way her eyes lit up when she smiled, and he liked to hear her laugh. She was great company.

"So what about you, Nicole, are you married?"

"No, I am not married, and I have never been married. I am very much single and satisfied," Nicole said, answering a question that he already knew the answer to.

"So you're not with anyone."

"I date, but as far as an exclusive relationship, no." Nicole lifted her fork and slowly slid a small piece of broccoli off of her fork and into her mouth. She chewed, raised an eyebrow at him, and smiled.

"So you don't have a love life?"

"Oh no, don't misunderstand me. I do have a love life." She smiled at Don. He couldn't tell if she was purposely peaking his curiosity or if she was just being her flirtatious self. But he indulged her.

"Are you monogamous?"

Nicole frowned and said, "Didn't I answer this question already?"

"I don't remember asking that question."

"Yea, but I think I answered it. You just weren't paying attention."

Don pretended to try to recall when he'd asked her that question as Nicole finished her dinner and waited patiently for him to say what he really wanted to say.

"Don, do you know what inference is?" Nicole asked. Don nodded. "Of course, you do. Inference allows you to draw conclusions based upon the information provided. Am I right?"

"Correct." Don nodded.

"So based on the information given. By me," Nicole said, pointing to herself. "Am I monogamous?" Nicole wanted to see how bold he was; she wanted to see if he was easily intimidated. Don smiled and nodded.

"So why aren't you in an exclusive relationship?"

"I was monogamous, my ex wasn't."

"Hurtful"

"Yea, a little. Deceitful mostly." Nicole shrugged her shoulders and said, "C'est la vie."

"You are so beautiful, Nicole. I can't imagine that any man would want to let you go."

"Beautiful woman don't get cheated on?"

"No. I'm not saying that. It's just that you are." Don's face contorted, as he tried to find the words to express himself. "I dunno, you're just beautiful. A lovely woman to be with."

"Well, Don. I'm glad you're having a nice time. I'm having a nice time too."

The lights in the restaurant are a bit too dim for a casual dinner. The setting too romantic for two friends getting better acquainted. Candles flickered and waved. Quiet conversation and gentle murmuring could be heard in the background.

"Don, do you know who you look like?"

"Oh no. Here we go."

"No, seriously. You look like Kevin Costner."

"Huh?" Don said, with a look of confusion on his face.

"You haven't heard that before? I'm sure you've heard that before."

"No, I don't think that I have."

"Not No-Way-Out Kevin Costner, but Mr. Brooks Kevin Costner."

"Oh," Don laughed. "I look like Kevin Costner when he played a psycho serial killer."

Nicole laughed, "No, no, no. I didn't mean it like that. You look like an older, more-mature Kevin Costner. You are really a handsome man."

"I am, am I? Well, why didn't you say Matthew McConaughey or George Clooney?" Don turned his head to the side, showing Nicole his profile. "How about now?"

Nicole laughed. "You really look like Costner now. What's wrong with Costner? He's a great-looking guy. He is just older and more distinguished looking now. And he has those sexy, blue eyes."

"Are they blue?"

"I don't know. I think they are."

"You say Costner like you know him personally."

"I've never met Kevin Costner before. I'm not sure what color eyes he has. But I'm looking at you, and your eyes are clear and blue." She looked at him and smiled.

"You are a flirt."

"You think so?" Nicole said, wrinkling her nose. "I don't think so," Nicole said shaking her head. "What's the matter, Don? You feel like I'm coming on to you? Do I make you feel uncomfortable?"

"Quite honestly, yes, you do." He laughed. "I don't know how to take you."

"I don't flirt, Don," Nicole said with a grin. "I'm very straightforward. Leaves no room for the wrong interpretation."

Don took a huge gulp of his drink. It burned as it went down. What interpretation should he be getting from all of this, he wondered. Was this a proposition of some sort?

"Do you plan on being single forever?"

"I have no intention of going through life hopping in and out of relationships, becoming more and more vulnerable and bitter with each one. It weakens you. I'd much rather date and enjoy the company of many men. No strings attached. No commitment necessary." Nicole paused for Don's response and then said, "Sound like somethin' you'd be interested in?"

Don could barely contain himself. He could feel himself rising in his shorts. He wanted to raise a finger and say, "Check please." But instead, he said, "Nicole, you intrigue me."

Nicole smiled. Don asked for the check and left a generous tip. Nicole was going to his hotel room with him, and Don couldn't get there fast enough. Nicole and Don didn't do too much talking from the restaurant to the hotel, partly because Don was afraid of saying the wrong thing and changing Nicole's mind. It had been a while since he had been intimate with a woman. Don was single too, and he hadn't the time or the energy to start, let alone maintain a long-term relationship. So this invitation of Nicole's was right up his alley.

He was excited but understandably nervous. Once they got into his hotel room, Don offered Nicole a drink, but she declined.

"No need for formalities," Nicole said as she tossed her purse on a nearby chair.

Don stood in front of her and asked, "Does size matter?"

"Sure it does," Nicole answered without hesitation.

Don was surprised at her answer. He'd hoped she'd be kind. Don stood fully clothed, staring at Nicole, wanting her. He knew he didn't have the ideal body. He was lean, but not muscular, average height, not tall. His short graying hair framed his head like a salt-and-pepper bed skirt. He had a small protruding paunch that could be seen through his button-down shirt. He rubbed it, giving it the unwanted attention he was trying to avoid. As much as he wanted her, he was afraid of what she was going to think. He was athletic in his day, but he hadn't played baseball in years.

Nicole sensed that he felt uncomfortable. She stepped out of her shoes because they made her appear taller than him. She approached him slowly, seductively, trying to ease his nerves.

"Your attraction to me is sexy. Knowing that you want me is appealing to me," she whispered in his ear. Her warm, sweet-smelling breath made the hair on his neck stand on end and sent chills down his spine. She was right. He wanted her. He wanted her like he'd wanted no other woman.

They stood in front of each other. He couldn't be further from her type than what he was. He smiled at her. She smiled back. If he only knew. This night would determine if he'd be a regular on her callback list. Or just a one night stand. They stood in front of each other. She smiled, trying to contain her laughter.

"Why are you laughing?" Don laughed nervously too. Don tore open a condom and began to unbuckle his pants.

"Wait," Nicole said, "how long has it been since you've done this?" she giggled. "Take off your shirt." Nicole helped him unbutton his shirt. She threw his button down to the floor and pulled his T-shirt over his head. Not bad for a forty-seven-year-old accountant. He didn't have bulging pecs and biceps, but he was fit.

Nicole smiled and pulled him close to her by his belt as she gently kissed and sucked his mouth. She heard the clink of the belt buckle as his pants hit the floor.

Nicole reached around into his boxers and held his butt in her hands; she pulled him closer to her and whispered in his ear, "You have such a little booty."

Don sighed and said, "Oh, for a minute there, I thought you were gonna say I had an ass like Kevin Costner's too." Nicole laughed and continued kissing him.

"It's been a long time."

Nicole stopped kissing him and said, "Okay, did you really mean to say that out loud? Seriously, Don. If you want your dry spell to end tonight, then you'd better get it together. You're too nervous man." She looked him in the eye and smiled.

"I have but one rule, don't go trailing off thinking about your one true love. My name is Nicole, and I like to hear my name repeatedly."

"Sounds like more than one rule to me."

"One rule, two, call it whatever you like. But break it and I'm out. I'll stop right in the middle, and I'll go right home and I'll act as if this night never happened." Nicole smiled and put her hand on the side of Don's face, to make sure that he was looking her in the eye. Don turned his head slightly and kissed her palm.

Don had wanted Nicole for a long time. Olivia was his past. She'd been married for many years and had a family now. The only reason he'd kept her photo in his wallet all these years was to remind himself never to settle.

Nicole and Don got off to a slow start, but it didn't take long for Don to get his bearings. Don was eager to explore every part of Nicole's body with wild abandon. Nicole unzipped her dress and slid it to the floor. Don watched as the dress slithered down every ferocious curve of Nicole's sexy body. She unhooked her bra and flung it to the floor too. Don admired her breasts as if it were a rare work of art. He wanted to reach out and touch her, but he let her finish. Nicole let her hair down, literally, and her long curls fell to her shoulders. She walked over to the bed as Don followed closely behind her and lay down on her back. Her hair forming a halo around her head on the mattress. Wearing nothing but her thongs, Nicole invited Don on the bed with her.

Don's foreplay seemed endless. He was such a tender lover. His thin lips were soft on her skin. He was gentle. And he obeyed her rules. He didn't have anyone but Nicole on his mind. He savored every moment with her. He wanted to remember the smell of her skin, her taste, her touch, forever.

The first time Don called her name, she smiled. She enjoyed him immensely. He was surprisingly very well endowed, and she told him so. He followed directions well too. Their bodies twisted and contorted into various erotic positions with great ease. He had tremendous stamina too, and he was an excellent lover. But Nicole didn't tell him so. Instead, she rewarded Don by showing him she had a few tricks of her own.

Aniyah walked past pictures of Matthew's children as if walking through a haunted mansion. It was dark and eerie and Aniyah felt as if she didn't belong there. She was there for one purpose and one purpose only, and even though she was ashamed of herself, she couldn't bring herself to leave. Matthew led her upstairs to his bedroom, just like he did when she was fourteen. But now it was a different place, a different time and they seemed as if they were two different people. Aniyah had it set in her mind that she would not be like the vulnerable, naïve teen that he knew so many years ago. She was a grown woman now, wiser and more mature, and she would prove that to him tonight.

Matthew's home was beautiful, but she tried not to soak up the details. She didn't want to become too familiar with his home, because she had no plans on returning to it. She looked away from the family photos in her attempt to become as detached as possible. Aniyah's heart pounded. She eagerly awaited what was to take place. She wanted it over and done with. She'd have this one night, this one secret rendezvous with Matthew, and go back to her life with Nathan. A life that up until this point she was perfectly content with.

The lights in Matthew's bedroom were off. They were on a dimmer switch, and Matthew dimmed the lights so that a little more than their shadows and silhouettes could be seen. Matthew thought he still knew her, Aniyah thought to herself. She was not the same little girl afraid of her own nakedness. Her body was fully grown and flawless, and she was proud of every womanly curve.

"Turn it up," Aniyah said to Matt, his hand still on the dimmer switch. Matthew turned the knob, and Aniyah told him when to stop. The light was bright, but not too bright. Matthew picked up a remote and pointed it to a small shelf stereo in the corner of the room. Maxwell's "Bad Habits" blared through the stereo's sound system. He adjusted the sound to a lower-volume setting, to set the mood he'd wanted to set.

He approached Aniyah, looked into her eyes, put his hands on her shoulders, and worked his way down her arms. He kissed her, and she felt her legs turning to jelly. She was swooning over him. His touch sent sparks of electricity through her body. He kissed her neck as he untied the straps to her dress. He unzipped it and peeled it off her; she let it drop to the floor. He backed her into his bedroom wall, kissing her ravenously as if he'd been waiting a lifetime for this very moment. Aniyah unbuttoned his shirt, kissing him and running her hands over his chiseled chest and abs. Insatiable was the only way she could describe this hunger she was feeling for him. Aniyah unzipped his pants and slid his boxers down along with them. She stared at his erection, as he slid a finger into the waistband of her thongs and hooked them and pulled her closer to him. Aniyah kicked his pants and his underwear out of the way and moved his hands, sliding her panties off. He admired her nakedness and shook his head thinking of the many ways he'd pleasure her tonight.

Chapter 12

WHOSE THAT GIRL

It was Monday morning, and neither Eric nor Serena had early-a.m. classes today. Serena didn't want to sleep in this morning though. They'd ordered in all day yesterday, and she was ready to get up and get out. Eric was still sleeping, so Serena gently eased him awake while rubbing his back and kissing the back of his neck.

"Get up baby, take a shower with me," she whispered in his ear. I want to go out and get some breakfast. I'm hungry." Eric had a bachelor's empty fridge and a few snacks in the cupboard, but Serena wanted real food. "Eric, come on." Serena didn't really want to take a shower with Eric. Eric liked the water too hot, and she'd always leave the shower beet red and tender. But Serena knew he liked to, and if that's what she had to agree to in order to get Eric up, then she'd agree to it, because she was starving.

Eric yawned and stretched, then turned over facing Serena. "What do you want to eat?"

"I am starving, I want a big breakfast. Bacon, eggs, sausage, hash browns, and pancakes," Serena said licking her lips.

"Yea, you're hungry. 'Cuz you're not going to be able to eat all that."

"Whatever. Come on. Let's go."

Eric was awake now, so Serena hurried and took her shower first, before she had to make good on her deal. She changed her clothes, and Eric showered after her. Serena threw on an old T-shirt. The sleeves were cut off and frayed on the ends, and she'd cut around the neck of the T-shirt so that it hung off one shoulder. She wore a pair of sexy, blue jean cutoff shorts and a pair of flip-flops. She looked so cute. Serena had a flair of her own, and she had a way of making the everyday look stylish. She wore an old beaded leather pouch over her shoulder and across her body so that the pouch hung on her left hip. She put a little moisturizer in her hair and was ready to go.

"Eric, hurry up," Serena yelled in to Eric, as she sat down on his sofa.

"I'm comin'," Eric said as he pulled on an old T-shirt and a pair of jeans, body still wet from his shower.

Serena bounded down the stairs like an excited child, leaving Eric at the top of the stairs, taking one stair at a time.

"Come on, old man," Serena said, yelling up at him from the bottom of the staircase.

Serena rubbed her eyes and licked her lips, then reached into her little leather pouch, pulled out some cherry lip gloss, and put some on. She rubbed her lips together and waited for Eric.

Eric was tall, much taller than Serena, and he was brown skinned, the color of buttered toffee. He wore his hair in a bald fade, which meant he had to get his hair cut every week in order to keep it up. Serena liked it when his hair grew out; she preferred Eric's hair longer. Eric's hair was dark and thick, and she loved the way it felt on her hands. Eric also wore a neatly trimmed moustache and a pencil-thin beard. Serena didn't like the beard at all. She kept telling him he'd look so much better if either he'd choose to cut it off or wear it full. But Eric thought he looked so fine with that pencil-thin beard, and apparently, all the girls did too.

Eric walked slow. Serena wasn't sure if it was a cool stroll he had going on or what. Usually, it didn't bother her. She liked to walk behind him and watch him walk; he had a sexy walk, and his butt was one of his best assets. But on this particular morning, she was hungry and her stomach was growling, and his sexy stroll and that butt were the furthest things from her mind.

"So where are we going?"

"I don't care. I'll let you pick."

Eric unlocked the car doors, and Serena hopped in. Serena immediately started flipping through the radio stations until she found a song she liked.

"What's this?" Eric said holding a flyer that he'd pulled off the windshield.

"I don't know. I didn't even notice it." Serena looked up at Eric. He was holding a white sheet of paper folded into thirds. "It's probably just some trash. Or somebody advertising a party or cabaret or something. Come on, let's go," she said, pounding her fists on his dash.

Eric sat in the car and unfolded the piece of paper. Serena sighed, folded her arms, and looked out the passenger-side window.

"Whoa," Eric said as he laughed, holding the piece of paper open with both hands.

Serena stopped looking out the window, to look over Eric's shoulder, and she couldn't believe what she was seeing.

"Can you believe this?" He laughed. "Do you know whose desk that is?"

Serena didn't answer. She didn't say a word. Her eyes said it all. Her stomach wasn't growling anymore. She was nauseated now. She was staring at a picture of herself naked and exposed for all the world to see. She had called Hakeem's bluff and had lost. She couldn't believe he had done this. She stared at the writing at the top of the piece of paper and written in bold red letters were the words, Whose That Girl? As if a challenge to whomever the reader was. Eric stared at the picture smiling, which Serena thought was such an insult, considering that he hadn't realized that he was staring at his own girlfriend's naked silhouette. Hakeem would have recognized her body immediately, Serena thought to herself.

"Hun-gry," Serena said to Eric, trying to keep her composure. She wanted to snatch that piece of paper away from him, ball it up, and hit him in the face with it. She wanted to find Hakeem, curse him out, and beat his ass if she could. She wasn't mad at herself right now. No, she was mad at the idiot staring at the picture and the idiot who had given him the picture to stare at. "Eric!" Serena said.

"Oh, yeah," Eric answered still smiling and holding the piece of paper in his hands. "She fine, but she ain't got nothing on you," Eric said and leaned in to give Serena a kiss.

Serena turned her head. "Baby, don't be mad. I'm just trippin,'" he said with a laugh. "I can't believe nobody would be so stupid. Who would do some stupid shit like this?" he said, holding up the piece of paper. "I mean there's gonna be some consequences behind this," he said, waving the piece of paper in his hand. He looked at Serena as he spoke, then reached in front of her, opened up his glove compartment, and placed the paper inside. Serena wanted to tear up the paper and curse his ass out for being so disrespectful to her. True, it was her own body in that picture, but apparently, Eric didn't know that and to reach in front of her and put it in his glove compartment as if filing some important paper, how dare him!

Serena didn't say anything though. She knew she was in a world of trouble. But she was really surprised at Eric. As hard as he stared at that picture, he couldn't see the woman in it was her, and it hadn't occurred to him that it was mighty strange that the picture was on his windshield and no one else's in the parking lot. Serena had peeked around; there were no other pieces of paper on anyone else's windshield. She was in trouble and she knew that picture was going to pop up again and she didn't see a way out.

"After we eat, I'm gonna need you to drop me off at my dorm."

"You left your books at my place."

"I'll get them later. The books I need for today are at my dorm."

"Okay."

Serena could barely eat. Her eyes were bigger than her stomach. Once they made it to the diner, she wasn't as hungry as she was before she'd seen the picture, and it didn't help that Eric wanted to talk about it all the way there and the entire time they were in the diner.

"Listen, Eric, I don't want to talk about that picture anymore. Please, let me enjoy my breakfast in peace," Serena said as she pushed her scrambled eggs around on the plate.

Eric smiled at her and agreed to let it go. But he hadn't. He kept thinking about it, smiling and shaking his head. "What an ass," Serena thought to herself. She seriously considered dumping Eric right then and there. Eric didn't talk about much of anything. He couldn't get that picture out of his mind. He wasn't sure if it was the image on the picture or the fact that somebody at the college was so bold as to actually get into the dean's office and pose right on his desk. He wasn't sure if it was the boldness of the act or the act itself that had him so absorbed.

Eric's phone rang, and as soon as he answered it, his eyes brightened. It was his friend Ron, and he'd received the picture too; in fact, there were copies of the picture all over campus, and all of them had the heading Whose That Girl? scrawled across the top. Serena didn't know what to do. She figured if Hakeem had gone so far as to distribute these pictures all around the campus and to make a special trip all the way to Eric's place; eventually, he'd reveal who the mystery girl was, and then everyone would know that it was her in the picture.

She knew that Hakeem would be getting in touch with her. But he had played the only bargaining chip he had left. Serena glanced over at Eric. He was on the phone laughing and smiling and grinning. Sitting on the phone with Ron, the two of them were giggling and gossiping like a bunch of teenaged girls. She could hear everything Ron was saying on the other line, telling Eric all the things he could do to the mystery girl on the paper. And Eric laughed with him, not knowing that the girl he wanted to do all those freaky things to was his girl.

Eric dropped her off at campus, but not before taking her back to his apartment to pick up her things. Eric was very preoccupied, Serena could tell. Normally, Eric didn't want to leave her. He'd go through the whole "I love you, I'll miss you, I don't want you to leave" ritual before succumbing and seeing Serena off to her dorm. Serena wasn't sure if it was her imagination or not, but it seemed to her that Eric was all too eager to drop her off.

Serena saw the pictures. She saw groups of students holding them in their hands. She didn't wait around to see what they were saying. She had a one-track mind, and she couldn't wait to get to a phone.

"La Maya, he did it."

"He did what?"

"He made copies of that picture of me on the dean's desk, and he's been spreading them all around campus."

"Oh. My. God."

"Oh, no. It gets worse. He even drove over to Eric's apartment and put one on his car. Can you believe that?"

"What did Eric say?"

"Nothin'. He doesn't even know that it's me."

"He can't tell?"

"Apparently not, 'cuz he's been on the phone with his friends, giggling about the mystery girl in the picture. Isn't that crazy? I can't believe he doesn't know it's me."

"Well, you said he made copies on a piece of paper. I'm sure it's not photo-grade copy paper, and it's probably not that clear."

"Believe me, it's clear enough."

"Well, trust me it could be a whole hell of a lot clearer. Poor picture quality is a good thing. You don't want anybody identifying you, do you?"

"Of course not."

"Well, then, it's a good thing that your boyfriend can't recognize you in those pics. So don't be so hard on him."

La Maya paused. There was a long silence on the phone as if La Maya was trying to think.

"Do you know that Hakeem even had the nerve to write on the top of each copy, Whose That Girl? As if there's some sort of contest to identify who the girl in the picture really is. And he didn't even spell it right. He spelled it like w-h-o-s-e instead of like who is that girl, you know what I mean? What an idiot."

"No, maybe it's not a question directed at the students or anyone else for that matter. Maybe it's a challenge to Eric." Serena got quiet. She'd never thought of it like that. She sighed into the phone. "Forget I said that, Serena. I don't want to speculate. My god, girl. Is this what you all do in school. Girl, it's like a soap opera. A real-life soap opera. This shit has gone too far! You're really gonna hafto call your mama now."

"I'm not telling my mama, and don't you go telling her either," Serena said, as she tried to think. "This is our secret. Okay?" La Maya didn't answer. "La Maya, I can't hear you."

"Okay," La Maya said, clearly irritated.

"This is between me and you. I'll figure out something."

"Serena, girl, this is out of your hands. Don't you think that somebody in administration is gonna get their hands on that picture? Maybe even the dean himself. Girl, please, this is seriously going to affect your future at that school, your future period."

"You're right. The key word being *my* future. So I'm gonna handle it."

"Serena, why do you even call me with this stuff, if you won't even listen to what I'm sayin'?"

"I don't need any advice right now. I just need someone to listen. Someone that I can bounce ideas off of."

"What ideas? I haven't heard one idea yet."

"Listen, Maya. I just need someone that I trust, to confide in. Okay?"

"Girl, I can't take it. You're about to send my blood pressure up."

"I'll be okay. Don't worry about me. And don't go telling anybody," Serena added. "Promise." La Maya didn't say anything. "Promise, La Maya."

"All right. I promise."

"Thanks, cuzzy. I love you."

"I love you too, baby doll. And why does cuzzy sound like you're calling me a huzzy on the sly?"

Serena got off the phone with her cousin. La Maya was right; she didn't have any ideas. Serena didn't know what she was going to do. She didn't know what Hakeem was thinking and why he was doing this to her. True they didn't break up amicably, but hell, he was cheating. She didn't owe him a thing. Not a damn thing. And she wouldn't be forced into maintaining any type of relationship with him if she didn't want to. She'd said "No," and she meant it.

Serena was right; she didn't have anyone that she could confide in about this. She had some really great friends, but none that she could entrust this information to. Niko would go into panic mode, and as much as she loved him, Serena knew that he couldn't keep a secret to save his life. Justin would go into defense mode and would want to fight anyone who had anything negative to say about the girl in the picture. Tammey and Laura would be very supportive too, but not supportive enough not to blow her cover.

Serena went to her classes as planned, keeping her ears open. She was dubbed The Mystery Girl, and she found what the guys had to say about her differed from what the girls had to say. But what both groups agreed on, was that The Mystery Girl was stupid as hell to put herself in such a position with her education and that the punishment would be severe.

"Breaking and entering. That's breaking and entering."

"Well, she didn't actually break anything. Because if she did, we'd have heard about this before now."

"You don't actually hafto break anything for it to be called breaking and entering, you dork. Just the process of entering into a space that you don't belong in, or don't have permission to go into, constitutes breaking and entering or at the very least illegal trespassing. Look it up. I'm sure she didn't have Dean Carmichael's permission. All I'm saying is this broad is gonna be in a shitload of trouble," a tall, muscular guy said as he held the picture up to the light. The shorter dark-haired guy with the black-framed glasses looked up at the picture with the jock. "Great body though," the jock said.

"Yea," the dark-haired guy agreed.

"Great tits."

Serena walked around campus eavesdropping on different debates that the students were having about The Mystery Girl. She was the talk of the day. The females hated her, but most of that was body envy. Serena looked damn good in that picture and in all the other's Hakeem had taken. Hakeem had had her posed in a way that accentuated every voluptuous curve of her body. Her full breasts sat up perfectly even as she lay on her back perky, full and perfect.

"They ain't real!" One girl said to a young man admiring the pic.

"They look real to me." The young man replied.

"Ain't nobody with titties that big gon' stand up like that. The bitch is fake!"

"Whatever," the guy laughed. "You're just a hater."

"Whatever, I ain't got no reason to hate. Because I am stacked, baby," she said as she did a slow turn, switching her full hips and displaying her endowments. "Anyway, it looks like a white girl."

"I don't think so. Not wit all dat ass."

"Shut up, Charles, you can't even see an ass in that picture."

The two looked at the picture together. The others in the crowd either looked at their own pic or they looked at a copy with a friend. Each of them looking for a booty.

"I see it. That's a sista's booty."

The arch of Serena's back was a perfect semicircle, and it accented the roundness of her hips and butt. It was beautiful. Not trashy and offensive as some made it seem. "Yea, it's so round," a dark-skinned guy said, pretending to lick the page. A small light-skinned girl smacked him in the back of the head. Everyone laughed.

"Well, there's one thing that I can say, at least I'll still be in school. 'Cuz this heffa is gone," the buxom girl said as she waved bye-bye, balled up the picture, and tossed it to the ground. Everyone laughed. The guy and girl who had been debating back-and-forth high-fived each other, then walked off together carrying their books.

A few times, Serena was tempted to speak up for herself, but she didn't because she knew that that would be foolish. She hadn't heard the members of the faculty mention anything about the picture, but she didn't know what they were saying behind closed doors.

Serena met up with her friends later that night for dinner at a little sports bar, not far from campus. It was a humid night, but it was also nice and breezy, so they decided to eat outside at one of the little tables with the umbrellas. Serena loved this place; it wasn't too loud when there wasn't any major games broadcasted on the TV, and it was so cozy. Serena loved the little white lights that were strung throughout the outdoor eating area. They reminded her of fireflies.

They ordered drinks right away. Justin and Niko ordered Coronas. Niko ordered two. Tammey and Laura each ordered Margaritas. Serena asked for ice water with a wedge of lime. When the drinks came, Niko waited for the waitress to walk away and then he slid one of his bottles of Corona over to Serena. Serena put her lime wedge over the open bottle neck and took a swig. She wouldn't be twenty-one for another week.

Tammey commented on Niko's T-shirt; it was black, with the words Eat Me printed across the front in big white letters.

"How did you get away with wearing that all day?" Tammey asked Niko. Serena loved to hear Tammey talk; she loved the way she pronounced her words so precisely. She stressed every syllable of each word when she spoke, as if she always had something really important to say.

Niko didn't say a word; he just rearranged his big, fringed, black-and-white checkered scarf around his neck so that it completely covered the word Eat.

"Aaah," Tammey said nodding. "Very clever, young Niko."

Niko wore a small, black-rimmed hat and a pair of skinny jeans. Laura teased Niko by commenting on how she liked how the jeans showed off all his junk. Everyone laughed like crazy.

"So, baby girl, are you still headed home on Friday?" Niko asked.

"Yes, sir," Serena said, taking another swig of her Corona. "Plans have not changed. I can't wait to see everybody. My sisters are supposed to have something really big planned for my twenty-first birthday. I can hardly wait. Did I tell you Mariah's having twins?"

"Yes," everyone at the table said in unison. Serena had mentioned the twins five times on the walk to the sports bar.

"I'm sorry," she said with a dimpled smile. "I'm so excited. It's our first set of twins."

"Uuugh!" I am so glad that this day is over!" Laura said as she took a sip of her Margarita. "I am gonna take a hot bath and chill as soon as I get back to my dorm room. This day has been hell on wheels," Laura said as she slunk down in chair with her arms hung over each side. Laura had big, expressive, green eyes, long wavy, red hair, and freckles. She had a big gold ball in her tongue, a piercing that she flicked about and played with as she talked.

"I know what you mean. This has been one mess of a Monday. Dr. Travers is crazy and his tests are just as weird as he is," Tammey added as she sighed. "I am mentally and physically drained." Dr. Travers was Tammey's psychology professor with whom she'd had a huge crush on at the beginning of the semester.

"How do you think you did?" Serena asked and took another swallow of beer.

"Okay, I guess. I'm sure I passed. But hell, who wants to pass? Psychology's my major, I wanna ace it." Tammey smiled and winked at Serena. Serena smiled.

Music played in the background as the friends talked, laughed, and ate. They ordered five appetizers and shared each of them. The appetizers were so huge that there was no need to order a main course, and they were cheaper too. Perfect for a college student's meager budget.

They were a melting pot. Niko was of Japanese decent; he was about five foot ten with wiry-jet black hair that he kept cut wispy and wild. Justin was Caucasian with the deepest baby blue eyes, wavy blond hair, and a gorgeous tan; he had a great body, and he was about six foot two. He looked like a surfer dude, but he was far from it. Justin was afraid of water, due to a boating accident when he was younger. He carried that surfer look well though. Tammey, with an E, had short dark brown hair that she wore in a pixie cut. Her skin was fair and her eyes were hazel and she wore glasses whose frames were as dark as her hair. She had a small gap in her two front teeth that she hated, but Serena loved it. She thought it gave her character.

"So is your mom gonna let you stay with Nicole?" Laura asked as she munched on chicken fingers.

"I am a grown-ass woman. I can stay wherever I want." Everyone stopped chewing and looked at Serena. Then Serena said, while fumbling with a mozzarella stick on her plate, "Yes, my mama's gonna let me stay at Nicole's." Everyone laughed.

"Is Eric going with you?" Justin asked.

"No way," Serena answered with a smile. "He wants to go, but I told him, 'Not this time.' We're not there yet. Ya know?" Serena had only been dating Eric for a few months. She didn't think it was time to be introducing him to family.

"Well, he's in love," Tammey said.

"Whatever," Serena said as she blushed.

"Eric and Serena. Together forever," Niko said jokingly.

"Hope he doesn't turn out to be obsessed, like Hakeem," Tammey added.

Serena didn't say anything. She reached over and picked up a loaded potato skin and double dipped it in sour cream. She didn't want to get on the subject of Hakeem, because she wasn't sure if she was strong enough not to tell on herself.

"I really thought that Serena and Hakeem were great together," Laura said; she was a self-proclaimed psychic. She wanted to be a relationship therapist or a marriage counselor. Serena thought she'd be good at that.

"Oh, here we go," Niko said. "Yea, it's your fault that they didn't work out." All but Laura laughed.

"No, really. I was the one who told Serena to give him a chance, ya know, after she found out about him and that girl Stephanie," Laura replied.

"Don't worry about it. I didn't listen," Serena said.

"Yea, thank God," Laura said.

Hakeem had been trying to talk Serena, since she'd broke up with him. He had been trying to explain, but Serena didn't want to hear it. She didn't want his explanation. She thought they had a good thing going; apparently, Hakeem didn't agree. Because if he did he would have been faithful.

Serena was in her comfort zone. Good food, good friends, and good conversation. The perfect end to a grueling day. Serena had almost made it through the entire meal without anyone mentioning The Mystery Girl. Almost, that was.

"Did you guys see this?" Laura said as she pulled the infamous mystery-girl picture out of her folder. It didn't have a wrinkle or a fold, not even a crease. Laura started to sit it on the table, but there was no room and she didn't want to get it covered with grease or food.

"Who hasn't?" Niko said.

"It's all anyone's been talking about all day," Tammey said.

"I know and I'm sick of hearing about it," Serena said without looking any of her friends in the eyes.

"Let me see it?" Justin said, holding out a greasy hand.

"No, you're gonna get it all greasy."

"I'll wipe my hands," Justin answered as he reached for a napkin to wipe his hands off with.

"No," Laura said, slipping the picture in her green folder.

"What?" Niko said, laughing. "Look at her. What are you saving it for?"

"Dude? It's beautiful. It's artsy. It's lovely. It's just a really cool photograph."

"It's not even a clear picture. What are you keeping it for?" Justin was irritated that Laura didn't give up the picture.

"Justin, you saw the picture already. There were so many of them. You could have grabbed a couple for yourself."

"I just wanted to take a peek at it again," Justin said, sulking like a little boy.

"Here, Justin! Look, but don't touch," she warned as if she was pulling out her boob.

Laura opened up her folder and held the piece of paper by the very edge of it.

"I don't know who she is, but she sure is sexy," Justin said as he stared at the paper.

Serena looked at Justin as he lusted over the picture. She laughed and wondered if he'd still find it as sexy if he knew it was her naked body on that page.

"Beautiful, isn't she?" Laura said.

"Yea, she's a knockout," Justin said, still staring at the photo.

"I wish it were clearer. I'd love to frame it," Laura said.

"You're obsessed," Niko said jokingly.

"I just appreciate true beauty," Laura said and flicked her pierced tongue at Tammey. Tammey flicked her tongue back at Laura. Everyone laughed.

"Serena, you're mighty quiet over there."

"I was just thinking, everyone keeps talking about The Mystery Girl but no one is talking about the person who actually took the pictures."

"What pictures?"

"Excuse me," Serena cleared her throat and corrected herself. "Picture."

Serena wished she hadn't said anything. She almost gave herself away; pictures, why would she say pictures?

"Well, I don't know. Whoever the photographer is, he did an excellent job at capturing beauty, sensuality, and mystique all in one piece. He's really a talented artist. I'd like to see the rest of his work."

Tammey laughed. "You are such a nut job."

"No, seriously. He or she captured an image that has had the entire campus talking all day. I mean that's some really thought-provoking shit." The table burst out in laughter.

"That's it," Tammey said, "no more Margaritas for you. You can't express yourself without using profanity." Always a clear-cut sign that Laura had a bit too much to drink.

"I know," Laura said, giggling. "I do feel a little buttered."

When their dinner ended, the guys walked the girls to their dorm rooms. Justin and Niko always made sure the girls made it back safely. Everyone thought Niko was some sort of martial-arts sensei. He'd go around campus, striking poses, doing kicks, and waving his arms. He looked pretty convincing. But the inside joke was that Niko held no belts and he had no formal training, and if attacked, they'd all be in trouble. Tammey joked about Niko's jeans as Niko pretended to pull something out of his front pocket and pulled out his middle finger instead.

As they laughed, talked, and walked, Serena thought about how blessed she was to have such good friends. They were uplifting and positive and true. She treasured time spent with them, and she valued their friendship as well as their opinions. Each of them played a very special part in her life. She loved their view of the world. Serena liked that Laura looked at the picture and saw something creative and beautiful. She liked that none of her friends talked about how stupid mystery girl was and that no one was unkind. They were gentle and considerate, not off-putting and judgmental.

Serena was the last one to be dropped off. Justin and Niko walked her to her door and waited until she was safely inside. Serena hadn't gotten a chance to write anything in her journal, and after an entire weekend with Eric and a long, eventful day of eavesdropping, she needed to get to her journal. She went into her overnight bag and went into the pocket of her blue jeans and pulled out a journal entry. She had so much that she needed to write down in her journal, and everything came flooding into her mind at once. She hated that, because she didn't want to miss anything or leave out any important details.

Serena lifted up the side of her mattress and reached her hand underneath, but she didn't find her journal. "That's odd," she thought as she moved her hand around underneath the mattress and patted down the box spring. When she came up empty handed, she lifted the mattress all the way up and looked underneath. It was gone. There was nothing. Not even her pen. And there wasn't a note left in its place. Serena panicked. She knew who had done this. But she couldn't understand why. What had she done to make him treat her this way? Why was he trying to ruin her life?

Serena began to cry. She was exhausted. It was too much work trying to figure Hakeem out. She couldn't understand him, and she never would. She tried to calm herself down before making that inevitable phone call, and she didn't want him to hear the defeat in her voice and think he'd won.

Chapter 13

THE MORNING AFTER

When Aniyah opened her eyes, she found herself in an unfamiliar bed, wearing nothing but her jewelry. Then all the memories of the previous night came flooding back into her head.

"Good morning," Matthew said into her ear. He was spooning with her, and he held her close to his body. She'd forgotten how it felt to lie that way. She was afraid to turn to him and look him in his face. She hadn't meant to fall asleep there. She didn't know how she'd let that happen. It was as though sex with him had drained her of every bit of energy. The last thing she remembered was lying, quivering in his bed. She hadn't meant to make that morning after walk to his car, wearing the same clothes that she had walked in with. And she hadn't meant to enjoy the other night as much as she did.

Aniyah had to hand it to him. He was still hands down the greatest lover she had ever had. This wasn't an infatuated child's opinion, but the opinion of an experienced woman. He was gentle and attentive, and he discovered erogenous zones that she didn't even know she had. It was markedly the most intense sexual experience she'd ever had.

Matthew kissed her neck. She could see her beautiful dress rumpled on the floor. Matthew ran his hand along her hip and down her thigh. She trembled a little, involuntarily. Presumably, aftershocks from the previous night. She could hear her phone beeping in her little clutch purse, but she didn't feel comfortable getting up to get it.

Matthew got out of the bed and walked over to the side of the bed Aniyah was lying on. She wanted to close her eyes and lie very still and pretend that she was still sleeping. But Matthew knew that she was awake, and before she could think about it any longer, Matthew was kneeling beside her and planting a kiss on her mouth. His mouth tasted minty and fresh; her mouth didn't.

Mathew was wearing a pair of brown paisley boxers and a big satisfied grin. "I know you have to leave me soon," he said; his voice was deep and sexy. "So I ran you a hot bath. I have everything set up for you in there," he said pointing to his master bath.

"I'll make you breakfast before you go."

She didn't know what he was trying to do, but she knew she needed to hightail it out of there. She had to be at work for her double shift by three thirty this afternoon, and she needed to go home and freshen up and reflect on a few things. But for some reason, she felt weak as if she couldn't move or speak, as if she was suffering from post-climactic intoxication, and her body was in post-climactic shock. She smiled at that thought, to imagine that a man could put it on her so tough that it would actually have her silent and unwilling or unable to move.

"I really hafto go, Matthew. I've got a long day ahead of me." Aniyah stood and walked toward the bathroom. "Thanks for breakfast, but don't bother. I'll grab something to eat when I get home."

Matthew watched her as she got out of bed. She acted as if she wasn't aware that his eyes were on her. She walked into the bathroom as if moving to her own sultry theme music. The power she felt from making this man's mouth drop from her nakedness was exhilarating. The large, white bathtub was full of bubbles. She didn't recognize the scent, but it smelled so good. Aniyah smiled as she looked around his bathroom. It was beautiful but plain. Definitely a man's bathroom, it lacked a woman's touch. But it was so clean and white. It wasn't colorful or cluttered like her own bathroom. It didn't have a his-and-hers vanity like her own bathroom did, but it had a large vanity with plenty of light and a lot of counter space. His color scheme was black and grey, and all his bathroom fixtures were shiny and silver, including the old-fashioned tub's clawed feet.

Matthew had laid a silver gray washcloth on top of an oversized silver gray towel next to the tub. Aniyah tested the water with her foot before getting inside. The temperature was just right, and the pulsating water jets felt wonderful as she eased her body down into the fragrant water and the bubbles.

"Mmmph," Aniyah said to herself. "I must have really put it on him last night." She giggled. The ends of her hair were getting wet, but Aniyah didn't care. She figured it couldn't look any worse than her leaving from his house at ten o'clock in the morning, wearing a dress that she had picked up off the floor.

She was ultra relaxed. She felt like she didn't have a care in the world as she soaked in that tub. Despite the fact that she hadn't been home all night and her boyfriend was probably wondering where in the hell she was. She lathered her washcloth with a good-smelling soap she didn't recognize and hoped that it wouldn't irritate her sensitive skin. But as she bathed, she figured if she would have stayed at home and out of Matthew's bed she wouldn't have had that to worry about. Matthew had gone overboard on the bubbles as men usually do. They never quite know how much bubble bath to add, since they don't usually use the stuff for themselves. It was difficult for her to rinse herself off because the bubbles didn't melt or dissolve. So Aniyah stood and rinsed her body with the shower hose.

Matthew knocked and spoke, but she didn't hear him. When he knocked a second time, he'd mistakenly thought she'd told him to come in. When he opened the door, he saw Aniyah with her head thrown back and her eyes closed, rinsing the soapsuds and bath bubbles off her body. She was beautiful. The arch of her back, the round, firmness of her butt, her full perfect breasts, that fit like grapefruits in his palms, she was the ideal woman. Sexy and beautiful and as confident as she appeared to be he was sure that she didn't even know it. He wanted to join her, but instead, he closed the door, realizing she hadn't invited him to come in.

Matthew had placed a toothbrush still in its packaging on the counter top along with a travel-sized tube of toothpaste. Aniyah brushed her teeth after toweling off. When Aniyah came out of the bathroom wrapped in a towel, she found a pair of plaid shorts and a big old T-shirt on the bed. "I'm not sure if you can fit the shorts, but it's worth a try. I know the T-shirt is pretty big. I can't help you with the shoes though.

The T-shirt was pretty thick, and it was sunshine yellow. The plaid shorts were way too big for Aniyah. "I'm not going to be able to fit these shorts. Are you giving me this T-shirt?"

"Sure, I don't need it back."

"Got a pair of scissors?"

"Sure," he said again. "Hold on a second."

Matthew came back with a large pair of scissors with big orange handles. Aniyah worked her magic on the T-shirt and slipped it on over the bath towel, then let the towel slip to the floor. She cut the neck out of the T-shirt; she cut the sleeves off and cut a slit in the side and tied it in a knot. Then she grabbed her clutch and put on her strappy shoes and was ready to go.

Aniyah was grateful for the heavy T-shirt. She knew it wasn't just a matter of going from his house, to his car, to her condo. It was a matter of leaving his house, getting into his car, going back to the restaurant where her car was, then going home to her condo. She looked like sunshine, and she worked that dress, giving any runway model a run for their money.

Matthew told Aniyah that his brother and sister-in-law had kept his children for him overnight and had dropped them off at summer camp this morning. He worked from home, so he had some work to get to after he dropped Aniyah off, but he told her that he would love to see her again.

"I can't," Aniyah said.

"Why?" Matthew had asked.

"I can't keep doing this."

"Doing what? I know you enjoyed yourself as much as I did," Matthew replied.

"That's not the point. I did what you asked me to do," Aniyah answered.

"Which was?"

"You asked me to spend the night with you and I did."

"So you're saying that you don't have any feelings for me?"

Matthew looked at her, and without turning away, Aniyah said to him, "I hafto go back to my life."

Aniyah's decision was very upsetting to Matthew, but he said he was going to keep his end of the bargain as he promised. He didn't argue with her about it. He had too much pride. Aniyah thanked him before getting in her car and driving away. She was glad that they drove in opposite directions, because she didn't want him to see her crying. She couldn't believe that she'd done something so stupid. Aniyah pulled over when Matthew's vehicle was out of sight. She reached into her purse and took out her cell phone, and when she heard Nate's voice on her voice mail, she felt horrible.

Aniyah was so mad at herself. She wished she'd never had any contact with Matthew. She was already confused about her feelings for Nathan; now she'd added Matthew to the mix. Aniyah had two other messages. Both were from her job. Both of her shifts were cancelled; she'd asked to be the first on the list to be cancelled if they were overstaffed because she was starting her vacation tomorrow. Normally, this would have been great news for her, but working kept her mind occupied. Now she would be free to think about what she had done.

Aniyah drove to her condo. She went up the back way. Much less traffic in the hallways. As soon as she got into the house, she stripped off that bright yellow shirt and pushed it down deep into her trashcan. She walked into her bedroom, grabbed her cordless phone, and called Nate. He was happy to hear her voice.

"Hey, baby! Where you been?" Aniyah usually loved the excitement in Nathan's voice. Under normal circumstances she would have been happy to know that he was excited to hear from her. But instead she'd felt so guilty and ashamed.

"Long night." Aniyah answered.

"You get enough rest?" Nathan asked.

"Yea, I guess," Aniyah said as she sighed. "Not really."

"You're talkin' crazy. Baby, you okay?" Nathan asked, his voice sounded concerned.

"I'm okay, baby."

"Good, 'cuz I can't talk now. I gotta go."

"All right."

"I'll call you later," Nate said.

Aniyah was glad that she was off today. She was so upset with herself. She threw on a nightgown, closed the blinds in her bedroom, and lay in her bed and cried. She didn't cry because she had lied or because she had cheated. She cried because she wanted more.

Nicole had a great night, and she was back home by two in the morning. She started her day bright and early, feeling fresh and rejuvenated and shockingly satisfied. Her personal assistant, Aaliyah, was there with notepad open, daily planner open, and pen in hand, arranging dates and times to accommodate Nicole's busy schedule.

Nicole's full house staff was there too. She had a small but devoted household staff that consisted of a chef, a maid, and gardeners to maintain her sprawling lawns. Her pool was maintained weekly by a company she retained, and today was Monday, the day scheduled for routine maintenance.

"I hate Mondays," Aaliyah said with a sigh.

"I love Mondays," Nicole said, grinning from ear to ear, displaying her deep-dimpled smile.

Aaliyah looked at Nicole, smiled, and shook her head. Nicole put her hand on Aaliyah's cheek and made kissy faces at her, teasing her about her Monday-morning blues. Nicole loved having Aaliyah around. She was bright, young, and efficient. She was such a valuable asset to her company, and she was thankful to have her.

Aaliyah never complained, no matter how difficult it was to juggle Nicole's appointments. She was very professional, and she knew how to conduct business in a professional and orderly manner.

"Okay, so we took care of your granny's car. The brakes should be done by four o'clock today. The rental car was dropped off this morning. Your grandmother has the keys, and she knows your little brother is not to drive it."

Nicole smiled.

"The car will be dropped off to her when the work is completed. They are going to check the car out thoroughly, if there is any more work needed, they know to give me a call and then I will notify you, and of course you can determine if you want the additional work done and if you are satisfied with the fee." Nicole nodded and smiled. Aaliyah was so thorough. "Naturally, if there is any additional work to be done on the vehicle then that will affect the estimated time of completion and when the van is returned. But the rental is for three days."

"What did granny pick for the rental vehicle?" Nicole asked.

"A white 2008 Chevy Impala," Aaliyah answered.

Nicole laughed. "Did she pick that or did Tye?" Nicole shook her head. Aaliyah didn't answer the question. She was sure it was rhetorical.

"Nicole, you have two events scheduled on the same day, at the same time. Next Saturday at 5:00 p.m. One's a charity auction, the other is a viewing of an art gallery showcase. Actually, no," she said, reviewing the calendar, then Nicole's appointment book. "You are scheduled to attend the charity auction, but this artist has extended a special invitation to you for the art showcase. Do you want me to pencil it in?

"Who's the artist?" Nicole asked.

"It's a Jeremy Clarke."

"Jeremy Clarke." Nicole let his name roll off of her tongue. "Jeremy Clarke," she repeated again. Her eyes brightened when she said his name again. "Sure, pencil him in."

Aaliyah sat with her legs crossed. She was tall and statuesque and no more than a size zero. She wore her hair in a short, wrapped hairstyle. She had high cheekbones, thin lips, and a small nose. Her skin was smooth and brown, and she looked like an entirely different person when she smiled. Aaliyah didn't smile much; for some reason, she didn't think it was professional. So her countenance stayed serious most of the time. She was professional and business-like at all times, but she held a special fondness for Nicole. She viewed her as more of a mentor than an employer. There was so much that she felt that she could learn from her. Nicole had exposed her to so much that she would not have ever been exposed to if it hadn't have been for her employment with her. She didn't want to leave Nicole, but if she ever did, her resume would look great. Aaliyah aspired to having her own business someday, and she truly appreciated Nicole for showing her the ends and outs.

Nicole didn't come from old money. Sure her mother was a hardworking woman, had been a hardworking woman all of her life. But it was through her own blood, sweat, and tears that she'd accumulated her wealth. She'd worked very hard for other people for many years until she'd discovered that it would be more profitable for her to work just as hard for herself. Nicole's mother had several streams of income, but all of her businesses massed together could not compare with the wealth Nicole had attained.

Tamani was a very lucrative business venture birthed from Nicole's vision and funded by the insurance money left to her by Daddy Ray. Daddy Ray had made Nicole the sole beneficiary of his many life-insurance policies, and he'd collected insurance policies like some collected rare coins.

Daddy Ray had a fear of dying. He'd feared that it would be a quick onset and he'd die slowly suffering. And he was right. He'd been diagnosed with pancreatic cancer, and he'd died painfully slow. By the time it was discovered, the cancer had spread to distant lymph nodes and other organs. He refused treatment and died one year after being diagnosed.

It was hard for Nicole's mother to fathom why Ray would leave everything to Nicole. But that wasn't the cause of her bitter hatred of her daughter. She'd cut her out of her life when she was seventeen years old, and she hadn't looked back. The fact that Ray had made her his beneficiary only added fuel to the fire.

Daddy Ray was the one who told Nicole that she was beautiful and that she'd be a force to be reckoned with someday. He was the one who made her feel that no matter what other's said she looked like on the outside, she was going to feel good about herself on the inside. When Nicole felt sad and low or hurt because others had teased her and called her cruel names, he gave her support and lifted her spirits. He praised her sun-kissed skin and told her that they would all eat their words one day. He made her feel special and important. He was the man behind the woman that Nicole was today.

"Nicole, you know you have that twelve-noon lunch meeting with Sebastian Humphries," Aaliyah said.

Nicole nodded. "Are you okay?" Aaliyah asked, noting the melancholy look on Nicole's face. Aaliyah didn't want to get in Nicole's business. But she needed her to be focused as she went through the day's highlights with her.

"Yea, I'm fine," Nicole said as her face brightened into a smile.

"Also," Aaliyah said, as she looked down into Nicole's date book, "it looks like you have that appointment at three fifteen with a George Margiano."

Nicole frowned a little, trying to figure out what that appointment was for.

"Remember? He wants you to be a guest speaker at the GCEA dinner next month."

The Greater Cleveland Entrepreneurial Association had invited Nicole to speak at a benefit dinner about the success of Tamani. Nicole felt honored for being given this invitation. She had been a guest speaker at events such as this before. The last speaking engagement was in Sacramento, California. Nicole loved it there. The warmth and the sunshine were what she missed the most. She'd grown accustomed to Cleveland's ever-changing climate, but enjoyed the thought of yearlong warm, sunny weather.

Aaliyah and Nicole sat in Nicole's office. Her office was on the second floor at the rear of her house. It had an amazing view of her property. Her beautifully maintained lawns and colorful garden looked like a perfectly framed picture through the glass of her bay window.

"You're unusually cheerful this morning," Aaliyah said, as she looked at Nicole suspiciously.

"This is a beautiful morning," Nicole replied.

Mariah was happy to see her sister, and as soon as she walked through the threshold of her doorway, she wrapped her arms around her neck, gave her a big squeeze, and kissed her on the cheek. She hadn't seen or heard from her since they were in the hospital, and she was glad to see that she was all right. She didn't complain of migraines, and she didn't speak about the seed that was growing in her belly. But she was happy to be there for her sister if she needed to talk. If that was what she wanted to do.

"Want something to eat?" Mariah asked as they sat at her kitchen table. Mariah was clearing plates and washing breakfast dishes.

"No, I haven't been too hungry lately," Fatimah answered.

"Well, you need to eat something," Mariah said, looking at her sister with concern.

Fatimah looked at her with a raised eyebrow.

Mariah didn't push it. She had leftover bacon, eggs and sausage from the breakfast she'd prepared for her family. They'd eaten, and Carl had dropped the children off to their various destinations before going off to work. So Fatimah was welcome to it.

Mariah had asked Fatimah where the kids were, and she told her they were at vacation Bible school and that they'd be going over to Granny's house later on. Fatimah said they'd been asking to go for a while and Granny said she was missing them too and that it was okay.

Fatimah was really funny acting about her children. They were very sheltered, and she carefully watched who they associated with, family included. Fatimah wouldn't even let Mariah keep her children overnight. It was rare that she'd let them visit. She claimed they acted differently when they got back home to her. As if Mariah and her family had soiled them somehow.

Mariah didn't care about Fatimah's opinions she didn't care what she had to say about her kids. But Fatimah felt that Mariah's children were too mouthy. She felt that they had way too much input in adult conversations and that they were borderline disrespectful. Mariah knew how her sister was, and as long as it didn't affect her children, then she wouldn't say anything to Fatimah about it.

"You know what, Teemah? That's a good idea. I think I'll take the kids over to Granny's too. They haven't seen their cousins in a while." Mariah smiled. "What time are you dropping them off?"

Fatimah sighed, "Don't you think that's a bit much for Granny?"

"What are you talking about?" Mariah asked with her back to her sister as she scrubbed scrambled eggs from her skillet.

"My kids, your kids. I mean that's ten kids."

"Uh-huh. My five and your five." Mariah kept her back turned and continued scrubbing. She didn't know what her sister was driving at, but she had to remind her, in case she'd forgotten, that they both had five not just her.

Fatimah sighed and shook her head. Mariah turned and looked at her.

"What?" Mariah said.

Fatimah closed her eyes and shook her head in that persnickety way that she does.

"Disrespectful," Fatimah said under her breath.

"Excuse me?" Mariah said, turning around, her hands full of soapsuds.

Fatimah doesn't respond.

"Who's disrespectful, Fatimah?"

Fatimah crossed her arms over her bosom and didn't speak.

"I thought so," Mariah said as she turned around and continued washing her pots.

Fatimah mumbled something under her breath, and Mariah turned to her sister and said, "Disrespectful? Fatimah, my children are not disrespectful."

"They most certainly are. They sit in grown folks' faces as they talk. They interject as they see fit and that oldest one," Fatimah said with a huff as she rolled her eyes up in her head.

"My baby has a name!" Mariah looked at her sister. She was so worried about her and happy to see that she was okay, and this is what she got for all of her care and concern? "Fatimah, don't come over my house talkin' 'bout my kids. My children are fine, they are very well mannered and well behaved."

"Where is your dog?" Fatimah said with arms crossed as she looked into Mariah's eyes.

Mariah squeezed her lips together tightly as if that could control her tongue. There were so many hurtful things that she could say right now.

"Fatimah, just get out," Mariah calmly said, pointing a sudsy finger toward her kitchen doorway.

"What did I say?" Fatimah said as if she was totally oblivious to what she had just insinuated.

"You are so hateful," Mariah said as she shook the soap suds off of her hands and into the kitchen sink. Mariah reached for a kitchen towel and dried her hands. She approached Fatimah as she rubbed her protruding belly with one hand and braced her aching back with the other. "Come on," Mariah said, motioning for her sister to get up. "I can't deal with you right now."

"Why are you overreacting?" Fatimah said to Mariah, laughing nervously. She was embarrassed. She wanted to kick herself. Fatimah hadn't intentionally driven all the way over to her sister's house to offend her and then be kicked out of her home.

Mariah raised her voice at her sister, "Fatimah!" Mariah grabbed the back of the chair that Fatimah was sitting in, held it firmly in her hands, and shook it. "Fatimah, I am so serious. Get out. I want you to leave." Mariah didn't not raise her voice this time. She had just gotten out of the hospital, and there was no need to have her blood up over Fatimah's evil behind.

"What?" Fatimah asked. "What did I do?" Fatimah laughed sheepishly as if she was an innocent victim of a misunderstanding. But Mariah was tired, and she wasn't laughing. She wanted Fatimah to go, and she wanted her to go now.

"You are a huge gloom. You're like a humongous rain cloud." Fatimah looked at her sister as if in shock and shook her head nervously. "I don't know why, but you're miserable and you want everyone around you miserable along with you. Well, not today. Get out."

Fatimah picked up her purse and got up out of her sister's kitchen chair.

"Mariah, I'm sorry." Fatimah's eyes softened; she seemed to be sincere, but Mariah had fallen for that wide-eyed innocent act before and had been sorely disappointed.

"Uh-huh," Mariah said as she showed Fatimah to the door. "Good-bye."

"Really, Mariah, I am. I apologize."

"Okay," Mariah said as she escorted Fatimah to the door.

"Mariah," Fatimah's voice was soft and sincere.

"Good-bye, Fatimah," Mariah said as she unbolted the door and unlocked multiple locks. "Bye." Mariah bucked her eyes at her sister as wide as she could and opened her steel security door. Fatimah exited Mariah's home like a scolded housecat.

Mariah slammed the door behind her. Fatimah could have sworn that she heard her sister call her a bitch under her breath. Fatimah couldn't blame her.

Fatimah walked down the front steps and to her car parked in Mariah's driveway. She unlocked her car door and slid inside. She was so angry with herself. She had had every intention of pouring her heart out to her sister and crying on her shoulder, but instead, she'd insulted her children and underhandedly suggested that they'd killed their beloved pet.

The one person that she felt comfortable enough to confide in, she'd alienated. Fatimah wanted to cry. She stuck the key in the ignition and began backing out of the driveway. She wanted to use her cell phone to call Mariah and apologize again and tell her that she really needed to talk. She wanted to tell Mariah that her husband had hurt her so badly that she felt that she was in constant agonizing pain. She wanted a moment to release her anguish with someone that she loved and trusted. There were things Fatimah wanted to share with her sister that hurt her from holding them inside for so long. She knew that Mariah would listen to her, embrace her, cry with her, and would never tell another living soul. But pride prevented Fatimah from calling Mariah and running back to her door. Fatimah struggled to fight back tears so hard that her eyes burned for the remainder of her ride home.

Nicole left Aaliyah to completing the rest of her duties. She knew exactly what she was going to wear for her meetings with Sebastian Humphries and George Margiano. She wore her strapless sundress and her sexy summer sandals. The shoes were gold, and the dress was hot pink with splashes of blue, yellow, and gold. She wore her large, gold, concave bracelet and her long, gold chain with one white pearl, one large gold seashell, and a smaller star pendant that dangled on the end of it. The dress was long and billowy, and it flowed as she walked. Nicole loved how it made her feel, and she looked great in it.

Nicole thought about Jeremy as she prepared for her meeting with Sebastian Humphries. Jeremy was such a sweetheart. He was modest and unassuming. The exact opposite of Darren. He wasn't a braggart, Jeremy let his talent speak for him. He flirted with Nicole and pursued her at the same time as Darren, but not quite as aggressively as Darren had. Darren had won out simple because Nicole had been too exhausted to continue to ignore his advances and eventually his persistence had worn her down.

Jeremy was about six feet tall, brown-skinned with brown eyes. He had very little facial hair and he wore his hair in a short but neatly trimmed afro. After getting to know Jeremy better, Nicole was surprised at how shy he was. He hardly seemed like the type to approach a woman, let alone actively pursue Nicole as eagerly as he had.

*   *   *

"There's a package for you Ms. Turner!" La Tika had called out as she signed for the package and closed the door behind her. Nicole's housekeeper, La Tika's had attempted to drag the large flat package wrapped in the stiff, brown paper, but it was much too heavy for her to move. "I can't move it!" La Tika said. "Don't try to move it La Tika, I'm coming." Nicole had called out to her. Nicole had imagined La Tika attempting to move it and damaging it somehow. La Tika was loud and nowhere near as professional as she needed to be, but she was very sweet and trustworthy and she could clean a house like nobody's business, so Nicole had kept her on as part of her staff. "Your painting has come," La Tika had said in her rich Indian accent.

When Nicole had seen the large package propped against the wall, she was a bit confused. "I think they sent me the wrong one." Nicole said as she approached the package. "Open it! Let's see." La Tika replied. Nicole tore open the brown paper. La Tika helped grinning, excitedly. "Oh, it's beautiful," La Tika had said as she smiled and placed her hand over her mouth. "They sent me the wrong one." Nicole said as she looked at the picture of Myra and Tatiana."

Jeremy had sent Nicole the painting of the mother and child as a gift. She'd purchased the painting of three children, a little boy and two little girls splashing in the rain for Aniyah. She'd thought that Aniyah would like that since she hadn't been able to go to the art showcase with her. It had reminded Nicole of Aniyah, Serena and Tye when they were young and she'd hoped it would remind Aniyah of that too. But that painting hadn't arrived. Instead she had been sent the painting that she had been admiring that entire evening. The painting of mother and child.

Nicole had searched for Charmaine Sanders's phone number, the woman who had hosted the art showcase.

"Hello Nicole. Great to hear from you. Did you enjoy yourself the other night?"

"Yes, I did. It was wonderful. Thank you so much for the invitation. I was really impressed."

"Yea and you weren't the only one who was impressed." Charmaine had said with a laugh.

"Oh. Did he have a good night."

"He had an awesome night. Excellent for his debut."

"Glad to hear it."

"Yea, but that's not what I'm referring to." Charmaine had chuckled and continued. "I see that you caught Mr. Darren Dunlap's eye."

"Who is that?"

"The big, tall well dressed man, that followed you around the entire evening."

"Oh, him." Nicole had answered rather unenthusiastically.

"Seems he was rather taken by you."

"Unfortunately." Nicole had replied.

"Do you know who he is?" Charmaine had asked Nicole.

"Is he a friend of yours?" Nicole had asked.

"Not really. It's ironic that you called though. Because he just called me inquiring about you."

"Well, I am not interested. I just called because the wrong painting was delivered to my house."

"Hmmm." Charmaine had replied. "I think you need to contact the artist about that one, Hun."

*　　*　　*

Nicole met with Sebastian Humphries for lunch at twelve noon as planned. Mr. Humphries was a tall light-skinned man with a nice tan. He appeared to be in his mid—to late—forties. But he looked good for his age. He looked very dapper in his perfectly tailored, sage green suit. His salt-and-pepper hair was cut low, as well as his neatly trimmed goatee and his teeth were so perfect and straight that Nicole wondered if they were his own.

"So, Ms. Turner, I'm glad you agreed to meet with me today. Before we get started, I have a few questions I have to ask you."

Nicole nodded in agreement. Nicole didn't order any food; instead, she sipped on sweet tea as he spoke. Mr. Humphries ordered a cup of coffee.

Nicole was impressed with his presentation, even though she felt as if she'd heard it before. Sebastian was very knowledgeable and well spoken. He was selling himself hard too. Nicole had already determined that she wasn't going to go with their company. But because he'd traveled so far and had gone to so much trouble to meet with her in person, she felt that she should at least give him the opportunity to try and convince her to reconsider.

"I must admit. You do have me rethinking my decision. But let me ask you, do you feel that I need an image consultant? Is that the impression that I've given you today."

Sebastian smiled as he spoke, "Well, Ms. Turner, that's a loaded question. So I'll just say this: Hiring an image consultant does not suggest that you or your company are lacking as far as professionalism is concerned. Image consulting can enhance and improve any business."

"This was a suggestion made to me by a colleague of mine, and I told him that I would consider it. It's just recently that I have been in the public eye. I have been behind the scenes of Tamani for most of its early years, and with its growing popularity, I've been kind of thrust into the forefront. So I realize why he felt the need to suggest this to me."

"You weren't insulted, were you?"

"I was at first. But Clinton knows me. He knows that I am very outspoken and no nonsense. So lovingly," she said with a smile, "he made that suggestion. Really I don't see the need for it right now. I have had quite a few interviews and speaking engagements that I've handled pretty well. I am very careful when screening new hires and have trained my employees likewise. So I don't feel the need for any workshops at this time," she said as she moved a strand of hair away from her face, tucking it behind her ear. "Professionalism and customer service is of utmost importance to me, and I think that that's reflected in my business. I honestly don't see the need to hire image consultants at this time."

"Please don't be insulted by what I'm about to say," Mr. Humphries said. Nicole nodded and braced herself. "What many people starting new businesses don't realize is that as their business grows and expands so should their mind-set. There are so many new and innovative ways to improve your business, and image consulting is only one of them. Always think improvement, with your company's growth, there should be changes made. Maybe not in the outlook, I mean as far as that's concerned every business owner's outlook is generally the same to grow and to make money. But what I'm saying is, is that I am sure the suggestion was not made as an insult to you or with your own personal image in mind. I am sure that it was made in the effort to improve a business that is already thriving." Nicole appreciated his pitch and how he tried to compliment her on the sly, but she knew that Clinton had suggested image consulting with her in mind.

Nicole had not been honest with Sebastian. Clinton was not a colleague of Nicole's. Clinton Russell was one of Nicole's oldest and dearest friends. He had known Nicole since she was eleven years old, and he knew Nicole very well. He knew about the arguments and the knock-down—drag-out fistfights she'd gotten into with her sister Fatimah. He knew about the feelings that Nicole's mother had for her, as well as other unsavory things about his friend Nicole. He was a photojournalist and he knew that with money came fame, came popularity, and he knew how the truth could destroy lives. He told her that she'd needed an image consultant in case any of those things came out. Nicole said that she didn't care, nor was she worried about what others thought about her.

Nicole made no apologies about her relationship with her mother or her sister Fatimah. She'd done nothing wrong to either of them. She had always loved Fatimah and treated her just as well as she'd treated all of her other siblings. She'd never mistreated her mother. And she gave her mother the utmost respect, even though it meant that she had to avoid her as much as possible and that she couldn't attend many of her family's social events because her mom would be present.

She couldn't explain what would cause her and Fatimah to come to blows. It wasn't unusual for Fatimah to make mean and cutting remarks to Nicole. It didn't hurt her or at least she didn't think that it did; Nicole just thought that there were some things you didn't say unless you expected to get popped in the mouth. It was sad really, because they were only one year apart and they use to be really close at one time.

Sebastian liked Nicole. He liked the way she carried herself. She was very personable, and she was easy on the eyes. He told Nicole that he was very sorry that they couldn't do business together, and he passed her his card.

"Do you mind if I call to check on you periodically? To see if you changed your mind," he said, correcting himself. He didn't want it to sound like he was hitting on a potential client.

"Sure. I don't mind."

Nicole knew she wouldn't change her mind. Sebastian Humphries suspected that Nicole wasn't interested when she didn't order anything but an iced tea. He'd paid for their drinks and walked her to her car. Nicole drove off and hadn't given him a second thought.

Aniyah had left her a message, asking her if she had time to talk. She'd said that she'd be home all day and that Nicole could stop by if she had the time. Nicole's next appointment wasn't far from Aniyah's place so she stopped by.

Aniyah's apartment was dark. The shades and curtains were drawn, and her sister came to the door, wearing an oversized T-shirt and wrapped in a throw blanket.

"Why is it so cold in here?"

"I have the air on high."

"Why are you wrapped up in this blanket?" Nicole asked as she opened up Aniyah's living room blinds. Aniyah pulled the blanket over her eyes, shielding them from the light like a vampire does with his cape. "Girl, what's the matter with you?"

Aniyah squinted, looking at her sister, then opened her eyes a bit wider, admiring her dress. "Nicci, you look cute. I like that dress. Ooh," she said, looking down at Nicole's feet.

"Those shoes are so cute."

"What's the matter with you?" Nicole asked again, frowning at Aniyah.

"Nothin'. Just sleepy."

"Well, what did you call me over here for?" Nicole slung her keys and her oversized bag on the couch and then sat down beside it.

Aniyah sat down next to Nicole as she bundled herself up in her blanket. "I don't know, I was a little down when I called. I'm better now," Aniyah lied.

Nicole could read her sisters like a book. Some were easier to read than others. She looked at Aniyah, and she didn't say a word. Nicole knew that something was wrong; she'd seen her like this before. She watched Aniyah as she crossed her legs and sat on the couch facing Nicole. She was wearing oversized socks that sagged at the ankles. It was the middle of the summer, and Aniyah was dressed like it was wintertime. She pulled the blanket tighter around her shoulders as she shivered from the air conditioning. Nicole put the back of her hand on her sister's nose. It was ice cold.

"Aniyah," Nicole said, shaking her head.

"Huh?"

"Why do you hafto act crazy when you start feeling down? Did you invite me over here to turn off your air conditioning?" Aniyah didn't say anything. "How did your date go yesterday?"

Aniyah wanted to tell Nicole that it wasn't a date, but thought that she didn't like the way that sounded, considering that she'd slept with him when the night had ended.

"Fine." Aniyah answered.

"Did you work that dress?" Nicole asked with a smile.

"Yea, I worked that dress all right. I worked it right off my body and onto the floor." Aniyah thought to herself.

But instead, she smiled and said, "Yea, Nicci, I worked that dress."

"I knew you would," Nicole said as she smiled at Aniyah and gave her a wink.

Aniyah didn't say anything more, and Nicole didn't ask her anything more. Nicole told her about the art showcase next weekend and invited

Aniyah to go with her. Aniyah enjoyed attending events with Nicole. She always had a blast, and Nicole thought the exposure did wonders for Aniyah's self-esteem. She was Nicole Turner's beautiful younger sister, and she'd smile bashfully when people told her so. Nicole told Aniyah that she'd help her pick out something special for the event.

Nicole turned down the air conditioner, and Aniyah was talking and smiling and laughing before she knew it. Aniyah had thrown the blanket off her shoulders and was up talking excitedly about next Saturday. Aniyah wanted to confide in her sister about the other night. She wanted to tell her about the mixed emotions she was having. But she didn't say anything. Instead, she laughed and talked with her sister as if nothing ever happened.

Aniyah was glad that she'd asked Nicole to come over. She felt so much better, and for at least a little while, she didn't think about the predicament she'd gotten herself into.

"Have you heard from Fatimah?" Aniyah asked.

"I tried to call her earlier this morning, to see if she felt any better. But I couldn't reach her," Nicole answered.

"Neither did I," said Aniyah.

"I didn't really think anything of it," Nicole replied.

"Yea, Fatimah can be a trip," Aniyah said.

"Fatimah's got something goin' on that she don't wanna talk about," Nicole said as she winked and smiled at her sister, indicating that she knew that she had something going on that she didn't want to talk about either.

Nicole looked at the clock on Aniyah's living room wall. It seemed to be ticking louder than usual. And time was really flying by as if affected by the loud ticking of the clock. She'd be leaving soon, and she wanted to leave her sister excited and upbeat.

"You are gonna have a ball next weekend. Those art showcases are always very lively and very interesting. Who knows you might even see something there you like."

"That art is way too expensive. I could never afford it."

"I wasn't talking about the art." Nicole gave her sister a little wink and a smile, and then she was off to the bathroom. Nicole took her big ole hot-pink Chanel bag with her. Aniyah's bathroom counter was cluttered, but it was clean. Nicole knew that Aniyah didn't use half the stuff that she kept on the vanity, but there everything was, all in the way. Nicole fluffed her hair with her fingers and freshened up her lipstick and played with her lashes a bit. They were her own, and they were long. Sometimes, they'd get in the way or would fall into her eyes. She absolutely hated that feeling, and she hated removing anything from her eyes. Anything touching her eyeball really freaked her out, so tending to her eyelashes were part of her regular daily-maintenance regimen.

Nicole wasn't in any way suggesting that her sister pick up a man at the art showcase. But Nicole felt that Aniyah needed to practice and perfect her flirting skills. She believed it helped her build her self-esteem. Nicole also knew that Aniyah felt that these wealthy and affluent men were out of her league. Nicole wanted her to know that no man was out of her league. Nicole didn't have anything against Nate. Nicole wasn't suggesting that Aniyah should find a man better than Nate. But Nicole wanted Aniyah to know that she could do better than Nate if she ever wanted to.

Fatimah thought Nicole was a troublemaker and a shit starter, but Nicole simply loved her sisters and she encouraged them to raise their standards. She raised hers, and Nicole didn't want anything less for her sisters than she would want for herself. It was true that Nicole was unapologetically promiscuous, but she didn't encourage her sisters to be. She didn't flaunt her lifestyle. They never associated with any of the men she slept with. The only way that they had an inkling of it was that Fatimah announced it to everyone like she was a town herald. And her facts were always wrong.

When confronted by her sisters about Fatimah's accusations, Nicole simply said, "I am a single woman." It didn't really answer their question, but they knew not to ask her again. So everyone assumed that she was sexually indiscriminate, and because she never denied it, everyone believed it to be true. But Nicole didn't give a damn what anyone thought because as far as she was concerned, she was happy and she was very sexually satisfied.

When Nicole exited the bathroom, she saw that all of the blinds were open. Aniyah had changed her clothes and combed her hair. Nicole smiled at Aniyah, and Aniyah smiled back. Nicole was happy to see her sister in better spirits. She wanted to say, "My work here is done," but she just hugged Aniyah and gave her a kiss on the cheek as Aniyah handed her keys to her.

"Well, they canceled me for my double today. So my vacation starts today."

"Fatimah and Mariah are on vacation this week too."

"Yea. I can't wait for Serena to get here."

"I'm surprised she hasn't been calling us. She gets so excited and anxious when it's time to come home," Nicole said.

"Maybe she's maturing," Aniyah said. Then Nicole and Aniyah looked at each other and busted out laughing.

"I can't believe baby doll will be twenty-one on Saturday."

"I know. It snuck up on us. I'm gonna stop over Granny's house, then I'm gonna check on Mariah and Fatimah, make sure they're okay."

"Okay. Well, keep me posted."

Nicole headed to her next appointment eager to see what the GCEA had planned for the evening. Nicole had been the talk of the town here lately, and she was eating it up. Everyone wanted to hear what Nicole had to say. Nicole was a private person; she didn't care much for the popularity or the possible notoriety that might come with it. But she loved Tamani. She loved talking about it, and she delighted in the success of it. It made her proud.

She met Mr. Margiano at a quaint bistro on the upper west side. The Bistro boasted a plethora of savory dishes. Nicole had heard great things about it, but had never been there before. She liked the dark shellacked wood and the stiffly, starched, white linen napkins. It was filled with the scents of roasted chicken and seasoned potatoes in addition to other scents she couldn't readily identify. The air smelled so delicious, and the food looked delicious too. The presentations were beautiful.

Mr. Margiano arrived before Nicole. A hostess showed her to his table, and he stood with hands outstretched and invited Nicole to sit down. George had a nice smile. He was a big man, clean shaven, with dark features, and he had thick, dark hair. Mr. Margiano's navy suit jacket was draped across the back of his chair. There was an open folder sitting on the table in front of him. He closed it as Nicole sat down. A faux-leather-covered menu was placed in front of her. The cover was a vibrant red. It was embossed with the words The Bistro on the cover in black, and the letters were trimmed in gold. Nicole traced the letters with her slender fingers before looking inside.

"This is really nice," Nicole said to Mr. Margiano.

"Yes. My wife Connie and I love this place," he said, looking around the restaurant.

"You hungry?"

She smiled at Mr. Margiano. She wanted to say that she was starving, but she nodded instead.

Mr. Margiano was very excited to meet Nicole. He told her that the GCEA really appreciated her taking the time to speak with them. And he thanked her for accepting the GCEA's invitation as guest speaker at their upcoming dinner. Nicole was quite flattered.

Mr. Margiano was a wide man, and his girth prevented him from sitting comfortably in front of the table. Nicole wanted to scoot her chair backward and pull the table toward herself. But the table was too heavy, and she didn't want to embarrass him; she figured if he really got too uncomfortable, then he would speak up. He breathed heavily and wiped sweat from his brow with the back of his hand as he spoke. The restaurant was pleasantly cool, but Mr. Margiano continued to sweat profusely. But it didn't seem to bother him. Nicole tried not to stare as the sweat rolled from his hairline as he wiped it out of his eyes with his white handkerchief. She tried to look away from the dampness on his collar caused by his perspiration on his neck. But she found it very distracting. So she smiled and averted her eyes.

The one thing that kept Nicole from staring so hard was his very interesting story about his family history. He told her of his grandfather and his great uncle and how they came to this country as poor Italian immigrants, who settled in Cleveland and started lucrative family-owned businesses, leaving a legacy for their families. He spoke about how most, but not all, of his family still live in Cleveland. Although, he has a brother that is a lawyer and one that is a doctor that live on the West Coast. He and his elder brother along with their sons still live in Cleveland and run their family-owned businesses, and they continued to thrive.

They ordered their meals, and as they waited, Mr. Margiano spoke with Nicole about what made this particular event so special. He stated, "We are especially proud of our business owners who are Cleveland born and bred and who currently live in the city of Cleveland."

Nicole smiled. "Mr. Margiano, I don't currently live in the city of Cleveland."

"I realize that Ms. Turner and I didn't intend to put my foot in my mouth." They both laughed.

Mr. Margiano went on to say that he was looking forward to hearing what she had to say about growing up in Cleveland and attending Cleveland Public Schools and what Cleveland meant to her in general. He told her that they basically wanted her to incorporate Cleveland into her speech about Tamani. Mr. Margiano had a prepared list of questions to ask Nicole. He needed to verify her contact information, emergency numbers, as well as her home and e-mail addresses. He asked if they could take photographs of her along with a host of other questions.

Nicole and George talked and ate. He really enjoyed his food. He talked about how he loved this place; he claimed that he could taste the freshness of the ingredients in every bite. Nicole's meal was delicious too. Nicole ordered roasted chicken, with roasted red-skinned potatoes and a side of bread crumb encrusted parmesan zucchini and summer squash casserole sans the marinara sauce. Mr. Margiano recommended the casserole; he said it was simply scrumptious, and it was. It smelled delicious and it looked even better, but Nicole knew that she wouldn't be able to finish it all so she asked for a to-go container before she even got started and packed all but about a third of her meal in the container. Nicole tried to calculate how many miles on the treadmill and on what speed it would take to burn this heavy meal off, as George ordered a to-go meal for his wife Connie.

Mr. Margiano thought that Nicole was a charming young woman, and as he walked her to her car, he told her how fantastic it was to finally meet her. He told her that he would be calling her frequently to keep her updated. Then Mr. Margiano said, as he smiled and leaned over into Nicole's passenger-door window, "Seems you have an admirer, Ms. Turner." Nicole looked at George bewildered. He smiled as he discreetly looked over at the car he was referring to. Nicole followed his eyes and saw Darren sitting conspicuously on the other side of the street in a car she didn't recognize. He looked angry, not to mention the fact that his nose was slightly off center, an indication that she had broken his nose.

Darren was alive unfortunately. So much for wishful thinking. She wondered how long he had been following her. She'd hoped she had kept him entertained.

"Someone you know? Mr. Margiano asked. Darren hadn't done anything, but there was something about Darren that had him concerned for her safety.

"No," Nicole said. It was someone she *thought* she knew.

Nicole checked her voice-mail messages as she waited for Mr. Margiano to drive off. She had several missed calls. None were from Jermaine or Don. Fatimah hadn't called her either. Nicole wondered if her sister would have headed over her house as quickly as she had done if she'd suspected that something was wrong with her. Nicole thought she knew the answer, and she didn't let it bother her. Fatimah had been like that for years, and it would take more than one incident to change her. Nicole doubted that Fatimah would rage a thunderstorm at the slightest thought that she was in danger or in harm's way. But Nicole would do it again if she had to. Because whether Fatimah liked it or not, that was her sister.

Nicole looked over at Darren and made eye-contact with him. She balled up her fist, pretended to punch herself in those nose, then pointed at him and laughed. She thought she saw steam coming out of his ears. Nicole decided that if Darren wanted to follow her; then she would gladly accommodate him. Nicole made a U-turn in the street. Darren pulled off behind her. She led him all the way to first district police station. He left when Nicole parked and went inside. She didn't file a police report or anything. She knew that there was nothing they could do. She could and would handle Darren on her own and in her own way.

It had been two days since her altercation with Darren. She may not have mortally injured him, but she had left him to stew in his own juices for a while. Nicole figured that the phone calls would start up again soon. Since he had made him self-known. And she'd be ready for them.

Aniyah left a message on Nicole's voice mail telling her how much she liked Granny's rental car and that Granny had been riding around in her shades in the white Impala all day. Nicole could hear other people in the background, and she could tell that Granny's house was full. It was good to hear that Aniyah was feeling better. Nicole could hear it in her sister's voice.

Nicole called Fatimah and got no answer. Not even the kids had picked up the phone. She'd called several times earlier, and no one had answered. Mariah had called Nicole too and had left a message for Nicole to call her back when she had time. Her message was "I spoke with your sister. Call me back when you get a chance."

Nicole called Mariah back as she ran a few errands. Mariah told her about Fatimah and how earlier she had to tell her to leave. She didn't tell her more than that though she didn't have to. Everybody knew how Fatimah was. Mariah said she'd stopped by Granny's house to drop the kids off and that the kids were still there, Fatimah's children too. Mariah told her sister that Tye's baby boy was there too. Mariah said that he was so cute and getting so big.

Nicole smiled. She liked the thought of seeing her family all together. Mama wasn't there, so she didn't have to worry about her stares of contempt. Fatimah wasn't there, so she didn't have to worry about dealing with the funk that she was in and she'd get to see all her nieces and nephews. Especially Fatimah's children, Nicole didn't get to see them too often.

Nicole made it to her grandmother's house at about seven thirty that night. Granny's house was packed. There were cars parked in the streets and in the driveway. Aniyah was still there. Nicole could see her car parked in the driveway. Big Daddy's car was there and a few other cars that Nicole didn't recognize. Nicole parked and approached the house. It seemed as if every light in the house was on, and she could hear the television and the music playing before she even got to the door. She knocked on the screen and then stepped in. Granny didn't have a security screen door. She had an old-fashioned wood-framed screen door. The kind that you have to replace the screens with the storm windows for wintertime.

As soon as Nicole stepped in, everyone said, "Hey," almost in unison. They stood to greet her and came over to give her hugs and kisses. Her oldest niece eased her sunglasses out of her hands and ran off to try them on. Great-granny, otherwise known as GG, sat in her chair. Her very own recliner chair. Nicole had purchased it for her years ago, back when GG could get around with just her cane. GG had picked it out herself. Nicole had told her not to worry about the cost, and GG didn't. She was sitting in the top of the line remote-controlled recliner chair, and she loved it.

GG was sitting in front of the TV with her glasses on, feet up, totally relaxed, with remote in hand. When she saw Nicole, she had the biggest smile on her face. Nicole watched as GG slowly let the feet of the recliner down. She kneeled down to hug GG, and GG planted a big wet kiss on her cheek. GG's silver gray hair was curly, and she wore it in three thick braids, one at the top and two in the back. The top braid was tucked, and the two back braids were beginning to unravel. Nicole stood and braided the loose ends as GG rubbed her arm. GG didn't talk much; she just smiled a lot. She'd be so quiet that it was easy to forget that she was even there, until one of the children would trip over her feet and she'd reach out smiling, trying to brace their fall.

Nicole walked into the kitchen to say hello to everyone. Granny hugged Nicole around the neck like she hadn't seen Nicole in years. Nicole kissed her on the cheek. Granny's breath smelled like coconut rum and pineapple juice. Granny told her that Aniyah had fixed her a drink and that it was delicious. Big Daddy, Granny's beau, sat at the kitchen table. Granny sipped her drink and rubbed Big Daddy's back as he sat at the table, eating fried chicken, green beans, and rice. She smiled at Big Daddy as if she was young and in love as she rubbed his back. They were trying to get a bid whist game started, Tye and Aniyah didn't want to play so Auntie Cookie and Uncle Clyde were on their way over from across the street to play.

"Baby, you hungry?" Granny asked.

Granny made the best fried chicken, and when she made it, she made a lot of it. There were peach cobbler and chocolate cake for dessert if anybody wanted any. The kids played all through the house keeping up noise. But that was the way she liked it. She enjoyed having her family around her. She like seeing all her babies together.

Granny pulled out a chair and patted the back for Nicole to sit. Nicole washed her hands and dried them; then she sat her purse on the floor and sat down.

"Fatimah stopped by here an dropped the kids off. She was in a very funky mood. I told her, 'Cain't nobody help you if you don't want to talk about it.'" Granny stopped talking to Nicole briefly to chastise her grandchildren. "You all stay out of GG's room. I tole y'all to stay outta there!" Four children came running out of the room.

The children were so happy to see each other. They were able to talk and laugh and play together and just have a good time. Aniyah was sitting on Granny's deck on her cell phone. She hadn't seen Nicole when she came in. Tye came down the backstairs and into the kitchen, holding his baby boy. Tye's little boy was so fat. He had on a T—shirt that wasn't long enough to cover his little buddha belly and his cheeks were so big and saggy. He was sucking on a chicken drummette that he held tightly in his chubby little hands.

Nicole stood and smiled and held her arms out to her brother, Tye, so that he could pass the baby to her. "Hey, Nic," Tye said as he kissed Nicole on the cheek. He passed the baby to her, and his little T-shirt rose up like a belly shirt.

"Tye, wassup wit da shirt?" Nicole laughed. "It's not even covering his belly." Nicole held her heavy nephew with one hand and pulled the T-shirt down with the other.

"Dat shirt is too small for dat baby. Tye put it on him 'cuz of what it says on da front. Did you read it?"

The front of the T-shirt read Yung-Ty.

"You see it got da baby's nickname on it. Dat's why Tye put it on." Granny looked at Tye and shook her head.

"Yung-Ty," Nicole read.

"Yea, dat's my boy."

The baby took the drummette out of his mouth and held it in his hands. He stared at Nicole with his little mouth open. As his head bobbed slightly like a bobble-head doll.

"Give Auntie a kiss," Tye said. The baby leaned forward and gave Nicole a sloppy wet opened-mouth kiss on her cheek.

"Awww," Nicole said as she smiled at him and gave him a kiss on the cheek. It made a big smacking sound.

Granny grabbed a napkin and handed it to Nicole, and Nicole wiped the drool away.

"Baby, that dress is so pretty. Let me take him 'fore he mess up dat pretty dress."

"It's okay, Granny. I'm fine." She kissed the baby on his forehead and then on his little fat greasy cheek.

"Tye, go upstairs and check on the two little ones," Granny said. Fatimah's and Mariah's two youngest children were asleep on opposite ends of Granny's bed. Tye went up to check on them.

Granny took the drummette from the baby's hand and he started to cry, but Granny gave him a look and he quickly shut his mouth. Nicole laughed. Granny chucked the drummette in the trash and then used a clean dishtowel to wipe off the baby's hands and mouth. He whined a little but didn't take his eyes off Nicole.

"Baby, let me take him. He's gonna get that dress all messed up." Nicole had the baby's little greasy handprints on her shoulder, but she didn't mind. Granny took the baby from Nicole and when Tye came down to tell Granny that the little ones were still sleeping, he took his son back upstairs with him.

Granny was jazzy, and she stayed young and vibrant. She had to, because as she would always say, she had "so much work left to do." Everybody took such good care of her because she had taken such good care of everybody else. She'd raised Tye from a baby, and she took Nicole in when her mama had kicked her out and she had nowhere else to go. She'd outlived two husbands and was working on a third (Big Daddy wasn't her husband, but she'd said he was as close to one as she was going to get). And she didn't have a gray hair on her head, and she had all of her own teeth.

She was the original Headturner. She had a natural switch in her hips that had everybody talkin'. She had a bad-ass body for an old lady, and she was still turning heads after all these years. She was beautiful inside and out, and at seventy-two years old, she didn't look a day older than fifty-two. She had survived an abusive first husband and a philandering second husband. And after years of infidelity and abuse, she could finally say that she was content. She didn't deny that she wanted the company of a man; that was where Big Daddy came in, but she most certainly didn't need one. Big Daddy was a good man, and he made her happy. That was the only reason Granny kept him around. They weren't married and they didn't live together, but he was her man and she loved him.

Auntie Cookie and Uncle Clyde came in. They heard Uncle Clyde before the screen door slammed shut. Aniyah heard him and came into the kitchen. He had a loud, boisterous laugh and a smoker's cough, and his eyes were always beet red, as if he'd been drinking. Once one of the children had asked him why his eyes were always so red, and before anybody could scold them, he'd answered, "That comes from rough livin', baby, rough livin," then he busted into one of the laughs he was so famous for.

Uncle Clyde was so much fun to have around; it was like having a comedian in the family. He was always so upbeat and he was the life of the party and everyone loved having him around.

"Hey, Nicci. I thought I heard your voice. What time did you get here?" Aniyah said.

"I haven't been here long," Nicole answered.

"You see the baby?" Aniyah said.

"Yea, I saw him," Nicole said with a smile.

"Isn't he big?"

"Yea, he has gotten so big."

"Yea, really. What is Jeanette feeding him?" Aniyah said.

"I don't know, but he is huge. But he is so cute. He looks just like Tye when he was a baby give or take a few pounds."

Nicole could hear Auntie Cookie and Uncle Clyde talkin' to GG and the kids. They seemed happy to see the children, and they could hear Uncle Clyde picking with the kids. Auntie Cookie was Granny's best friend. They were like sisters. When she married her brother Clyde, it made Granny the happiest woman in the world to actually be able to call her best friend her family, her sister. Auntie Cookie walked in the kitchen first and hugged and greeted everybody.

"I ain't seen you girls in a long time. Y'all just as pretty as y'all can be." Auntie cookie smiled and pushed up her glasses to get a better look at Aniyah and Nicole.

"Well, Delores," she said talkin' to Granny, "I thought you needed me and Clyde to play, but you got yo' two girls here. You don't need me and Clyde." Auntie Cookie laughed at herself so hard that her eyes closed. Nicole thought she looked cute when she laughed like that.

"Girl, sit yo' butt down here," Granny said as she pulled out a kitchen chair. "You ain't 'bout to git outta dis game dat easy." Granny and Auntie Cookie laughed and laughed as if granny had just said the funniest thing. Nicole and Aniyah looked at each other like "Did we miss something?" But it wasn't what Granny had said that had brought a smile to their faces. It was just being in each other's company. Those old gals loved each other. They were true blue friends, who had had a long history together. They had shared so many stories and so many memories that they could keep the family entertained for hours.

Sometimes, granny would get that faraway look in her eyes and say, "We been through so much together, her and I," and they would both get a little misty eyed. Nicole and her sisters used to wonder what it was they'd been through, what secrets they'd shared. But Granny would always say to them, "Treasure a true friend. They are worth their weight in gold. You can't pick your family, but you have a choice who your friends are."

Uncle Clyde came into the kitchen and gave Big Daddy a friendly smack on the back. Big Daddy smiled and held out a greasy hand to Uncle Clyde. Uncle Clyde kissed his sister on the cheek, saying, "Hey, Sis," and gave both of his nieces, each big bear hugs, lifting them off of the black and white tiled floor.

"Hey, Uncle Clyde," Nicole and Aniyah said. Uncle Clyde smiled wide, showing off gapped spaces where his molars use to be. Granny offered Auntie Cookie and Uncle Clyde a plate as she topped off Big Daddy's chicken wings.

"Yea, Dee. You can make me a plate," Uncle Clyde said. She asked Uncle Clyde what he wanted as if she was a waitress taking his order, and Uncle Clyde answered, "What cha got?"

Granny made Uncle Clyde a plate and piled it high with everything, but dessert. Everyone sat in the kitchen around Granny's old gray formica table. Nicole sat in an old chrome-and-vinyl step stool that Granny had had since before Nicole was born. The seat was a little cracked, but it was comfortable. Granny, Big Daddy, Auntie Cookie, and Uncle Clyde sat at the kitchen table in the black, high-backed vinyl chairs with the chrome legs. The table's design was ugly Nicole thought. Who would have thought to design a gray kitchen table, trimmed in black flowers. She thought about Granny making bread in this kitchen and kneading homemade dough at this table, and then the table didn't seem as ugly.

Aniyah sat on a tall, black bar stool that she swiveled from side to side as she sat. When her cell phone rang, Aniyah hopped off the stool and went back out to the deck and slid down in one of the deck chairs as she talked on the phone.

Nicole enjoyed talking to "Granny and them," but she wanted to spend some time with her nieces and nephews. Nicole knew that as long as grown-ups were in the kitchen talking, then it was off limits to the kids and they stayed out. Nicole excused herself and went into the living room. All of the children were in the living room. Fatimah's and Mariah's toddlers were awake and sitting on the floor with their siblings. The four oldest children sat on the couch with Tye. Yung-Ty sat on Leah's lap, and they all sat in front of the TV. They were quiet too. Nicole assumed it was from pure exhaustion. They had been going nonstop since she got there. They were in relax mode now.

The kids made room for her on the couch. Nicole looked over at GG; she was in her chair knocked out. When Nicole sat down on the couch, Lana sat on Nicole's feet and leaned back on Nicole's legs as if she was sitting in a chair. They were really into their television program, and they didn't say a word. Even Tye was glued to the TV screen. The children gravitated over to their aunt. They missed her too. Before she knew it, they were lying and leaning on her. She liked how they loved her. She didn't have any children of her own. She wasn't physically able to. She didn't think that she would if she could.

Lana was the first one out. She fell asleep on Nicole's legs. One by one, they dropped like dominoes. The oldest ones sat on the couch, fighting sleep. Even Tye struggled to stay awake as his namesake lay sleeping on his chest. It was only nine o'clock. Aniyah was still on the deck on her cell phone, and "Granny and them" had finally gotten their bid whist game going. They were having a good old time. Nicole eased her way off the couch. The front door was open, and the screen door was unlocked.

Nicole didn't recognize the car but saw the blinding headlights as the car drove up the apron of the driveway. When her mother stepped in the door, she felt it was her cue to leave, but she figured if her mama hadn't wanted to see her, then she wouldn't have stopped by. Mama knew that she was there. She could see her car parked outside.

Nicole was standing when Mama came in. She started to speak to her, but Mama turned her head and did not acknowledge Nicole's presence, so she didn't open her mouth. Mama came in loud and made sure she woke up everybody in the house. She even startled GG. She took Yung-Ty away from his daddy and woke him up kissing him all over his face and neck, and the baby started to cry.

"Aww, Nana's baby," Nicole's mother said as she continued kissing him on his cheek. The baby held his arms out to his sides and blinked and trembled as if he thought he was going to fall. Mama had picked him up too fast. He cried with his bottom lip stuck out, and he held out his arms toward his daddy.

"Mama, you woke him up," Tye said frowning.

"Hush up, boy. I just wanted to see ma widda suga," she said as she gave the baby one last kiss before handing him over to Tye. One by one, she went through kissing on her groggy grandbabies, waking them up as she went along. GG went back to sleep with no problem at all. Mama kissed GG on her forehead, and she didn't even flinch. But she walked right past Nicole and into the kitchen to see the rest of the family. She didn't speak to her. It was as if Nicole wasn't even there.

Granny was surprised to see her daughter. Mama went around the table, kissing everyone. Granny could smell the liquor on her breath. Mama had toned down her drinking for a few months, but had started picking up where she'd left off since the announcement of her decision to move to Baltimore.

"Ooh girl! Who's drivin'?" She frowned, looking her daughter in the eyes. She definitely smelled as if she'd been tossing back a few. Tangie didn't answer her mother. It didn't matter who was driving because Cleo was waiting in the car, but he was just as fucked up as she was.

Aniyah heard her mother come in. She was still on the phone. She hugged and kissed her mother, frowned from the overwhelming smell of liquor, then headed back out to the deck. Granny ignored Tangie as she laughed about nothing and talked in her half-slurred, drunken gibberish. Granny was somewhere between embarrassed and ashamed, but this was her daughter and this had been her daughter for many years. She was either a happy drunk or a confrontational drunk, and right now she was happy. Granny hated seeing her like this, and if her babies weren't there, she would have cursed her out and told her to take her ass upstairs and sleep it off. But right now she wanted her to leave. Just go. Tangie went over to the stove to make herself a plate.

"Tangie, what chu you doing back there?"

"I'm making me a plate, Mama."

"Girl, go on. Sit down somewhere. I'll make you a plate." Granny put her cards face down on the table and stood to fix Tangie a plate. She sighed as she put her daughter's food in a large storage container, to go. Everyone at the table was silent. The kitchen was still, except for the nothingness that was spilling out of Tangie's mouth. She wasn't stumbling drunk, but she wasn't far from it. Granny packed Tangie's food and put it in a plastic grocery bag, and she felt guilty as she sent her on her way.

Tangie stepped over her grandbabies and headed to the door. Nicole had gone to the bathroom and was walking down the stairs and back into the living room. But before Mama could open the front door and step outside, they heard a loud noise that sounded like firecrackers, coming from outside. Pop! Pop! Pop!

"What the fuck!?" Mama said.

"Get down!" Tye yelled. All the children were lying on the ground. Tye laid his son on the floor, and the baby began to cry. Tye swiftly but carefully grabbed GG by her legs and slid her to the floor, carefully guarding her head. The children began to cry. Big Daddy and Uncle Clyde were on the kitchen floor with their women, shielding them with their large body's. Nicole had run down the stairs and knocked her mother to the floor.

Mama was mad.

"What the fuck?!" Mama repeated.

Pop! Pop! Pop! Again. Then the distinctive sound of glass shattering. The next thing they heard was the screeching of rubber against pavement as a car peeled off down the street.

"Stay the fuck down!" Tye said as Zenobia tried to raise her head to look around.

"Everybody okay in there?" Uncle Clyde yelled from the kitchen. Granny and Big Daddy were talking over top of one another, both with the same message, "Stay down!"

"Get the fuck offa me!" Tangie said to Nicole, but Nicole ignored her and just pressed her body harder into her mother's back pinning her to the living room floor.

"Aniyah!" Granny yelled.

Aniyah didn't answer.

"Aniyah!" Granny yelled. Her voice was panicky, and it was shaking. Nicole could tell her grandmother was crying.

"I'm okay, Granny! I'm down!" Aniyah yelled from the deck.

Nicole and Tye were the first to raise their heads. Aniyah had called 911 on her cell phone, and as the dust settled, she crawled back into the house. The security door slammed hard behind her.

"Everybody okay?" Aniyah asked, still on all fours, crawling into the kitchen.

"Yea. Everbody okay in there?" Uncle Clyde asked.

"Okay in here," Tye answered.

Startled children lay on the floor, babies cried, and the older children lifted their heads out of curiosity.

"Get the fuck off me!" Tangie said as she gave her daughter a push. Nicole got off the floor and let her mother stagger to her feet.

Nicole walked out the front door to see the extent of the damage. When she stepped onto the front porch, she saw that Granny's neighbors were forming a crowd outside. Nicole didn't walk toward the crowd; she walked around the front porch, examining the outside of Granny's house. No broken windows as far as she could see. When she stepped off the porch, she could see Cleo sitting in the driver's seat of Mama's Cadillac. He was scared shitless.

"What the fuck just happened?" he said, shaking and staring straight ahead, as he clutched the steering wheel.

Nicole walked right passed him, totally unaware of what he had just said. Something of more interest had caught her attention. She slowly approached the growing crowd, surrounding her car. She felt like she was having an outer-body experience as she walked toward it. Not knowing what it was she was about to see. She had no idea what condition her car was in. Too many people in the way. She could hear off in the distance; more family members had started filing out of Granny's house. Granny included. But she couldn't see anything, but the crowd surrounding her car. It seemed as though it took her an eternity to get to them, but when she did, the crowd parted like the Red Sea.

Bullet holes. Her heart was beating like a bass drum. She could feel it pumping through her chest. Her carotid throbbed as if it were about to burst. Bullets holes. They'd pierced the front and the rear windshield. There were bullet holes in the driver's side door and one in the driver's side window. One lone bullet had pierced the driver's seat precisely at the point where Nicole thought her heart would have been, had she been sitting in the driver's seat. The streetlights shone down like a spotlight on

Nicole's car and on the bits of broken glass on the driver's seat, making them sparkle like diamonds.

"Man, they fucked that car up!" one onlooker said.

"Look at how the bullets went right through the seat. Got-damn! Good thing nobody was in there," another said.

"Day-um! Is that her shit?" another neighbor said.

Nicole stared at her car in disbelief. So many questions flooded her mind. She knew the Who, the What, the When, and the Where, but she didn't know the Why. She didn't want to reflect on the possible messages this man could be trying to convey to her. That was so unimportant right now. She didn't feel threatened or afraid as she should have. She felt pure, unadulterated fury. She was hot. She felt like she was a pot about to boil over. How dare he bring this shit to her grandmother's house. To the house where her family was.

Nicole crossed her arms, brows furrowed and lips clenched together tightly. She thought hard about the Why. What would make him do this? Why would he do this to her? Then a smile spread across her face. She thought about the explaining he had to do when his wife came home and found him lying on the ground with his ego as well as his manhood bruised. She smiled picturing him stammering trying to explain what the fuck had happened to leave him lying in the driveway physically and mentally wounded. She smiled and saw her fractured reflection in the shattered driver's side window of her Porsche, and she thought, "Yeah, you got me, Darren, but now it's my turn."

Chapter 14

ANIMOSITY

When the police arrived, they wanted to talk to everybody, but especially to the owner of the candy apple-red Porsche Boxster. The one with the holes in the door, the window, and the windshields.

Two units were dispatched to the scene. They questioned potential witnesses before questioning Nicole and her family. Cleo had given his report to the officers from the inside of Mama's Cadillac. He had pissed himself and didn't want to get out of the car. He said he hadn't gotten a good look, but that this big guy had driven around the block once; then when he came back the second time, he drove up slowly, fired a shot at Nicole's back windshield, then stopped next to Nicole's car, and started firing.

Cleo stressed the fact that the culprit hadn't driven by and randomly shot into the night, but that he'd stopped next to Nicole's vehicle and had intentionally aimed directly at it and started shooting. The description given was Darren's. Cleo had described a big man, light-skinned and tall. Cleo hadn't told the police officers that it was Darren, but he'd tell everybody else that later. He said he didn't get a good look at him because he was too busy ducking down, pissing on himself. The police could smell the liquor on Cleo, but didn't bother him about it. The events that had just occurred had sobered him up for the moment.

The police asked a bunch of useless questions, Nicole thought. She didn't volunteer any information about Darren though. They asked Nicole if the descriptions given sounded like anybody she knew, and she answered, "Yes." She knew that it was Darren's ass. But when they asked if she had any idea why he might have done this, she said she had absolutely no idea. One of the detectives took pictures at the scene; they gave her a card with her case number on it and told her they would be in touch. Her car was towed away, and she watched as her Porsche sat on the flatbed tow truck and was driven off into the distance.

Nicole didn't recognize the description that Cleo and the neighbors had given of the car that the suspect drove. It was a late model Cutlass. Darren didn't own one that she knew of, but then again, Darren was full of surprises.

Granny was tearful; Auntie Cookie was pretty shaken up, but she wasn't crying. Tangie was livid.

"No, Mama! I am serious! She brought this shit to your house, Mama. *She* did," Tangie said, pointing at Nicole. "We could have all been killed. Any one of those babies in that house could have been killed."

"Stop talkin' nonsense, Tangela! This is not Nicole's fault. She's a victim here too!"

"Victim hell!"

Aniyah stood next to her sister in shock. She was shaking. One of her biggest nightmares about her sister's ex was coming true. Nicole may not have cared about his message to her, but Aniyah did and it scared her to death.

"Nicci, you need to get a restraining order against that man! He's crazy! He was clearly trying to tell you something!"

Nicole rubbed her sister's back reassuringly, and then she said one of the stupidest things Aniyah had ever heard her sister say, "He's not that crazy, he's just acting crazy."

"An act? Nicole, wake up? He just shot up your car. Your car was just towed away as evidence. He just shot at your car!" Aniyah said repeating the most obvious indicator that the man was crazy.

"You're not protecting him, are you?" Aniyah said.

"Hell no," Nicole said, frowning in disgust.

"He is fucking crazy! If he could do this, imagine what else he could do. Nicole, are you listening to me?" Aniyah recognized that look on her sister's face; it was as if what she was saying was going in one ear and out the other. "Nicole?" Aniyah said, snapping her fingers in her sister's face.

"Yes, Aniyah,' Nicole said. "I'm listening."

"No, you're not."

Retaliation was what had brought Darren to Nicole's grandmother's house. Nicole had humiliated him and had raised a lot of difficult questions for Darren to answer to his wife. He had to let Nicole know that it was not over. She did not call the shots; he did. Literally. He had gone from wanting to hide Nicole from his wife to simply not giving a fuck. He was married sure enough, but when he confessed it to Nicole, he was trying to come clean because he loved her and he wanted to be honest. Of, course, he had no intention of leaving his wife, but why should that have mattered to Nicole? She didn't give him the impression that she'd wanted to get married to him or to anybody else for that matter. Their relationship was just perfect the way that it was. He spoiled her. He gave her the time and attention that she wanted. He'd taken her to family functions. She'd met his colleagues at dinner parties, and he'd taken her with him out of town when he had to go away for business. Shit, he was good to her. Damn good to her. Hell, he was being nice. He didn't have to tell her he was married at all. They had a good thing going. Why did she have to go and fuck it all up?

Darren thought about what he missed most about Nicole. He missed having sex with her. He couldn't even sleep with his wife anymore. He couldn't get it up, let alone keep it up, because he couldn't lie with her without thinking about Nicole and the things they used to do. The things she used to do to him. He tried, but his wife just didn't compare. He'd felt sorry for his wife when she'd asked him what it was that he'd wanted, what could she do to please him. She'd tried everything, but it didn't matter. He wanted Nicole. He loved his wife. Hell, she was the mother of his kids, but he didn't desire her. He was no longer physically attracted to her. Because he wanted Nicole.

He was obsessed. He knew that he was. But he felt that it was more like an addiction than an obsession. He couldn't even function anymore. He'd followed her to different hotels. Sat in different rental cars outside of restaurants. Most times, he couldn't even see inside, but he'd sit in the car, trying to imagine what they were talking about and becoming enraged as he'd follow them to various hotels. She hadn't even waited. The filthy bitch. Nicole belonged to him, and here she was fucking all these men. And what was up with the white guy? She knew he was just sleeping with that guy to spite him. She couldn't possibly have seen anything in him. He wasn't even her type.

Darren sat in his home away from home, the apartment that he'd always brought Nicole to during their year together. Darren couldn't understand why Nicole had gotten so upset about the scarf. She liked it rough, she said so herself. Darren sat it in the chair in the dark room, illuminated by the light of the big, flat screen, TV. He watched his favorite of the "home movies" he'd made of him and Nicole. Nicole was on all fours at the edge of the bed, ass in the air, back sloped, flat and low. Darren stroked himself as he sat with one leg thrown over the arm of the chair watching himself entering Nicole from behind. Warm, wet and as tight as a virgin he pushed himself into her. "Aaaah," He heard himself say onscreen, as he sighed deep and low, lifting her torso up as Nicole threw her head back tossing her hair and slowly flattening her back returning to her sloped position. Darren held his dick firmly in one hand and make a twisting motion with it in his other hand as the KY jelly seeped through his thick fingers. He watched as Nicole gyrated her hips and backed up against him as he pounded away as hard as he could. He was so impressed with himself. He was fucking the shit out of her and she loved it. Nicole arched her back like a cat and flattened it as she rhythmically moved her hips in circles. He fought orgasm as he watched her round butt, jiggle and bounce against his every thrust. He was rough with her, so rough that he thought that he'd break her. But just when he'd thought that she'd had enough, she'd look back at him and smile that sexy smile of hers and say to him, "Harder, daddy. Harder!"

He'd captured it all on tape. The very acts that had sent him to the moon and back, he had right there in front of him to view at his leisure, as many times as he'd wanted. He cupped his balls in his hand they were still very tender. Nicole had hit him in the nuts so hard that past Saturday, that he'd fallen to the ground hitting his head on the driveway giving himself a concussion. The pain had been excruciating, he never thought that he'd stop vomiting. He'd wanted to kill her that night. He wished that he had. Darren turned his attention back to the TV screen. He watched himself grabbing a handful of Nicole's thick, curly hair and pushing the side of her head into the bed into the soft comforter that lay on top of the bed just behind him. Darren turned and looked at the bed then back at the screen that had pictured the very same room in a totally different light. He didn't want to miss a thing.

He should have had the TV on mute, but he wanted to hear every sound, from the subtle rustling movement of the two of them changing position on the bed, to the moans of ecstasy and the sexy pillow talk. Nicole was great at that. He missed it and he missed her.

Everybody was okay. Her family had calmed down, and the streets cleared as neighbors gradually went back into their homes. Mariah and Carl came by to check on the family. Tamia had given them a call. Tamia was more excited than she was scared, but Mariah was scared to death. They were happy to see that everyone was safe, but she was taking her babies home with her where they'd be under her roof and under her care. Fatimah's children, on the other hand, had stayed with Granny; no one could get in touch with their parents.

Tangie had gone and had taken Cleo with her. Granny had told her to go and had prayed that they'd make it home safely. She couldn't deal with all of Tangie's negativity, and she could see the confrontational drunken Tangie rearing its ugly head. Auntie Cookie and Uncle Clyde had gone home too. It was way past their bedtime, and all the excitement had made the couple exhausted. Uncle Clyde had said he hadn't had to hit the floor like that in years. He'd laughed and said he was amazed that he could get down there so fast.

Mariah and Aniyah stood in Granny's living room, trying to convince their sister to file a restraining order against Darren.

"I will."

"Did you tell the police that he's been stalking you? Did you tell them about the pictures?"

Aniyah wanted to know what were on those pictures, so she listened intently hoping to get a little more detail.

"No, Mariah. I didn't mention the pictures. What's up with you and those pictures? It wasn't as if there was anything lewd or indecent on those photos." Nicole couldn't understand why Mariah was so stuck on those pictures.

"Nicole! That is not the point. They were pictures that a man who is stalking you had taken. That's the problem. It's not the content of the pictures! It's the fact that he'd followed you and had taken the pictures in the first place." Mariah was angry and frustrated, not to mention the fact that she was afraid for Nicole. Aniyah had gotten the information that she was looking for, and she felt the fact that Darren had been stalking Nicole was just as disturbing to her as pornographic pictures would have been.

"No, Mariah, I didn't tell the detectives about the pictures. It totally skipped my mind," Nicole said to Mariah with a smile.

"Stop patronizing me, Nicole. I hate when you do that. This is serious business. A man just shot up your car!" Her voice was shrill and high pitched, the more excited she became.

"Okay, Mariah, where are the pictures?" Nicole asked her sister. Nicole knew that the pictures were gone. Mariah's expression changed as she'd realized that she had deleted the only evidence that they had, in her attempt to keep them from their mother. "You deleted them, right?" Nicole asked. Mariah nodded.

Nicole hunched her shoulders. "I love you guys, and I know that you all are concerned about me, but I'm gonna be okay. And Mariah, I'm not patronizing you." Nicole hugged her sister. "I'm telling you. You have nothing to worry. He crazy, but he ain't that crazy."

Aniyah offered Nicole a ride home, but Nicole declined. Granny and Big Daddy tried to convince Nicole to stay. When she declined, Granny told her to take the rental car. But Nicole frowned and shook her head "No." Carl and Mariah offered Nicole a ride home too. Nicole told them she'd take a cab home.

Granny squeezed her hard and held on to her longer than usual when she hugged her good-bye. Nicole looked at her and smiled. She couldn't understand why everyone was being so dramatic. Everybody had that "you are so dead" look on their face. They had the same sad expressions on their faces as if they were looking at her dead body in a coffin.

The ride home was long, but it gave Nicole the opportunity to reflect on a few things. Nicole was deep in thought, but she could see the driver staring at her through the rearview mirror. She'd caught him a few times and he didn't look away when she did and he didn't smile. Nicole was glad that he didn't talk to her during the ride home. In fact, he hadn't spoken to her at all. Nicole thought he was creepy. She'd imagined that he'd have a ghoulish accent when he spoke. She imagined that he was going to drive her to the underworld, and she'd never see her loved ones again. She was beginning to frighten herself, so she avoided meeting his gaze.

Her grounds were always well lit. She looked around her property carefully as they drove up the long drive and parked in the half-moon driveway in front of her house. She paid her fare and tipped him generously. That was the first time she'd seen him smile the entire trip. He looked even more frightening with the smile on his face.

It was about seventy-five degrees outside. The temperature was perfect. Brisk gusts of wind rustled through the tall, green maple trees that lined her property. Stars twinkled against the backdrop of the darkened sky, and the moon was full and luminescent. Nicole looked out onto her property and imagined werewolves bounding toward her in every direction as she struggled to find the right keys to unlock the door to her home. That was the sort of night that it was, like a scene out of a graphic horror movie. And she was the damsel in distress.

Her cell-phone ringing startled her and snapped her back into the present. She answered it as she disarmed her security system and unlocked the doors to her home.

"You miss me?" an unfamiliar voiced asked.

"Who is this?" Nicole asked, as she walked into her foyer, sitting her bag and her keys on a small, round, marble-top table by the door.

"Oh, so that's the impression that I made?" the man on the other line said, trying to appear to be cool, but Nicole could tell he was uncomfortable.

"Jermaine?" Nicole asked.

"Yea, it's me," he said with a smile, relieved that she hadn't gone through a list of names before coming to his.

"I'm sorry. I didn't catch your voice at first. It's been a rough night."

"Really? What's going on?"

"Nothing in particular. It's just been a very eventful evening," Nicole said with a sigh. "So what's up with you?"

"Not much." He paused. "Umm. I've been having you on my mind ever since the other night. I didn't want to pressure you or anything, but I'd really like to see you again."

Nicole smiled as she armed her alarm and stepped out of her shoes. She tossed her keys in her bag and carried the bag over her shoulder. She carried her shoes up the stairs by its straps, as she held the phone to her mouth and spoke. Nicole wondered if he wanted to go out for drinks or if he just wanted a repeat session of the other night.

"This really isn't a good time."

Jermaine could feel the brush off and it stung a little. In his pursuit of Nicole, his pride had taken a beating. "I'll make it worth your while."

Nicole frowned; she couldn't imagine that he could do anymore than what he had done the other night. He'd pulled out all the stops that night, and although Nicole was completely uninhibited, she still had a few tricks left in her bag.

"And how would you do that?" Nicole asked.

"Just trust me. I will make it worth your while."

Nicole wanted to laugh. She didn't bother asking him what that meant. He might as well have said he was going to do it to her all night long or some other overused line.

All she wanted to do was hit the sack and end this night as soon as possible. She wanted to hop in the shower, relax, and drift off to sleep. She didn't want sex tonight. She didn't want company. She wanted to enjoy the new day without rushing a stranger out of her bed before dawn.

"I can't tonight. I'm tired, I'm going to hop in the shower and go to bed."

"So you're gonna make me beg," Jermaine said. She wasn't sure if that was a statement or a question. She appreciated this young man's persistence, but she wasn't going to bend. She stripped off her clothes and tossed them to the floor and went into her bathroom. Her eyes were heavy; she was completely worn out.

"No, don't. I don't want to make you beg. It's just really been a rough night, and I've got to get some rest."

She'd shot Jermaine down and had gotten off the phone. She thought about what he must have been thinking. How he probably was replaying their conversation over in his head, wondering what he could have said differently to make her change her mind. She pictured him sitting in his little apartment, questioning his sexual prowess. He had made an impression on Nicole, but apparently not as big of an impression as she had made on him. Nicole showered and tucked herself into bed and went to sleep without giving Jermaine a second thought.

Nate couldn't get to Aniyah fast enough. He went straight to her place without even changing his clothes.

"Baby, you okay?" Nathan said as he embraced Aniyah. She hugged him back and laid her face on his chest. He smelled like food. He always did when he got off work. He was an executive chef at a thriving fine dining restaurant, and his chef jacket always smelled like food. He catered on special occasions, but he never smelled like food when he catered. Those fifteen-hour work shifts were killing him. His feet were bad, and he slept a lot. But he said it was worth it. Someday soon, he'd have his own restaurant. Their schedules were always conflicting, but they always managed to spend some quality time together. It was difficult, but they managed to pull it off.

Nathan kissed Aniyah on the top of her head. "You all right?"

"I'm okay," she said, holding on to him.

There was something about his embrace. It was warm and comforting. She could stay in his arms forever. His body was so warm, and she felt safe there. He made her feel that he wanted to be with her to make her feel safe and secure. She wondered if this was what love felt like. Was she loving him right now or was she just scared? She hated not being able to identify her feelings for him. She hated that she'd put herself in such a compromising position and that she had to struggle to keep another man out of her mind. Nate pulled her away from him by both her arms and took a good look at her.

"You sure, you're okay?"

"I'm okay," she said, and she wrapped her arms around him again and buried her face in his chest. Nate was overworked and tired, but he wanted to be there for Aniyah and to make sure that she was alright.

"Okay, so tell me what happened," Nathan said, peeling Aniyah off him and looking into her eyes. Aniyah sighed.

"Darren shot up Nicole's car. We were all at Granny's house, and Nicole's car was parked right in front of the house. I was in the back on the deck. Granny, Big Daddy, Auntie Cookie, and Uncle Clyde were in the kitchen playing cards. All the kids were there, and Tye was there with the baby. Tye had to snatch GG out of the chair and pull her to the floor. Nicole had to knock Mama on the floor and hold her down. It was crazy."

"But everybody's okay, right?"

"Yea, we were all a little shaken up, but okay. That man is crazy though."

"Well, they'll arrest him. They're not gonna let him get away with shootin' up somebody's car. Especially in a residential neighborhood."

"A few people got a good look at him, but they couldn't positively identify him. Hell, they were all too busy duckin'. Oh, and Cleo was sitting in Granny's driveway in Mama's Cadillac when it happened."

Nate laughed. "I know he was scared as fuck."

"Yea, he was. He peed on himself in Mama's car," Aniyah continued. "He didn't even get out when the police came. Him and Mama came over Granny's house all drunk and shit. It was embarrassin'. Mama tried to make a scene sayin' that it's all Nicole's fault for bringing him around, but Granny made her go. Mama was up to no good when she came over in the first place. She knew Nicole's car was there. If she didn't want to see her, then she should have kept on driving."

"That's messed up. So he shot up her Porsche."

"Yea, we heard the Pop, Pop, Pop," Aniyah said, using her hand as if it were a gun. "I couldn't believe it. It didn't even sound like gunfire. It sounded like firecrackers going off, and the shots weren't right after each other, it was like he was aiming. It's just crazy, that's all I can say. He's crazy."

Nate loved Aniyah, but he couldn't think of anything that she could do that would make him do anything that stupid. He loved her, but he wasn't going to do any jail time over her. He had worked too hard establishing a good relationship with the community. His reputation was very valuable to him, and he wanted to keep it clean and pristine. And he couldn't see where he'd let any woman get in the way of that, including Aniyah. He did love Aniyah very much, and he was glad that he had finally found himself a good girl. Aniyah was perfect for him, but he wouldn't allow any of his feelings for her to change the man he was, the man he was brought up to be.

Nathan was a hardworking man, and he was very industrious. At age fifteen, he'd worked in his neighborhood, finding useful things that he could do for others that could make him a little extra money. He stayed away from drugs, doing them and selling them, and he stayed very productive. He was the youngest of six children, three boys and three girls They were taught to work hard to get what they wanted. Sure, there were plenty of times that Nathan had the opportunity to work hard in other ways in his neighborhood, but he chose a good path and as his mother would say, "He was blessed because he made good choices." Nathan had been gifted his family's home when he graduated from culinary school. It was paid in full by his parents. His parents had planned to move to Florida to retire, but when his father died suddenly, plans had changed.

Gifting wasn't as easy as it sounded. There were a few legal hoops he had to jump through and some land taxes he had to pay, but he felt honored to be asked to take over the family home and he kept it in immaculate condition. Every time his mother came over, she'd say how proud she was of him, and she would comment on the overall good condition of the house.

Nathan's parents had every intention of spending their last days in a nice, warm climate, free from Cleveland winters and close to their only grandchildren. But when his daddy died of a massive heart attack, his mother decided she wasn't leaving. She couldn't imagine starting a new life without the person she was supposed to spend the rest of her life with. She felt God had played a cruel joke on her, and she was left behind to brave those bitter, cold winters alone. So she stayed at a pricey retirement village in Beachwood with a "bunch of old folks" as she would often say, waiting to shrivel up and die. She seemed so out of place there, Nate thought. He offered to let her stay with him. There was plenty of room. But his mother would always say, "Who wants a grown man who still lives with his mother? You'll never get a wife if you move me in there." Nathan couldn't tell if she secretly hoped that he'd beg her to live there with him, or if she'd rather just live alone. He kind of figured that his mother was still sad and lonely, missing his father and she'd be bitter and depressed no matter where she'd lived. Especially in the home she'd shared with his dad.

Nathan stripped off his clothes and tossed them on the floor in Aniyah's hallway. Aniyah picked them up and draped them across the back of the chair in her bedroom.

"Do you want me to wash them?"

"No, don't worry about it. I don't have to be at work 'til two. I have time to stop home before then."

Nathan didn't take long showers, especially after a long day's work. He couldn't wait to get in bed. He wouldn't be particularly interested in sex either. He'd likely fall asleep with Aniyah's bare breasts in his hand or with his hand on her butt, before rolling over on his side.

Nathan did as Aniyah had predicted, and Aniyah was up and off to the den to visit with her computer. She went through the ritual of deleting unwanted e-mails and visiting her social sites. She never commented much, but she added pictures quite often. But tonight she felt the need to type in something under the "Thoughts of the Day" section. She typed in big letters as if making an announcement: LADIES: BEWARE OF CRAZIES. THEY ARE MASTERS OF DISGUISES. She had Darren in mind when she made that post. Aniyah had intended for that to be her last and only post for the day, but the comments rolled in immediately.

Lucy commented, "Girl, ain't dat da truth! Lyin' next to one right now. Lol."

Aniyah: Huh?

Lucy: Sitting up in bed on my laptop.

Tina: I know what you mean. That's why I'm single today.

Bill: Is that really why you're single today? I've seen your profile pic. Lol.

Tina: Shut up, Bill. Lol. This conversation is for the ladies.

Nora: No. let 'um speak. Like 2 c wat he has 2 say.

The comments went on and on. Aniyah didn't stick around to see them all. Instead she logged out and slept next to the man who claimed he loved her.

Chapter 15

GOOD-BYE

Jason Thomas had the perfect life. He had a beautiful, vivacious wife. Five beautiful children. A nice home in the suburbs. And an easy, stress-free job that he absolutely loved. He attended church with his family twice a week, and although he was not on a ministry, he attended faithfully. He read his Bible; he could quote scripture, but he couldn't stop cheating on his wife.

Fatimah and Jason were high school sweethearts. They attended college together. They graduated together. They had done everything. Together. Jason was voted the best-looking boy in high school. Fatimah was voted most likely to succeed. They were both voted best couple. And they were for a while.

Jason couldn't explain what drove him to infidelity, but he felt as if there was some unseen force that would propel him into the arms of these other women. Pastor said it was the devil. He tended to believe him, but Fatimah said it was his dick. He simply couldn't control himself.

He loved Fatimah, but she wasn't the woman he had married so many years ago. She was suffocating and cold. He'd begged her to keep the marriage together after his first affair, but in hindsight, he wished he would have let her go, because in small ways, she'd made his life a living hell. He'd paid for cheating on her daily even though she'd promised that she'd let it go and put it behind her. She said she would, just like that. But she'd lied. She'd ration out sex when she thought he deserved it, and she'd withhold it when she thought he didn't.

Plus, she loved to remind him that she was watching him. And she was. She was watching him like a hawk, and he hated that she felt she couldn't trust him. Not because she could, but because it made it more difficult for him to get out there. It made it harder for him to cheat.

New pussy added spice to his humdrum life. It wasn't as if sex with his wife wasn't good. It was great; well, at least it used to be. But it was just sex. Not that just sex wasn't okay, it was just not what you're looking for when you're lying with your wife. At least not as far as Jason was concerned. He missed his wife telling him he was the best; he missed her shrill cries of ecstasy when she climaxed. He missed that "who am I, where am I" look on her face when she was spent and exhausted afterward. And he missed how she'd say she loved him and he could see it in her eyes. Now all he got was that "I hate you" look as if she wanted him to hurry up and get off her when he was done.

He looked down at his watch. Fuck! How could he have let time get away from him like that? He was supposed to pick up the kids from their granny's house hours ago, but he was way late. He'd had turned off his cell phone; he figured the kids could call their mom if they needed anything or if they wanted to get home sooner. But he'd fallen asleep and had totally lost track of time. When he turned the phone on, the message that he heard was "Where the fuck are you? Leave the kids over Granny's and get home. We need to talk."

Jason had gotten another message from his oldest daughter, Leah. She was a daddy's girl. She was crying and distraught, and she said, "Daddy, I want to go home. They've been shooting over here, and I wanna go home."

Jason called Granny right away and apologized. He asked her what had happened and Granny had said that the kids were just fine and she'd tell him more when he got there. Jason headed over Granny's house. It was pretty late when he arrived. Granny got up and let Jason in to see his kids. His two oldest children along with Granny told Jason their versions of what had happened. Jason asked them if their mother knew, and they'd said they couldn't reach her. Jason asked Leah if she still wanted to go home, and she answered, "Yes." "Good," Jason thought, "she could be his buffer," because Fatimah was going to be pissed, and he hoped that the shooting would calm Fatimah down and put her mind on other things besides him coming in after twelve in the morning. Jordon wanted to stay, and Jason told Granny that he'd take Leah home with him and that he'd pick the others up later. He thanked Granny as Leah grabbed her things; then Leah gave Granny a hug and kissed her good-bye.

Jason talked to his daughter; she told him how afraid she was and that everybody was talking about how they thought Darren was going to hurt her auntie Nicole. Leah described Nicole's car and the damage as much as she could see of it, because none of the grown-ups would let the kids go outside to get a good look, but Uncle Tye went out and took pictures.

"Were you cryin'?"

"Yea, I was cryin'. I didn't know what was goin' on. We all had to get on the floor and Tye pulled GG on the floor and the baby was crying, and Tori and Christian was cryin' 'cuz they didn't want to stay on the floor."

"What was Josh and Lana doin'?"

"Josh didn't cry, he just stayed down on the floor, and Lana was sleepy so she did as she was told. Uncle Tye cussed and told Zenobia to put her head down, and he didn't get yelled at or anything, because everybody was so scared."

"You feelin' better now?"

"Much better," she said as she looked over at her daddy and smiled. "I can't wait to tell Mommy about it."

"Well, if Mommy is sleep, we'll just let her get her rest, okay?"

"Okay," she answered.

Leah fell asleep in the car as her father drove her home. He glanced over at his daughter sleeping soundly. She was a beautiful girl, tall and thin. She looked just like his oldest sister when she was a teenager. All of Fatimah and Jason's children favored him. They were very light-skinned with curly hair; all but Lana had his hazel eyes. Lana had eyes like her mother. They were exotic-looking children. Fatimah would say that people would look at her funny when they were all together as if she couldn't possibly be the mother of their children. Jason told Fatimah that she was just being paranoid, but he had noticed it too.

Jason told his daughter to be very quiet as they entered the house so as not to wake Fatimah. Leah was too old for Jason to lie and tell Fatimah that he had gotten in earlier than what he'd actually come in, but at least, they wouldn't fight until the morning.

When they stepped in the house, there were boxes everywhere. The house was in disarray. This wasn't like Fatimah. Everything had its place, and Fatimah kept them neatly in it, whether it be a person or a thing. Leah tiptoed into the house, bleary eyed, unsure of what she was seeing. The house was dark except for the illumination of the streetlights that shone in through the curtains and the blinds. Things were packed, but not everything. Things were thrown in the boxes in a disorderly manner half in and half out of boxes, more like she was throwing out trash.

"Daddy, what's goin' on?" Leah asked.

"Go on upstairs, baby."

Leah rubbed her eyes and walked up the stairs to her room.

"What the fuck?" Jason said under his breath as he clicked on the living room light to get a better view.

Jason rifled through the boxes. "This is all *my* shit," Jason said as he moved from box, to box, to box. There were his trophies, his plaques, his diploma. His degree sat at the top of one of the boxes, with the frame cracked and the glass broken. Pictures of him at various family events and special occasions were piled in boxes ready to be packed away or discarded. "Fatimah has lost her mind," Jason said to himself.

Jason jogged up the steps and burst open the bedroom door. Fatimah wasn't there. He searched the other bedrooms and no Fatimah. He went into the basement and looked around. She wasn't there. He went into the kitchen to get the garage-door opener. It was sitting on the window ledge, just above the kitchen sink. He used it to see if Fatimah's car was in the garage. As soon as he saw Fatimah's car inside, he pressed the button again and lowered the door.

Jason was puzzled and confused. It wasn't like Fatimah not to be around for her children. She'd never ignored her cell, especially when her children were out of her sight. It didn't matter who they were with; she didn't trust anyone with her babies but her. It was totally out of character for her to be out at this hour without anyone knowing where she was. It hadn't occurred to him that maybe, just maybe, his secrets had been exposed. That maybe she knew about the newborn that he had fathered.

Jason called Mariah at about six in the morning. He said that he was worried about Fatimah. She hadn't come home all night, and she hadn't called. He told her that she hadn't been answering her cell phone either and that he didn't know where she was.

"Well, did you call the hospitals?"

"Yea. I called them last night."

"Well, did you call any of her friends?"

"You mean the members of the church?"

"Well, those are her friends."

"I don't wanna embarrass her. And I don't want them all in our business."

"Jason, is everything all right over there, or is there something you're not telling me?"

"Mariah, I don't know what's goin' on, and I'm worried about her. We came home last night, and there were packed boxes scattered all over the living room. And she's nowhere to be found. I don't know what to think."

Mariah was suspicious, but she was worried. This was totally out of character for Fatimah. Mariah told him that she would call her sisters and they'd make some calls and be over there later. Jason said he had to go to work for a few hours, but for her to call him if she heard anything.

Mariah made a few phone calls before calling Aniyah. Mariah wasn't having any luck, and surprisingly, Aniyah had a few pretty good suggestions, but their efforts were in vain, no Fatimah.

When Mariah called Nicole, with Aniyah on the three way, Nicole said, "Fatimah has finally gone and lost her mind."

"That's not funny, Nicole."

"I'm not laughing. I'm serious. All that trying to be Ms. Perfect has gone to her head."

"Well, we need to find her."

"Have you guys thought that maybe she's not missing? Maybe, she doesn't want to be found. She's been having those migraines. She might have found a quiet place to chill out." Nicole replied.

"Fatimah wouldn't just leave her kids like that. You know how Fatimah is."

"They were safe," Nicole said.

"Still Fatimah would never do anything like that."

"Whatever," Nicole said. Nicole knew her sister. Fatimah wasn't all that. She cursed like a sailor, she could drink any one of them under the table, and she knew for a fact that Jason was not her first, not even her second for that matter. She didn't knock folks who wanted to change their life. But keep it real. Know where you came from. "Did y'all try Donna?"

Donna was Fatimah's best friend in high school. Fatimah kept in touch, but she kept her distance. Donna drank, smoke, and got high and she'd sleep with her man, your man and anybody's man she could get her hands on, but Fatimah trusted her, because she always had her back and she could talk to her about anything.

"Oh yeah. I remember Donna." Aniyah replied.

"I don't know. You really think Teemah still talks to Donna? You know, Donna was a trip." Mariah said.

"Everybody needs a friend, and she was Fatimah's friend." Nicole was becoming irritated; they had asked for her suggestions, but didn't want to hear what she had to say.

So she told her sisters that she had things to do and asked them to call her back after they'd gotten in touch with Fatimah.

"What up?" That was how Donna had answered the phone.

"Hello. May I speak with Donna Miles?" Mariah said.

"Who dis?" Donna answered.

"It's Mariah, Fatimah's sister. I was wondering if you've seen her."

Donna laughed. "I knew who dis wuz. I seen it on the caller ID. Hey, girl, how you been? Yea, she here. Hold on a second. Day-Day, go tell Fatimah she got a phone call."

Mariah and Aniyah could hear a little boy yell, "Auntie Teemah. Da phone!"

They could hear Fatimah coming to the phone, and she answered, wondering who in the world could be calling her over Donna's. She hadn't told anybody where she was.

"Hello?" Fatimah answered, wondering if she'd recognize the voice on the other line.

"Fatimah, we've been worried about you. What's goin' on with you, girl?" Mariah asked.

"Nothin'. I'm fine," Fatimah answered.

"Something's goin' on. This isn't like you. You sure you're okay?"

"I'm fine. I just needed to get away for a minute."

Donna's house wasn't a quiet place to relax. There was music playing in the background, and people were talking loudly over it. It sounded like they were having a party, at eight o'clock in the morning.

"Fatimah, come home. Something's wrong, and we need to talk about it. Okay?" Mariah said.

Fatimah didn't even put up a fight. "Okay, I'll meet you at my house in about an hour."

Fatimah asked Donna to take her home. Donna hated to see her go. They had so much fun together reminiscing about high school and talking about life back then before college, before marriage and kids. Donna hadn't gone to college. She barely made it through high school. She had two children by age eighteen, and for her, college was not option.

Donna made horrible first impressions. She was loud. She dressed provocatively, leaving very little to the imagination. And she put the P in promiscuous. But she had always been such a true friend, and no matter how much time had passed between them, they were always able to pick up right where they left off. Donna's self-esteem was low, but Fatimah thought she was beautiful.

Fatimah kissed each of Donna's children good-bye. They asked her when they could come over her house to visit, and she'd said she'd let them know. Donna's oldest son Ricky was there visiting from college; she was so happy to see him all grown up. She hadn't seen him since he was fifteen. He was nineteen years old now.

Donna was a great host. She struggled to make ends meet, but somehow she kept it all together. She worked at a local salon as a nail tech. She made good money, but she spent it as fast as she made it. She kept her kids in designer gear, because she wished she had it when she was a child. She said she remembered what it was like to get picked on at school. But it was difficult for Donna trying to keep up with the Jones's, she was barely keeping her head above water.

Fatimah left her some money on her nightstand. Donna said it made her feel like a prostitute. Fatimah told her to considerate it a gift for the kids. Donna accepted it with much gratitude. Besides, Donna's kids called her Auntie Teemah, and they had never met their "cousins," no more than a picture or two that Fatimah would pull out of her wallet during her rare visits.

Donna got her children situated; her oldest boy kept an eye on them while she drove Fatimah home. Her little ones wanted to tag along, but Donna wanted to talk grown-folks stuff with Fatimah, so she made them stay at home.

"You need to let his ass go," Donna said as she gripped the steering wheel. Her nails were long and colorful and meticulously designed. "Just kick his ass out. Puttin' you through all dat bullshit. You have been a good wife and mother to his kids. You don't deserve that."

Fatimah didn't say anything.

"Wit his pretty ass. Dat's da problem. He think he too cute." She glanced over at her friend, then looked straight ahead, and mumbled, "Pretty ass."

Fatimah didn't say a word. She sat quietly as Donna talked to her all the way home. It was a shame that she lived right here in the city of Cleveland, and she didn't even keep in touch with Donna. Donna knew everything about her. She knew the real Fatimah. She knew how Fatimah used to sneak and get high with her after church while she was still in her church clothes. She knew that Fatimah let Reverend Johnson's son get to second base with her after choir rehearsal on Wednesday night. She knew it all, and she kept her secrets as if they were hidden in a vault.

No one was at the house when Fatimah got there. She showered and changed her clothes and prepared for her sister's arrival. She didn't have a clue what they wanted to discuss. Mariah acted as if they had some sort of intervention planned. She was still herself. She was still Fatimah. She was just tired, fed up, had it up to here Fatimah.

When she was ready, she gave Mariah a call. Mariah told her that they'd be over shortly. She could tolerate Mariah, but she didn't want Nicole coming over. Nicole was the last person she wanted to get advice from.

The girls were there in no time. Nicole included. Nicole saw Fatimah roll her eyes at her. Nicole didn't want to be there either. She only came because they had asked her to come. Quite frankly, she had other more important things to do than to talk to Fatimah about her problems. They all knew that she was very private, and they all knew she had a shitty attitude.

Mariah and Aniyah hugged Fatimah as they looked around at all the packed boxes. Fatimah looked around too as if there was absolutely nothing unusual about them.

"So Fatimah, what's goin' on?" Aniyah asked gently. She spoke as if she was talking to someone about to jump off a roof.

"Nothin'," Fatimah said, looking around the living room. Pictures were missing from the walls, and pictures were removed from the mantel.

"Well, what's going on here?" Mariah asked.

"Nothing, just packing," Fatimah answered.

"So, uh, are you moving and you didn't tell anyone? What?" Aniyah asked.

"This isn't my stuff. It's Jason's," Fatimah answered calmly.

"Okay, Fatimah, what's going on? Something is obviously wrong." Mariah was tired. The babies were kicking and she really wanted to have a seat.

"Nothing is going on. I am fine. I just needed a little time away, and now I am back."

"Are you sure you're okay?" Aniyah asked.

"I'm fine, Aniyah."

"You obviously are not fine. We come into your house, and it's in disarray. Boxes packed all over the place. Pictures taken down off the wall. Your husband can't find you. Your children can't find you, and the person you have watching your kids can't even find you. You don't answer your phone. You don't leave a number. I mean, let's just keep it real, if Mariah hadn't asked you to come home, you probably wouldn't even be here." Nicole was tired of the bullshit. She didn't have time to play with Fatimah. And she was not going to come all the way over her house to walk on eggshells just because her ass had gone crazy.

"I don't need you to teach me about being responsible. You're the last one to teach me about being responsible." Fatimah retorted.

"Fatimah, I am a single woman. I don't have a husband, and I don't have children. I did not want that responsibility, so I don't have it. But this isn't about me, it's about you. You have a husband, you have children, these are the responsibilities that *you* have chosen."

Fatimah opened her mouth and raised a finger, preparing to tell her sister off. But Mariah stopped her.

"Last night, while the kids were at Granny's house, shots were fired."

"What?" Fatimah said as she turned to Mariah with fear and concern in her eyes.

"It's okay. Everyone is fine. The kids are fine. But no one could reach you, and Leah was scared. She called and called, and you never called back." Fatimah dropped her head and tears welled up in her eyes.

"What happened? Were they shooting at Granny's house." Fatimah had assumed that it may somehow be related to someone that Tye associated with in the streets.

"No," Mariah answered. She didn't want to go into detail about it. She didn't want to tell Fatimah that there was a possibility that Darren was responsible.

"No. It was Darren, and he shot up Nicole's car," Aniyah blurted it out just like a little kid as if she wanted to be the first one to say it. Nicole and Mariah turned and looked at Aniyah like they did when she was a child when she tattled.

"What? Your boyfriend put my babies in danger?"

"Not my boyfriend. My ex boyfriend."

"What difference does it make! You brought his ass around," Fatimah said, walking slowly and approaching Nicole as she spoke. Aniyah and Mariah hoped that Fatimah didn't walk up on Nicole, neither of them were in the mood to break up a fight.

"Fatimah, you'd better back the fuck up. 'Cuz if you think you've got problems," Nicole warned. "You'll have a whole 'nother set of 'um if you step over here." Fatimah stopped in her tracks.

Nicole felt guilty about last night. But it wasn't as if she brought just anyone around her family. She loved them, and she would never, ever do anything intentionally to harm them. She had dated him a whole year before she'd brought him around. She thought he was the one. She really, seriously thought he was the one.

"Why did you bring her here!" Fatimah asked Mariah.

"You're right. Mariah should have called your friends from church," Nicole said, rocking back and forth, clapping her hands, and tapping her foot.

"You know you reap what you sow, Nicole."

"Oh really?" Nicole said calmly. She wasn't phased by Fatimah's remark. "So what's your excuse? Huh? Did you sow this shit here?" Nicole asked with her arms spread as she looked around at Fatimah's dismantled living room. "What did you do to deserve this?"

Fatimah wanted to smack her, and her eyes burned as she fought back tears. Scriptures ran through her mind, and they scrambled on top of each other. She wanted to hurl each of them out at Nicole, throwing them at her like daggers.

Fatimah was jealous of Nicole. She was jealous of her confidence and her fearlessness. She was jealous of her ability to reverse a negative situation and come out victorious. Why didn't she care about what people thought of her? Why didn't it matter to her that she acted like a whore? Where was her shame? How could she walk around with such a laissez-faire attitude? It mattered to *her*.

The truth was Fatimah hated her life, and though she tried so hard to disguise that fact, Nicole could see right through it. Honestly, Fatimah thought if given the opportunity, she could leave everything, that job, that husband, that sham of a marriage, even her beautiful babies.

They didn't need her. Not really. She felt if she died today that no one's life would be affected. Jason would continue seeing other women. Serena would continue to make silly decisions, Mama would still be Mama, and life would go on. Eventually, no one would even remember that she ever existed. Her ministry didn't really impact anyone's lives. She struggled to control her anger, and no matter how hard she tried, she just couldn't stop cursing. People inevitably did what they wanted to anyway. How could she minister to anyone when she absolutely hated her sister?

Nicole defied everything that Fatimah had been taught. She never suffered for her actions. She was rich and successful and she seemed to be genuinely happy, and Fatimah hated that about her.

Nicole was the first to leave. She knew that Fatimah didn't want her there anyway. As Nicole walked down Fatimah's front steps, Fatimah repeated, "You reap what you sow, Nicole." Nicole continued walking to her car. She didn't turn around; she just waved an okay sign with her fingers above her head. Fatimah stood in her doorway with her arms crossed, and she continued, "Maybe they'll put that on your tombstone."

"Fatimah!" Mariah said in disbelief. "Fatimah, how could you say something like that!"

Fatimah couldn't believe she'd said it herself. She did have a problem. Why was she so hateful?

Her sisters were gone, and the first thing she did was call Leah and apologize to her. She called her granny and told her she loved her as she apologized wholeheartedly. She called Mariah and told her that she really needed to talk to her, and Mariah came right back over to her house.

They sat amongst the boxes as Fatimah told Mariah about the repeated phone calls, the migraines, and the one-month-old child. Mariah sat quietly and listened as her sister cried and told her that even though she'd been through the cheating before that it was hard for her to keep it together this time. She said she couldn't pretend that it was okay just to keep her family together. She didn't know how her children were going to handle it, but as far as she was concerned, the marriage was over. She said she couldn't let him mess with her sanity anymore. She felt as if she was losing her mind.

Mariah hugged and consoled her sister. She told her that she couldn't blame her and that she wished she would have come to her sooner. They talked a while longer; then Fatimah asked her sister if she could keep the kids for her overnight because she hadn't confronted Jason yet. Mariah told her that she would.

Fatimah picked her children up from vacation Bible school. The little ones were excited to show her the crafts that they'd created.

"Lana, where's yours?" Fatimah asked.

"I don't wanna talk about it."

"What chu mean, you don't want to talk about it?"

"Mommee. I don't wanna talk about it," Lana whined.

"Why what happened?"

"I'm too hungry to talk about it."

"Is everybody hungry?"

"I'm hungry for ice cream," Joshua said.

"I'm hungry for ice cream too," Jordan added.

"Who wants real food?" Fatimah asked.

"I want real food, Mom," Leah said.

"Me too," Jordan said.

"Okay, let's get something to eat."

"And some ice cream," Lana added.

Fatimah took her children to a restaurant where they sat down and ate and talked about the other night at Granny's. She was having a great time with her children. She laughed and talked with them and told them how much she loved them. Fatimah sat there with her children, admiring what a great job she'd done with them. They were terrific kids who she'd nurtured into wonderful little people. She had done a great job.

She watched how they interacted with one another. She wondered how resilient they'd be when separation and divorce hit. Would they be there for each other or would they be distant like her and her sister Nicole? She'd hoped not. She'd raised them to be close to one another and to love each other no matter what. Unlike her mother who'd stand back watching her daughters fight and argue, adding fuel to the fire. Fatimah's children loved and protected one another. They'd be just fine.

Jason got home from "work" at 7:00 p.m. Fatimah still hadn't cleaned up the mess she'd made. His kids weren't there, and neither was his wife. He checked the kids' rooms. Everything was in place. Fatimah hadn't left and taken his kids way from him. One of his greatest fears. When Jason went to the kitchen, he saw a note on the refrigerator door, stating that the kids were spending the night with Mariah, but that was all it said.

Jason assumed he'd be getting an explanation of her actions and her whereabouts when she returned home tonight.

Jason grabbed a snack and went up to the bedroom and lay down on the bed. He turned on the TV and watched a little Tuesday-night primetime until the telephone rang. It was Mariah.

"Hey, Jason. Um, Leah and the kids are over here. I wasn't sure if you knew." Mariah hadn't wanted to call. She didn't feel comfortable hearing Jason's voice, after the things she'd heard today.

"Yea, Fatimah left a note on the fridge. Did she tell you what's going on?" Jason asked.

"Yea, but I'm sure she'll discuss that with you," Mariah answered. "I was calling because Leah would like to come home."

"Now?" Jason asked. He was tired, and he just wanted to relax.

"Yea, now," Mariah answered.

It took all that she had not to tell Jason to just get his sorry ass up and get his daughter and not ask so many questions. Leah felt badly for wanting to go home, but Mariah understood. It wasn't her fault that she wasn't used to sleeping over her auntie's house. Tamia was a little hurt though; there were no girls her age to play with. She looked forward to Leah spending the night, and now she was going home. Tamia would get over it though. Her daughter knew how to keep herself entertained.

Jason came by to pick up Leah. He honked, and she came out. He was tired and irritated. Natalie had been putting a lot of pressure on him about seeing the baby. She promised that she'd keep everything on the down low if he'd come see his child. He'd asked her if she'd contacted his wife, and she said she hadn't. It was too much work trying to figure out if someone else had, so he didn't worry about it. He wasn't going to tell on himself this time. So if Fatimah knew something, then she was going to have to spill it.

Leah went up to her room, and Jason went to his bedroom to finish his nap. It was a hard job trying to satisfy everybody's needs. They all expected different things from him, and he felt pulled in so many directions. You would think that it would be so much easier just to break it off, but that would be the worst thing he could do. He wouldn't be able to handle the aftermath. But with the birth of his new daughter, everything was coming to a head.

Jason woke up at twelve o'clock exactly. Fatimah wasn't there. He checked the house. No sign of Fatimah.

"This is some bullshit," Jason said as he raised the garage door and closed it again after seeing the grill of Fatimah's car.

It felt like déjà vu. It was after midnight, and his wife wasn't home. He had no idea where she was, and she hadn't bothered to call. He didn't call her cell phone. He knew that it would anger him more if she didn't answer. He crossed his arms and stood in the living room wondering where in the world his wife could possibly be.

He wasn't worried about her being out with another man. Fatimah wasn't like that. She cared too much about what other people thought to be unfaithful. He was angry because she knew better. She had done this once this week already, and he didn't want it to become a nightly thing.

Jason sat on the couch. He fell asleep again. He didn't know why he was still so exhausted. But it felt so good to rest. He didn't have to think about what a mess he'd made out of his life. Juggling women was a hard job. But keeping them all a secret from one another was harder.

At about 2:00 a.m., a dark car pulled into the driveway. Jason moved the slats of the blinds and peered out. He hadn't seen this car before. He figured that it was his wife, but he couldn't see into the car well enough to tell for sure. He waited. He expected to see Fatimah come rushing in the house trying to explain, but she sat in the car for a few minutes, gave someone Jason didn't recognize a hug, and she stepped out of the car leisurely and walked up to the front door. Jason could hear her keys jingling, but he didn't unlock the door. He wanted her to open the door and see him standing there. He wanted her to realize she had some explaining to do.

Fatimah walked in. She looked like herself. She was dressed neatly and conservatively. Her hair was perfect, and she seemed to be in good spirits.

Jason clicked on the lights and asked, "What is all this?"

"Did you look in the boxes?" Fatimah asked.

"Yes, I did," Jason answered.

"Well, what did you see?" Fatimah inquired.

"I saw all my shit in the boxes," Jason replied.

"Well, then you already know what's in the boxes. So why the fuck are you asking me what is in the boxes, if you looked in them already and saw your shit in them?" Fatimah smacked her lips and mumbled the words, "Dumb ass," as she started up the stairs.

"Wait a minute, Fatimah. Get back down here. What the fuck is goin' on here?"

"Where are the kids?" Fatimah asked, totally ignoring his question.

"Over your sister's house where you left them." Jason didn't mention that Leah was upstairs. He didn't need a buffer. He was as mad as hell, and he wanted to know what was going on.

"Good. 'Cuz we need to talk," Fatimah said as she walked down the stairs, stepped out of her shoes, and left them at the base of the staircase. She walked past her husband and into the living room amidst the boxes.

"So what are you doing? Throwing my shit out?"

"No," Fatimah said as she shook her head.

"Well, then, what the fuck is going on?"

"Quite honestly, I didn't know what I was doing at first. My head hurt so badly. I was in so much pain that I couldn't even think straight. When that woman called me and told me that you had a one-month-old child, I was so beside myself that I just didn't know what to do," she said, as she dramatically laid a hand on her chest. Fatimah spoke as calmly as she would discussing the weather.

"Let me explain," Jason said.

"Oh, there's no need to explain. I wouldn't except an explanation anyway, an outside baby is an outside baby, that's a deal breaker as far as I'm concerned. I thought that's what had me so pissed off," she said as she raised a finger, "but that wasn't it. I have finally figured it out after all these years. I have finally figured it out," she'd said as if she'd discovered something of really great importance.

"Have a seat," she said to Jason as she pointed to the couch. Jason sat.

"Twice today, I've had someone say to me, 'What did you do to deserve that?' And I thought about it, and it didn't take me long to come up with the answer. So I figured now is as good a time as any to come clean about a few things. First of all, let me dispel the myth that I stopped working for Dr. Stevens for you. I know that everyone believes that I left Dr. Stevens's office because you asked me to. But that's not true at all. I left Dr. Stevens' office because I knew that if I continued my affair with him that I would have left your sorry ass for him a long time ago."

"What the fuck!" Jason said as he began to stand to his feet.

"Sit down!" Fatimah said, pointing to the couch. "Let me finish." She took a deep breath. "I knew I was wrong, but Lord help me, it felt so right." She closed her eyes, then opened them to look at her husband. His lips trembled in anger. "So I know how you feel. I can relate to you. I know how it feels to be unhappy every single day. I know how it feels to play the role and act like everything's just perfect, and I know what it's like to want someone for so long and be stuck with someone you just don't love anymore."

Jason couldn't believe what he was hearing.

"What are you saying?"

"I'm saying that it's over."

"So you're kicking me out?"

"Oh. No," she said, shaking her head. "You're gonna need to be here for your kids."

Jason looked at her, totally confused. He watched her as she pulled two large suitcases and a roll-away bag from the hallway closet under the staircase. He watched her, speechless as she dragged them to the door.

"Fatimah. What are you saying?"

"Isn't it obvious? I'm saying good-bye."

Fatimah closed the front door and dragged the bags outside to the dark car that waited for her in the driveway. Jason hadn't noticed that the car that had dropped Fatimah off had never left the drive. And Fatimah hadn't noticed her daughter sitting at the top of the staircase when she'd said, "Good-bye."

Chapter 16

DAMAGED

"She left me! My wife fuckin' left me." Those were the words that Mariah woke up to at two thirty in the morning.

"What?" Mariah answered, still sleepy. She grunted a little as she tried to adjust herself in the bed. "Jason, could you say that again?"

"She left me, Fatimah fuckin' left me!" Jason said as he paced the floor.

"Wait a minute, Jason. Calm down. Now start over."

"Fatimah packed her shit and she left me."

Carl rustled in the bed; he can hear a man's voice on the phone, and he doesn't like his tone.

"Who is that?" Carl asked.

"It's Jason," Mariah answered, as she covered the phone receiver with her hand.

Carl looked up at the alarm clock on the nightstand. "At two thirty in the morning?"

"He says Fatimah's left him."

"She couldn't have gone too far. Don't we have her kids?"

"Yea," Mariah said. "Jason is hysterical," Mariah said to her husband, still holding her palm over the receiver.

"Jason, did you and Fatimah get into a fight or something? What's going on over there?"

"She's gone. She started talking about how she had an affair with that doctor she used to work for and how she didn't like being married anymore, and she left. She grabbed her bags, and she left.

"Did she say where she was going?"

"Naw. At two o'clock this morning, a car brought her by the house; she picked up some suitcases and she left."

"Well, what did she say, Jason?"

"She said good-bye."

Mariah tried as best as she could to calm Jason down. She told him to get some sleep and that they would talk about it in the morning. But Mariah couldn't sleep. Her sister had really lost her mind. How could she do that? How could she just leave her children that way? What was wrong with her? Mariah didn't call her sisters. There was no reason for them to lose any sleep. She'd tell them everything in the morning.

Nicole was having a horrible night. She tossed and turned, and she just couldn't relax. She stared up at her stuccoed ceiling, as her mind wandered. Her eyes were heavy, but not heavy enough to stay closed. Her body was tired, but her mind was wide awake and active. "Dammit! I have got to get some sleep," Nicole said to herself as she turned over in a huff. She pulled her heavy embroidered comforter over her nakedness.

Nicole sighed and flipped over on her back. She stared at the ceiling again. It was too dark to see the detail in the ceiling's design, but she saw patterns in it as if she were looking up at the clouds. "This is some bullshit," she said as she sighed. She felt as if she needed to get up and walk around a bit. But she knew if she got up, it was a done deal. She wouldn't go back to sleep. She considered getting up and making herself some warm milk, but she didn't see how getting up out of the bed going all the way downstairs and into the kitchen would help her to sleep. So instead, she stayed in her bed staring up at the ceiling.

Nicole rolled over and grabbed the remote to her stereo off of her nightstand and turned it on; "Have Faith" by Floetry played. She closed her eyes and tried to will herself to sleep. She tried to clear her mind of everything but the music that played over the speakers. But her mind was busy. She thought about Don and how she hadn't spoken with him since their dinner date. She thought about Mr. Humphries and how sure he was that she could use his services.

Mr. Humphries. She smiled as she repeated his name in her head. He was sexy. She didn't mention to him that she knew who he was. Nicole wondered if it would have mattered if she'd told him that she knew he was the CEO and that he had traveled all the way to Ohio to meet with her. She didn't know whether to be flattered or offended. She was aware that she was a little rough around the edges, but only around family and a few select friends. And she knew that Mr. Humphries had come to speak with her as a favor to Clinton, and though she appreciated the effort, she was going to stick to her guns. At least for now.

She thought about Darren and had wondered how she could be such a poor judge of character. Why couldn't she sense that he was mentally unstable? Perhaps because she was so busy enjoying other aspects of her relationship with him.

"Hmmm," she thought to herself. It was such a shame. Once she got past his arrogance and ego mania, they actually had pretty good chemistry. He was by far the greatest lover she had ever had. He was confident and sensual, not to mention very well endowed. He handled Nicole's body as if she was an instrument that only he could master. He was a tender lover. He was a generous lover too, which was in stunning contrast to his narcissistic tendencies. But he was married. He belonged to someone else, and Nicole didn't want to share.

Many would describe Nicole as being cold, but she had taught herself how to keep her emotions in check. Emotional people had a tendency to lose control, and it was important that she always maintained control of herself and her immediate surroundings, as much as possible. She couldn't control everything that happened in her life, but she could control how she reacted to it.

Nicole had experienced so much in life that she'd become very cynical.

Nicole remembered a time when she had absolutely no say in her life. Back when she was a little girl, when she was Tangie's pride and joy. Nicole was a smart child. She was exceptional. She attended honors classes and excelled academically. Mama had Nicole and Fatimah in dance classes, and they both played the piano beautifully. Nicole was brilliant and received numerous awards and accolades. She always made her mother proud, and Tangie beamed when she spoke about her. Nicole and Fatimah were close back then too. Fatimah lived in Nicole's shadow.

Nicole lay on the bed and remembered a time when things were beyond her control. A time when she couldn't put a stop to things, no matter how hard she tried. She couldn't stop Mama from drinking and staying away from the house. She couldn't stop Mama and Daddy Ray from fighting, and she couldn't stop Daddy Ray from creeping into her room at night while Mama was gone.

Nicole had learned at a very early age, that she hadn't been the only one who had experienced unwanted late night visitors. She'd had friends that had so called uncles and such that couldn't keep their hands to themselves too, so Nicole didn't feel alone. Even though she never felt comfortable enough to share her plight with others, she would have no problem with being a support to those of her friends who felt the need to share their situation with her. One friend in particular had an especially troublesome situation. She had been raped by an older brother and when she'd confessed it to her mother, her mother did nothing. In fact she'd told her not to bring it up again. She never acknowledged it or addressed it at all. It was as if she'd never told her mother what had happened. This friend's name was Tara. And Tara's mother knew what she had said was true, but she ignored it as if ignoring it would make the problem go away. Tara had said that she hated that she'd ever told her mother. She'd said that her mother looked at her differently and that she'd acted as if somehow it was all her fault. Tara's relationship with her mother had eventually gotten worse as the years went by and Tara ended up committing suicide. She hung herself in her mother's closet. Her mother was the one who'd found her with a note pinned to her T-shirt that read: IGNORE THIS. Nicole wished that she could have saved her. She wished that she could have stopped her somehow, but she had problems of her own.

Nicole had another close friend who had similar issues. She was being visited by her mother's boyfriend late at night too. Only, she hadn't shared this with Nicole. Nicole had discovered her secret when she'd spent the night over her friend's house and he'd entered the room that Nicole and her friend were sleeping in.

*　*　*

He'd entered the room quietly. Nicole had become accustomed to sleeping lightly. She was very aware of her surroundings especially when she was sleeping in an unfamiliar place. She'd noticed when the bedroom door opened slowly. The bolts at the door jamb creaking eerily. She'd seen him creeping into the room, and she'd watched him slowly closing the door behind him. She was sharing the bed with her friend, Sasha. Sasha had slept on the side of the bed facing the wall. Nicole had slept facing the door. Nicole slipped her head under the blanket and had shut her eyes. She could hear this man kneeling beside her at the bedside and she heard the covers rustle as he slid his hand inside and placed them on her bare thigh. Nicole was wide awake, but she didn't flinch. She didn't move his hand away. She let him move his hand up her thigh and between her legs. She didn't move his hand as he moved her panties to the side and fondled her. Nicole moved the covers off of her head and looked at him. He had his eyes closed. One hand in his pants and the other hand between her legs. She couldn't believe how bold this man was, with Sasha lying in the bed right beside her. Nicole had looked him in his face and he'd opened his eyes exhaled and smiled at her. Nicole could remember how foul his breath had smelled and she wondered what woman would want to lie next to him. Nicole had smiled back at him. He'd looked surprised. Nicole took him by the hand. The hand that he had been fondling her with, she wrapped her hand around his middle finger and placed her thumb firmly against the side of his finger tip. He'd smiled at first, assuming that she was going to simulate a hand job on that finger. But instead she squeezed it tightly and she pressed her thumb securely against his finger tip. She wondered if he would snatch away once he'd felt her grip getting tighter. Nicole had wondered if he'd call out or slap her as she pushed her thumb against his fingertip as hard as she could until she felt the joint snap. He'd snatched his hand away and yelped like a wounded dog. Nicole had stared at the man with a big mischievous smile on her face as he held his lips tightly together and jumped up trying to zip up his pants with one hand. With one quick movement Nicole had snapped his finger tip with as little emotion as she would have had snapping a green bean. She knew that Sasha had to be awake by then, if she'd ever even fallen asleep at all.

That next morning, Sasha's mother's boyfriend wasn't at the breakfast table. Sasha's mom had said that he'd had to go to the emergency room because he had slammed his finger in the car door. Sasha had looked at Nicole and smiled. Nicole didn't smile back at her. She just continued eating her cereal. Nicole was thirteen and she didn't think that it was possible, but she'd wondered if she could have snapped the tip of his dick off the same way.

*　　*　　*

Nicole had that dream again. The same dream that she'd had when her cousin La Maya was over to visit. Had she known this was what she was looking forward to, she wouldn't have tried so hard to fall asleep. Darren was there, taunting her, luring her into that strange tent. She couldn't scream or curse at him and tell him to stop. What did he want her to see? She felt as if he was trying to expose her somehow. He laughed at her, and she could hear the others in the tent gasping in disgust. She didn't want to go inside, but she had no control as she was being drawn into the tent.

Fatimah was there, but she was a little girl this time and she kept saying, "I saw you! I'm telling Mama!" She was crying and shaking and she was talking to Nicole, but Nicole was a little girl too. Nicole was wearing the little lavender, satiny gown that her granny had bought her for her birthday. Fatimah was barefoot and was wearing a pair of pink pajamas, the same pink pajamas she wore when she was a child. Nicole looked around, and they weren't in the tent anymore; they were now in the home they grew up in. Fatimah was standing in the hallway, and she kept crying saying, "What are you doing? I'm telling Mama! I saw you!"

Nicole was panicking, and she was trying to calm her sister down. But Fatimah kept saying, "I saw you. I'm telling Mama." The last thing she remembered before waking up abruptly was the hallway stretching and extending longer and longer as Daddy Ray stood in the doorway, as her sister hid behind her bedroom door.

Her heart was racing, and she was sobbing like a baby. She hadn't cried like that since she was a little girl. Nicole threw the covers off of her and went into the bathroom. Her eyes burned from the brightness, as she flicked the bathroom light on. She grabbed a washcloth off the rack and wet it in the sink. She didn't look at herself in the mirror; she felt weak and vulnerable, and she didn't like seeing herself that way.

That whole situation with Darren had screwed her up so bad and had her questioning who she was and reviewing the major events in her life that had made her the adult that she was today. She was remembering things that she had repressed for so long, and although she could push these things down and out of her day to day life, she couldn't prevent them from creeping up in her dreams.

Every now and then, when things in her life went haywire, she would revert back to that helpless nine-year-old girl afraid of her secret after hours visitor. The same little girl who was instructed to sneak in her Mama's bedroom after dark while Mama was gone and her younger sisters were asleep.

Forced to satisfy the desires that Mama wasn't there to fulfill. How ironic it was that the only man that she ever really loved was the one who had left her the most damaged. Many years had passed from the time she was nine until at age seventeen when that secret relationship was cut short by Mama's discovery. When force through fear transformed into coercion, and coercion transformed into numb compliance.

Although Daddy Ray never hit her, he put a mental hurting on her that she couldn't escape, even when she was old enough to say "No." She loved him, and she didn't want to displease him. He had been the only one who made her feel special and important. He praised her when she did well in school when Mama didn't have the time. He came to her defense when others used to pick on her, and he protected her. He was the daddy that was always around, because Daddy Otis couldn't be. He was daddy, and as Nicole had gotten older, she felt her body was such a small price to pay for his approval.

It was strange. She knew that it was, and she couldn't explain it. That was why she never did. Nicole knew that Daddy Ray had a sexual appetite that couldn't be satisfied by Mama and that eventually it wouldn't even be satisfied by Nicole. So she would be the sacrifice. She complied and as long as she did, she never had to worry about Daddy Ray approaching her younger sisters. Nicole believed that as long as she cooperated, her little sisters were safe.

As time passed, she had mastered disconnecting herself from her body; by the time she was ten, she couldn't see him, feel him, or taste him on her tongue. By eleven, the nightmares stopped, and she almost never dreamed at all. By the time she was a teenager, she was numb. She could let him do whatever he wanted without so much as a second thought and still call him Daddy as if nothing had ever happened. No one ever suspected a thing. That was, not until she was seventeen.

*   *   *

Mama smacked Nicole so hard that the spoon that she was eating her cereal with flew out of her hand and slid across the kitchen floor. Little bits of frosted cereal and marshmallows landed on the kitchen table and onto the linoleum.

"What did I do, Mama?" Nicole asked, looking at her mother in shock with tears in her eyes.

The girls gasped, but they didn't say a word. Mariah and Aniyah's mouths dropped; they didn't know what was going on. All they knew was that their mother had come into the kitchen without saying a word and had open hand slapped their sister in the face. She'd slapped her so hard that the spoon had cut into the corner of Nicole's mouth.

Nicole had no idea what had happened to cause their mother to react that way. Mama's face was wet with tears, but she was sober. She was beet red, and she had hell in her eyes. Before Mama could leap onto her, Daddy Ray grabbed her; she struggled fruitlessly to break free, screaming, "Get offa me dammit! Get the fuck offa me!"

Mama fought and wrestled violently, but Daddy Ray was strong; he'd had a good hold of her.

"You let her alone! Let dat girl alone! Don't act this way! Look at you! You got the girls all scared! Don't act this way, Tangie!"

Nicole was scared, and her heart beat wildly as she tried to figure out why her mama was acting so crazed.

Her mind was working. What had she done? Had the school called? Couldn't have been school. She was an A student, quiet, and studious, and she stayed out of trouble. Was there a chore that she hadn't done? No, and even if there was, that couldn't have been the reason that her mama was acting like that. Nicole strained to think of what could have caused her mother to behave that way. But none of those things would have provoked such a violent reaction. But just then, the worst had popped into her mind. Her eyes had met her daddy's. And he just looked down at his feet as he held tight to Tangie, who was trying with all her might to get to her daughter to rip her head clean off.

"You get yo' shit, and you get outta here! And I mean that! I don't want to see your fuckin' face! I mean it! I want you gone!"

"No, Mama!" her sisters said as they started to cry. Mariah was there. She was fourteen years old. Aniyah was there too. She was boo-hooing saying, "No, Mama, please, don't make her go!" She was only nine years old. Mariah was crying and saying, "No, Mama, don't! What did she do? What did she do?" Serena was three years old, and she was crying because everyone else was crying, from all the confusion and excitement. Conveniently, or so Nicole had speculated, Fatimah wasn't there; she'd spent the night over her girlfriend's house.

Nicole was seventeen when she was booted from her mother's house. What they didn't know at the time was that Mama was pregnant with another product of her addiction to Otis. Tangie never told anyone why she'd kicked Nicole out that day. Nicole's sisters didn't know, and Tangie never told her mother. Granny had no idea why she had to take her granddaughter in, on the eve of Nicole's high school graduation. The graduation that Tangie didn't attend. But Nicole knew; it turned out that Tangie had found a pair of panties tangled in her sheets when she came home that morning. She knew they were her daughter's because she was the one who'd bought them for her.

Nicole had blamed everybody but Daddy Ray for that incident. She had somehow gotten it in her mind that Fatimah had set her up. Back when Nicole was ten years old and Fatimah was nine, she had caught Nicole coming out of Mama's room one night, while Mama was gone. Fatimah said she saw something, and Nicole hadn't even asked what she had seen; she just told her to be quiet and go back to bed. Nicole had told Fatimah that she didn't see anything and told her to be very quiet and just go back to bed. But Nicole knew when they heard the rustling behind Mama's bedroom door that when Fatimah ran to her room, that she hadn't done as she was told. Nicole knew that she was lurking behind her bedroom door peeking through the space between the door and the doorjamb to see if Nicole was going to go to her own bed or back into Mama's room.

Nicole walked back into Mama's room that night, and Fatimah and Nicole's relationship was changed forever. Nicole didn't blame Daddy Ray. Even though she thought that the right thing to do would have been to confess his wrongdoing to Tangie and to tell her that he'd been "doing" her daughter since she was a fragile nine-year-old girl. But it made it much easier for him to allow Tangie to go on the assumption that her voluptuous seventeen-year-old daughter had seduced him. Nicole had no idea how Mama and Daddy Ray's conversation had went when she found those panties in the bed, but it certainly hadn't gone in Nicole's favor.

Nicole had moved in with Granny that very morning. Mama had left the house, so Nicole could freely move about and gather her things. Granny picked her up, and Nicole had cried all the way to her granny's house. Granny didn't know what was wrong, and Nicole couldn't bring herself to tell her. Granny had just figured that it all had occurred as a result of one of her daughter's numerous drunken binges. But Nicole knew that that wasn't true. Her mother was sober, and she knew exactly what she was doing.

Nicole graduated high school with honors. She could have attended school anywhere, but she chose to go to school close to her sisters'. She'd gotten hired at a law firm as an executive secretary through an apprenticeship program through her high school. She worked there as she earned her BS in business management and business administration.

Tye was born in December of that year, and he stayed with Granny from the time that Mama brought him home from the hospital. Tangie had claimed that because Daddy Ray couldn't have any babies that Tye would be the last straw and she didn't feel comfortable having Otis's baby boy around him. Granny told her she sounded crazy as hell. But she wouldn't turn away a grandchild, no matter how lame the excuse was. Granny thought that Tangie's problem was that she didn't want any kids; she just wanted the man. But as crazy as Otis was about his first and only boy, it still had not made him leave his wife and it didn't make him want Tangie anymore than he'd wanted her when she'd had his girls.

Mama regularly dropped Nicole's younger sisters off at her granny's house for them to "spend some time" with their grandmother. But Nicole knew the truth; she had been her sisters' primary caregiver all of their lives, and that wouldn't stop just because she'd kicked Nicole out. Nicole didn't mind though. Because she loved her sisters, she loved taking care of them, and that way, she could keep a watchful eye over them, protect them, and make sure that Daddy Ray was keeping his hands to himself.

At age nineteen, Nicole rented the downstairs of Uncle Clyde and Auntie Cookie's two-story house, across the street from Granny. It was available because their elderly tenant had passed away. Nicole cleaned it up and made it her own, and when Mama would drop her sisters off at Granny's, she'd take them across the street to her place. She'd help them with homework and school projects, made sure that they got their baths. And did their hair, and got them ready for school each day. She would stay home with them and fix their meals, watch television with them at night, and send them to school each morning, with either a bagged lunch or lunch money. All Mama had to do was pick them up from school and drop them off at Granny's house every day. But Nicole didn't mind because she knew that they were safe with her.

Uncle Clyde and Auntie Cookie charged Nicole very little for rent. They felt so guilty about how she was being mistreated by her mother. But nobody could say anything to Tangie without being cursed out or getting into a screaming match with her, so nobody tried. Nicole took such good care of the girls and of herself that nobody wanted to say anything. They felt it was in the best interest of Nicole and her sisters to keep their mouths shut.

Mama never mentioned it, but she knew where her daughters really were every day. But twenty-four seven was still a new business, and she still had a lot to do and a lot to learn. It was so convenient to have someone she knew and trusted to keep her girls and take good care of them as she worked and went on with her life. Because of this convenience, life hadn't changed for her. But it had changed drastically for Nicole.

Fatimah went to college out of state, and she'd had a ball. Nursing was her major, and she "went all the way," earning her master's degree and becoming a nurse practitioner. She made Mama so proud. She'd gotten married and made her plenty of grandchildren, and they had a nice home. She thought Fatimah had made the perfect life for herself, until it had gotten out that her husband was a compulsive cheater.

Nicole helped Fatimah out while she was in school too. She sent her money and care packages. When Fatimah wouldn't do something Mama wanted her to, Mama would withhold money saying, "You so grown, figure it out for yourself." Then Fatimah would call Nicole, and she would handle it. "How soon they forget," Nicole would often say to herself.

Nicole helped everybody. She had always done so. She put her little sisters first. She loved them and sheltered them and protected them, then let them go as if she was their mother and they were her own children.

Nicole wrung out the cool washcloth and pressed it against her face. She flinched. It was cold and wet on her skin. She rubbed her eyes with it, draped it over her face, and sighed deeply into it. She opened her eyes wide and stared at herself in the mirror as she held the washcloth in her hands. She stood up straight with her shoulders back, relaxed her eyes, and looked at her face. She leaned into the counter with her hands gripping the edge and looked deeply into her own dark eyes. She wondered if they were really the window to her soul. She hoped not.

Nicole remembered what GG used to say about praying, and she wondered if things would have been different if she would have gone to church with her more. She wondered if she knew how to talk to God like GG did, maybe Daddy Ray never would have come to her room.

Nicole blinked a few times and then dismissed those thoughts from her head. She'd reasoned that no matter how hard you try to avoid life's pitfalls, things were just going to happen whether your eyes are opened or closed, whether you're on your knees or standing up on your feet.

Nicole wasn't bitter though. This was just a rough night. Things would all be better when the sun came up. Darkness and solitude could do this to a person sometimes, force them to think about the things they had buried inside. Things that waited like demons to creep out of the darkness when you least expected.

Mariah woke up to a new set of problems. Problems that were not her own. She made breakfast for the kids. Then she headed upstairs with a cup of coffee for her husband as he got ready for work.

"You need me to stay home with you and the kids?"

"No, baby, I need you to work," Mariah said as she handed Carl the mug of hot coffee. Mariah had taken the week off, and they needed every penny. She had plenty of vacation time to cover the time off, but there was no need for upsetting their household's routine over Fatimah's issues.

"It'll be fine, I mean, this is something that Fatimah and Jason have to work out. There's nothing we can do."

"So what's Jason gonna do?"

Mariah leaned back against the footboard of her bed, her huge belly protruding in front of her. "He didn't say, but I know one thing, he needs to talk to his children before they get home and see that their mama is gone."

Mariah crossed her arms and shook her head. "Never in a million years. I never saw this comin'. If anyone would have told me that Fatimah would have done some shit like this, I never would have believed 'um. This is just crazy."

"Well," Carl said as he pulled a white T-shirt over his head, "if he needs the kids to stay while he works out some things, it's fine with me."

Mariah stared straight ahead as she thought about her sister's situation. "You know what? This is what Jason gets. All that cheatin' and messin' around and thinkin' that somebody's at home holdin' it down, makin' sure his shit don't stink. Now he's stuck over there dumbfounded. He don't know what to do."

"You really think your sister ain't comin' back?" Carl asked, turning to his wife as he brushed the waves in his hair.

"I don't know if Fatimah's serious or if she's just going out of her way to teach Jay a lesson. But whatever the case is, he's gotta do something. He's got kids," Mariah continued, leaning against the footboard with her arms crossed. "Somebody's gotta think about the kids."

"Where you think she's at?" Carl asked.

"I have no idea."

It was not the beautiful morning that Nicole was expecting. Her head hurt like she had a hangover, and her body ached as if she had the flu. She finally did get a little dream-free sleep, but it was very little and not quite enough for her to function.

Nicole went into the bathroom, stuffed her hair into a plastic shower cap, and stepped into the shower. The water fell from the shower's ceiling like raindrops. She leaned up against the wall and was tempted to fall asleep right there. Nicole pulled off her shower cap and slung it to the floor; it wasn't really keeping her hair from getting wet anyway. She closed her eyes and let the warm water run down her face and through her long, thick hair. It was so refreshing. She was starting to wake up and feel rejuvenated again. "Aaaah," she said to herself as the water awakened her body. "A new day a new opportunity."

Nicole towel dried her hair and then blew it dry with her hair dryer. She flat ironed it super straight and gave it a little bump on the ends. She preferred it curlier and full, but it had taken so long just to dry it and get it straightened that she didn't want to spend any more time curling it. She checked her voice mail and got the message from Mariah about Fatimah leaving Jason and the kids. Nicole shook her head. She always said that she saw it coming, but she didn't want to say "I told you so." She felt sorry for Fatimah's kids. She felt it was sad that doing the right thing could make a person go crazy. She got a call while she was changing her clothes.

"Hello?"

"Hello, Nicole," said the voice on the other line. Nicole didn't recognize the voice at first. He sounded really weak and weary.

"Is this Don?"

"Yes," Don said. He groaned as he repositioned himself in the bed. "I want to apologize for not getting in touch with you sooner. I had a bit of a mishap that morning after I dropped you off." It had been three days since she'd heard from Don. But she thought nothing of it.

"What's the matter? What happened?" Nicole asked.

"I was attacked in the parking garage of the hotel."

"Oh my god. Are you okay?" Nicole stammered in disbelief. "What happened?"

Nicole thought that Don would say that he was robbed. That he was hit over the head after his wallet having been stolen, but Don said, "I was just about to enter the stairwell to the elevators when this big, huge guy came behind me and punched me in my back."

"Oh my god," Nicole said again. She covered her mouth with her hand; she couldn't believe what she was hearing.

"I mean this guy was huge, and I'm not just exaggerating for the sake of the story. He punched me hard, right in the kidneys. Mmmph," Don said as he paused to reflect on the incident. "I didn't even know what he wanted at first. He didn't take any money. He didn't take the keys to my rental car. He just kept beating me. I couldn't get a good look at him. I wish that I could have gotten a better look at his face. But he was careful not to stand in front of me. He didn't want me to be able to identify him."

"Did you go to the police?" Nicole asked.

"Yea, but not right away. Luckily, someone found me passed out in the stairwell. I have no idea how long I was out. The last thing that I remembered was him grabbing me from behind and wrapping his forearm around my neck. My god, it felt like he had my head in a vice," Don said as he rubbed his neck.

"Don, are you okay? Is there anything that I can do? I can't believe that happened to you. Were there any cameras around? I'm sure there had to be cameras around."

"Well, no. Ironically, the cameras were out of order right in that vicinity. Isn't that crazy? If I'd been attacked just a few more feet closer to the elevator, it would have all been caught on tape. It was as if he knew exactly where to strike."

"Awww, Don. That is terrible. I am so sorry."

"Believe me, I am too. This is really very embarrassing for me. To call a woman and to tell her about the thrashing I just received. But I had to call you."

"Oh, Don. I'm glad you did," Nicole said, voice full of concern. She stopped pulling up her jeans and sat down on the bed.

"I was really groggy after all of the pain killers, and I was hallucinating a bit from all of the Dilaudid. He cracked my ribs pretty good."

"Oh my god," she gasped.

"I wasn't quite sure at first, after everything had happened, but now that a few days have passed and my mind is clear, I remember something. Something that my attacker said."

"What was it? It could be a clue. Did you tell the police?"

"No, I didn't," he said with a sigh. "I thought that I might have been hallucinating, a side effect of the medication I'd been taking. I remember him saying, in my ear as he was choking me, right before I blacked out."

Nicole sat up to the edge of the bed as if anxious to hear what his attacker said, as if those words would give some much-needed clue to his identity. "Well, what did he say?"

"He said, 'Stay away from Nicole, or I'll kill you.'"

Nicole thought that this should have been the first thing he said when he called. But it wasn't any less disturbing, being that it was the last. Darren had lost his rabid mind. Nicole had intended on playing his little tit-for-tat game with him, but he had gone too far. She'd taken the shots at her car as being a mere destruction property. The fact that it was parked right in front of her grandmother's house was simply payback for what she'd done to him in his driveway. But to actually assault someone, now that was taking it too far, and she knew she needed to stop it here, because she wasn't willing to take that next retaliatory step.

Nicole told him she'd call him back. She sat there with her jeans pulled halfway up her thighs as she scrambled to figure out what to do. She had greatly underestimated Darren and how far he was willing to go to prove his point. She didn't fear for her own safety. He knew that she didn't, but he was well aware of her concern for the safety of her loved ones and others around her, and she didn't want to be responsible for any of them being put in harm's way.

She considered going to the police with this new information; perhaps, by putting two and two together, they could arrest Darren as a suspect of both of these crimes. But they should have gotten to Darren by now. She'd given them his home addresses, both the one he took Nicole to and the home he shared with his wife. She had provided his work and cell phone numbers as well as his e-mail address. She was pretty thorough; that was why she couldn't understand why her sisters acted as if she wasn't doing enough.

Nicole wasn't an emotional woman; she didn't cry and tremble in fear and panic like her sisters did. It wasn't that she didn't feel any fear; she just wouldn't be displaying it for all of the world to see. She didn't open herself up to criticism. She had nerves of steel, and she didn't wear her emotions on her sleeve. She'd deal with Darren in a calm and rational manner. And in her own way.

Aniyah woke up facing her bedroom wall, with her butt resting in the small of Nathan's back. She scooched back on the bed and pushed her buttocks snuggly in the crook of his back as she reached back and ran her hands across the smooth skin of his muscular thighs. Aniyah didn't care if her touch disturbed Nathan, and she didn't care if it woke him up. She had to do something to keep her mind off this other man. The man that was invading her thoughts and her dreams. She lay there, with her head resting in the crook of her left arm. As she'd slept, she thought about Matthew, and he was the first thing on her mind when she woke up. She was off again today. She had absolutely nothing planned, and that left plenty of time for her mind to wander.

Aniyah got up and headed straight to the shower. She hopped out soaking wet and grabbed an oversized bath towel from her linen closet. She tied the big, purple towel around her body and went to the kitchen. Her kitchen counter was lined with appliances that she never used. Most of which were products that she had purchased impulsively as a result of watching late-night infomercials. "Those potato peeling gloves seemed like a good idea at the time," Aniyah thought to herself.

Nathan didn't have to be at work until two o'clock this afternoon, but Aniyah knew he wouldn't wake up until around 1:30 p.m. Aniyah reached over her as-seen-on-TV appliances and opened her kitchen cabinet. She reached for a box of cereal that was too far back for her to grasp, but that didn't stop her from leaning and reaching and trying to get it down.

When she saw Nathan's hand pick up the cereal box, it scared her. She gasped and turned to look at him, holding the towel tighter by the knot that she'd tied it in.

"What?" Nathan said, handing her the cereal box.

"You scared the mess outta me," Aniyah replied.

"Why? Did you forget I was here?" he said with a smile.

"Of course not. You were just so quiet. You shouldn't sneak up on folks like that." Aniyah frowned, and her heart was beating a mile a minute.

"Speaking of sneaking," Nathan said, as he pulled Aniyah close to him by her towel. "Who is Matthew?"

"Excuse me?" Aniyah said as she looked at Nathan, trying not to let the surprise show on her face. "What are you talking about?" Aniyah said, ready to deny everything if she had to.

"Math-thew," he said. "That's the name you were calling in your sleep," Nathan said.

"The only Matthew I know is this guy I went to school with. And I don't have any reason to call his name. He used to pick on me in high school," Aniyah answered; she figured half the truth was better than no truth at all. "How many times did I say it?"

Nathan looked at her with a raised brow. "How many times were you supposed to say it?"

Aniyah frowned and pushed Nathan away. "Believe me, Nathan, Matthew is the last person you hafta worry about." Aniyah turned away from him and walked over to the refrigerator to get some skim milk. She was not a good liar, and she certainly couldn't keep up the lies for too long without it eventually showing all over her face.

Aniyah sat the milk on the counter next to the cereal. She went into the cabinet and grabbed a small blue bowl. She sat on a stool at the counter and poured some cereal into her bowl and covered it with milk.

"Nathan, can you pass me a spoon?" she said without turning to look at him.

Nathan grabbed a spoon out of the silverware drawer and handed it to Aniyah. It was one of the biggest spoons he could find.

She turned to Nathan and smiled. "You know you play too much," she said as she handed the large spoon back to him. Nathan laughed as he took the spoon from her and replaced it with a smaller spoon.

"So this is what's for breakfast?"

"Yea, for me," Aniyah answered as she put a big spoonful of bran cereal in her mouth. "What? You want me to fix you something?" Aniyah said, talking with her mouth full.

"Naw, I'm going back to bed," Nathan said as he stood in front of her in his navy blue boxers and stretched. She watched as his sexy, chiseled abs and obliques lengthened and tightened. He yawned and stretched his arms way above his head, as he growled and exhaled fatigue from his body.

"Are you sure you don't want me to fix you something?" Aniyah asked again, desperate to change the subject.

"Naw, I'm okay. I'll grab something before I go to work. I just wanted to let you know that I'm not gonna close tonight. I'm gonna have one of the kitchen managers close, so we can go out and have a late dinner. I'll get off at about eight," he said as he wrapped his arms around her waist and kissed the crook of her neck. "I want to be with you tonight."

Aniyah smiled, put her spoon down, and turned facing him, swiveling the stool she was sitting in. She wrapped her arms around his neck and kissed Nathan as he held on to the rim of the counter behind her. She closed her eyes. She loved the way this felt, and she thought she loved him too. Aniyah asked herself, Is this what love feels like? Aniyah hugged

Nathan's neck tighter and whispered in his ear, "I love you, Matthew." Nathan pushed away and looked her in her face. But before Nathan could get out a word, Aniyah opened her eyes, winked, and smiled, then said, "Gothcha!"

"That's not funny, Aniyah," Nathan said with a look of uncertainty on his face. Aniyah giggled and held his face in her hands and kissed him all over his lips and his cheeks. A smile gradually appeared on his face. She pulled him close to her and gave him a big hug, giggling in his ear. She stared at the wall behind his head and mentally reminded herself to be more careful. She hadn't intentionally called him Matthew, but her play-off was perfect.

Chapter 17

THE COLOR OF FIRE

The picture spread through campus like wildfire. Even some of the students who had gone home for the summer knew about the mystery girl. Everyone was talking about the hot girl lying naked across the dean's desk.

It only took a day or two before Dean Carmichael sent out a mass e-mail to administration and had made an official announcement to the student body, concerning the photograph. Serena didn't care about any of that though. All she could think about was her journal. Had he read it? Did he destroy it? Had he planned on keeping it? Or was he planning on exposing all of the dirty little secrets inside?

Serena didn't know what she was going to do. She had nothing planned, and she didn't even want to think about. Her journal was like a missing child, and she wanted it back safe and sound. She didn't want to deal with Hakeem to get it back, and she couldn't imagine what he'd want as "ransom."

Serena had poured so much into her journal. Her thoughts, her feelings, her vision for her future. She had entered college as a nursing major. She'd taken prerequisites while still in high school, and her mother had been grooming her for nursing for as long as she could remember. Serena never had any choice in the matter. All of Tangie's girls went to school for nursing. The only daughter who didn't was Nicole, and she became very successful on her own without having to obey everything that her mama said.

Mama didn't know that as soon as Serena was able to, she had changed her major from nursing to English and she minored in music. She'd studied classical piano since she was a child, and she was quite good. Too shy for big Carnegie Hall dreams, but she loved the solace that her music gave. She had been writing and composing music, but shared it with no one. She reveled in the quiet solitude that she shared with her thoughts and her feelings, in her journal. How dare he take that away from her?

She saw Hakeem today on campus; he looked her in her eyes as she walked past him, and he had the nerve to smirk. She rolled her eyes at him and snatched her arm away as he'd grasped it when she walked past. "Don't touch me." Serena thought to herself as she walked past. "I am in so much trouble because of his ass."

She hadn't talked to Eric all day. He'd been trying to get in touch with her, but she ignored his calls. She overheard him talking about the mystery girl saying what he would do "wit dat ass," if it was his. Not only was the statement ignorant, but it was disrespectful. She knew that he was just talking amongst friends and that he hadn't intended for her to hear him. But she did, and she was pissed. She was mad about the disrespect, and she was mad that he didn't even realize that he was talking about his own woman. She was so tempted to say, "It's me. Dumb ass. The girl in the picture is me!" But she didn't. She wouldn't be telling anyone.

"When are you leaving?"

"On Friday."

"I am gonna miss you so much," Stacey said as she picked up a few of the fries that she was sharing with Serena.

"I'm only gonna be gone a week," Serena said as she took a bite of her cheeseburger.

"I know, but a week is a long time."

"I hope it doesn't go fast. Time flies when I go home to visit."

"Yea, I know. A week feels like a weekend when I go back home," Stacey said. "I know Eric is really gonna miss you."

"Yea, whatever."

"Why you say that?"

"Eric is too busy worried about the mystery girl. He's not thinking about me leaving him for a week," Serena said, washing her burger down with her vanilla milkshake. Stacey laughed.

"No, seriously," Serena replied. "I wouldn't be surprised if he looked for her while I'm gone." Stacey laughed louder, and Serena smiled picturing Eric scouring the campus for the mystery girl, not knowing that the mystery girl was really her.

"You know I really feel sorry for her."

"Why?"

"She's really in deep trouble. I bet she didn't think her little stunt would get her in this much of a mess. Everyone's looking for her now—faculty, administration, even the students."

"Well, I don't think that anyone's gonna figure it out. I think it's gonna stay between The Mystery Girl and whoever took her picture."

"Not if they offer a reward for information on her."

"Hmmph," Serena scoffed. "No one knows who she is or they would have said something by now. Besides, you can't even see her face in that picture."

"Well, I bet her man knows it her. You can't have a body like that and be single." Stacey giggled. At about fifty pounds overweight, she was convinced that if she was a little bit smaller, she wouldn't be single or unhappy.

"Nah, I betchu her man doesn't even know that it's her, not unless he was the one who snapped the picture. Even so, he would have said something by now. He would have wanted to tell somebody that he was nailin' the mystery girl. Seems that's what all the guys are talkin' about. Screwin' the mystery girl."

"Not Eric. He's a sweetheart. You should see the way he looks at chu," Stacey said.

"No, including Eric. He's a man. He just like any other man."

Serena finished up her burgers and fries. She was sitting almost in the exact spot she was sitting in when she'd met Eric.

"You know what I would do if I was her?" Stacey said. "I'd turn myself in."

"What?" Serena said, looking at her as she took a big sip of her milkshake.

"I sure would. I wouldn't give anyone the opportunity to turn me in. I'd walk right into Dean Carmichael's office, wearing my sexiest dress, and I'd tell him it's me, aaaaall me."

Stacey sat up straight, sticking her bosom out. She put her hands on her hips and switched her hips from side to side in her seat as she spoke. The girls laughed hysterically.

"That's what you would do, Stacey?" Serena asked, laughing.

"That's exactly what I would do, Serena. Anyone who has the boldness and the confidence to pose naked on the dean's desk has the confidence to walk right into his office and lay her cards on the table."

"Wouldn't she get in trouble?"

"I don't think so. But if she did, I bet she'd handle it like a woman. She seems tough like that," Stacey said. She spoke as if she knew her, the mystery girl that was. Serena wrinkled her forehead and smiled. Laura had been right; that photo sure was thought provoking. Serena tried to picture it in her mind. She didn't see herself as bold and confident, but somehow Stacey had gotten that out of the picture and Hakeem had gotten it out of Serena on film.

Serena headed back to her dorm room. She'd had her last class of the day, and she was tired. She missed her roommate, Tiffany, but she was so glad that Tiffany was out of town for the summer visiting her family. Tiffany was messy and loud, but she loved having her around, because she was so much fun. But she also enjoyed the peace and quiet.

As soon as she stepped into her room, she cried. She didn't know why she was being so emotional. Maybe it was a combination of her plight and the fact that her journal was stolen. Or maybe it was just because she was homesick. She missed her sisters, she missed her little brother, she missed her nieces and nephews, and she even missed her mother. Serena wanted to hug her granny and kiss GG on her soft smooth cheek, and she missed her friends. Serena sighed and wiped the tears off her face. She sat her cell phone on the table next to her bed and tossed her book bag to the floor. She hated feeling this way. Feeling scared and confused was a terrible combination. It made her feel like a little girl instead of the mature, grown-up woman that she was telling everyone that she was.

Serena lay back on the bed and thought, "Not a bad idea Stacey had come up with." If only she was that bold, confident, hot girl that Stacey and the others saw in that picture, she would go straight to the dean's office in her sexiest suit and lay her cards down on the table.

But what cards were she holding? What exactly would she say when she got a moment alone with him. She would go in like a woman and come out like a sniveling child. She had no idea what to say to the adult who held her future in his hands.

Serena fell asleep. She had several weird dreams, some about home, some about school, some about Hakeem. She'd met Hakeem when she first started college. She didn't date him right away, but there was an instant attraction. He could feel it too. Hakeem was dating a girl named Trinity at the time. Trinity was beautiful; her father was Hawaiian and her mother was black. She had long, straight, dark hair, beautiful china-doll eyes, and a pretty smile.

She was very tall and thin and very attractive. But she was mean. She had the nastiest attitude, and she would always refer to Serena as the little girl. Serena dreamed that Hakeem was still with her, flaunting this pretty girl in her face. She didn't think that Trinity and Hakeem were a good couple. They were both beautiful people, but not such a good match. Trinity was haughty and snobbish. Hakeem was witty and down to earth.

* * *

Hakeem had told Serena that his name means wise, intelligent, and insightful. He told her that the first day they were formally introduced. She didn't know why he told her that, but she was impressed that he knew the meaning of his name. Serena had told him that her name meant peaceful and cheerful and had added that its origin was Latin. Hakeem had smiled and said the origin of his name was Arabic.

"So you weren't ever gonna call me." Serena was startled by his voice.

"What are you doing in here!" Serena said as she hugged her pillow and scooted up to the head of the bed. Hakeem sat at the foot of her bed facing her.

"How did you get in here?" Serena said. She noticed her journal sitting on the bed. She grabbed it and stuck it behind the pillow, and pulled the pillow close to her body.

"I have access to keys," Hakeem said as he looked at her. Serena couldn't bring herself to look away. Hakeem reached out and touched her leg, and Serena pulled it in closer to her. "So when were you planning on talking to me?"

"I wasn't."

"What do I hafto do?"

"You don't hafto do anything. Just get out of my room!"

"Why? Why are you acting this way?"

"Hakeem! Do you know what you've done?" Serena looked at Hakeem like he'd lost his mind. "Why would I ever want to talk to you? You're trying to ruin my life!"

"Nobody's trying to ruin your life. I just wanted to get you to talk to me. That's all I wanted. Just a chance for you to hear me out."

"Hakeem, I don't want to hear you out. It's over. I have bigger things to worry about, thanks to you!"

"Listen, it's not that serious."

Serena felt herself getting more upset and excited by the minute. "What do you mean it's not that serious? Don't you understand what you've done to me? Those pictures were supposed to be between me and you. When I agreed to take 'um, you promised me that they'd never get out. You promised me."

"It's not a big deal. Easily rectified. No one can see your face anyhow. It was the only way that I knew to get you to talk to me."

"It didn't work, you had to break in to my room to get to me."

"Didn't break in. I used a key."

"Hakeem, get out of here!" Serena leaned forward, gripping the pillow tighter. Her voice was getting higher and squeakier. She was trying hard not to get herself excited. She didn't want anyone overhearing their conversation.

"Look, calm down. Do you want my help or not?"

"I don't need your fucking help. Now get the fuck out of my room."

"Listen, Serena. Just hear me out. I wanted to talk to you about Stephanie."

"I don't give a fuck about you and Stephanie? Oh my god," Serena said as she held her face in her hands. She shook her head and sighed as she struggled to hold back her tears.

"Don't you understand what you've done. Don't you understand what you've done to me? You've humiliated me in front of all of my peers, in front of the faculty and staff. You have sabotaged my academic career."

"Serena, stop being so dramatic."

"Dramatic? Oooh! Hakeem, get out of my room!" Serena said, pointing to the door.

"Look, since I'm already in here. Let me just explain. Okay?"

Serena didn't say a word.

"I have been tryin' to get you to talk to me since you broke up with me. All I want is for you to hear me out. I'm not tryin' to scare you. I'm not tryin' to ruin your education. I just want to talk to you."

Serena still didn't say a word.

"Okay," Hakeem said, as he took a deep breath. "I never, ever, cheated on you."

"Yes, you did!"

"No, I didn't."

"Yes, you did!"

"Let me finish," Hakeem said. "I never ever cheated on you. I don't know who told you that I did, but whoever it was is a liar. We had a good thing going. Why would I want to ruin that?"

"Yea, you did. You had a great thing goin'. You just wanted someone that you could control. You had me doin' all sorts of crazy stuff."

"I didn't make you do anything you didn't want to do. I only introduced you to some things that you would have been afraid to do otherwise."

"Yea, whatever."

"You know I'm right." He scooted closer to her in the bed.

Serena scooted away.

"You hafta admit those pictures are good."

Serena sat up. It was getting late, and the room was getting dark. She was afraid of Hakeem. She was fearful of his influence over her. She'd done anything he'd asked. Anything he suggested. And she loved it. It was such a rush. But it was dangerous. With Hakeem, she had no self-control. He wasn't mild mannered and calm like Eric. Eric would do whatever *she* said, whatever *she* suggested.

"We didn't have a healthy relationship." Serena said.

"What was unhealthy about it? We had fun together. We made memories together that we can someday tell our grandkids about."

Serena pressed her face in her pillow; she couldn't hold back the tears. Her eyes felt like they were on fire. She was so angry. She felt like she was a child, with no voice and no control. She didn't want to lift her head, but she wished that when she did that Hakeem was gone. She hugged her pillow, pressing her face into it trying to muffle her cries.

"I hate you, Hakeem. I wish I never met you. You are the worst thing that ever happened to me."

"So what is Eric? Is he the best thing that ever happened to you?" Hakeem asked. Serena didn't say a word. "I bet he doesn't even know that it's you in that picture." Serena didn't answer him.

"He hasn't cheated on me."

"Don't be so sure."

"Get the fuck out of here! I don't want to have this conversation with you. I hate you." She tried to say the word "hate" with such emphasis that it was as if she was grinding the word down into his very soul. The release of that picture was just a further act of manipulation. But he wouldn't be dangling her by those puppet strings today. She wanted him gone, and she meant it.

"I wouldn't have cared if you did or if you didn't fuck Stephanie. I just didn't want to be with you anymore. I wanted us to be over. I was glad when I found out that you weren't faithful, because it gave me an excuse to dump yo' ass." Serena leaned forward as she squeezed her pillow and looked deeply into Hakeem's eyes. She could read the hurt all over his face, and she was glad. She wanted him to hurt too.

How could Hakeem ever claim to have loved her and hurt her as badly as he did? How could he be so ignorant so as not to see what he'd done? And how could he have the audacity to think that she'd ever want to see him again or have him in her presence?

"You can tell everybody it's me in that picture. I don't care. I don't care if they kick me out of this stupid school. I want to go home anyway."

Serena cried as her body shook. She felt so stupid and naïve and fragile. She hated that she turned out to be the stupid little girl that everybody thought she was. Her sisters were right; she should have stayed in Cleveland where everybody could keep her safe. She obviously wasn't capable of making mature adult decisions on her own.

Hakeem looked at her, speechless. He reached down at his feet and tossed an envelope on her bed. "I would never have gotten you into something I couldn't have gotten you out of."

"Don't bother. I'm a grown-ass woman. I can take care of myself."

"Serena, I swear I never ever cheated on you. After three years, three years, Serena? You won't even give me the benefit of the doubt? I love you," Hakeem begged.

"You are nothing but a fucking liar. Get the fuck out."

Hakeem left her room. He was stubborn, but he didn't fight it anymore. It was crazy, but Serena did love him. She enjoyed her time with him, but it felt too weird. It felt too much like an outer-body experience. Hakeem had her sneaking into the auditorium at night to play the college's grand piano as he sat in the audience listening. He'd clap and give her a standing ovation when she was done. Then they'd make love backstage or in one of the other forbidden areas of the campus. Hakeem made her feel alive.

*   *   *

"Hakeem, you're gonna get me into trouble," Serena had said as they snuck in past the huge mahogany doors of the auditorium.

"No, I'm not. We'll be fine. We just hafto hurry up. We'll be in and out."

"What if somebody hears us?"

"Don't worry about that. I've got it covered. We'll be in and out," Hakeem had repeated as if he had any control over who heard them.

"How much time did you say we have?"

"I didn't. It depends on how long it takes you to play." The stage was lit, and sitting center stage was a beautiful grand piano. Serena had run down the aisle as fast as she could; she was nervous and excited, and she couldn't wait to run her fingers across the piano's ebony and ivory keys.

Serena had felt like a kid at Christmas time as she ran toward the stage. She had an adrenalin rush, and she knew that time was of the essence. Serena walked around the sleek, black, lacquered grand piano, a gift from one of the school's wealthy alumni. She ran her fingers across the glossy, shellacked wood of the lid and the rim of the fine instrument. She admired its beauty giving it the respect it deserved. She stood downstage and took a bow, as Hakeem whistled from the back row of the auditorium. She was happy to be right there at that moment in that forbidden place. Her heart raced with excitement and anticipation. She grinned like a Cheshire cat as she approached the bench. She sat down, back perfect and upright. She was poised as if accompanied by the finest of orchestras.

Serena had intended on warming up first, but as she'd sat at the wooden bench, she couldn't help but start playing. She couldn't control herself. It was so quiet in the auditorium that you could hear a pin drop, that was, until she filled the air with music. She'd closed her eyes as her fingers danced across the keys.

Serena played the intro to Christopher Cross's Sailing, just as she'd heard it in her head. She played it note for note just as she'd remembered it; she didn't change a thing. It needed no embellishments as far as Serena was concerned. It was perfect just as it was, and Serena was more than happy to play it for her audience of one.

She played as if there was a fire deep inside her that couldn't be extinguished. Her playing had been so passionate and heartfelt that she felt her heart was full to bursting. She sang the words in her head as she played. She'd held her eyes closed as if when she'd open them, she'd find herself swept away to a destination of her choosing.

When Serena had finished playing, there was nothing but silence. Serena had to squint to make sure Hakeem was still there in the audience, cuffing both hands above her eyes to look out in the distance. But then she could see Hakeem standing and clapping slowly then faster; then he'd started hooping and hollering and whistling. Serena had blushed and smiled in a way that made her dimples look their deepest.

Serena had recalled when Hakeem approached the stage and as he walked up the steps toward her. She'd asked him, "Did you like the song I chose? Or did you think it was corny? It's always been one of my favorite songs to play," Serena had said, rambling on like a teenager, giddy with excitement. Hakeem had known that he'd ignited a flame in her, fueled by both her creativity and her desire to experience knew things.

The expression on his face could be best described as being somewhere between admiration and a deepening desire for her. He had been so impressed by her performance that he was in awe. He knew that she was beautiful and he knew that she was artistic, but her talents were boundless. He approached her and stepped to her slowly as she backed up against the grand piano.

"That was beautiful" was all Hakeem had said as he leaned into her, bent down, and pressed his lips against hers. He loved her and he had felt more than honored to be the one that she had shared these new experiences with, and he longed for a day when he could expose her to new and exciting things without sneaking, copping keys, or trespassing.

*　　*　　*

Hakeem hadn't intended on hurting Serena, and he hadn't intended on taking this thing this far. It wasn't that he'd felt bad about the pictures; if he had to do it over again, he wouldn't have changed a thing. And it wasn't that he felt guilty about leaking the infamous, mystery-girl photo. It was beautiful, and he loved that picture. That picture as well as others had captured a side of Serena that she didn't even know she had. It was beautiful; it wasn't trashy at all, and it had sparked conversation on and off campus. It had people talking to each other who wouldn't have conversed otherwise. It was a masterpiece, and Hakeem was the genius who had captured it.

As Hakeem walked to his car, he thought about what he could have done differently and of all of the things he should have said. He wondered how he could have changed the outcome of this situation. This was not what he had planned. He wanted to sit and talk to Serena and have her reminiscing over the great times that they'd had. He wanted her to believe him, when he'd said that he hadn't cheated. And he wanted to find out who had told her that lie in the first place.

Hakeem acted like he didn't care. He hung out with Stephanie, hoping to make Serena jealous, but Serena moved on with such ease as if she'd never really loved him at all. Hakeem slammed his car door and sat in the driver's seat trying to think of what to do next.

Serena held her journal close to her heart like it was a living, breathing organism. She was glad that he'd returned it with the little gold lock intact. Along with her special ink pen, with the poof on the end. Serena had enough inside of her to fill the pages of that journal, even if she just stuck to the most significant events. She wanted to write relentlessly, but she wouldn't be corrupted by the poison of other people's cruel words. Serena sat her journal on her bed. She didn't bother opening the envelope that Hakeem had left. She didn't need any more surprises; she was having a hard enough time dealing with the last package that he'd left.

Serena got out of bed and clicked on the lamp on her nightstand. It wasn't too bright, but it was bright enough. She thought about what Stacey had said to her in the cafeteria. It was the closest thing to a plan that Serena had heard since the pictures had shown up. She went to her small closet and slid the hanging clothes along the aluminum bar by their hangers. Tons of clothes that she'd never even worn, most of which her mother had picked out for her. Clothes that made her look like a woman instead of a boy, at least that was what her Mama had told her.

There were several pairs of blue jean capris in her closet. They were cute, but Serena thought they made her butt look too big. She'd worn a pair once and had gotten so much attention that she'd sworn off capris forever. Her tiny little waist and her thick hips and thighs were next to impossible to hide in any pair of pants, but those formfitting capris really had the fellas going, and she couldn't handle the attention.

Serena wore an intricate lower-back tattoo that she had difficulty hiding, especially in hip-huggers and in low-rise jeans. The tattoo started at the small of her back and extended outward toward her full hips. She had a "low crack," according to the tattoo artist, a good friend of hers, so he was able to be more elaborate with his original design. It was in black ink, and it looked beautiful on her bronze skin. It accentuated her coke-bottle body and brought even more attention to her full, round butt. Men would catch a glimpse of it, then would stop and stare, wondering what the rest of the tattoo looked like beneath her jeans.

Serena had cut her long, curly hair after about a year of college. That infuriated her mother; she loved her long hair. She had grown tired of being called the little Latina girl; after all, she was black, just like her sisters, and even they would pick on her about being the lightest of the girls. She stayed away from the girly gear and preferred more ambiguous clothing, but nothing that she could wear could camouflage her hourglass figure. She didn't wear makeup; she didn't need to. Serena, like her sisters, had inherited their mama's naturally long eyelashes and her dark brows had a natural arch that she didn't have to maintain at a salon.

Serena crossed her arms and leaned on one hip as she stared into the closet. Then she saw it. Just what she'd been looking for, a formfitting, navy blue, cotton dress, pleats at the waist, a plunging neckline, with two short slits at each side. It was sexy, but not trashy, and it would give her the sophisticated look that she was going for, while accentuating her fabulous curves. She took the dress out of the closet and held it close to her body by its hanger, as she ran her other hand through her hair. She would have to have her hair done. She would wear a bit of makeup and put on the sexy, black, sling-back, peep-toe heels. Perfect for her meeting with Dean Carmichael. The meeting he didn't know anything about yet.

Serena e-mailed Dean Carmichael. She'd gotten his e-mail address off the college's Web site. She didn't know what she was doing, but she wouldn't think too much about it for fear of changing her mind. Something had to be done, and it had to be done soon. She'd be going home tomorrow, for the week of her birthday, and she didn't want this mystery-girl situation festering while she was gone. She wanted it addressed because Serena knew it wouldn't just go away, that it would only get worse.

She wrote a very casual message. She didn't concern herself with grammar or punctuation. They were beyond formality; after all, she'd been sprawled out naked on the very desk that he'd probably be reading this e-mail. Perhaps on the very spot where she'd left the butt print from her well-oiled body. Serena tapped away on her laptop. Her message was short and to the point:

Dean Carmichael,

I am the woman in the photograph, and I'd like to meet with you off campus at a location of your choosing. If this is agreeable to you, please notify me. I'd like to apologize to you in person.

Serena didn't post her name. He wouldn't find out her true identity unless he agreed to meet with her. She pressed send and waited to be notified via her cell phone. She found a new hiding place for her journal and put Hakeem's envelope with it. The envelope was thick and stiff. Serena speculated that he probably had put a gift of some sort in it.

It angered her to think that Hakeem thought that he had the right to invade her privacy the way he did. How in the world did he think that she would feel after he exposed her the way he did? Besides, Serena trusted the person who had told her that Hakeem was cheating on her. Her source was reliable, and he was a good friend and had no reason to lie. Justin had said he'd seen it with his own two eyes. She trusted Justin, and there was nothing that Hakeem could say to make her believe otherwise.

It was Thursday morning, and Serena had gotten several e-mail alerts on her cell phone. She ignored all but one, Dean Carmichael's message. Of course, he'd paid attention to propriety. It was as if it were an official letter from his office. His e-mail was very wordy, but it basically stated that although this was highly irregular, he would agree to confidentially meet with her at an eatery about ten miles off campus, at about 2:00 p.m. today. He hadn't asked if that would interfere with her classes. He probably didn't care. But the fact that he seemed eager to meet with her was an indicator that she may have made the right decision by sending her e-mail. Serena sent her reply right away; a simple "Okay" was all she'd e-mailed in response.

Serena contacted the campus "beautician" to ask if she could fit her in today as soon as possible. She said, "Sure." She couldn't wait to get her hands in Serena's hair. She'd often tell Serena that she wasted all that good hair wearing it in that "curly little afro." Now she'd have her chance to show her what she could do.

Serena met Rita, the campus beautician, at a mutual acquaintances house. Rita told Serena that she had this sharp cut that she'd like to try on her. She said that it was sort of funky and that she thought that Serena had the face and the persona to pull it off. Rita didn't have a picture, but Serena trusted her. She was a gifted stylist and she was responsible for some of the hottest looks on campus. And since Serena wasn't quite sure what she wanted anyway, she told Rita that she could do whatever she wanted.

Rita shampooed Serena's hair with a sweet-smelling shampoo. Serena didn't ask what it was, but it smelled so good. She massaged Serena's hair vigorously, and she felt as if she could fall off to sleep.

"Girl, I cannot believe you are here!" Rita said as she scrubbed Serena's scalp with her little round shampoo brush. "I have been waiting for you to let me get in this head."

Rita was a heavy, dark-skinned woman with a big toothy grin and a large gap in the front of her mouth, which made her look as though she had a missing tooth. Her teeth were straight and white, and when she smiled, she poked the tip of her tongue between her gapped teeth. She had a small pimple in the middle of her forehead on her otherwise smooth skin, which she kept rubbing with the back of her hand. And she had wide hips and big drooping breasts that dangled over Serena's head as she washed her hair. At one point, Serena thought they were going to fall right out of her V-neck shirt and hit her dead in the face.

"Watch those things, will ya?" Serena said of Rita's breasts bobbing over her head.

"Don't worry, girl," Rita said with a throaty laugh. "I've got those babies strapped in good." They both laughed.

"What are you using on my hair? It smells so good."

"Just some white-girl shit I picked up. Does smell good, doesn't it?"

"I am not white," Serena said. It seemed she was always defending her ethnicity.

"I know, I know. But chu got good hair, girl. I can't go usin' all those black products on your type of hair. It's too heavy, it'll weigh it down."

"I put oil in my hair, it gets dry," Serena said as if trying to prove her blackness.

"I see," Rita said, referring to the oils on Serena's wavy, curly hair. "Don't worry. I put a little clarifier in the shampoo. It'll get all dat shit out. Trust me." Serena pouted, but Rita didn't notice. Rita just blissfully continued to work a light conditioner into Serena's hair. "Ya see, you have da type of hair that is full of natural oils. It's not all dry and nappy like nigga hair. Excuse my French. You hafto take care of your hair differently. It just need a different kind of care."

It didn't matter how Rita put it, Serena was still offended. If she could choose between her hair and Rita's hair, she'd choose Rita's hair any day. She liked Rita's thick, course hair. She thought that Rita's kinky twists looked good on her and thought that she would look good in that style too, but her hair wouldn't lock and Mama had a fit when she had tried it about a year ago.

Rita cut Serena's hair while it was still wet. She was amazed at how long Serena's hair was. She'd have to cut it much shorter to put it in the style that she had in mind.

"Ooh girl, I'm gonna hafto cut a lot of this hair to do it like I want to do it."

"I don't care. My hair grows back really fast."

"As simple as dat, huh?" Rita said with a laugh.

Serena smiled and hunched her shoulders. She didn't know what was so funny, but she was happy that she had kept her so easily amused.

"Girl. Most women would have a fit if you go talkin' 'bout cuttin' off their hair. But you have dat good hair. So I guess it don't matter much to you," Rita said with a laugh.

Serena was sick of hearing that shit, but she didn't say anything, because Rita was her lifesaver right now. She was going out of her way for Serena, and she certainly needed the favor.

Rita put some product on Serena's damp hair and set the front of Serena's hair in extra-large rollers to give it more body. Then she molded the back and the sides.

"Girl, you are gonna love this. I mean this style is made for you," Rita said as she lowered the lid to the dryer down over Serena's head. Serena's hair wasn't very porous, so it didn't take it long to dry.

Serena didn't flinch when she heard the buzz of the clippers. She'd told Rita that she could do "whatever," and she meant it. She didn't think that Rita would have her looking crazy. So Serena closed her eyes and relaxed, moving her head in whatever direction Rita told her too. When Rita finished, Serena ran her fingers along the back and sides of her head. It was really short, but not short enough to see her white scalp. It was straight and flat too.

Rita removed the large rollers from Serena's head as she gushed; she was proud of her creation already. "Girl, I seen this in my head, and it is lookin' just the way I pictured it." Rita smiled as she rubbed a glossifier into the palms of her large hands and worked it into Serena's tiny head. Serena's head moved and jerked as Rita massaged the gloss into Serena's hair and scalp with the tips of her fingers. Serena's eyes closed. It felt so good. It had been a while since she'd had another person's hands in her head.

Rita used a flat iron and some of the tiniest curling irons Serena had ever seen. She used the tiny irons on the center of the back of her head. Rita put some sticky liquid stuff in Serena's hair to make her hair stick up a little in the front. It smelled minty, and it made her scalp tingle; it was refreshing, Serena thought. Rita teased a small piece of hair in the front with the rat-tail end of her comb, as it came to a bit of a point at the center of her forehead. Then Rita stood back to admire her masterpiece.

Rita started smiling and clapping and said, "Girl, I am bad! I am da shit!" Rita reached around and patted herself on her back.

"Are you done?" Serena said with a smile.

"Oh yea," Rita said, nodding, "I am done."

Rita handed Serena a mirror and escorted Serena into the tiny bathroom. As soon as Serena saw her hair, she gasped.

Rita smiled.

"Rita! I love it!" Serena said as she held her hand over her mouth. She turned her back to the mirror and held the other mirror in her hand as she further inspected her hair.

"Girl, you are so creative!" Serena examined her hair in awe.

"This is my version of the 'fauxhawk,'" Rita said because it looked like a Mohawk, but it wasn't. The sides and the back were the same length, but Rita had used the smallest Marcel irons to give the shortest parts in the center and back of her head the illusion of length. It was "So Serena," and she was working it like it was a style created especially for her.

"I'm so glad that you like it. You don't have to wear it like dis all the time. It's really very versatile."

"Girl, I love it! How much do I owe you?" Serena said, still checking out her hair.

"It's on the house. I always told you if you let me do your hair, I'd do it for free."

Serena smiled and put fifty dollars in Rita's hand. Rita took it with a smile and didn't give it back. Serena knew that Rita had an arrangement with Charles to use his apartment to do hair and that she could really use the money.

"Girl, your man is gonna love this cut on you."

"Yea, Eric will love it," Serena said; she was still upset with Eric, so she didn't know when he would actually get to see it.

"Who's Eric? I'm talkin' about Justin."

"Justin who?" Serna said, wrinkling up her nose and looking at Rita.

"The white boy I always see you with. The one with the nice tan and that great body."

"No. Justin and I are just friends. Just good friends."

"Hmm. Well, somebody needs to tell him that 'cuz that's not what he said."

Serena didn't question Rita anymore, but she did assure her that there was nothing going on between her and Justin. That they had been close friends for many years and that her boyfriend was Eric.

"Well, I never met that Eric but that Hakeem. Ooh, he was so fine. Big ole tall sexy man and those dreads. Girl, puhlease! Think he could handle a big, fine woman like me?" Rita laughed at herself and then nudged Serena. "I'm just playin' wit cha, girl. I know you were in love wit chu some Hakeem. Didn't see one without da other."

Serena didn't pay Rita any mind. She was still thinking about what she'd said about Justin, and she was fuming, but she didn't have time to worry about Justin; she had a meeting to go to. She could only handle one dilemma at a time.

When Serena left the small room and turned a corner to leave, there were a bunch of classmates sitting in the living room, listening to music and chatting. A few were smoking cigarettes. Everyone was going crazy about her hair. She thanked them, and smiled. It was about eleven o'clock in the morning, and Serena had to get going. She had a few more things that she needed to do.

Everyone ranted and raved over Serena's hair. Even strangers. She liked her hair too, so she didn't mind the attention that she was getting. She was turning heads wherever she went, and she got a lot of compliments and plenty of double takes. She needed to be a knockout at least for this afternoon.

"Baby, what's the matter with you? I've been trying to get in touch with you since yesterday, and you haven't been returning my calls."

"I've just been really busy, Eric. I've had a lot on my mind, and I've gotta get some things together before I go home tomorrow."

"Speaking of that, you sure you don't want me to come with you?"

"It's too soon, Eric. Besides, you wouldn't have any fun anyway. That's gonna be a very busy week for me."

Serena was growing tired of Eric always begging to go with her to see her family. He acted as if she couldn't do anything alone. She definitely needed some "me" time. She wanted to be free to visit her family and friends without dragging Eric along with her and having to worry about keeping him entertained.

"Well, I wanna see you."

"I want to see you too, but I have a lot planned today. Let me handle a few things, and I'll get back to you."

"I'll be here all day. I don't have any classes. I'm gonna take a nap, so call me when you're ready."

Serena didn't want to see Eric today; she hated that she was so fickle, but she just wasn't feeling him anymore. She couldn't explain why. She wanted to tell him it was over and end it right there on the phone, but instead, she stuck with her lie and told him she'd try and see him later.

She didn't mention to him that she'd overheard his mystery-girl comments, but she wondered if he was really serious or if he was just showing off for his friends. She had planned on finding out though. Plus, the comment that Hakeem had made about Eric had really gotten to her. She dismissed it as just one of Hakeem's little mind games, but she couldn't help but wonder if Eric had been cheating on her too. Serena headed over to Eric's apartment house; she didn't go to the door. In fact, she hoped that he hadn't seen her. She'd typed up a note and left it on his windshield. Eric was a heavy drinker, and she knew that he would be heading out sooner or later to grab himself a beer or something. He'd get her letter then.

Serena had told herself that no matter what the outcome was, that her meeting with Dean Carmichael should take no longer than one hour. She had no intention of pleading or begging him for anything, because ultimately he was going to do whatever it was that he wanted to do anyway. All she wanted was for him to at least hear her out, and as she headed to the restaurant, she rehearsed in her mind what she wanted to say.

Dr. Charles Carmichael was a good-looking man. He was balding, but if you didn't know it for sure, then you'd never be able to tell it. Because Dr. Charles Carmichael wore some of the best, most natural-looking rugs that Serena had ever seen. He was a good-looking man, and many of the female student body thought so. He was tall, distinguished-looking, and graying at the temples with a thick beard and moustache.

Serena thought that he was strange. It was something in his eyes. She thought that his preoccupation with his appearance was unusual, and she saw how he looked at the female students like he was a kid in a candy store.

Serena and Hakeem thought that it would be hilarious for her to pose on his desk that way. Hakeem had said that Dean Carmichael would have been more upset about not being asked to participate, than he would be that she'd posed on his desk at all. Serena though it was funny at the time, back when she'd thought no one would ever see it.

Dean Carmichael and Serena arrived at the restaurant at the same time. He hadn't recognized her, and he did not know that she was the mystery girl, but he stared at her as if he could see right through her clothing. She smiled at him as he opened the door for her, and she caught him staring at her behind as she walked in.

She turned to him and held out her hand with a smile and said, "Hello, Dr. Carmichael."

He gave her a firm handshake and a smile. She felt as if she was on an interview. But she was calm cool and collected.

"Table for two?" the hostess asked.

"Yes," Dr. Carmichael said with a nod. He boldly placed his hand on the small of Serena's back as the hostess led them to their seat.

Serena walked toward the table as Dean Carmichael walked behind her. He watched her walk, he watched the rhythmic sway of her hips, and he inspected her pretty legs as she walked in her heels. He admired the definition of her calf muscles as she walked ahead of him. He was impressed with this young lady, and he hadn't even heard her speak.

Serena sat down first; then Dean Carmichael sat across from her. He crossed his hands and sat them on the table. He smiled at her, and she smiled back.

A waiter came over to see if they were ready to place their order. They both said they needed more time. Neither opened their menus.

"Well, young lady. I'm waiting."

Serena smiled and looked Dean Carmichael in the eyes. "First of all, Dean Carmichael, I'd like to apologize to you. I am very sorry for my actions. I never intended to disrespect or desecrate your office in any way. I never thought that you would ever see that picture. I never thought that anyone would ever see it. It was never my intention to publicly embarrass you in any way."

Dean Carmichael held up his hand to stop her from finishing. He smiled at her like a father would smile at a daughter before scolding them.

"Young lady, what were you thinking?"

"That's just it. I wasn't thinking. It was just something that I did on an impulse. My boyfriend had access to the keys somehow. I don't know how. I never questioned him about it."

"You don't even seem like that type of girl. Seems like he was a bit of a bad influence."

Serena didn't answer him. She'd wanted to come off like this hot vixen, but she felt more and more like a little girl playing in her mother's makeup and clothes.

"What's your name?"

"Serena Turner," she answered.

"Serena Turner. Hmmm. You are a beautiful girl. Did you know that?"

"Strange question," Serena thought.

"Thank you, sir," she answered as she reached into her purse and then sat it back on the table. She smiled at him, and he smiled back at her. She felt his eyes turn toward her cleavage. They stayed there awhile before returning to her face.

"It looks like we have a bit of a dilemma here, Serena," Dr. Carmichael said.

Serena listened. She knew that before they'd sat down. She needed a resolution, not a restatement of the facts. "You see everyone is expecting me to handle this situation in a way that would be acceptable to the university and fair to the student body," he continued.

"Well, Dean Carmichael, why does anyone hafto know how you've handled it. Why can't you just tell everyone that the situation's been handled. That you handled it. No one has to know."

The waiter came back over to the table, and neither was ready to order. So Dean Carmichael ordered himself an iced tea, Serena ordered one also, and then the Dean told the waiter that he would call him over when they were ready to order.

"It's not that easy," the dean answered, after the waiter walked away. They stopped talking when the waiter came back over to the table to drop off their drinks; then they resumed their conversation when he walked away.

"You can do whatever you want to do. Just say that you don't want to do it. Don't pretend that you can't," Serena said, unable to control her frustration.

"Serena, you are in no position to make demands. Do you realize the seriousness of this situation?"

"Yes. I do. But no one is at this meeting except you and me. You can do whatever you want to do. If I didn't think that you had the authority to resolve this, then I never would have arranged this meeting with you."

"I'm sorry, Serena, I can't help you."

"Well, I came here to apologize and I did. I am truly sorry. I didn't come here to beg or to haggle. I have apologized, and I'll accept my punishment. Enjoy the rest of your day."

Serena reached for her purse and rose to stand when Dean Carmichael placed his hand over hers.

"No, Serena, sit." Serena stopped and looked at him; then she sat back down. "Maybe I can be persuaded to change my mind."

Serena smiled. She smiled as if those were the words she had been waiting for.

"I'm unclear, Dean, what are you saying?"

Dean Carmichael looked both ways, then leaned in, and said to her, "I said that maybe I can be persuaded to change my mind. Surely, I don't have to go into detail about my meaning."

Serena toyed with the charm hanging from the delicate gold chain around her neck. She let it go and watched the dean's eyes as he watched it dangle between her supple breasts.

"I really need for you to be clearer. I don't want any misunderstandings."

He smiled but didn't repeat himself, nor did he clarify his statement.

Serena crossed her arms on the table and leaned forward, resting her breast on her folded arms. She spoke just above a whisper, but loudly and clearly enough for the dean to hear.

"Dean, I never asked you. Did you like that picture? The one I took on your desk."

He continued to smile as he enjoyed an unobstructed view of her bosom. "What did you think when you saw it? Did you recognize your office right away? Did you recognize your desk? It was so cold in there that night," she said, biting her lower lip sensuously.

While still leaning forward, Serena grabbed the charm again, and she ran it seductively up and down her thin gold chain, moving it slowly from side to side. The dean's eyes followed that charm with his eyes as if he were watching a tennis match. He licked his lips. He salivated a little; Serena saw it, and she continued, "I remember because my nip—"

Dean Carmichael cleared his throat and interrupted her. "One night."

"Excuse me?" Serena said.

"Just spend one night with me, and you can have whatever you like."

"Whatever I like?" she asked.

"Whatever you like. I assure you. You give me this one thing, and you'll never have to worry about that picture again. Just one night. Tonight. You won't be disappointed."

Serena smiled her most seductive smile. Dean Carmichael couldn't wait to get his hands on her. He didn't mean for this meeting to go in this direction, but he had no idea that the young woman he would be meeting would be this beautiful. He'd seen her body, at least the silhouette of it. But he hadn't imagined that this young woman would be so captivating.

"How is Mrs. Carmichael?" Serena asked. The smile left the dean's face as if he'd been abruptly awakened from a wet dream.

"What?"

"There is a Mrs. Carmichael, isn't there?"

"Yes."

"Does she know that you've met me here?

"No, why would she?"

Serena pulled her mini tape recorder out of the purse that she had sitting between them on the table. The one she used to support her notes in class.

"Well, if you don't want her to know or anyone else for that matter. I suggest that you ignore that picture and go back to your office and pretend that it's been handled."

"How could I do that?" he said, raising his voice.

"The same way you would have if I would have slept with you. Or aren't you a man of your word?" Serena said, raising her voice too. Dean Carmichael squinted at her with rage in his eyes. Reality had set in. "Look, I didn't ask you to meet with me to solicit sex from you. I called you here because I didn't want my education to suffer because of my indiscretion. You did this to yourself. I didn't come here to set you up. I only wanted to record whatever agreement that you'd make with me in case you reneged. Who knew that you wanted to sleep with the mystery girl," Serena continued to talk as the tape rolled.

"Look, I never said that!"

"Would you like me to rewind the tape?" Serena said as she realized she had gained control of this meeting.

"What do you plan on doing with that?"

"It depends. What do you plan on doing?"

Serena looked at him, and he looked at her. He tried to read her, but he didn't want to gamble.

"You won't have to worry about that picture," Dean Carmichael said.

"Sir, I'm not worried about that picture. I'm worried about the consequences of that picture." She needed him to be precise in his statements. She needed him to be specific.

"There will be no consequences concerning that picture."

The dean held out his hand. Serena frowned at it. "What's that for?" she said as she shook his hand as if sealing the deal.

He frowned and snatched his hand away. "I don't want to shake your hand. I want the tape."

Serena looked at him as if he'd just lost his mind. "Do you think that I'm crazy? I'm not handing over this tape."

"What guarantees do I have?" the dean said.

"You have my word."

"What does that mean? That means nothing to me," he said, raising his voice at Serena.

"Okay, well, then try me. I'll bet your reputation and your career mean a whole lot more to you than going to your university means to me."

"The school could prosecute you for trespassing and for breaking and entering."

"Well, you go right ahead. I'll be prosecuted, and you'll be humiliated and unemployed. Good luck finding another job. Excuse me." Serena corrected herself, "Another career. How old are you, sir? Far beyond the age of age discrimination. Even if I were prosecuted and went to jail, I'd bet that I'd still get out in enough time to go on and have a healthy, happy life. But let's not think about me. Let's focus on you." Serena rewound the tape and played it. He listened intently as his recorded voice played in the background. "Hmmm? The choice is yours," Serena said as she looked down at her watch.

"Like I said, there will be no consequences," the dean said.

"Thank you," Serena said with a smile.

"But if that tape leaks out, then all bets are off."

"Agreed," Serena replied as she reached out her hand to shake his, and he reluctantly extended his hand to shake hers.

Serena stood up, smiled, and thanked the dean again. He nodded and Serena walked away. She walked to her car feeling confident that she didn't have to worry about any consequences. The meeting had gone better than she'd hoped. She sat in her car and waited for her next appointment. If she guessed correctly, he should be arriving shortly. Serena watched as Dean Carmichael left the restaurant with his head down and with his tail neatly tucked between his legs. She watched as he drove away in his shiny, new BMW. Serena guessed that even if he didn't love his wife, he loved his career and the respect that his title brought him, and if he played his cards right, his reputation would remain unblemished and he'd have his position well into his sixties.

Serena watched as the silver blue '98 Ford Escort drove into the parking lot. She watched as its driver stepped out and walked into the eatery.

"Boy, does he look fine." Serena said to herself. She watched as Eric walked his fine self into that restaurant, wearing what looked like a fresh haircut and an outfit she'd never seen before. She bet he smelled good too. She smiled as she stepped out of her car and walked into the restaurant. Eric had been seated. He couldn't see her, but she saw him sitting at the table and he looked really nervous from where she was standing.

"Oh you're back," the hostess said as she looked into the dining area. "I think your date has left already."

"Oh, no," Serena said with a smile. "He wasn't my date, he is," she said, pointing at Eric. Eric still didn't see Serena, or at least, he didn't recognize her. She couldn't wait to surprise him with her new look.

"Oh, okay," the hostess replied. Serena could tell that the hostess was confused, but that was neither here nor there. Serena was on a mission.

The hostess started to lead Serena to the table, but Serena told her that was okay and she'd get there herself. She also declined a menu. As Serena walked over to the table, Eric had the biggest smile on his face. "Awww," she thought to herself. "Had he really missed her that much?" It hadn't been quite two days since they'd last seen each other, but he seemed very happy to see her approaching the table. The closer that she got to the table, the more his smile seemed to fade. The look of excitement in his eyes was replaced with confusion. Eric stood to embrace her.

"Baby, you look so good. I love what you did with your hair. What are you doing here?"

"Well, I could ask you the same question. What are you doing here?" she said with a sly smile.

"I just thought I'd have a little lunch," he said, looking around the restaurant nervously.

"Baby, what's wrong wit chu? What are you looking for?" Serena said as she looked around the restaurant to see what he was looking for. "Are you expecting someone?"

"Naw, baby. You said you were going to be busy today, so I figured I'd, you know, I'd go out and get a little something to eat." Eric laughs nervously, while scanning the restaurant's dining area with his eyes.

"Eric, since when do you go ten miles out of your way to go and get something to eat all by yourself? Who are you supposed to meet here?"

"Nobody, baby."

"Eric, tell me the truth."

"I'm not lying to you."

Serena didn't say anything. Eric avoided her gaze. Serena reached into her purse and removed a folded piece of paper. She opened it and laid it flat on the table.

"Is this who you were looking for, Eric?" Eric looked down at the paper; it was a picture of the mystery girl. "Huh? Answer me."

Eric didn't say a word.

"Did she leave a typed note on your car telling you how attracted she was to you and that she wanted you to meet her here at three o'clock? Hmmm? Did she?" Eric's eyes widened. "How do I know all of this? Is that what you're asking yourself?" Serena asked as she leaned forward and nodded at Eric as if encouraging him to say the word, "Yes." "I know because I wrote the damn note. I overheard you talking about her on the phone with your friends. I was going to give you the benefit of the doubt, but this tears it."

"Serena, let me explain."

"No need to. I don't wanna hear it."

"So you set me up, and then you get mad that I take the bait? It's not like a fucked her!" Eric said, suddenly getting defensive.

Serena shook her head. He didn't even understand. He was totally oblivious to the fact that he already had the woman who he was fantasizing about. It hadn't even occurred to him that she was the mystery girl and that everything in her note was true. She'd hoped that he would see her and discover for himself her secret identity instead of looking so disappointed when she'd approached his table. She had hoped that he was so enamored by her and her new look that he wouldn't be able to take his eyes off her, but instead he searched for the mystery girl, while she sat right in front of his face.

"You know what, Eric, you want her. You can have her. But believe me that's as close as you'll ever get to her," Serena said as she balled up the piece of paper and threw it in his face. It bounced off his nose and landed on the table.

Serena stood to leave, and Eric grabbed her arm. Serena snatched away and headed for her car. Eric was on her heels.

"Wait, Serena. Don't go. You are overreacting. I didn't sleep with anybody. I didn't talk to anybody. The note was left by you, and you're here. What did you come all the way out here for?" Eric said as he chased her to her car as onlookers watched, curiously.

"I'm killing two birds with one stone," she said as she slammed her car door.

Serena drove back to her dorm. She had taken care of the mystery-girl situation and a potentially unfaithful lover. Serena wondered how far Eric would have gone if given the chance. She certainly wasn't going to stick around to find out. It was a shame that instead of Eric being satisfied with what he had, he was too busy wondering what more was out there to be had. Well, he could have it. He could have it all. Serena had left him to his devices.

Serena had gotten so many compliments on her hair. Men as well as women had given her a double take. She was wearing that dress, and Rita was right—the hair was definitely her. Her new do had her feeling really good about herself. It gave her a sexy, funky look and was that much-needed change she'd been longing for.

She was so proud of herself for handling her very grown-up problem without anyone else's help. "Thank you, Stacey, for the suggestion," Serena thought to herself. It had worked like a charm. She didn't have to tell Mama or any of her sisters about her problem. She had handled everything all by herself. And she'd handled it beautifully. She wished she could have shared it with somebody, but it would be her own little secret.

She had told Eric "Good-bye," without so much as a second thought, and she hadn't waited until it would be too difficult to do. She did it while the hurt was still fresh and while the words were clear in her head.

Before going back to her dorm, she called her friends and told them to meet her at the sports bar because she had a big surprise for them. It was about five thirty in the evening. She felt like she wanted to change, but not before they got a chance to see her. She couldn't wait to see what they would say.

Serena had arrived there early. Her friends had gotten there all at the same time. She giggled as they all walked right past her. They sat at an outside table about four tables down from hers. She walked over to them; they were looking right at her and didn't even know who she was. They didn't recognize her until she smiled. Her smile was unmistakable. She put her hands on Niko's and Justin's shoulders and leaned in and said, "Hey, guys."

Their mouths dropped.

"Oh my god! Is that really you?" Laura said as she touched the front of Serena's hair."

"Nice," Niko said as he looked at Serena and nodded.

"Oh, Serena, that is hot," Tammey said, as she pointed at her and nodded as well.

"How about you, Justin. What do you think?" Serena held her arms to the side and did a little spin. Justin was speechless.

"Close your mouth, darling, you're starting to drool," Tammey said as she took her hand and lifted Justin's dropped jaw. Her friends all laughed.

"So, girly, what's the occasion?" Niko asked.

"Well, as you all know. I'm leaving tomorrow."

"Aaaw," the table said in unison.

"I know, right? The time really snuck up on me. But umm, I thought I needed a change," she said, running her hands through her hair.

"Well, I think your mom's gonna love it," Tammey said.

"Oh and your sisters will too," Laura added.

"I can't get over how great you look. You really look awesome," Tammey said, grinning at Serena.

"Really and I love that dress. Cleavage anyone?" Laura said.

"I am busting out a little," Serena said, looking at Justin.

"Well, if you got it, flaunt it, that's what I always say," Laura replied.

"Since when have you ever said that?" Niko said.

"Shut up, Niko. I do always say it. I just don't ever say it around you." She winked and smiled at Niko.

"You do look great, kiddo," Niko said. "But you've always looked great to us."

"You're so sweet, Niko," Serena said as she threw an arm around his neck, pulled him in, and gave him a big loud kiss on the cheek.

"Service sucks today. Nobody's come over to offer us any drinks," Niko said as he looked around. "There isn't a server in sight."

"Yea, and they're really packed tonight. Is there a game on or something?" Tammey asked.

"No," Justin answered.

"I'll get somebody," Serena said, and she got up and walked inside the dark restaurant; she walked over to the bar and asked for a little assistance. The bartender tried to flirt. Serena smiled politely. As she walked back to the table, she could see Justin looking at her. "What's the matter with you, Justin? You haven't said much," Serena said and brushed her hand against his cheek.

"Nothin', nothing's wrong," he said, shaking his head with a half smile. He looked a little sad.

"You know, guys, I've been thinking. I've decided to give Hakeem another chance."

"What?" Laura said. "What about Eric?"

"Eric is history."

"What happened?"

"It's a short boring story. It's just over."

"Sorry to hear that?" Niko said, unsure of really what to say.

"Why do you feel as if you just hafto be, with anyone. Why can't you just stay single and give yourself some time to find the right guy. Who knows, he could be sitting right in front of your face."

"That's highly unlikely," Serena said with a smile. "And besides, I know Hakeem, we had a good thing going, and he's been really going out of his way to show me how much he cares." Serena knew that she was pushing all of Justin's buttons, but she wanted to see just how far he'd go.

The server came over to the table and apologized, then took everyone's drink order. No Corona for Serena tonight. She'd ordered iced tea.

"I just don't think it's a good idea," Justin said, looking around at the others for support.

"Hakeem and I had some really good times. We had lots of fun together and I miss him," Serena said, trying to look Justin in the eye, but he looked away.

"Do whatever, Serena. I don't care," Justin answered.

"What are you getting so mad about it for," Laura answered. "You've been acting strange since we got here. You all right?"

"I'm fine. I just hate to see her make another dumb decision."

"Another? What was the first one?" Serena asked.

"Eric," Justin answered.

"What was wrong with Eric?" Serena said to Justin.

"Something was obviously wrong. Didn't you just say you dumped him," Justin answered.

"Well, did you see something wrong with Eric, Justin? Because it's plain to see that you thought that something was wrong with Hakeem."

The entire table was quiet. No one knew what was going on between Justin and Serena, but they could tell that something was amiss. Serena really cared for Justin. She really considered him among the closest of her friends. She had had every intention of pulling him to the side and discussing this with him alone. But as the conversation progressed, she couldn't help herself. She wanted to know why. She wanted to know why he had lied and accused Hakeem of something that had led to her ending her relationship with him. Because of her faith in her friend's word, she had ended possibly the best relationship she'd ever had. Everyone could see that they were happy together. A true friend would want her to be happy, would root for her happiness. The silence was uncomfortable. Serena sat her elbows on the table, held her hands together, rested her chin on her fists, and stared at Justin. He looked up at Serena, but Serena looked away.

Niko, Tammey, and Laura looked at each other. They didn't know what the hell was going on.

"Justin, did you really see Hakeem kissing Stephanie?" Justin looked away; everyone at the table looked at Justin, waiting for his answer. "Justin, you told me that you saw my boyfriend kissing and feeling up Stephanie Johnson outside of her dorm. You told me you saw him go up to her room and that you saw him leaving her dorm that morning. Was that true?" Justin didn't answer. Serena looked at Justin and talked to him as if there was no one at the table, but him and her. "I broke up with Hakeem and never even gave him a chance to explain. I told him that I hated him and that I never wanted to see him again. I made him into some type of a monster in my head, because I valued your friendship. I valued your word."

The server sat the drinks in front of everyone at the quiet table. Poor little naïve Serena. She couldn't think for herself. All she needed was one word from someone that she trusted, and she didn't need to follow her own mind. Did Justin think that he could lie about all of her boyfriends until she realized that he was the man for her? Had he ever expected Serena to grow up, come in to her own, and think for herself?

"Listen, I love everyone sitting at this table. I consider all of you my closest and dearest friends. But at this time in my life, I need to surround myself with people who support, uplift, and upbuild. Lies do exactly the opposite."

This group of friends had always been the most positive of all of her friends. She had friends in Cleveland that she was really tight with, but these four were special. She was hurt by Justin's lies, because he was just as manipulative as he had accused Hakeem of being. How could Justin have thought that it would have been better for her to replace one manipulative man with another one.

Serena enjoyed the rest of the evening with her friends. The uneasiness gradually left the air, and little by little, merriment settled at the table with the circle of friends. They sat at the table eating and drinking and having a good ole time. At the end of the night, everyone gave Serena hugs and kisses and wished her a safe flight to Cleveland. The friends walked back to their dorms together as they always did on nights like these. The guys dropped off the girls one by one.

When Niko and Justin had gotten to the door of Serena's dorm, Justin gave Serena a big hug and a kiss and whispered his apology in her ear, further confirming that he had lied to her. She squeezed him back and accepted his seemingly heartfelt apology. But his lies had hurt her and had caused a chain of events that had almost spiraled out of control.

Before she pulled off her clothes, Serena checked on her journal. It was right where she'd left it. She tossed it on her bed, opened it up, and wrote and wrote and wrote. She added notes that she'd scribbled on scrap paper and included the events of the past few days. She wrote that it was the end of her relationship with Eric and that she wouldn't be going back to collect anything that she'd left at his place. She wrote about the resolution of the mystery-girl situation and of the taped meeting she had with Dean Carmichael. She wrote about how empowered she felt handling her problem without the help of her mother or her sisters. She also wrote about her new look and how much she loved it. She wrote about the betrayal of a good friend and how she'd handled that too. She ended her note with how excited she was to get home to her family and friends.

Serena was so proud of herself. She'd gotten a lot accomplished in a day. She was on fire, she thought to herself as she slipped off the shiny, navy blue cotton dress. The one that had her turning heads all day. She draped it over her computer-desk chair. She didn't take off her little, black, peep-toe, sling-back heels. They made her feel sexy as she tiptoed around her room with her matching black bra and panties on.

She turned on her CD player. But when she opened up the door to place in a CD, she saw a disc that she didn't recognize. "Hakeem," she said to herself. He must have left it when he returned her journal. Serena pushed the disc in and pressed play. She sat on her bed and listened to Stevie Wonder's "Rocket Love" playing through her speakers. She smiled. She loved this song; the music did something to her, and the words were so beautiful.

She loved Stevie Wonder. He had the ability to write about the things that he felt with such clarity. This song moved her. It always had. She knew the words, but she listened to them more intently now. She knew that this was a message to her from Hakeem.

Serena opened the manila envelope that Hakeem had left her with. In it was that infamous picture of her on the dean's desk, and it was framed. The background was totally dark except for shadows, but her body had a luminescent glow. Beneath her was a beautiful blue flame where the desk should have been. The flames enveloped her, but she was not burning at all. It looked like it could have been the picture on an Alternative Rock CD cover. It looked so Goth. But she had to admit it. It was so beautiful. The frame had an inscription; it read, On Fire, But Not Consumed. She stared at it and traced the inscription with her fingertips.

Hakeem was so creative. But so extreme. He had gone overboard trying to get her to talk to him. Extreme Hakeem. All he'd wanted to do was talk, but he couldn't just knock on the door to get Serena's attention; he'd blown up the damn door, possibly destroying what he was trying to get to on the other side. Serena had felt like that was what he'd done to their relationship. The methods that he used to get her to talk to him were so extreme that he'd ruined any chance that they'd have to start over again. He'd obliterated it.

On Fire, But Not Consumed. She stuck the picture back into its envelope and wrote about it in her journal. She wrote about the inscription on the frame. Her sister Fatimah would have thought that it was blasphemous, but Serena thought it was one of the greatest compliments she'd heard all day.

Chapter 18

SOUL SEARCHING

Jason was angry. He was more than angry; he was livid, as he dug through boxes and boxes of his broken and shattered belongings. "She didn't have to do this shit," he said out loud as he sifted through piles of the things he'd accumulated in his thirteen years of marriage.

Jason picked up the busted picture frame that held his and Fatimah's marriage license. The license was torn, and the frame was bent and broken as if Fatimah had tried to break it over one knee. Jason couldn't believe this was happening, as he stared at the broken frame. His eyes watered a little, and he squeezed his lips tightly together. He wiped his eyes with the back of his hand. He had to hold it together. His kids needed him, and his daughter had been upstairs in her room bawling since last night. She'd finally fallen asleep, and he didn't want her to come downstairs and see him weakened. He had to keep it together for their sakes.

Jason worked diligently to get the house looking as close to normal as possible before he brought the rest of his children back home. What would he say to them? He wondered if Mariah had said anything to them yet, to soften the blow. He couldn't believe that Fatimah had put him in such a fucked-up position. Why couldn't she have just come to him and tell him about the phone calls? They could have sat down and talked like civilized adults about it and worked things out like they always did. He wasn't planning on going anywhere. He would never leave Fatimah and the kids. He loved them. He needed them. He needed to be able to come home to a family, a regular life. It kept him grounded.

Jason had always reasoned that cheating was just something that men did. His father had other women and his father before him. His Mama never stopped loving his daddy, and his grandparents had just celebrated their fiftieth wedding anniversary. Jason looked down into the bottom of the last box; something glistening had caught his eye. It was Fatimah's wedding ring. He held it in his fingers and watched it sparkle. He could remember when he'd presented that ring to her. He remembered how in love with him she was. She was so in love that she couldn't see anyone but him. Or so he thought, until Fatimah came in talking about fucking that damned doctor.

Jason shoved the ring in his pants' pocket. He flattened all the boxes and bound them with heavy twine, then took them out to the backyard. He stored them on the side of the garage so that they could be discarded on garbage day. He wasn't looking forward to this day. He couldn't imagine it getting any better than it had started. He still had the task of talking to his children and keeping his home together until he decided what to do.

He hadn't called his family. He didn't know what to say to his children, let alone his mom and dad. Besides, they couldn't help him out anyway, and he wasn't going to fuel any family gossip.

Jason dialed Mariah.

"Hello?" Mariah answered.

"Hey, Mariah. How are the kids?"

"They're fine. They're playing right now."

"Did you talk to them?"

"No, I didn't mention anything. I didn't think it was my place. But if you need me to be with you for support, I can do that."

"Mariah, I don't even know what to say to them."

Mariah didn't know what he should say to them either, but she knew he had to say something, especially since Leah had overheard the conversation and she was distraught about it. Her siblings would find out about it sooner or later.

"All I can tell you to do is pray about it. Ask God to help you find the words to talk to your children." Mariah wasn't religious, and she was surprised that she had to offer this suggestion to someone who attended church regularly.

Jason was so disgusted. He wondered if Mariah or any of Fatimah's other sisters had seen this coming, and he wondered why they hadn't stopped her. He didn't know what he was doing. He had no idea how he should handle the situation. He wanted to just get the kids together and tell them that their mother had lost her mind, that she had had a nervous breakdown, but he didn't know how that would help the situation.

Jason headed upstairs to check on his daughter. Leah was awake lying on her bed, staring out the window. Jason knocked twice on her door. It was partially opened. She didn't turn to the door; she didn't say come in.

"You okay, baby?"

"Uh-huh," Leah said as she sat up on the bed. She wished she would have stayed over her aunt's house with her brothers and sisters. If she'd stayed over her aunt's house, then she wouldn't have heard her mother say those things to her daddy and she wouldn't have seen her mother walk out that door.

"We've gotta go get your brothers and sisters, Bay."

Leah got up and put on her sandals and walked past her daddy and down the stairs. Her father touched her hair as she walked past him. Leah didn't take her purse. Her first act of defiance. Fatimah had always taught her that a young lady carried her purse at all times. Leah wouldn't be carrying hers today.

"Leah, baby. You okay?"

"Fine," Leah said as she opened the front door and walked out to the car.

Jason sighed.

It was a beautiful Thursday afternoon. A picture-perfect day. The sun was beaming, the sky was clear and blue, and the clouds were white and wispy as if painted in the sky. It was a breezy eighty-two degrees. The streets were a buzz with summertime activity. It had the appearance of a beautiful day, but Jason thought this was the worst day of his life. He felt like something inside him had died.

He drove with his eldest daughter curled up in her seat, leaning against the passenger-side door, staring out the window. He didn't say anything to her. He tried as best he could to give her comfort and reassurance when her mother left, but he felt he needed someone to help him and tell him what in the hell was going on.

Jason reached over and stroked his daughter's hair. He wondered if she was mad at him or if she was just hurt and angry at the situation. He didn't want Leah to be mad at him. Up till now Jason had been like a superhero to Leah, but this whole situation with Fatimah had exposed him as the weak and fragile man that he was.

As soon as Leah came into the house and saw her aunt, she ran right into her arms. The children were upstairs playing and they couldn't hear her crying, but Jason and Mariah could and it broke their heart. Jason's eyes watered as he turned away with his hands in his pockets. Leah buried her face in her aunt's chest and cried. Mariah held her in her arms and rubbed her back.

"Oh, baby," she said, rubbing Leah's back and stroking her hair. She jerked and cried aloud, muffling the sound into her aunt's bosom. Mariah walked with her into the family room, holding her, and then she slid the large dark wooden doors closed behind them. Mariah asked her if she wanted to talk about it, and Leah shook her head No. Mariah just sat in the room with Leah, holding her niece as she cried. Leah just needed to get it all out. She was perfectly content with being in the security of Mariah's embrace.

As Mariah sat there holding her niece, she thought about how dysfunctional her family was. She comforted Leah and thought to herself that enough was enough and somebody had to step up and stop this cycle of dysfunction.

After Jason had left with the children. Mariah checked on her own. She wanted to make sure that they were okay, and that they hadn't heard what was going on. She had them all in an upstairs bedroom watching a video, and they were obediently doing just what she'd asked them to do.

Mariah called Fatimah on her cell phone, and Fatimah answered on the second ring.

"Hello?"

"Fatimah, where are you?"

"I'm with a friend."

"Well, when are you coming back?" Mariah said to her sister. Fatimah didn't answer.

"Fatimah, your children need you."

"They don't need me," Fatimah replied.

"What? Fatimah, you're talking crazy. What's wrong with you? This is disturbing to your children. You know that. You've worked so hard to try to make things so perfect for them. How could you do this to your children?"

"What would be more disturbing? Me walking away or me staying and slitting my husband's throat?"

"Fatimah?" Mariah said, shocked that her sister would speak this way.

"What?" Fatimah was cool. Too cool and there was a strange calmness in her tone.

"You're right, Fatimah, you're no good for your children right now. Not talking like that. You really need help. I am so serious, because what you've done to your kids will affect them for the rest of their lives. All the hard work that you've put into raising these children and you'd throw it all away. Just like that?"

Fatimah didn't answer.

"Did you know that Leah was home when you left?" Mariah asked. "She heard everything that you said. Can you imagine how your baby is feeling right now? She's devastated." Fatimah sighed, but still didn't say a word. Her eyes filled with water. One lone tear rolled down her cheek, slow like molasses. Fatimah smashed it into her face and smeared it away with the palm of her hand. "Fatimah, you need help. I think you need to talk to a professional about what you're feeling right now. You can't ignore these feelings. The fact that you think that you're too unstable to be with your kids is a problem."

"Mariah, I am not mentally unstable. I just feel like, enough is enough. I want *my* feelings to matter."

"Well, when you have kids it's not about you. Or Jason. It's about them. They didn't ask to be here. They didn't choose either of you, but they're here. You have five children wondering what happened to their mother. What about them? I refuse to believe that you're that selfish, Fatimah."

Fatimah was that selfish though. She had always been. She loved her children, but the way she was feeling now, she could jump on the first flight out of Cleveland and leave them all and not look back. There was a side to her that no one ever knew about—a side that struggled with what was good and what was right and doing the right thing. What was doing the right thing, really?

She battled with herself daily to enjoy the ritualistic activities of her daily life. She kept telling herself that doing what others had told her was the right thing to do would make her happy in the long run and would make her a better person. But being good got her here. It had gotten her to the place in her life where she was the most unhappy. She didn't feel comfort in the mothering of her kids, and she was ashamed to say that while separated from them, she'd sat lining them up in her mind from the child she'd miss the most to the one she'd miss the least.

What kind of monster was she? She did love her children, all of them. At least, she thought she did. She'd never say these things out loud though. She knew her thoughts were wicked, and she tried to suppress them. But the closer that she came to her world falling apart, the more that the inner Fatimah came creeping through.

Fatimah had always been taught that if you didn't speak on something, then it was as if it had never happened. Suppress, suppress, suppress. But to suppress a thing doesn't diminish its intensity. And the things she was suppressing were fighting its way to the surface.

"Fatimah, you there?"

"Yea, I'm still here."

"I know just the person that you need to see. And you don't have to go alone. You know your sisters will always be here to support you. We love you. Are you with me?"

Fatimah didn't say anything.

"For your kids' sake," Mariah said.

"I'll go," Fatimah said reluctantly.

"Good and I think all of us should be there, Mama too."

Fatimah grimaced at the thought of Mama being there. But she still agreed to go. Mariah told her that she'd make the appointment as soon as possible. She didn't give Fatimah anymore details, but said she'd get back with her when everything was all set up.

Fatimah didn't talk about going home; she hadn't even given Mariah a message for her babies. Mariah just wanted to slap some sense into her sister. She was not the only one in the world to ever be cheated on. She had made the choice to try to stick it out with Jason. She knew what she had when she married him. So Jason's sorry ass was not the only one at fault. She could blame herself too for accepting the shit in the first place.

Mariah thought about her nieces and nephews. She didn't know what Jason had said to the children, but they'd cried as if they were at Fatimah's funeral. Mariah couldn't stand to hear it. It hurt her and had made her cry just listening to them. Mariah's children stayed upstairs and played while Jason talked to his kids. They never came down, and Mariah was glad; she didn't want to have to explain to her kids why the others were crying.

When Mariah called Aniyah about going to counseling with Fatimah, she said, "Sure." Aniyah knew there was going to be big drama. Mama, Fatimah, and Nicole all in the same room to talk about Fatimah's issues? That was a catfight waiting to happen.

"Did you ask Mama? What did Mama say?" Aniyah asked.

"She didn't say anything, because I haven't asked her yet. I'm just biding my time. I haven't said anything to Nicole about it either. Anyway, I have to make the appointment. I'm hoping to make it as soon as possible."

"How soon?"

"As soon as she can see us. Fatimah needs to get back here with her children."

"Well, if you think she's so sick, then why are you rushing her back home to her kids?"

"She's not sick, Aniyah, she's just hurt and confused. She's depressed."

"Whatever. Just let me know when. You know Serena's coming home tomorrow. Too bad she's got to come home to this mess," Aniyah said.

"Our family is nothing but a big mess. It's crazy. Mama won't talk to her daughter and a sister hating a sister the way Fatimah hates Nicole. It's just crazy. We all need help," Mariah said. "We've all been dealing with this shit for years. Something's gotta give." Mariah rubbed her belly.

"You think Serena's gonna wanna come?"

"I'm sure she will. She'll be mad if she's excluded. Anyway, let me go. I have some more calls to make," Mariah said.

Mariah called Nicole, and she agreed to go. Mariah wasn't surprised. She was always very cooperative when it came to family. The problem was Mama. Nobody had told her that Fatimah had walked out on Jason and the kids. And when Mariah had told her, she was beyond furious. But it seemed that she was more upset about not being informed than she was about what Fatimah had done.

"What?" Mama said. "When did this happen?"

"Last night," Mariah answered.

"Well, what the hell is goin' on over there?" Mariah didn't say anything. Then Mariah heard, "Mmmph, mmmph, mmmph. I cannot believe it. I just cannot believe it. Well, where is she now?" Mama asked. "I don't know, she didn't say." Mariah answered.

"Well, how are the kids?"

"Sad, confused, but okay. I guess. They just need our love and support."

"I know. I need to see my babies."

Mariah wanted to tell her mother to leave them alone and that she'd only make things worse, but she was their grandmother and she had a right to be concerned. So instead, she told her, "They're off somewhere, spending time with their dad."

"Hmmph," Mama said.

"So, Mama, are you goin'?"

"Yea, I guess. How else am I gonna find out anything. Y'all asses won't tell me nothin'."

Mariah made an appointment with Dr. Kendra Muhammed, a certified licensed therapist. She had heard many great things about her through an associate of hers. Mariah had been interested in going to meet with her, but hadn't gotten up enough nerve to make an appointment. But now was as good a time as any. Mariah was able to speak directly to Dr. Muhammed. She was very sympathetic to Mariah's plight, and she said that she could meet with them as early as tomorrow evening. Mariah thanked Dr. Muhammed immensely and made the appointment for the following day at 6:00 p.m. She knew that Serena may be a little jet-lagged, but she saw no reason to postpone it any longer, because Fatimah's family was at stake.

One by one, Mariah informed her sisters and her mom about tomorrow's appointment. She didn't call Serena. She knew that her baby sister was excited about coming home, and she didn't want to take away her excitement. She'd hear about everything soon enough, that was, if Aniyah didn't blab everything.

Nicole wasn't looking forward to counseling. She thought it was a bunch of bullshit, and she didn't have time for it. Fatimah was the crazy one as far as Nicole was concerned. "Let her ass go to counseling" is what Nicole wanted to say. But all of her sisters were involved, and she wanted to give her support too.

Mama didn't act like it, but she couldn't wait to go to counseling with Fatimah. She had a lot of things to get off her chest, and she wanted to get to the bottom of the Jason-and-Fatimah fiasco. Aniyah was a little bit nervous about the whole thing. She didn't know what might come out of this. Fatimah was acting crazy as hell, and it scared Aniyah to think that someone that you thought you knew so well could lose it just like that.

Jason was mad at Fatimah, but he wanted her to come back. He was angry, but he wanted her, he needed her. She was the one who held it all together. He'd sat with his children over Mariah's house and told them that their mother was okay, but she'd be gone for a while. There were many questions, and there were tears. They didn't pretend to understand. Jason told them that Daddy had done some things to hurt Mommy's feelings and that she needed some time alone to think about some things.

He thought that was a good idea until Lana kept screaming and crying saying, "What did you do, Daddy? What did you do?" It took Mariah to calm her down and smooth things over.

What had he done? His actions had provoked a series of actions that would change his children's lives forever, whether Fatimah had returned or not. Jason told his children he loved them. He kissed and embraced them all and told them that they were going to be just fine. He spent the entire day trying to assure them of that. Too bad he couldn't convince himself that that was true.

When the children returned home they could tell that something was different. Pictures were removed from the wall. Pictures whose frames had been broken and crushed. Not to mention the fact that their mother was not there and they didn't know when she was coming back. Each of them secretly hoped that she would be there when they got home.

It felt as if they were coming home from a funeral. It felt like death and loss lingered in that house. Jason's head was hurting. He needed a release, someone who he could pour his heart out to. But he felt he had no one. Not once did he think of calling anyone from his church. He was afraid of what they might say, and he didn't want anybody judging him. Appearance had always meant so much to him, and it still did.

Jason knew how to pray. He'd often led prayers. He'd opened in prayer, and closed in prayer in church and on holidays at family gatherings. He was good at it. He had been praised as a brother who had given some of the most anointed and heartfelt prayers that many had ever heard. But when it came to praying for himself and his family, he just could not find the words. He felt that he was so unworthy that he shouldn't even bother. But he had prayed just as Mariah had suggested.

This was such a nightmare, he thought to himself as he sat in his room on his unmade bed. He folded his hands and laid them in his lap and cried. He cried with his head dropped low as his broad muscular shoulders jerked from the sheer emotion of his tears. He muffled his cries with a clenched fist to his lips. He felt completely and utterly broken. He prayed silently and fervently for answers. He had so many things to think about. He not only had to concern himself with the well-being of the children that he had there, by his wife. He also had to worry about the infant daughter he had with Natalie.

Natalie was a young woman; she was only twenty-five with four children. Saroya, his infant daughter, was her only girl. Natalie would often complain that he didn't come and see them enough. A few times, she'd threatened to give Saroya up. But Jason had convinced her not to. He had considered telling Fatimah everything and asking her if they could take the baby in, but he decided against it. He knew Fatimah wouldn't go for it, and he wasn't ready to expose himself at the time.

The house was unusually quiet. The children had cried themselves to sleep. His three-year-old Tori had fallen asleep in the car and was sleeping in her bed now. It was too early for her nap, so he expected to be up all night with her.

Lana was closest to Fatimah, and she was very angry with her father. As far as she was concerned, it was all his fault; he had said it himself, and he was the reason that Mommy had gone away. Natalie had texted Jason several times, and he didn't answer her. She didn't want anything important, and he had bigger fish to fry. She couldn't hurt him right now anyway. His wife had left him, he'd been found out, and his life was in shambles.

Nathan had just left for work; he'd kissed Aniyah and told her that he'd see her tonight. But she couldn't stop thinking about Matthew. She couldn't get him out of her head. Nathan's kiss was still fresh on her lips, and still her mind kept wandering into another man's bed. She couldn't focus on anything. She was too preoccupied with reliving her night with Matthew.

Aniyah hadn't anticipated that she'd feel this way about Matthew. She hadn't spoken to him since that night, but she wanted to. She didn't want to seem desperate, so she didn't call. But it was crazy how he stayed on her mind. Aniyah found herself smiling out of the blue as she pictured Matthew's face in her head. She blushed like a little girl as she recalled the way his lips felt on her neck and his hand on her thigh. She sat with her mind wandering off as she thought about the way he gyrated his hips when he was inside of her. She tried, but it was next to impossible for her to get this man out of her mind.

She hadn't worked out in a couple of days, so she decided to go to the gym. It was a beautiful day. The weather was perfect. "Now this is what summertime is supposed to feel like," Aniyah thought to herself. The sun's rays beamed down, brightly but sparing everyone from its heat and intensity. Children played and hung out, enjoying the quickly fleeting days of summer. Aniyah felt like she should be enjoying the summer sun too. She thought about planning a getaway for her and Nathan. They always had such a great time together when they traveled. She'd even considered a weekend hotel stay next weekend, if Nathan could get the time off. Something, anything, to get her mind off this other man.

Aniyah worked out for about an hour as the men, young and old ogled her. She hadn't even noticed. She had so much on her mind. She felt badly for not being a better support to her nieces and nephews, but she didn't know what to say to them. She wasn't good at dealing with domestic situations like that. She figured that she'd probably make it worse. Mariah and Nicole were better with situations like that anyway.

Aniyah considered driving past Matthew's house just to see if he was there, but it felt too much like stalking so she left that alone. She wanted to snap herself out of this state she was in. What was wrong with her? She had a good man who loved her. Was she really so self-destructive that she would jeopardize her relationship with Nathan for a man who had hurt her so long ago? She wanted to call her best friend Asia, but Asia gave the worst advice. Then too, Asia was at work right now; she was married with two small children, and she loved to live vicariously through Aniyah. She'd never cheat on Tom, but she'd probably tell Aniyah to go for Matt, just because running off with a sexy lover was a fantasy of hers. She'd call Mariah to talk to her about Matt, but she had enough going on and she didn't want to burden her with her problems. So she kept it to herself. At least for now.

Nicole tried to push the image of Don's badly bruised face out of her mind. She hadn't seen him, but she could picture it in her head. She felt badly for him, grunting in pain with every deep breath he took and he didn't get the okay to return home, because flying could possibly worsen his condition. She wanted to see him, just to see how he was doing. But after the threat he'd received from Darren, she didn't think it was a good idea.

Nicole felt like she had to do something, but what? She could hardly think without the word retaliation ringing in her head. The police were involved, but she still hadn't gotten any word from them. Nicole wanted to get him back once and for all, to show him that he couldn't fuck with her. But how?

Nicole felt like a hot mess; she didn't look like it, but she felt like it. Like a hot stinking mess with flies on it. She hadn't gotten but a drop of sleep, and she was feeling it in every fiber of her being. She stood with her back facing the full-length mirror in the hallway. She placed her hand on her flat, toned stomach and turned to look at herself from behind. She had to admit that she sure looked good in a pair of jeans. She reached behind her head and pulled her hair over to one side in order to get a better look at herself.

"Huh? My smile," she said to herself. "It's not my smile, it's that onion that's got 'um goin' crazy."

Nicole looked good coming and going. She had on a pair of traffic-stopping, hip-hugging jeans and a beautiful red satin blouse. She couldn't hide her curves, so she didn't try. She was perfectly proportioned, and everything she wore looked good on her.

Nicole only had one thing on her schedule, and that was lunch with her best friend, Charisse. They had so much to catch up on. She considered stopping by Tamani's corporate office today, just to see how things were going, but she quickly changed her mind. No need to interrupt their day with a surprise visit from the boss. At least not today anyway.

Nicole never thought that Tamani would become so popular. She never expected it to cross over the way it did. She realized that there was a high demand for it in the black community. She knew women of color knew all about ashy, Tamani was a godsend to women who had particularly dry skin. But woman of other ethnic backgrounds loved the scent and feel of Tamani on their skin and the fact that it had sunscreen in it too.

She kind of missed the days when Tamani was smaller and more manageable. It kept her on her toes. The more that Tamani expanded, the more her role had changed. Instead of doing, she was delegating. And although this was what most business owners dreamed of, it would sometimes leave her with a lot of time on her hands. Tamani was a well-oiled machine, and it was able to function whether she was present or not. She had hired others to do the things that she used to do herself, and this gave her lots and lots of free time. So she called Charisse, to see if perhaps she'd like to get together earlier.

"Hey, Charisse"

"Hey, girl! What's up?"

"What are you doing right now?"

"Hmm. I am driving on Rockside Road. Why?"

"You wanna go shopping or something?"

"Sure, honey," she said with a smile. "I never get tired of shopping. When do you want to meet? Before or after lunch?"

"Before."

"Okaaay, well, you're going to hafto make a run with me."

"Fine. Where are we going?"

"Do you know what day this is?"

"Thursday," Nicole answered.

"Yes, ma'am! And what do I do every Thursday?" Charisse asked.

"I don't know. What do you do?"

Charisse laughed, "I go visit my psychic friend."

"Girl, puhleese. I forgot you did that shit. I'm not goin' to no psychic."

"You don't hafto. You can just sit there and wait for me."

"No, thank you."

"Come on, Nicole. You know I've been trying to get you to go for years," Charisse begged.

"No, I am not into that shit."

"Don't be scurred," Charisse said, laughing.

"I'm not. But you should be. Wasn't yo' daddy a preacher?"

Charisse laughed. "That doesn't have anything to do with this? Just admit it. You're afraid."

"No, I'm not."

"Yes, you are. You're afraid, and you've always been afraid."

Charisse was laughing, and it irritated Nicole being teased like a child.

"I'm not afraid of anything."

"You're afraid of Madame Kalushka."

"No, I'm not," Nicole said. Nicole thought that Kalushka was a fitting name. It sounded like the name of a psychic to Nicole. She pictured an elderly woman with stringy, silver hair braided in one long greasy braid going down her back. She even pictured a tattered scarf tied around her head. She'd pictured Madame Kalushka wearing a long embroidered skirt, with several missing rotten teeth, sitting behind a round covered table wriggling long, twisted arthritic fingers around a large crystal ball. "I just don't play with stuff like that. Tarot cards and stuff."

"Is it against your religion?" Charisse laughed. She didn't realize that she was upsetting Nicole. If she did, she would have stopped, but she didn't so she kept going.

She mocked and teased Nicole until she said, "Fuck it. I'll go."

Nicole met Charisse at this little storefront on Larchmere. It was quaint and not as eerie as Nicole expected. The building was brick, but the storefront's wooden structures were painted white. It looked homey. There was no parking lot. They parked along the curb. Nicole had parked her truck right behind Charisse's olive green Hummer.

"This is it," Charisse said as she got out of her truck and slammed the door.

She looked at Nicole and started waving her body in circles and wriggling her fingers in front of her face. Charisse said, "Oooooh," as if she were a ghost, then burst into laughter.

"You're not funny," Nicole said to her friend as Charisse held the door open for her.

"No this is yo' shit, you go first." Nicole held open the door, and Charisse walked in ahead of her.

Nicole walked in. Her heart raced; she was afraid. But she didn't want Charisse or Madame Kalushka to know it. Nicole had never ever given in to peer pressure as a teen. Now as a grown-ass woman, she was being led by a friend to a place that she had always been warned against going.

"Welcome," a woman said as she stepped out of the back room.

"Hello, Madame Kalushka," Charisse said. Nicole didn't say a word. She wasn't intentionally being rude, though. Her senses were being overwhelmed by the distinct smell of several different incenses. Sandalwood and patchouli were two scents that she recognized. The lighting was dim, but Nicole could see that Madame Kalushka had a fondness for antiques and diverse taste in art.

"Hello, Charisse," the woman said with a smile. She looked nothing like Nicole had expected her to look. She was a pretty middle-aged woman with thick, brown, wavy hair. Her features were dark and she looked to be of Middle Eastern decent and she had an accent that Nicole didn't recognize. She offered the women something to drink. Charisse accepted. Nicole declined.

"So you've brought a friend," Madame Kalushka said as she looked at Nicole and smiled.

Nicole smiled back at her. "She's a very beautiful woman," Madame Kalushka said to Charisse."

"She ah-ight," Charisse said and smiled and winked at Nicole.

"So who's first?" Madame asked as she looked at both Nicole and Charisse.

"I am. She's not here for a reading," Charisse said as she sat down at the table. Madame Kalushka sat in front of her.

"Are you sure, young lady," Madame Kalushka said, turning to Nicole.

"Positive," Nicole said with a smile.

"All right," Madame Kalushka said as she pulled out a deck of tarot cards and shuffled them in her hands. She laid them in a semicircle in front of her on the table and asked Charisse to pick a card.

Nicole was so afraid. She tried to look away but couldn't. She sat facing Charisse, but behind Madame Kalushka. She listened to Madame Kalushka, and as soon as Charisse looked up at Nicole, Nicole mouthed the words, "Dis is some bullshit," to Charisse and smiled. Charisse smiled back at her, but she could tell that she was taking her reading very seriously. So Nicole left her alone.

Charisse asked Madame a bunch of questions, about her family, her marriage, and her kids. Madame Kalushka had nothing but positive things to say. Charisse held out her palm, and Madame interpreted the meaning of the different lines. Nicole wondered if she'd gotten this done weekly too. She hoped not; how much could your palm change in a week?

It wasn't as bad as Nicole had thought. Gradually, her fear went away. It was as if Madame Kalushka could sense this. Because as soon as Nicole felt comfortable, she asked, "Are you ready, young lady?"

"Huh?" Nicole said. "Had she not heard Charisse when she told her that she was not there for a reading?" Nicole thought to herself.

"It's your turn," she said, extending a hand to Nicole. "Don't be afraid. I won't bite."

Nicole smiled politely and shook her head No.

"Come on, Nicci. I've been coming here for years. It will be just fine."

Nicole gave Charisse a look. She recognized it; she'd seen it before. Nicole didn't want to be coaxed into doing anything that she had made clear that she didn't want to be a part of. She didn't want to come into this woman's establishment and insult her. But she wanted to tell her, "I am not into this demonic bullshit." But Madame Kalushka had very kind eyes, so she told her, "Not the cards, you can read my palm but not the cards."

Nicole sat in front of her. Madame Kalushka looked into her eyes as if she could see right into her soul. Nicole had always had a very tough exterior. She would never allow anyone to make her feel uncomfortable, especially not another woman. She held out both palms. Madame Kalushka asked her if she was left—or right-handed.

Nicole said, "Right," and smiled. She wondered why Madame couldn't guess if she was right—or left-handed for herself, if she was such a good psychic. Madame stared into her palm and traced it with her fingertips. She furrowed her brow at Nicole's open palm, then looked at her with concern.

"I see a very sad little girl."

Nicole looked into her palm and said to her jokingly, "And where do you see that at?"

Madame Kalushka ignored her sarcasm and closed her eyes. She shook her head and moaned a little as if she could see something that really disturbed her. "I am sorry," she said as she stroked the center of Nicole's hand with her finger. Then she pushed Nicole's hand back toward her.

"What's the matter? What did you see?" Charisse said as she walked over to the table and stood behind her friend.

"I saw nothing," Madame Kalushka said sternly.

"You did. You did see something. What did you see?" Charisse's eyes widened. Her voice was loud. She had convinced her friend to do something she was opposed to, and then in the middle of the reading, Madame shuttered, then pushed her hand away. Oh, no. Madame was going to give her an explanation, and she was going to give it to her right now. "You tell me what you saw!" Charisse demanded.

Nicole had opened up her hand and had invited Madame Kalushka into her world and Madame Kalushka hadn't liked what she had seen. Nicole smiled at the thought of having that much power in the palm of her hand. She giggled at the idea of transferring her fears to someone else by the mere extension of her hand and the connection of a touch. Then she quickly dismissed her thoughts as wicked.

Nicole stood. She could see her friend poking out her chest. In a minute, she would be snatching off her earrings and stepping out of her high-heeled shoes.

"It's all right, let's go," Nicole said and smiled at Madame Kalushka. She took Charisse by the arm to escort her out of the door.

Madame Kalushka turned to Nicole and waved her hand to Charisse. "I am so sorry," Madame said to Nicole. "I am so sorry," she said and squeezed Nicole's hand and rubbed it, as if consoling her. Nicole looked at the woman. Madame Kalushka was misty eyed.

"Dammit! What did you see?" Charisse yelled at Madame Kalushka. Madame Kalushka said nothing; she just shut the door behind them.

Charisse's eyes welled up with tears, and she embraced Nicole.

Nicole gently pushed her off her and said, "Get offa me, drama queen."

Charisse wiped her eyes and smiled. Charisse had gone into Madame Kalushka's, upbeat and confident, and was now on the sidewalk crying like a baby. Nicole had come out feeling better than she did when she went in. She was not afraid. It didn't matter what the woman thought she saw. She wouldn't allow a stranger to dictate how she felt.

Eric wouldn't stop calling Serena, but she didn't want to hear his apology. He'd told her that it was a big mistake, and she agreed with him, right before clicking the end button to disconnect their call. She'd asked Eric what he would have done if that girl had shown up? What would he have done if the tables were turned and she was meeting with some man that he'd overheard her fantasizing about? How would he like it if she'd driven ten miles out of her way to meet with him, a stranger who claimed to have a secret crush? It didn't matter how he answered, because her mind had been made up. It was true; she was very fickle, but a woman reserves the right to change her mind.

Serena had so much going on at school that she hadn't kept in touch with her sisters much over the past few days. Her tickets were purchased, and all arrangements had been made. Her bags were packed; all she had to do was print up her boarding pass, first thing in the morning. She would drive her car to the airport and park it in the airport parking garage, so she didn't have to ask anyone for a ride to the airport.

All of her friends had hugged and kissed her good-bye. She hadn't heard from Hakeem, and she hadn't called him. Serena didn't call Hakeem to tell him that she knew that he hadn't cheated. She didn't apologize to him for ending their relationship over a lie. She was going to relish being single again. She would console herself, in herself, by herself at least for a while. She'd packed her journal, the pictures that Hakeem sent to her, and the mini tape recorder along with the dean's taped conversation inside. She figured all those things would be safer with her.

Serena called her mother to see who was going to pick her up. She said that she was. Her mother sounded tired. She asked her mother how everybody was doing, and her mother told her, "You'll see soon enough." Serena didn't know what she meant, but she didn't like the sound of it.

Matthew didn't have the time to chase Aniyah. He wanted to, but his life kept him very busy. He didn't believe in his children sitting idly, so he kept them involved in sports, dance, and other productive activities. He would have loved to pursue Aniyah, but in order to do that, she would have to be a willing participant. Anyway, he'd promised that he would leave her alone, and he was going to at least attempt to keep his promise.

As he drove down Warrensville Center Road to pick up his daughter from ballet class, he thought about Aniyah. He tried to get her off his mind, but she lingered there like the sweet taste of her lips on his tongue.

When he parked his silver Mercedes in the parking lot, he sat in the car for a few seconds and imagined Aniyah sitting next to him in the passenger seat of his car. He pictured that sexy dress and those pretty caramel-colored legs, and he smiled.

He liked Aniyah. She was sweet and fun, and there was still something so irresistible about her. He wished that she could be a permanent fixture in his life. But he knew that was too much to ask. He realized that it was unrealistic of him to think that one night with him would make her leave her man and choose to be with him. It was silly of him to ask her for one night when he'd wanted forever. But he'd hoped that he'd given her a night to remember—a night that she would reflect on for years to come.

Matthew walked in through the big glass double doors of The Dora Jean Williams School of Dance where his daughter took ballet lessons. There stood his daughter, Abriana, waiting in her pale pink leotards, hair in a bun, holding her ballet slippers in her hand.

"Over here, Daddy," she said as she smiled and ran up to him. She gave him a big hug around his waist, pressing the side of her face into his stomach.

"Hey, baby!" He wrapped his arm around her, giving her a squeeze.

"Daddy, you should have seen me. I was awesome," she said as she stood upright and did a little ballet twirl. "I can't wait for the recital. There's this thing that I do," she said, clutching onto her father's waiting hand as she tried to demonstrate her little ballet move. They walked to the car together. Abriana talked about what she loved most in the world, dancing. Matthew opened the door for her, and she tossed her pink-and-brown book bag in the car, then leapt in behind it.

Abriana talked a mile a minute as Matthew drove them to pick up his son Aaron from football practice. Matthew was glad that the timing was so perfect. He hated trying to find something to do in between picking up his son and daughter. There was just enough time for him to gather up his kids without a lot of waiting. When both of his children were in the car, Matthew asked, "So, you two, what's for dinner?"

"I want a big, sloppy burger with a side of chili cheese fries," Aaron answered right away, licking his lips.

"Sounds good," Matthew said. "How about you, Abriana?"

"I am a dancer. I have to eat healthy. I can't stuff my face with those kinds of foods." She smiled at her daddy through his rearview mirror.

"Hmmm," Matthew replied. "So what do you want, a salad or something?"

"Well, I would liiiike," Abriana said with a finger to her chin, as she stared up at the roof of the car, trying to decide what she wanted for dinner

"Well, Abriana you'd better make up your mind or else your gonna be stuck with Daddy's famous ham and cheese sandwich."

"Nooo," Abriana whines.

"Well, make up your mind, kiddo. We're almost home."

Abriana made the decision as to what they ate that night as she did mostly every night. His son Aaron was pretty laid back; he stated what his preferences were and just waited to see what the outcome would be. Abriana was the princess of the house; whatever she decided was the final word. The Tullamore men were fine with that, and Matthew figured his daughter might as well learn early what it was like to be catered to. Perhaps when she became a woman, she wouldn't settle for anything less.

Abriana had decided that it would in the best interest of everyone involved, for Daddy to stop at the grocery store and to pick up the fixings for a healthy dinner and a healthy snack for dessert. Abriana had decided on a Rotisserie chicken, a spring salad with french dressing, potatoes for baking, and apple juice. For dessert, she chose plain vanilla ice cream and a package of frozen strawberries in syrup. Not bad for a nine-year-old.

When Matthew got home, the children climbed out of the car and raced to the side door. Once inside, they hurried to change their clothes and both headed into the kitchen to help their dad with dinner. Matthew always did most of the work, but he used this time to bond with his kids and spend a little quality time with them. He found out what was on their minds, and sometimes, they had a great deal to talk about.

"Daddy, did you tell everybody about my recital? You said you were going to make copies of my flyer. Did you make copies of my flyer?"

"Didn't get a chance to yet, Abriana, but Daddy's got chu. I will not forget about my baby girl's recital. I got chu," Matthew said, pointing his finger to his chest and smiling.

"Dad, have you seen my truck?" Aaron said, referring to the remote-controlled Hummer that his maternal grandparents had gotten him this past birthday.

"Yea, son. I think it's underneath my bed. I'm not sure. I know I've seen it around here somewhere. You need to keep up with that thing, man. It was expensive, and I know it would really upset Nana if somethin' happened to it."

"Okay, Dad. I know, I'll go get it now." Aaron had a fondness for all types of cars. He'd hoped to be a truck driver someday.

Matthew talked with his daughter as he microwaved a couple of potatoes. They were large, and he knew the kids couldn't eat a whole one to themselves. So he prepared two, one for them to split and one for himself.

Matthew often wondered if the kids were missing their mother. They didn't talk about her much. They were happy to hear from her when she called, but it wasn't as if they ever brought her up. Sometimes, it seemed they'd forgotten about her until someone had mentioned her name or she decided to call. He knew that the kids loved their mother, but Matthew had figured that his children had developed their own means of coping with her absence.

The last he'd heard from her, she wasn't doing too well. She had gotten a few acting gigs, but nothing to write home about. He kind of admired her for stepping out and going after her dreams, but he thought it selfish of her not to think about her kids.

He knew *he* didn't miss her. Matthew thought she was bipolar. She was too hard to please, and she complained about everything. No matter how hard he tried, he couldn't make her happy or at least she never appeared to be happy with him. She liked the concept of having a family with him, but the reality of it was that she felt trapped and smothered, and if it wasn't acting, it would have been some other excuse to leave him and the kids behind.

Matthew opened the bag of salad mix, and Abriana dumped it into a big wooden bowl. She rinsed grape tomatoes and sprinkled them over the salad and into the bowl. She cut up hard boiled eggs with a butter knife and sprinkled it over the salad too.

"Looks good, Boo." Mathew said to his daughter.

Abriana looked up at her daddy and smiled. She sprinkled shredded cheddar cheese over the top and said, "Voila," as she gave her fingers a snap.

They hardly noticed Aaron when he walked into the kitchen. He had a peculiar look on his face; he was holding something in his hands, and it wasn't the remote-controlled truck.

"What's up, man?" Matthew said as he stopped what he was doing and turned to him.

"What's this?" Aaron said, holding up a black piece of lacy material in his hand.

"I don't know. What is it?"

"Looks like panties. Where'd you find them?" Abriana asked, wrinkling up her little nose in disgust.

"Under Daddy's bed."

Aniyah had gone on her computer earlier today to leave a friendly message for Matthew, hoping that he would bite. She and Nate were going out, and she'd wanted to talk to Matthew before their date. She'd felt if she could just get in contact with him that maybe, just maybe, she could get him out of her system. She felt she was beyond feeling guilty about the other night. What had happened had happened, and as long as she didn't make any more slipups, then Nathan would never have to know. People cheated all the time, and she wasn't going to punish herself for doing something that she couldn't take back even if she tried.

As she winded down to prepare for dinner with Nathan, she turned on her stereo and slid in her Vivian Green CD. She played track 10, "Fanatic," because she had it on her mind, and that was what best described that feeling she was getting right then. It was a smooth mellow groove that kind of reminded her of that feeling that she had over the past several days.

She left her computer on, and every now and then, she'd go back to the screen to check it. She felt like a desperate woman. She didn't know why one-chance encounter would have her behaving this way.

Nathan called her from work.

"Hello."

"Hey, baby. I've got some bad news."

Nathan went on to say that he wouldn't be able to take Aniyah out to dinner. He had to close tonight and he didn't have any way around it, but he apologized and he promised to make it up to her. All that thinking about Matt and she was still disappointed about not being able to go out with Nathan tonight. She didn't know when they'd be able to get together again with his hectic work schedule. She was really looking forward to being with him tonight.

When Aniyah got off the phone with him. She walked into her den and got on her computer. She had several e-mail alerts, so she checked her messages. One of the messages was from Matt.

It read, "Nice to see you've been thinking about me. I've been thinking a lot about you too. Had a very interesting evening. I'd like to share it with you. Call me if you can."

He left his number. Aniyah looked at the time that the message was left, and she called him straightaway. She didn't have to worry about seeming desperate. Matthew had left that message several hours ago. She dialed his number with haste.

"Hello, Aniyah," Matthew said. "So glad that you called." She could tell that he had a smile on his face by the sound of his voice. She liked that he was happy to hear from her.

"How are you?" Aniyah asked.

"I'm doing pretty good. What are you up to?"

"Nothing much. I had plans to go out with Nathan, but my plans were cancelled." She had to mention Nathan. Keeping Nathan in the conversation would keep her from crossing the line.

"Awww, too bad. I'm so sorry that your man can't make the time to spend with you," Matthew said sarcastically with a light laugh.

"Yea, you really sound like you feel sorry for me," Aniyah said. Matthew laughed at her. He had a cute laugh.

"You know I'm just playin' wit chu. Man's gotta work, right? That is what he's doin', isn't it?"

"Yea, that's exactly what he'd doin'." She knew what he was alluding to.

"Well, I would invite you over here if I thought you'd come. But I just put the kids to bed. Well, actually they're supposed to be in bed, but they're upstairs watching TV and my daughter's reading a book."

Aniyah wanted to tell Matt that she'd come if he wanted her to, but she didn't. She was fighting hard not to appear desperate in any way, and she was struggling.

"You know I really enjoyed the other night with you. The dinner part, I mean."

"Oh you enjoyed the dinner part?" he said with a little laugh. "Well, what about the other part, did you enjoy that?" Aniyah blushed. She did enjoy that part too. She enjoyed it immensely, but she wasn't going to tell him that. He knew that he had made her feel uncomfortable, and he was enjoying it. "I had a great time with you too. I'm so glad that you came. Came to the restaurant, I mean," Matthew said and laughed. "Let me stop messing with you, before you get embarrassed, and you get off the phone. Are you still shy? Shy Aniyah?"

"I don't think I'm shy. I can be a bit reserved at times. But I wouldn't say shy."

"You know we met so briefly, there's still so much that I don't know about you. I'd like to get to know you a little better. It's been a long time. I'm sure you've changed a lot. You're a grown woman now."

Aniyah had never really thought about it, but she didn't think that she'd changed that much.

"I remember back in high school, you liked to dance and sing, and you performed in school plays. Do you still play the piano?"

"Not so much anymore."

"Have you lost interest in the arts?"

"No, I love music. I listen to music all the time. I like going to plays, and I still love to dance. But with work and trying to help my mom with her business, I haven't had much time to get into all that. The only reason why I'm not working now is because I was scheduled to work one double shift this week and I was cancelled. I started my vacation on Tuesday, so basically I'm just relaxing and trying to catch up on all the things that I like to do but can't when I'm working."

"Oh, so you're on vacation. Got any plans?"

"My baby sister is coming in town tomorrow morning and she's spending the week here, so we're gonna be doing some things together."

"You sure she's not just gonna want to hang out with her friends?"

"Oh, no. I'm sure she will. But I know my sister. She's still a tagalong. She's gonna want to be included in whatever her sisters have planned."

"I can hear my kids running around upstairs. I told them they could stay up as long as they stayed in their rooms. This is our wind-down time."

Aniyah thought he sounded like a mother. She had never dated any fathers who were single parents, and she didn't have any male friends who were single parents either."

"Speaking of my kids. Guess what my son found today?"

"I don't know? What?"

"I'll give you a hint? It is black and lacy, and it has Aniyah sweet scent?"

Aniyah frowned, trying to guess what he was saying. How was she supposed to know what his son found? But when she realized what it was, her eyes widened and her eyebrows raised.

"Oh, no. I am so sorry. That is so embarrassing."

"For me or for you?" Matthew said with a laugh. "Aaron came down holding it in his hands asking what's this? My daughter knew what it was, but she had no idea where he'd found it until he said, 'Under Daddy's bed.'"

"Oh my god. I am so embarrassed."

"It made for interesting conversation," Matthew said.

"Well, what did you say?" Aniyah asked.

"Not much. I took the panties from him and stuffed them in my pocket."

"Oh my god. You should have just thrown them away."

"Why would I do that. That's all I've got left of you." Aniyah was quiet. She didn't know what to say. "You need to tell yo' man to watch out. I'm gonna get you eventually."

"Whatever."

Matthew laughed. "What? You're fair game until you're married. I respect the bond of marriage.

"You'd better watch out. People get hurt thinking like that," Aniyah said.

"Who's gonna hurt me?" The conversation went from light to serious.

"I didn't mean it like that," Aniyah answered. She wasn't trying to insinuate that Nathan would hurt him. Although she didn't know what he would do if he'd found out about her and Matthew. "I was only speaking in general."

"Oh don't worry. I didn't feel threatened. But you'd better tell Nathan, what's that Beyonce says? 'If you like it, then you'd better put a ring on it.' 'Cuz if he doesn't, then I'm gonna pursue you as if you were a single woman. And you can tell him that for me."

Aniyah felt so uncomfortable. She'd hated that she called him.

"How would you feel if somebody said that to your woman?"

"Well, if my woman went out on a date with another man and slept with him that night, then she wouldn't really be my woman. I'm not trying to offend you," Matthew said. But Aniyah was very much offended. "If you were content with him, then you wouldn't have come to me. Something is lacking. You can't even say that you love the man."

"I do love him."

"Then why are you on the phone with me?"

"I thought that we could have a friendly conversation." Aniyah answered.

"Okay, well, just to be abundantly clear, here. Have I not given you the impression that I want more than just friendly conversation?" Aniyah didn't answer him. "Hello?"

"I thought that was a rhetorical question."

"It wasn't."

"Yes, you have."

"But yet you called me. Don't get me wrong. I love talking to you. I really want to get to know you better. You are everything that I have ever wanted in a woman."

"Hold on a second. Didn't you just say that there's so much that you don't know about me?"

"Yea, but what I know I like."

"Well, what if you got to know me better and then you decided that you've lost interest. Then I will have messed up what I have with Nathan for you." She hadn't meant to say that out loud.

"Well, I see you've thought about it." Aniyah couldn't deny that she had.

"Look, Aniyah. I have kids. I don't want to expose them to anyone who's not serious about me. I'm not going to play games with your emotions. I'm not into that. I don't have time for it. But if you'd just take a chance, you'd see that I'm really serious about you and I know that I can make you happy."

"I don't take chances. I can't afford to gamble. I've got too much to lose."

"And I don't?" Matthew said.

Aniyah couldn't understand why Matthew thought that just because he had kids that he had more at stake than she did.

"Nathan's a good man. I don't want to hurt him."

"Well, I'm a good man too."

"So are you asking me to sneak around? Are you so sure that I wouldn't do the same thing to you if I were your woman?"

"That's a chance I'm willing to take," Matthew answered.

Chapter 19

NO EMOTIONAL TIES

Nicole hadn't given Madame Kalushka a second thought. Charisse eventually calmed down, and they were able to have lunch together without doom and gloom hovering ominously over the two of them. But before everything had calmed down, Charisse had told Nicole that she'd always had a positive reading and that Madame Kalushka's interpretations were so nonspecific to her and her life that she could have given anyone off the street the same reading as hers, and they would have thought that it was specific to them. Charisse had also told Nicole that although she'd been going for years, that it was purely for entertainment purposes only and if it had ever gotten weird like it did today, that she never would have gone back. That was why she was so upset, she said. Charisse told Nicole that she never would have encouraged her to have a reading if she knew that that would happen.

Nicole reassured her friend that it was all right and that it was not her fault, and that she hadn't given it a second thought. But Nicole could see past Charisse's laughs and smiles, and she knew that she would be disturbed by that for a long time and that she'd never go to see Madame Kalushka or any other psychic again. Nicole was surprisingly unaffected by Madame Kalushka's reading. Oddly enough, it made Nicole feel powerful that this supposedly all-knowing, all-seeing psychic reader was intimidated by whatever she'd seen in the palm of Nicole's hand. And she wondered if it really could have been something that she had seen from Nicole's past, present or future that had left her so awe-struck and speechless.

Nicole hadn't planned it this way, but she ended her night with Benjamin. She'd told herself that she wasn't going to see anyone for a while, but she had that itch and she knew just the person to scratch it.

Benjamin was in love with Nicole, and she knew it. She'd been seeing him off and on for a while, before she'd met Darren, but had cut him off when she and Darren had gotten really serious. Benjamin had told her that he loved her and that he wanted more of a commitment from Nicole. But Nicole had told him that that was out of the question and that if he couldn't handle it, then he should just move on. Benjamin had chosen to stay and to take whatever Nicole was willing to give. He'd decided that a piece of Nicole was better than no Nicole at all.

When Nicole had gotten serious about Darren, Benjamin couldn't believe it. How could she tell him that she didn't want a commitment with him and then go and choose someone else? He was angry with Nicole for a long time about that, but he'd gotten over it after one phone call.

Benjamin was a younger man. He was nine years her junior. He was young and fine, and he liked to fuck. But that was all that he liked to do, and he did it so well. He was a tall yellow brotha with pretty hair that he kept braided to the back. He had dark, curly baby hair around his hairline that he had lined up with his clippers. He stayed neat and clean, and he kept himself looking sexy. He had dark, curly lashes and small, dark eyes that slanted as if he had a little Asian in his background. He was more pretty than he was handsome, Nicole had thought. She liked his lips; they were full and pink, and she loved the things that he would do with them.

He wasn't a man of means or of substance. The sex was all he really had to offer. But offer it he did. Over, and over and over again. Yea, Nicole was in the mood for her some Benjamin. She needed that release. When she'd called him, he had acted a bit attitudey, but when he thought she was going to hang up the phone, he eagerly agreed to meet her at "their place."

Once Benjamin had made the mistake of thinking that she was going to pay for the hotel. Nicole had raised so much hell that he was nearly counting pennies, trying to scrape up the money for a nice hotel room and a night with her. It was worth it though. It always was. There was something about Nicole that he couldn't explain, and he didn't try to. He just sat back and enjoyed.

Nicole had called Benjamin, because she knew that he would show her a good time. He knew her body well. He knew exactly what turned her on. But Benjamin was nothing more to her than a mere "fuck buddy" or a "boy toy." She could never have any future with him, because he couldn't handle a woman like her outside the bedroom.

Nicole met Ben in the hotel room. He had a drink ready and waiting for her, her favorite, Coconut rum and Coke. She took a big sip and walked over to Ben. He smiled when he saw her, his body anticipating all the ways that she would wake up his senses. He was so sexy. He worked out all the time, he took very good care of his body and he smelled so good. He was broke, but he could easily have any woman that he wanted to. But he wanted Nicole.

Nicole didn't waste any time. She knew what she had come there for, and she was going to get it. He loved the way she touched him, the way she kissed him. It was always a fight to the bitter end to maintain his composure and to keep himself from coming too soon. But just her nakedness and that sexy-ass walk was enough to make him explode. Benjamin was well hung and he had a little curve to his dick that gave him a little extra something and it drove Nicole wild. Benjamin called it his hook, and he'd said it would get 'um every time.

They had sex until she'd gotten her fill; then she lay exhausted on the bed. She had no intention of staying the night. Nicole forced herself off the bed and then went into the bathroom. She showered and then came back into the bedroom, wrapped in a large bath towel. Benjamin was lying on the bed on his back with his arms stretched out to his sides, his dick erect and bobbing slightly, as he made it dance, showing off his muscle control. He was smiling as if he'd just successfully completed a magic trick.

"Come on, Nicole, how 'bout it? One more go?" Benjamin said. He looked at her seductively without even trying. Benjamin was drop-dead sexy, but Nicole had to go. "Do that thing you do." Ben said with a wink and a smile.

"Naw, I'm finished. I'm going home," Nicole said.

"What?" he said, sitting up in the bed. "Do you know how much I paid for this room?"

Nicole just stopped and looked at him.

"Hello? Are you listening to me?"

"Boy, I don't give a fuck how much you paid for this room! You didn't pay for this ass! Now I'm going home."

"Oh is that what you want? You want me to pay for it now? Well, then, here." Benjamin leaned over the side of the bed, took his wallet out of his pants' pocket, pulled out two crisp one-hundred-dollar bills, and tossed them to the floor.

Nicole looked down at the fresh bills and then walked on top of them to get to the clothes she had draped across the chair. "Benjamin, you knew what this was. Don't get brand new."

Nicole didn't even look over at him. She picked up her lacey panties and slid them on; then she put on her matching bra.

"So what you're saying is that you're a whore." His words were cruel, but Nicole didn't even raise an eyebrow. She wasn't hurt by his statement. It was a legitimate question, she supposed.

Nicole turned to him with a vibrant smile and replied, "A whore is someone who is paid for performing services that she doesn't necessarily want to perform."

"So the difference between you and a whore is that you will do for free what a whore will do for a fee." Ben was trying to be hurtful, and he looked deep into Nicole's eyes to see if it was effective. But it was not.

"Yes, I guess you're right. Except there's a slight difference between me and a whore. You see with a whore, the client pays immediately, either before or after services rendered. I'm not quite sure which because that's never been my field of expertise. However, with Nicole, you may not pay immediately, but you'll pay eventually."

"Meaning what?" Benjamin asked. He didn't want to hear that gibberish. He wanted Nicole to stay and spend the entire night. He didn't know when he'd get to be with her again, and he felt cheated. Benjamin watched as she slipped on her heels buckling them around her ankles. She was so sexy, those long chocolate legs, smooth and brown. Her hair fell in her face as she leaned her long back over to buckle her shoes.

"What do you mean?" Benjamin asked again.

He knew exactly what she meant. He was forgetting the rules of the game. He knew what it was.

Nicole smiled devilishly. She stood and began picking pieces of her clothing off the chair. She stepped into her dress and pulled it up and stuck her arms through the short sleeves. It was a red formfitting dress, and she looked drop-dead gorgeous in it.

"I call it as I see it. You're a whore. A whore is a woman who indiscriminately sleeps with men."

"Okay, Ben, then I'm a whore. Happy?" Nicole put on her jacket and lifted her hair and dropped it over the collar. She looked Ben right in the eye as she adjusted her jacket on herself.

"Look, Ben, you can't hurt me, because I have absolutely no emotional attachment to you. You are at best a quick lay. Emphasis on quick." He tried to hurt her, so she tried to hurt him.

Nicole knew that she had struck a nerve when Ben had lifted her up in the air by the collar of her jacket and slammed her down hard on the firm hotel mattress. It hurt and she'd thought she heard her neck snap. But the expression on her face was of shock not fear.

Ben was on top of her, and he held both sides of her collar in each hand as he pressed her body into the bed. He was breathing hard; his nostrils were flared, and his lips were pursed as he spoke through clenched teeth.

"I have done nothing, but loved you," Ben said as he lifted her up slightly by her collar, then slammed her back down on the bed again.

"I do what I do because I like it. If I didn't like it, then I wouldn't do it with you or any other man." Nicole mentally prepared for a slap or some other form of abuse. But she didn't let it show on her face.

Ben released her and got off the bed. She scooted to the edge of the bed, adjusted her clothing, and then walked over to the door, leaving Ben naked and hurt on the bed. Nicole walked out of the hotel room and shut the door. Ben didn't try to follow her, and she didn't look back. She walked up the hall with her usual swagger, with dry eyes, and her heart feeling heavy in her chest. She wouldn't be seeing him again, and she wouldn't be accepting his calls. He obviously couldn't handle their arrangement anymore.

Aniyah talked to Matthew for hours. They had made arrangements to meet while his kids were at summer camp the following day, depending on what Serena had planned. She felt a little guilty, but she reasoned that if she didn't get Matthew out of her system, then she wouldn't be any good to any man. He told her that she could come over after he dropped the kids off and he'd make her breakfast. She told him that she'd see what she could do. But she knew that if all went well, then she'd be there.

Serena had called her last night before she went to bed. She was so excited about coming home that she couldn't sleep. Aniyah hadn't mentioned any of the drama that had been going on in Cleveland. She didn't want to upset her sister. Serena told Aniyah that she had a lot to tell her and that she couldn't wait to see her in the morning. Aniyah told her she couldn't wait to see her too and that she should hurry up and go to sleep so that she wouldn't miss her flight in the morning.

When Aniyah got off the phone, she thought about Matt and the mess she'd gotten herself into. She was so confused. She was upset with Nathan because he hadn't even called her to say good night. She thought sometimes that he'd avoided calling her after work because he was afraid that she might want to spend the night or vice versa. Her feelings for Nathan were very strong, but she often felt that he didn't love her like she wanted to be loved. He wasn't as affectionate as she'd like him to be, and that "turning away from her in bed" thing really turned her off. But, she had to ask herself, did that warrant her seeing another man? She'd have a fit if Nathan did this to her.

She thought about what Matthew had said as if it were a challenge to Nathan. Matt had had Aniyah second-guessing a relationship that she'd otherwise had no problems with. Aniyah lay in her bed, and she could still smell the scent of Nathan's cologne there. She loved the way he smelled. She hugged his pillow and lay on his side of the bed, inhaling his scent until she drifted off to sleep.

"Aniyah! Wake up, girl. We've gotta go pick up Serena."

"Wha'?" Aniyah answered groggily.

"Come on wake up. Ride with me."

"What's goin' on?"

"Mama was supposed to pick up Serena this morning, and she can't so I hafto go and get her. And I want you to ride along."

"Okay, I'll be ready in fifteen minutes," Aniyah said, voice full of deep sleep.

"I'll be there in ten."

Aniyah yawned and stretched, then hopped out of bed and ran to the shower. She showered as fast as she could, dried off, brushed her teeth, and combed her hair. She put on a cute little purple tube top and a pair straight-legged jeans. She put on a pair of heels that were the same color, purple, as her tube top, and she was ready to go.

"Aniyah, come on, honey. I'm waiting outside." Nicole had called her on her cell phone to tell her to meet her outside. Aniyah grabbed her purse, her cell phone, and her keys and headed downstairs.

When Aniyah got in the truck, Nicole told her how cute she looked. Aniyah was glad her sister had asked her to ride along. She had to talk to somebody, anybody.

"Nicole, I've got a problem."

"What's up?"

Aniyah sighed. She sat on her folded leg and turned facing Nicole. She held the heart-shaped charm around her neck and played with it in her hands. "Do you remember Matthew?"

"Nope." Nicole answered without really thinking about it.

"Yea, you do. The Matthew that I had such a big crush on. My first love, Matthew."

"Oh, yeah. I remember Matthew." Nicole said with a frown.

"Yea, well. I slept with him," Aniyah said abruptly, like snatching off a Band-Aid. Nicole didn't say anything, and she didn't turn to look at Aniyah. She just kept both hands on the wheel and continued to drive.

"Did you hear me?"

"Yea."

"Well, say something."

"Say what, Aniyah?"

"Say something. I just told you that I slept with Matthew."

Nicole sighed and looked over at her sister. What did she want her to say? That she was stupid. Did she want her to tell her that she had a man and that she should think about his feelings?

"So how was it?" Nicole asked as if she really cared to know.

Aniyah crossed her arms and stared at her sister. "See, you playin' and I'm tryin' to be serious."

"Well, Aniyah, what do you want me to say? What were you expecting to hear? This is your life. These are your choices."

Aniyah stared at her sister with her arms crossed. Nicole continued to look straight ahead and drive. "I guess I could ask you, why?"

"Why did I sleep with him?"

"Yea?"

"I don't know," she whined. "I don't know what I was thinking? Nathan had just told me he loved me, and I had all these confusing feelings about that. I guess somehow I was trying to sabotage my relationship with him."

"And what talk show did you get that from?"

"What?" Aniyah whined again.

"Aniyah," Nicole said.

"What?"

"You did what you wanted to do. I don't have a comment on it."

"Why?"

"Because you won't like what I have to say."

Aniyah didn't say a thing. She knew that she wouldn't like what she had to say either. But she wanted to talk about it, so she was willing to hear it.

"I'm telling you this because, I really like Matthew and I feel horrible about Nathan."

"How'd you happen to hook up with him?"

"He was on my high school's website, and he posted an apology on my page."

"Hmmm," Nicole said. She remembered what an emotional wreck Aniyah was over him, and she just couldn't fathom why she'd give him the time of day, let alone sleep with him.

It bothered Nicole immensely that her beautiful sister's self-esteem was so low. She glanced at Aniyah. Smooth honey-colored skin with a figure to die for. "Aniyah, you are beautiful."

"Yea, thanks," Aniyah said nonchalantly.

"I'm serious. I just don't understand you. You can have any man you want, and you choose to cheat on your boyfriend who you appeared to be happy with by the way, with a man who fucked you, then threw you away, and called you a bunch of bitches."

"He was a kid. He's not like that now. He has his own business. He's raising his two children by himself, and he's a good man."

"Uh-huh," Nicole said. "Good for him."

"Nicci?"

"What?"

"I really like him, and I don't know what to do."

"Well, I don't know what to tell you, Aniyah."

"Well, you can say something. Give me some sort of advice."

"Aniyah, I have no idea what to tell you, because the whole situation is off to me. I never would have given him a chance. I never would have known what a good man he is or how nice he is because he never would have gotten the opportunity to get back in. Hurt me once and I'm done. Period."

"He was a kid, and he apologized."

"Good. He should have. That's the very least that he could do." Nicole glanced at her sister and shook her head. "You deserve a hell of a lot more than an apology. Believe me, he got off easy. Now you're sitting here trying to decide between him and Nathan."

What was Aniyah thinking? Nicole wondered, because she couldn't even imagine it. A guy approached and apologized to a beautiful woman that he wronged many years ago, and not only did he get an acceptance of his apology, he also got a little ass on the side. "You are a gem. You are a jewel. You've got the whole package, girl, but if you don't see that, then what can I do?"

Aniyah's leg was falling asleep, so she stopped sitting on it and turned facing forward in her seat. She rested her elbow on the arm rest of the truck's center console and rested the side of her head on her fist. She listened to the radio and thought about the situation she had gotten herself in. She sat and thought that maybe she didn't really love Nate. Maybe she was just content with him. Perhaps, Matthew was right, that if she was satisfied in her relationship with Nathan, then it wouldn't have been so easy for her to let Matthew in.

"Who do you like the best?" Nicole said out of the blue.

"Huh?"

"Which one do you like the best?"

"Simple question. Why hadn't I thought of that?" Aniyah said sarcastically as she stared out the windshield.

Nicole laughed. "Yea, you got jokes, but that's what you need to decide, because you, Aniyah, you're never gonna be able to pull off this two-men-at-a-time thing."

Aniyah wanted to ask Nicole how she knew how much she could handle, but it had only been five days and already she'd called Nathan, Matthew. But she didn't say anything; she just rode along with her mouth shut, until Nathan called her on her cell phone.

"Hello?" Aniyah answered.

"Hey, baby. I miss you."

"Yea, and I missed your call yesterday." Aniyah replied.

"I know, I'm sorry. I was just so tired when I got home," Nathan said as he yawned into the phone. "Where you at?" Nathan asked.

"I'm headed to the airport to pick Serena up."

"Oh, yea, I forgot about that. I forgot she was coming in town."

"So what cha'll got planned?"

"I don't know. It depends on Serena. I don't know what she wants to do."

Aniyah sat on the phone with Nathan. She was sad, and she had a hard time disguising it in her voice.

"You sound like something's wrong. What's the matter? You miss me?"

"Why don't you ever cuddle with me?"

"What?"

"When we're in bed. I know how you like to sleep on your side. But you know how I like to cuddle. Why don't you ever compromise and cuddle with me?"

Nathan laughed. "Where did that come from?"

Aniyah had to ask herself the same question. But she assumed that it came from mentally weighing the pros and cons of her relationship with Nathan, so it just rolled off her tongue without her thinking too much about it.

"I don't know," she said and sighed. "Yea, I miss you," she said as she wondered if it was really him that she was missing or if it was Matthew.

"Why don't you stop by the restaurant, you and your sisters, and have lunch on me?"

"Why? So you can sneak out and give me a kiss, then run back in the kitchen."

"No," Nathan laughed. "Your little sister loves our food, and I was thinking you could spend time with your sisters and get to see me too." Aniyah smiled. Nathan was really thoughtful; that was a pro, and he was ambitious and industrious and he was sho'nuff sexy. Pro, pro, pro, she thought to herself as she put mental check marks in Nathan's pro column. She loved his sexy, bad-ass walk, his wide shoulders, his chiseled abs, and the little creases in his cheeks when he smiled. She wanted to cry. Nicole was right. If she had a little more self-esteem, then she wouldn't even be faced with this decision.

Aniyah thanked him and told him that she'd give him a call if they were coming. Nathan ended the conversation with, "I love you." Aniyah ended it with, "Me too."

Aniyah didn't know why it was so hard to tell Nathan that she loved him. She could only assume that she didn't.

Nicole's cell rang, and she answered it. It was Serena, and she was panicking.

"Hello?"

"Nicci, where is everybody? Where's Mama?"

"I have no idea, all I know is Mariah called me this morning and told me to go and pick you up from the airport, because Mama couldn't."

"Where are you?"

"I'm on my way, baby doll. Did you get your bags?"

"Yea."

"And you're at gate 14B, right?"

"Right," Serena said.

"Okay, we'll see you in a minute. We're almost there. I just hafto park. I'll call you as soon as we get inside the terminal. Okay?"

"Okay." Serena answered.

Serena knew that Mama could be a trip, and she kind of figured that something would come up. But it still made her mad. Because she'd just spoken to her, and she'd said, "Don't worry about it. I'll be there to pick you up."

Nicole had taken 480 West all the way to the airport; she made a right and exited at Snow Road. She parked in the short-term parking garage across from the hotel, and she and Aniyah hurried into the terminal to pick up their little sister.

They hardly recognized Serena with her new haircut. Nicole and Aniyah squealed with delight as they ran up to Serena and embraced her. They had caught her by surprise, because she was so busy spying out the airport, nervously awaiting their arrival.

"Girl, that is so cute on you!" Aniyah said, touching her younger sister's head.

"Ooh, I like your cut too, and I love the color."

"Thanks," Aniyah said, smiling and wrinkling up her nose a bit; she still hadn't gotten use to her hair. "Yea, I'm supposed to wrap it, but so far I haven't had to."

Serena hugged Nicole around the neck and gave her a big kiss on her cheek, leaving a glossy lip print in its place. "Thank you, Nicci, for coming to get me. I can't believe Mama played me like this."

"I tried calling Mariah and Fatimah, but I got no answer."

"Well, Mariah had a doctor's appointment today. And Fatimah," Nicole paused.

"Fatimah's got issues," Nicole said, curling up the corner of her mouth a bit.

"What issues? What are you talking about?" Serena asked, looking at Aniyah, then back at Nicole.

"You'll find out soon enough," Nicole said as she loaded Serena's bags in her truck.

Serena traveled light. Nicole had told her too. Nicole said if she needed anything, she would provide it for her, and that included shoes and clothing. Serena didn't argue; she loved shopping, and even though Nicole didn't particularly like her taste in clothes, she'd let Serena pick out anything she wanted as long as she'd wear a few outfits that Nicole suggested. Nicole's outfits were always killer, so Serena didn't mind.

"So what's this about Fatimah?" Serena asked; she was sitting in the backseat and leaning up to the front, between Nicole and Aniyah.

"She's been having some issues."

"She left Jason and the kids the other day," Aniyah blurted out.

"Aniyah?" Nicole said as she turned to her sister with a frown.

"She did what?" Serena said. "Hold on a second?" Serena said, closing her eyes and holding her hand out in front of her. "What?"

"Fatimah left Jason and the kids. Jason said she'd already had her bags packed and she left," Aniyah said.

"I can't believe that. Not Fatimah," Serena said in disbelief.

"Yes, Fatimah," Aniyah said.

"She must be having a breakdown or something. Fatimah always has it together. What about the kids?" Serena inquired.

"They're with their dad," Nicole answered.

"Have you been over to see them?" Serena asked.

"No, not yet," Nicole answered.

"We'll see them today. Sometime before therapy," Aniyah answered.

"What?" Serena said, unsure if she heard Aniyah correctly.

"Oh yeah. You don't know. We're supposed be going to therapy tonight with Fatimah."

"All of us?" Serena asked. She wondered if Nicole was going too.

"Yep, all of us. But you don't hafta come if you don't want to," Aniyah answered.

"Oh no, I'm comin'. Is Mama gonna be there?" Serena replied.

"Yep."

"Oh, well, I'm definitely comin'," Serena said. She knew there was going to be drama with her mother around. Mama was truly entertaining.

"And guess what else?" Aniyah said, looking at the side of Nicole's face. "Darren shot up Nicole's Porsche."

"Oh my god!" Serena exclaimed as she covered her mouth and gasped.

"Dammit, Aniyah! You have such a big mouth!"

"Well, she was gonna find out sooner or later," Aniyah said.

This was true because Serena had intended on cruising the city of Cleveland in her sister's candy apple-red Porsche this birthday weekend.

"I told you that man was crazy! I told you!" Serena said, and her eyes began to water. Nicole looked at Serena through the rearview mirror. She had a pout on her face similar to the way she did when she was a kid when she cried.

"There you go," Nicole said to Serena, then rolled her eyes at her sister Aniyah.

"Aniyah, you're always startin' shit."

"What did I do?" Aniyah said.

"Serena, sit back and stop cryin'!" Serena sat back in a huff and wiped the tears from her eyes.

"I feel like I'm riding with two little kids. This don't make no sense," she said as she looked in the backseat to see if Serena was sitting back like she told her to and she was. Then she looked over at Aniyah who had the same silly look on her face that she did when she was a kid and had done something wrong. "Two grown-ass women," Nicole said under her breath. Aniyah mumbled something smart under her breath. "What was that, Aniyah?" Nicole said, looking at her sister sternly.

"Nothin'," Aniyah answered.

Nicole was seven years Aniyah's senior, and she was thirteen years older than Serena. Sometimes, she found it very difficult to relate to them as two adult women. They thought so differently from her. Even though she couldn't control their thinking, she tried to encourage them to make wiser, more well-thought-out decisions, but sometimes it was to no avail. Nicole exited the freeway and headed to their grandmother's house.

"Where are we goin'?" Serena asked.

Nicole was tempted to say, "Sit back and ride," but instead, she answered, "Over Granny's."

"Mama's gonna be mad," Serena said.

"Well, Mama should have picked you up. Then she could have seen you and taken you wherever she wanted you to go."

"I'm not complainin'. I'm just sayin'," Serena answered.

"I know and I'm just sayin'."

Serena sat back with her arms crossed. Nobody said another word. Aniyah sat on her phone, texting someone with a big grin on her face. Serena, whom Nicole expected to be on the phone with family and friends to let them know that she was home, just sat in the backseat, sulking.

"You know our family is so fucked up. Why couldn't we be normal?"

"Nobody's family is normal, Serena. You'd be surprised what some other families are going through," Nicole answered.

Serena sighed long and deep and shook her head. She wondered what the night would bring. Nicole pulled up in Granny's yard; she parked in the driveway this time. The street was packed with cars, and it was only twelve thirty in the afternoon. Family had been awaiting Serena's arrival, and they would all be so happy to see her. Serena couldn't even get out of the truck good before everybody bombarded the vehicle. Granny held Serena's face in her hands and gave her a big kiss on the forehead. La Maya was there with her girls, and Mariah's kids were there too, as well as a host of other relatives.

"You ready for your birthday licks?" Tye said to Serena as he gave her a hug.

"Boy, you better not put cho hands on me," she said with a laugh.

"Girl, this head is sharp!" Auntie Cookie said as she rubbed the back of Serena's head.

"Ain't she cute wit her short self, come on over here and give me a hug," Uncle Clyde said as he gave Serena a big bear hug lifting her feet off the floor.

Mariah stopped over after her appointment. She'd stopped and gotten Fatimah's children so that they could see their auntie Serena. Not everyone knew what was going on with Fatimah and her family, but they were all so happy to see them and they showered them with much-needed family love.

"I got your message. I'm sorry that I missed you for breakfast," Matthew said to Aniyah.

"Yea, I unexpectedly had to ride with my sister to pick up my little sister from the airport."

"I understand, I'm just happy that you were going to come."

Aniyah told Matthew that she enjoyed getting to know him all over again, but that she had to stop what she was doing with him. She told Matthew that even though she couldn't tell Nathan that she loved him right now, that she wanted to give herself a chance to see where the relationship was going to go, and she couldn't do that with him around.

Matthew said that he understood, and Aniyah hung up from him with the intention of never speaking to him again. And almost immediately, Aniyah felt as if a burden was lifted off of her.

Mama came over to Granny's house without so much as an apology or an explanation for not picking up her daughter from the airport. She grabbed Serena, hugged her, and kissed her and told her that she loved her hair.

"Now dat's what I'm talkin' 'bout. Dat's my baby." Tangie said as she admired her youngest daughter's new haircut. Tangie missed Serena's long hair. She missed the way it flowed down her back and down her shoulders. Mama loved Nicole's long hair, but she would never tell her so.

Serena snuck away from everyone and called her sister Fatimah, but Fatimah didn't answer the phone. Serena wanted to talk to Fatimah before the therapy session. She didn't want therapy to be the first place that she talked to her, but she couldn't reach her on the phone.

Serena's voice mail was full. She had lots of messages from Eric, begging her to take him back. Hakeem had called several times, but he'd only said, "Call me when you get this message." She didn't call. A bunch of her friends from school had called saying things like they missed her already and asking when she was coming back. A few of her close friends stopped over Granny's house. The house was packed, and there was barely a quiet spot for them to chill and talk.

She talked to them about school and what was going on in their lives. Gretchen and Tootie had brought their children with them. Jada left her son at home with his dad.

"Girl, I'm so happy to see you," Gretchen said.

Gretchen bounced her six-month-old son on her lap. He was a beautiful baby boy with soft, straight, jet-black hair, with his mommy's cocoa complexion. Tootie held her nine-month-old daughter in her lap; she was chubby, and she had a head full of curly hair. The mothers took turns passing their children to Serena as she held out her arms for them. Jada was baby-free and happy to get the much-needed break.

As the day winded down, Granny's house started clearing out. Everyone tried to prepare themselves for Fatimah's therapy session. Serena wondered if the rest of her sisters were as nervous as she was.

Dr. Muhammed's office was at the Family Wellness Center on Kinsman Road. Of course, Mama had to complain about Mariah's choice of facility.

She asked, "Why we gotta go over on Kinsman?"

"Because that's where Dr. Muhammed is," Mariah answered.

"So? You couldn't have found some place else?"

"No," Mariah said calmly as she got into her mother's car. "That's where Dr. Muhammed practices, and she was recommended to me."

Aniyah and Serena sat in the backseat. Mariah felt like they were kids again riding along with Mama.

As they headed to East Cleveland to pick Fatimah up, they'd wondered who she knew over there. Mama drove straight down Euclid and complained the entire way. Aniyah leaned up and turned up the radio to drown Mama out. Mama smacked Aniyah's hand and clicked the radio off.

"Mama!" Aniyah yelled as she rubbed her hand.

"That was rude, Aniyah. I was talkin'. Don't try and shut me up."

Mama parked in front of a huge well-kept home. Fatimah stepped out of the house through a big red door. "She looked sane," everyone thought to themselves. Actually, she looked very good. She wore a short-sleeved white top with ruffles in the front. It was kind of low cut, but not immodest. It was a wrap shirt that tied on the side; the tie was long, and it hung gracefully over her right hip. She wore a pair of dressy beige capris and a pair of tight, brown, high-heeled leather boots, and she carried a small, brown, leather clutch purse to match.

She looked sharp, and her hair was freshly done. She wore it in a long bob cut, which neatly framed her face. It was in a wrapped style, and it had subtle highlights, which glistened even in the dimmed rays of the evening sun. She looked sharp and fresh and ready for her appointment.

Fatimah greeted everyone and gave Serena a big hug and kiss, when she got into the car. The Turner women were stunning—whether they tried to be or not. They were natural beauties. Even their mother, Tangie, who at fifty-one years old and battling an ongoing alcohol addiction, could give plenty of much younger women a run for their money.

The Family Wellness Center was a small, two-story, brown, brick building. The center's focus was community health and awareness, through various therapies, counseling, and education. It offered a multitude of services to benefit the health and well-being of the members of the community. It also offered summer programs for the children in the neighborhood as well as tutoring, during the school year.

Nicole had intended on wearing a pair of jeans and a nice blouse with a pair of heels, but she opted to wear her taupe power suit with a dressy pair of Manolo Blahniks. She pulled the strap to her purse over her shoulder as she entered the building. She scanned the directory for Dr. Muhammed's office once inside. It was on the second floor, room 216. Nicole rode the elevator to the second floor. She walked down the corridor on the stained tan carpet to the door marked 216. There was a note on the door directing her to the room across the hall.

The room was rectangular, about fourteen feet long and eighteen feet wide. There were chairs stacked in one corner of the room, and in the center of the room sat a small round wooden table with a box of tissues on top. Nicole looked around. "Dis is some bullshit," she said under her breath. She could hear footsteps and murmuring coming from out in the hallway.

It was her sisters, and everyone came into the room with an attitude, because someone had the bright idea to ride in the car with their mama. Nicole drove her Range Rover and had a big ole smile on her face.

Dr. Muhammed came in the room behind them. "Why the long faces?" she asked. The girls looked over to their mother.

"Don't y'all look at me. All I said was that we don't hafto pay nobody to tell y'all what cho problems are. I can run it down to each and every one of you for free. First of all," Mama said as she raised a finger. She was quickly cut short by Dr. Muhammed.

The Doctor instructed each of the ladies to grab a chair and to sit it wherever they chose to. Each woman grabbed a chair and looked around the room. Mama struggled a little with hers. It was heavy. Mama had a limp due to some trouble she had with her sciatic nerve, from moving a patient years ago. Every now and then, it would flare up, but most times people mistook it for intoxication.

The chairs were scattered around the rectangular room. Fatimah didn't want to sit next to Nicole, Mama didn't want to sit next to Fatimah or Nicole, and Serena sat in between Nicole and Mariah. Dr. Muhammed often used this exercise to gauge a family's feelings about one another by where that sat in relationship to each other.

Dr. Muhammed sat and watched patiently as the women got themselves situated. She was stunned by how lovely each of these women were. They had such pretty features and really beautiful figures. She found it extraordinary that there were so many beautiful women in one family.

"First of all, my name is Dr. Kendra Muhammed and I'd like to welcome you all to The Gwendolyn E. Johnson Family Wellness Center. I have been with this facility for the past ten years. I am a certified licensed therapist. I have an Ed.D in marriage and family therapy and an MA in social work. I have been in this field for twenty-five years, and I enjoy helping families. Would you all like to introduce yourselves?" The women went around the room, stating their names.

Dr. Muhammed continued to speak as she passed around a clipboard with various pages and info for them to sign. After the signing of the paperwork and her spiel, she said the dreaded: "So what brings you here?"

Everyone looked at Fatimah and waited for her to speak. But she just sat there and said nothing. In fact, she looked around the room as if waiting for someone else to speak. As if she hadn't been the reason that this meeting had been suggested in the first place.

Mariah rubbed her belly nervously and took a deep breath. "Well, Dr. Muhammed, as I told you over the phone. My sister Fatimah, just recently, became so overwhelmed at home that she decided to leave her husband and children. This is very much out of character for her, so I suggested to her that she get help through counseling and I told her that we would all be here for moral support and here we are." Mariah laid it all on the line. No need for pulling any punches, they were there and something had brought them there.

"So what do you think about that?" Dr. Muhammed asked Fatimah.

"Well, my sister is right. I did leave my family, and I did feel very overwhelmed. But I felt like I'd reached my breaking point, and rather than expose my children to feelings and behaviors that I had no control over, I felt it was best to leave. I personally don't see anything wrong with that, but of course, that's just my opinion."

Serena's mouth dropped. Mama sucked her teeth, and Fatimah rolled her eyes at her.

"What are you suckin' your teeth about, Mama?"

"Who were you with?"

"What are you talking about?"

"You know what I'm talkin' about. Who were you with?"

"What difference does that make?"

"Hold on," Dr. Muhammed said. "Let's give Fatimah some time to speak."

"She did speak," Mama stated. "She wasn't sayin' shit," Mama said, completely unconcerned about where she was.

"Let's just let her finish," Dr. Muhammed said calmly. "Go on, Fatimah," Dr. Muhammed said as she extended her hand toward Fatimah.

"I'm done," Fatimah said.

Mama looked at Dr. Muhammed, and she nodded at Mama so Mama continued, "You didn't leave those kids because you were overwhelmed. You left them for a man. Now, who was it?" Mama demanded.

Fatimah sighed and threw her hand up at her mother. She didn't know what she was talking about.

"Don't chu throw your hands up at me. You ain't left those kids 'cuz of no Jason. You knew he was a sorry ass long before you married him, 'cuz I told you so. You left those babies over somebody else."

"No, Mama. I'm not like you! I didn't leave my babies over no man."

"What are you talkin' about?"

"You know exactly what I'm talkin' about!"

"No, I don't," Mama said, getting up and slamming her chair down facing Fatimah. Mama sat back down and glared at her. "I never walked out on you girls."

"You might as well."

"I worked hard so that I could take good care of you girls, and I took damn good care of you all! You always had a roof over your head. A nice clean roof over your head. Ya'll never had to live with utilities being shut off. Ya'll never went a day without food. And clothes. Ya'll were some of the best-dressed heffas around. Ray was there when I wasn't there." Nicole, Mariah, Aniyah, and Serena didn't say a word.

"That's not what I'm talking about," Fatimah said.

"Then what are you talkin' about?"

"I'm talking about six kids, Mama? By somebody else's husband. Six, Mama. Six. You've got all these years of chasing after somebody else's husband under your belt so you're the one to talk."

"How dare you talk to me like that!"

"Somebody should have talked to you like that a long time ago. It could have spared us all some humiliation."

"Fatimah!" Mariah said.

"No, let's talk," Fatimah said. "Let's talk about it. The drunken nights. Staying out late and coming in early in the morning. Leaving yo' kids with a man that you didn't even love enough to marry. Chasing after a man who never loved you, never wanted you, and used you to breed his babies. And then sending us over Daddy's house every weekend so that his wife had to stare us in the face every two weeks. Thank God she was a decent woman, and she never took her hurt out on us. Thank God."

"How dare you speak to me this way!"

Serena was in shock. Mariah was appalled, Aniyah was nervous, and Nicole was entertained.

"I can't believe this. I really can not believe this. I am not the only one in this family with problems, and I am not going to pretend that that is the case." Fatimah crossed her arms and looked at Nicole.

"You hafto remember, this session is for healing. We don't want to attack our loved ones with unkind and bitter words," Dr. Muhammed said.

Fatimah raised an eyebrow at Nicole. "Care to talk about your problem, Nicole?"

"And what problem would that be," Nicole asked. "Enlighten me."

"The problem that you have with keeping your legs closed?" Fatimah answered. Aniyah, Mariah, and Serena gasped.

"And whose problem would that be?" Nicole asked Fatimah. "I'm just trying to see how that would be any of your concern."

"It's a problem when you're lying up with somebody else's husband," Mama chimed in.

"What are you two talking about? Darren? I am not with Darren anymore, and this session isn't about me and Darren. It's about cho crazy ass." Nicole said to Fatimah.

"You know exactly who I'm talking about," Mama gave Nicole such a hateful look, and Nicole looked away.

"Look, this is going nowhere," Serena said. "I am sick of our family behaving this way. Mama hates Nicole. Fatimah hates Nicole. I want to know why? What did she do to make you to treat her so badly. She's been nothing' but good to the two of you. What difference does all this stuff that you're bringing up make? This is crazy, I'm sick of feeling like I can't love my sister around ya'll. I hate that she can't come around on holidays because of you, Mama."

"How is she good to me?" Mama said.

"She shares everything she has," Serena said, defending Nicole.

"That money was supposed to be mine!" Mama yelled.

"If it was supposed to be yours, you would have gotten it," Nicole answered calmly.

"You know you are nothing but a whore. And that's all you've ever been," Mama said to Nicole.

"Mama!" Mariah said.

"No! Nicole, you tell them how you got that money!" Mama yelled over to Nicole.

"Mama! Stop it!" Mariah said to her mother.

"No, Nicole, you tell them!" Mama yelled again.

"This session is going nowhere," Aniyah said. "This is a waste of time."

"All right, I'll tell them," Nicole said.

Everyone sat calmly in their seats and turned their attention to Nicole. Nicole gave a full account of the abuse that she'd endured beginning at age nine. She described in unflinching detail every single act of abuse that she could recall. Her sisters gasped and cried, and they wanted her to stop, but she continued, recounting the years of abuse put upon her by the father that she'd loved with all of her heart.

"I paid for every late-night argument, I paid for every new child you brought home from the time that I was nine years old until you kicked me out at seventeen. I took care of my sisters when you weren't there for them, and I took care of your man when you weren't there for him too."

All of her sisters were crying uncontrollably. Serena was bent over, crying into her hands. Dr Muhammed walked over and rubbed her back and handed her a wad of tissues. She passed out tissues to each of the women including Fatimah, who was crying with a look of shock on her face as if she couldn't believe her ears.

It was as if Nicole had left her body; she couldn't see or hear anything that her sisters were saying or doing. She could only hear her own voice, and she could only see her mother's face. She didn't pay any attention to anything else going on in that room; she just stared at her mother. Her mother was crying too.

Nicole had made everyone cry. But she wasn't the slightest bit moved. They shouldn't have been pushing her so hard. Well, they got what they wanted. They wanted everything out in the open, and there it was. All out in the open.

Her sisters wanted to run over to her and console her, but they were too busy consoling themselves. They cried and cried and cried, quickly emptying Dr. Muhammed's box of tissues. None of them could believe what they had heard.

"Well, Mama, are you satisfied? Are you satisfied, Fatimah?" Nicole said without the slightest bit of emotion as she looked over at the two of them.

"I am so sorry," Fatimah said as she cried. "I didn't know."

"Fatimah, you knew!" Nicole exclaimed.

"How did I know? You never said anything." Fatimah sincerely had no idea what her sister was talking about.

"You told me that you saw," Nicole said to Fatimah.

"I didn't see anything. I don't know what you're talking about. I swear."

Fatimah found the entire situation so troubling, and it distressed her even more that Nicole actually thought she knew about it.

"Fatimah, don't sit there and lie. I know that you saw and I know that you told Mama and that's why she kicked me out."

"Nicole, do you realize how crazy you sound?" Fatimah said as tears streamed down her face.

"Fatimah, I was ten and you were nine and I was coming out of Mama's room and you said you saw." Nicole tried to make Fatimah remember.

"I swear to you I don't know what you're talking about, and do you honestly think that at sixteen, I would conspire with Mama against you to get you kicked out of the house? Why would I do that? Why would I go all the way back to an incident that happened when I was nine just to get you kicked out of the house?"

Nicole felt like she was crazy; she knew that that had happened. She had relived it over and over again in her dreams, but she knew that it had actually occurred.

"Maybe we were in the hallway, Nicole, but I swear I had no idea that Ray was doing those things to you. I swear." Fatimah sobbed. Nicole knew that there was nothing Fatimah could have done, even if she'd known. She hadn't meant to make any of her sisters feel guilty. She wasn't trying to hurt them. For years, she had tried to shield them and protect them from the truth. But they'd forced her hand.

Nicole looked at her mother. Her otherwise emotionless face was wet with tears. Her eyes were red, and she was sucking on her trembling bottom lip. Mama closed her eyes and took a deep breath and stood, bracing herself by the arms of her chair. Her gait was unsteady, and she looked as if she wanted to faint. She walked toward Nicole, and she gulped as if stopping herself from vomiting.

Nicole sat and readied herself for her mother's long-awaited tearful apology. She had waited well over a decade for it, and she deserved it, for putting up with all of her mother's hatefulness and evilness for so many years. She wasn't going to make it any easier on her mother either. Nicole didn't meet her halfway. She wouldn't stand and embrace her the way they did in the movies. She just sat there with her long legs crossed defiantly and with her arms folded eyeing her mother as she approached her chair. She wondered how she was going to feel when her mother said she was sorry, but she kind of wished she could hear her say "I love you, Nicole." It had been a very long time since she'd heard her mother say those words. She hugged her daughter and bent down in front of her. Nicole didn't know what to think.

"Forgive me," she said as the tears flowed down her face. She held her daughter's hands and pulled her close enough for her to whisper something in her ear. And what she said filled Nicole with complete and utter horror.

Nicole's mouth dropped. Mama stood and stepped away from Nicole with her head dropped in shame. Mama cried so hard that her shoulders shook. Nicole stood, holding her purse in her hand, as she looked at her mother with a combination of confusion and shock. Her eyes burned, and she ran out of the room, before her eyes filled with tears.

Chapter 20

CHOICES AND CONSEQUENCES

Nicole hadn't cried like this in a long time. It was a painful cry as if she was hurt down to her very core. Her vision was blurry, and she was sure she was driving as if she were intoxicated. The tears impaired her vision. She tried to blink them away, but that only made room for more tears.

Nicole had spent her life trying hard to accomplish the things that she wanted to accomplish. She did the things that made her the most happy, and she thought that she was fulfilled. But she wasn't. There was a hole in her heart. There was something missing, and it wasn't a man. She had longed to have a relationship with her sister, and she longed for the love of her mother. And she battled with that daily.

She put up with Mama's cruel remarks and with Fatimah's insults for years. Fatimah liked to call her a whore, and Mama liked to agree. Nicole acted as if she had a heart of stone, as if their words didn't bother her, but they did.

Nicole didn't drive home; she drove to her granny's house. She didn't care if anyone saw her crying. She had to get to her. She had to tell her what Mama said. Maybe granny could tell her how her daughter could be so cruel. When Nicole arrived at Granny's house, only Granny's van was in the driveway.

She knocked on the door, and as soon as Granny let her in, she started crying.

"Nicole? Baby, what's the matter?" Her grandmother held her in her arms and told her to have a seat.

"Granny, I've got something to tell you."

"What's the matter, baby?"

Nicole took a deep breath. She didn't know where to start. Would she tell her about what she revealed at her session and get her all upset? Or would she just tell her what Mama said? Nicole calmed herself down and took a deep breath. She blew her nose into a tissue that she had taken out of her purse after dabbing her eyes with it. She sighed again, then looked at her grandmother, and shook her head; then she began to cry all over again, as she remembered the reason that she'd come over there in the first place.

Granny rubbed Nicole's back, trying to console her. "What is it, baby? What's the matter?"

"Granny, there is just so much. It's too much. I've been trying to hold it all inside. I've been trying to keep it to myself. I didn't want anybody to know," Nicole said as she cried into her tissue.

"You can tell me, baby. Granny is a strong old gal. I can handle it."

"Granny, when I was nine years old," Nicole said and paused to sniffle. "I was molested by Daddy Ray."

"Oh my god! Oh, no!" Granny exclaimed Granny's hands shook as she held her hand to her mouth. "Oh my baby!" Granny said as she embraced Nicole.

"It went on for years, and I didn't tell anyone. I was scared. I didn't know what anybody would say or what they would do, and I didn't know who to talk to or how to say it. I felt so ashamed."

Granny cried; she felt so guilty. "Oh my Lord. Sweet Jesus, sweet Jesus," she prayed, as if helping to prepare herself for what was next.

"I told Mama and my sisters today. I didn't mean to, but Mama and Fatimah just kept pressing me. So I just said it, just like that. And I couldn't stop. I just kept going on and on and on, saying every detail." She sighed. "I never meant for it to come out like that." Granny was glad that Nicole had spared her the specifics. She didn't think that she could handle that right now.

"Baby, why didn't you come to me?

"I didn't think that there was anything that anybody could do. I was a child, and I didn't know. Ray never threatened me not to tell, but I didn't know what to do."

"Well, baby, what did ya' mama hafto say?"

"She told me that Ray was my father."

Tangie had left her daughters at The Family Wellness Center. They were ganging up on her, asking her what she had said to Nicole. But she wouldn't tell them. They'd all find out sooner or later. She had a lot more secrets to reveal, but she wouldn't be revealing them tonight. She didn't go all the way on Kinsman to be attacked. She was a good mother. She may not have been perfect, but she was a good mother and she wasn't going to let anyone tell her any different.

She dreaded this day. The day the truth came out about Ray being Nicole's biological father. At least, he was dead now; she wouldn't have to look him in the face now after hearing Nicole's shocking news. She wished he was alive, just so she could kill him dead and put him back in the ground again. He didn't beat her when he was alive, for all the dirt she had done to him especially for her running around with Otis, but he had gotten his payback by abusing their child all those years. Why she didn't see it, she really didn't know. She thought that he loved Nicole, loved her like a father. He was there with her from the time she came into the world. How could he do such a thing to her? She wasn't surprised though, because he was a man and she was use to men doing some foul-ass shit.

Ray may not have known that he was molesting his own daughter back then, but Mama let him know before he died that Nicole was his. She'd whispered it in his ear while he was on his death bed. She rarely visited him in the hospital, especially toward the end. She didn't see why she had to sit up in the hospital and watch him die. But when they'd told her it was close, she showed up, stood over his bed, and stared at him. She leaned over his weak and dying body and told him that he had fathered three of her children. He cried and he looked horrified. She'd thought that he had cried because she was cruel enough to wait until he was near death to tell him or perhaps he had cried because she'd said it with a smile on her face. He'd always thought that all of Tangie's babies were Otis's. Besides he only had one testicle and as Tangie would often remind him, the other one didn't work worth a damn.

Ray had known that Tangie could be cruel, but he didn't think she was a monster. She could have kept that to herself, but she didn't. She wanted to hurt him. She wanted him to die knowing that he had given her three children and that they all called Otis their daddy. Tangie had thought that it was Ray's fault that she had never gotten Otis. She felt that if Ray had never told him about her and him, then Otis would have been hers, and they could have lived happily ever after. But Tangie was completely delusional. Otis didn't want Tangie; he never really did. What he wanted from her, he got every time she offered it and that was the extent of his relationship with her.

Carl came to pick up his wife and her sisters. He didn't know what to think. Mariah was crying when she called him to pick her up. And she was still crying when he got there. Carl hated to see any woman cry this way, but especially his wife. He didn't know how to comfort her or her sisters that were crying too.

"Oh my god. I just can't believe it," Serena cried. She sat in the backseat holding a piece of tissue to her eyes.

"What's goin' on? What happened?" Carl asked as he looked over to his wife.

Mariah shook her head; she couldn't even talk.

Aniyah was crying hard, wiping snot away with her tissue and wiping her eyes.

Fatimah was crying too; she had a blank stare as tears streamed down her face. She couldn't believe the cruelty she had put upon her sister. Guilt lay heavy upon her chest, and she could hardly move under its weight. Tears flowed as she imagined the things that Nicole had said. She couldn't block her words out of her head. It sickened her that Nicole had been going through that horrifying ordeal under the same roof as her and her younger sisters. How could no one have known? Fatimah cried as she thought about her children and the damage she had done. She thought about how she was the cause of her world coming down around her, not Jason, and she cried.

Fatimah dialed her house, and Jason answered the phone. She could hear her children talking in the background; she wondered if they were okay.

"Hello?"

"It's me," she said, trying to hold back the tears. "I'm coming home."

Fatimah was dropped off in her driveway. Her children ran out to meet her as Carl drove away. The rest of the sisters headed over to Granny's house. They had gotten in touch with Nicole and found out that she was over there. Carl dropped them off and then went back home to the kids; Jean was watching them for him.

Granny hugged and consoled three more of her grandbabies. They asked her where Nicole was, and Granny had sent them up to her bedroom. Nicole was asleep, lying on top of Granny's old quilt. Aniyah sat down on the bed at her feet and gently touched Nicole's leg.

"Nicci," Aniyah said softly. Mariah and Serena sat down on each side of Nicole. Nicole roused from her sleep and looked up to see all, but one of her sister's faces. "Are you okay?"

"I'm fine," Nicole sat up on the bed and held her arms out to her sisters, and they all gave her a big hug. Serena started crying again; she just couldn't control herself. "I'm sorry, guys, I never meant to tell you all like that? Are you all okay?"

"I'm in shock."

"I just don't believe it. I can't believe that happened to you." Aniyah began to cry again too. Mariah wiped her eyes as a tear began to fall.

"Y'all don't start. I haven't cried like that in a long time. I don't want to start up again."

Nicole sighed. "I'm glad you all came. I know you all are wondering what Mama said to me."

The women nodded.

"Well, she told me that Ray was really my father."

"What?" Mariah said as her other sisters gasped in shock and disbelief.

"This is such a fucked-up day," Serena said as she cried. "How can it get any worse?"

Nicole looked at Aniyah and Mariah. They knew the answer to that, but Serena hadn't caught on yet. Serena pressed the used tissue to her eyes, hoping it would absorb her tears. She sniffled, and her face was red and sore. Serena looked up at her sisters. All eyes were on her. Then it hit her. Was Ray their daddy too?

Fatimah had only been gone a few days, but so much had changed. Her family missed her. Her children hugged her and cried and held on to her for dear life. Jason was there. He was happy that Fatimah was home too. Fatimah apologized to her children and told each of them that she would never ever leave them again. She told them that she loved and missed all of them and that she was so happy to be back home with them.

"Leah said that you weren't ever coming back. But I told her you would. Mommy, I prayed that you would come back home. I prayed so hard. I prayed every single day," Lana said as she squeezed her mother tightly. She held Lana and kissed her on the forehead. And was happy that she had been in somebody's prayers.

She was surrounded by her children, and her heart swelled with love for them. She hated herself for being so selfish and cold. Fatimah was so upset with herself by how she had handled her counseling session. She had entered the room defensive, and she had decided that she was not going to be made out to be the crazy one, when everybody else needed help too. But she didn't have the right to call anybody out the way she did. She knew better than that, but she couldn't control herself. She was angry at herself for being so mean to Nicole all these years just because she was jealous of her happiness. She never knew what Nicole had to deal with all this time. She never knew what her sister had been holding inside.

She owed Nicole an apology, but she wondered if she'd accept it. She wanted to apologize to her mother too, but she wasn't in such a big hurry to do that. She was glad that she'd gotten those things off her chest, but she was ashamed of her delivery.

That night Fatimah could hardly sleep. As she lay on the couch in the living room, she tossed and turned thinking about everything that had happened. She thought about what she had done to her children, and she decided that she'd take them to counseling with her. She thought about Jason and of how she didn't want to be married to him anymore.

None of her sisters had asked, but she was sure that they wondered if she was still pregnant, and she was, but she wasn't going to bring it up until she decided what to do about it. She still hadn't told Jason, and she wouldn't until she thought she had to.

When Mariah got home, she hugged her husband and told him everything. He couldn't believe what he was hearing. He knew his wife had a lot of drama in her family but damn. Mariah went in to check on her children; they were all sleeping quietly, and they were safe. What a blessing it is to know that your family is okay, safe in their beds without a care in the world. Then she thought about Nicole slipping into their mama's room at night to get in bed with her own father. She shuddered at that thought. It was bad enough that she'd been carrying around the burden of her secret abuse, then to find out that it was your own father. She was so disgusted, and she felt so sorry for her sister. She looked at her children, each of them, and wondered if they had any secrets that they'd been hiding. She stroked her belly and said a prayer over them asking God for his continued protection over them and thanking him that they were happy and healthy and safe.

It was early Saturday morning; the birds were singing. The grass was damp with morning dew, and the sky was clear and sunny. It was Serena's twenty-first birthday. Nicole had dropped everyone at home last night. Serena spent the night over Nicole's house. Nicole had planned on going shopping today to get her ready for the surprise that they had planned for Serena tonight, but they had to take care of some business first.

Nicole picked up her sisters; they all looked tired from a lack of sleep. Fatimah looked especially exhausted this morning.

"Happy birthday, baby doll!" each one said as they stepped into the truck. They hugged and kissed her and asked her how it felt to be twenty-one.

They knew that the drama wasn't over. All kinds of questions swirled through their minds as they tried to put the puzzle pieces together. Their family was more than dysfunctional; it was a disaster. Nicole couldn't believe that they were actually going over to their mother's house to see who their fathers were.

They all looked at Serena, and she began to cry. She was the only creamy sister with the good hair. Who really was her daddy? Serena had said that no matter what Mama said, that Otis was her daddy, and he would always be her daddy. Nobody wanted to claim the dead man who had molested Nicole for eight years. But nobody in the truck knew for sure, and none of them really wanted to know.

When they got to Mama's house, Nicole stepped out of the truck first, Fatimah was next, then Mariah, and then Aniyah and Serena followed. They walked up the front walk and to Mama's front door. It was open already; Mama was letting the fresh morning air in. Serena rang the doorbell. Mama hadn't even called to wish her daughter a happy birthday. Mariah was the first to approach Mama.

Mama said, "Look, I'm not talking about this! And you girls are not going to stand around me, trying to provoke me."

Fatimah said, "What? Mama, what are you talking about?"

"You shut cho mouth!" Mama said, pointing her finger at Fatimah. "You don't have anything to say to me. You've said enough!" Fatimah sighed, shook her head, and mumbled something to herself, then said, "Mama, I am sorry about disrespecting you the way I did. But this is about something entirely different."

Mama got up from her recliner with a grunt. She walked over to the buffet in the dining room and handed each of her daughters a manila envelope.

"I just can't get away from these things," Serena said under her breath.

Some envelopes were thicker than others. She handed Serena her envelope and gave her a dry "happy birthday." "Now go on," she said, waving them to the doors. "Don't go opening it up now! Just go on. Unless somebody else has some more shockin' news to tell me."

Nobody said a word. Tangie's words were cruel. It wasn't that she didn't believe Nicole. She just didn't know how to handle what she'd said yesterday. She didn't know what to say to console Nicole, and she didn't know how to apologize to her. So she just wouldn't address it at all.

"I did the best that I could do wit chu girls. The best that I could do." Nicole noticed that there was one envelope left in the drawer, so she asked about it. "That's Tye's envelope. What? You wanna see inside,"

Mama said, her eyes bulging threateningly. She was acting as if she wanted to fight.

"No, Mama," Nicole said calmly. "But I can stop by and give it to him," Nicole said as she held out her hand; Mama slapped it in her hand hard and glared at her. She wanted to tell Mama that Tye was just a child and that was no way to let him know who his father was, but her mother was so confrontational and if it was left up to her, she'd probably never tell him the truth.

Tangie wanted to kiss all of her girls, especially the baby; she cried the hardest. She thought she knew why. But instead, she stood against the wall as each girl left the house.

Mama walked over to the front window to see who tore into their envelopes, but each one got into their big sister's truck, clutching their envelopes in their hands. None of them opened it before Nicole had driven off.

Each woman examined the outside of their envelope; their names were written on the front. They felt it up like it was a Christmas gift, and they were trying to guess what was inside.

"Why would Mama do this to us?" Serena asked.

"Mama wasn't thinking about us. She was thinking about herself and what she wanted. And she wanted Otis," Aniyah said.

Aniyah was the first one to open up her envelope; she breathed a sigh of relief as she looked inside and saw a picture of Otis. Otis was her father, and she was glad. Mariah was next, and when she pulled open her envelope, she saw a picture of Otis too.

"I can't believe this is how we're finding out who our father is? Like we're on the Maury show."

Fatimah opened her envelope, and as soon as she saw Ray's picture, she slid it back into the envelope, turned her head, and stared at the passenger-side window. Nobody asked her any questions.

"I'm not opening it. I don't care who he is. This is my birthday, and I'm not opening it." Serena said. "What mother reveals something so intimate and important this way?" Serena pushed the envelope under the seat with her foot. She didn't even want to see it.

Nobody blamed Serena for being upset; the situation was really crazy. "No more surprises, guys. Not on my birthday, I can't take it."

Nicole invited her sisters to go shopping with them. Mariah and Fatimah said they had to get back to their families.

Aniyah said, "I'm goin'," like a big kid.

"This is your day, birthday girl," Nicole said as she gave her baby sister a pinch.

Serena smiled. "This is my birthday!"

For the rest of the day, Nicole tried her best to keep her little sister occupied. They had so much fun together riding around Cleveland, visiting family and friends. Nicole pinned a twenty-dollar bill on Serena, and Aniyah followed pinning on a ten, a five, and a five ones.

Serena played with her bills and said, "I'm reyotch!"

They drove downtown and parked at Tower City and walked around and shopped. Aniyah and Serena didn't look at price tags because they weren't paying. Serena kept walking around taking pictures of them.

"Serena, stop it with the pictures," Aniyah said, blocking the flash with her hand.

"What?" Serena said. "I'll be going back in a week. I need something to remember this day by," she said as she snapped more pictures. She'd taken pictures of Nicole and Aniyah together, and every now and then, she'd have them take pictures of her with one of them. "I can't wait till tonight," Serena said. She knew that her sisters had something big planned, but she didn't know what it was.

Serena's phone rang, and she answered it. It was Otis.

"Hey, daddy," Serena said with excitement. Otis was her daddy; she didn't care what Mama said.

"Happy birthday, baby doll!"

"Thank you, Daddy."

"Where you stayin' at?"

"With Nicole," Serena answered.

"So what ch'all doin' tonight? You gonna stop by here?"

"Sure, Daddy." Serena put the phone to her chest and said, "Nicci, do we have time to stop by and see Daddy."

"Yea, baby doll."

Serena stayed on the phone with the man who was going to be her daddy forever and ever even though she knew deep down in her heart that she wouldn't be pulling his picture out of her envelope.

"Serena, we have to get your outfit."

"Okay. Okay"

"You don't even know what you wanna wear. Got us drivin' all over the place."

"Shut up, you ain't even drivin'," Serena said to Aniyah.

"Hold up, I have this place that we can try, but it has grown-up clothes," Nicole said to Serena. Aniyah laughed.

"I'm talkin' 'bout you too, Aniyah. You don't know nothing 'bout bein' grown and sexy."

"Whatever," Aniyah said. "I know all about bein' grown and sexy."

"I'm talkin' about outside the bedroom."

Nicole took her sisters to Haughty, a couture shop on Chagrin Boulevard. Haughty was owned by a brother-and-sister team, by the name of Chazmine and Domingo Christian. Nicole called them the "dynamic duo." She said they were awesome and that nobody ever left their store dissatisfied.

"Nicci!?" a tall, thin, dark-skinned woman said as she approached Nicole with open arms. Nicole smiled at her and gave her a hug. "Now who are these young ladies? No, don't tell me. They look just like you. Must be your sisters." She embraced Aniyah and Serena warmly. "Domingo, guess who's here?"

"Domingo?" Serena mouthed to Aniyah. Aniyah looked at Serena and hunched her shoulders. The women looked toward the back of the store at a curtained doorway and out stepped a fine specimen of a man. He looked like a model. He was gorgeous, and he looked nothing like his sister Chazmine.

"Mandingo," Aniyah mouthed to Serena. Serena smiled.

When he saw Nicole, his face lit up. "Hey, Nicci baby," he said. He hugged Nicole and held her in his arms and squeezed her and wouldn't let go.

"Let go of me, Domingo. You're smothering me."

Aniyah and Serena looked at each other as they spied Domingo's bulging biceps as he held their sister close to him in his locked embrace.

"Come on, let go, Domingo," Nicole said. Domingo closed his eyes and kissed Nicole on her neck. He whispered something in her ear, and she giggled and said, "You are so not funny." Domingo laughed and let Nicole go.

"Domingo, Chazmine, these are my sisters Aniyah and Serena."

They said hello with a smile. Aniyah and Serena said hello and smiled back.

"They are beautiful," Domingo said as he looked at the sisters.

"I know, aren't they gorgeous?" Chazmine said.

"They look just like you, I mean just like you," Domingo said to Nicole.

"Yes, it's uncanny how much you all resemble each other." Chazmine said.

The sisters smiled.

"Guys, we really need your help. My sisters need something hot for tonight. We have something big planned for Serena's birthday tonight, and we need them to look hot."

"Well, ladies, take a look around. I am sure that you will find just what you're looking for," Chazmine said with a smile. Nicole shot Chazmine a glance; then Chazmine said, "On the other hand, have a seat ladies and let us bring that look to you."

Nicole didn't have time for her sisters to peruse the store indecisively looking for something to wear tonight. She knew that the dynamic duo were perfectly capable of eyeballing the girls and finding something that they would look ravishing in.

Nicole, Aniyah, and Serena sat at the back of the store in the plush velvet seats as Chazmine and Domingo brought different outfits to them, and they enjoyed trying them on as Nicole sat and watched. Nicole's phone rang, and she excused herself and went outside. Aniyah liked every outfit presented to her, but she loved the shiny silver jeans. They were sexy low-rise jeans, which showed off her small waist, flat-toned stomach, and her round butt.

"Oooh, Niyah, those look so cute on you," Serena said.

"I know, I like these, she said looking at her butt in the mirror. But what top would I wear with this?"

"This," Domingo said, handing her a flimsy sequined top. It was all black with silver sequins that sparkled like diamonds; the back was out except for two pieces of string that ran across the back to hold the sides together.

"Aniyah, that is hot," Serena said.

"All of my back will be out. I won't be able to wear a bra."

"You won't need a bra, trust me. Try it on." Domingo said.

Aniyah tried the outfit on, and it was so sexy.

"Ooh, Niyah! You have got to get that."

"I didn't call your house!" Nicole shouted into the phone as she sat outside in her truck. "I keep telling you that shit!"

"My wife told me that you called!"

"I don't give a fuck what your wife said. I don't have any reason to call her or you. I don't give a fuck about neither one of y'all." It had been a week since Nicole had left Darren lying in his driveway, a whole week, and here they were with the same argument all over again.

*   *   *

Just one week ago, Darren had accused Nicole of calling his wife and harassing her. Nicole had no idea what he was talking about. He'd called her and said, "Bitch, stop calling my house!"

"Hold on, what the fuck are you talking about?" Nicole had said. She was out at a night club, and Darren and his wife were the last two people on her mind.

"You heard what the fuck I said! Don't fuck with my family!"

"What? Are you fuckin' threatening me?"

"You heard what the fuck I said."

"Muthafucka, you don't scare me. Fuck you and your wife. I don't give a fuck about her. What the fuck I wanna call yo' house for?"

"Bitch, don't let me find you 'cuz if I find you—"

"You'll what?" Nicole had interrupted. "You'll start crying like a bitch begging me to come back to you?" Nicole had gotten the voice-mail messages, and she had heard the sniffling and the tears. "Fuck you. I wouldn't fuck wit'cho ass again if you were the last muthafucka on earth, do you hear me? Fuck Yoou." Nicole had drawn out that last word as if talking in slow motion. Anger had burned so deep within Darren that he wanted to smash her pretty face, like a porcelain doll."

"Let me find you! Just let me get my hands on you!"

"Find me? Find me muthafucka? As a matter of fact, look no muthafuckin' further. Here I come!"

Nicole remembered how angry she was, pushing through the crowd to get to her car. She didn't wait for the valet to get it for her. She had walked through the parking lot, her short satiny skirt billowing in the breeze as she walked by. She felt the eyes on her; she knew the men were stopping and staring. She had that effect on them. She watched as every head turned in her direction. The very air of her commanded respect and attention and had caused people to wake up and take notice. Beauty, poise, and confidence had exuded from her pores. She was a Headturner, no, The Headturner, for sure.

*　　*　　*

That was a week ago, and this was where keeping it real had gotten her. Her car had been vandalized, her friend had been assaulted, and she was still right where she had started, arguing with his sorry ass.

"Why ain't cho ass in jail?"

"Jail? Never that. As a matter of fact, I have no idea what you're talking about."

"Bitch, you know exactly what I'm talkin' about!"

"Fuck you!"

"Fuck you. Bitch," Nicole said, saying the word bitch with as much emphasis as she could muster.

"Slut!"

"Limp-dick muthatfucka!"

That made Darren angry, and he asked, "How's your friend feel? Your white friend."

"Ooh he feels so good," she said, simulating a sexy moan.

"Fuck you," Darren said.

"I should have known better than to make a bitch like you my woman."

"I'm not the bitch that you made your woman." Nicole replied.

"Fuck you Nicole."

"Fuck you Darren. You lyin', cheatin', sorry ass bastard! Don't call me no more!"

Darren hung up on Nicole.

She didn't know where Darren was getting this shit from. She had never called his wife. She had never wanted to call his wife. As a matter of fact, the thought had never even crossed her mind. Nicole kept reminding herself that as soon as she discovered he was married, she had let him go. No ifs, ands, or buts about it. Why was this man doing this to her? She couldn't get any closure.

So she continued to find comfort in sex. Because sex was for her what food or chocolate was for some other women. She had to have it, when she wanted to have it and how she wanted to have it. And she was glad that so many men were willing to oblige her.

When Nicole had entered the store, she saw that Aniyah and Serena had picked out just what they had wanted. Nicole loved their choices. She paid for their outfits, shoes, and accessories and thanked and hugged Chazmine and Domingo as she left the store. Serena was happy and enjoying her birthday so far. Nicole was glad because she had a very special surprise for her.

Nicole had a big soiree planned for her little sis, an extravagant birthday party, and Serena was going to arrive in style. Nicole had reserved Luscious in Velour, a Cleveland hot spot in the flats. It was a tri-level club, and it was the hottest nightclub in Cleveland. Luscious in Velour was very trendy. Not only did local celebrities and the Cleveland elite party there, but, celebrities from all around the country would come to Cleveland just to see what all of the fuss was about. Many after parties were held there also; it wasn't uncommon to see famous rappers, musicians, and comedians at Luscious in Velour. Serena was going to love it. It would be the best birthday ever. She would be so surprised.

Nicole had rented a white Hummer limo for Serena's birthday. And she had told six of her closest friends about it. A few of them were so excited about tonight's party that they hadn't spoken to Serena since she'd arrived in Cleveland, afraid that they'd ruin the surprise.

They were to meet Serena at Daddy Otis's house and wait for the limo to arrive; then they would take the scenic route downtown to the flats. All of her sisters would be there as well as a host of family and friends to wish her a happy birthday. Nicole had hired the best photographers in the Cleveland area to snap Serena and her guests pictures as they arrived in the club, and they'd pose in front of a free-standing board that would read, Happy Twenty-First Birthday Serena. Nicole couldn't wait to see the look on Serena's face. That was just the tip of the iceberg, and she had much more planned for her special day.

Nicole drove over to Daddy Otis's house. Barbara and all of their half sisters were there with their children to wish Serena a happy birthday. They fawned over their baby sister, and Serena ate it up. Serena was on top of the world. Nicole wondered if Serena secretly wondered the truth about Daddy Otis. Nicole wondered if Serena was secretly asking herself if he was her biological dad. Nicole loved Otis, but she couldn't help but feel sad, knowing the truth about him. Aniyah wasn't acting any differently at all. Otis was her and Mariah's biological dad. And even though neither of them talked about it, Nicole knew that they were so relieved.

How would Otis feel knowing the truth? Who would tell him? Would he regret all those years of loving children that weren't really his? Nicole wondered if the truth would hurt him as badly as it had hurt her sisters. Nicole knew she wouldn't be the one to tell him, and she wondered which one of her sisters would.

Serena was curious about what was in her envelope. Hers was thicker than her sisters', and that was what had really frightened her. Her elder sisters were able to simply pull out a photo, but Serena's envelope was thick, rather bulky. She knew that there was more than just a photo inside. Her sisters had noticed it too and had figured that was why she had cried the hardest.

When she saw Daddy Otis, she squeezed him tight, and she didn't want to let go. She had to stop herself from crying, but the tears started to show. Otis looked at his youngest daughter and smiled.

"I missed you, Daddy."

Otis smiled and kissed her on the forehead. "I missed you too, baby doll."

Serena had so much money pinned on her chest that she had to take some of it off and stick it in her purse. Cassandra, Camille, Michelle, and Lacey were so happy to see their sisters. The children hugged and kissed on their aunts; it had been such a long time.

"Ya'll, it don't make no sense that we live right here in Cleveland, and we don't get together more often," Cassandra said as she hugged Nicole.

"I know," Nicole said. "My schedule is so erratic. One minute, my planner is free and clear, and then the next, I'm bombarded with things to do."

"Girl, I know. You have been all over the place. I read your article in The African American Business Journal, it was awesome," Camille said.

"I am so proud of you, Nicole. I think I have that article around here somewhere," Barbara said as she looked around her family room.

"Don't worry about it, Mama. I believe you," Nicole said with a smile.

M-a-m-a. That was a four-letter word. It was a fighting word. Tangie would have beat down everyone in sight if she had known that any of her daughters, including Nicole, were calling any other woman by that name, especially Barbara. Ooh, there would be hell to pay if Tangie knew that all of her daughters called Barbara, Mama and that each of them loved Barbara with their whole hearts. The girls had a lot of respect for the woman who took them in every other weekend or more and treated them like they were pure gold. Despite the way they had gotten into the world.

Nicole and Aniyah stayed for about an hour, but they had to get going to plan for the rest of Serena's day. Nicole had a bunch of people in charge of Serena's party, but she was confidant in her ability to delegate responsibility. She had hired someone to oversee, the person who thought he was hired to oversee everything, just to ensure that this birthday party was a complete and utter success. Nicole knew that the party would go off without a hitch.

Nicole had stopped by Granny's house to talk to Tye; she knew who his father was. She had looked into his envelope after she had gotten off the phone with Darren's sorry ass. Nicole, Fatimah, and Tye all had the same daddy. Nicole could see that, now that she knew the truth. It was really something that after years and years of looking at her siblings and seeing all of their many physical similarities, that now she was unconsciously trying to identify the differences. They had all assumed that they had the same mom and dad, especially considering the fact that their mama had told them so. They all had the same eyes, the same nose, and the exact same smiles. They had all inherited Tangie's deep dimples and long lashes. Even Tye had women swooning over those pretty eyes and that gorgeous smile.

Nicole had not intended on telling Tye anything about his envelope or about his real daddy. She knew that Tye had been upset that he couldn't go out with his sisters to celebrate Serena's birthday. After all, it was going to be held at one of the most talked-about hot spots in Cleveland.

"Nicci, you know that you could get me in if you wanted to."

"It's not about that Tye. You are only seventeen, you need to be at least twenty-one to get in there," Nicole said to her little brother.

'Whatever, man," Tye said as he threw his hand up at his sister.

"Anyway, everybody is going over to Daddy's house to see Serena off, so you'll get to see Serena before she rides off in the Hummer limo."

"Man! I ain't tryin' ta hear dat," Tye said, as he pouted and waved his hand at his sister. "I want to go. I want to ride in the limo. I look twenty-one."

"Really? Is that what your driver's license says? 'I look twenty-one,'" Nicole said as she looked at her brother. He gave her a look, and she said, "Well, you said that like that's gonna make a difference." Nicole looked at her little brother and sighed. Tye was sorely disappointed. "Tye, you'll get your chance. Today is Serena's day. Your birthday is in December, I'll have something special planned for you too," Nicole said, and a little smile appeared on Tye's face, as he pictured a big birthday party in his honor.

"Yea, so stop whining like a lil beyotch," Aniyah said with a laugh, teasing her little brother.

Tye frowned at Aniyah and started to say something inappropriate.

"Boooy," Aniyah said as she gave him a look and raised her hand like she was going to smack him in the mouth. "Watch cha mouf."

"I didn't even say nothin'," Tye responded.

"You bet not had," Aniyah said, and she blew a kiss to Tye. Tye pretended to smack it down to the floor, as he frowned. Aniyah laughed.

Nicole felt really bad that she hadn't included Tye. She wanted all of them to get together as a family. If only he was a little older. She knew that she had a lot of pull and could get Tye in. Tye had known it too. But this was going to be a very important lesson for Tye: You can't get everything that you want, and you are not a grown man yet. Because Tye was so tall and thick for his age, everyone had the tendency to treat him like he was a grown man; then they would get mad at him because he wouldn't be able to make grown-up decisions. But Nicole would always remind Tye that you can't do everything before it's time or you'll have nothing to look forward to.

Nicole dropped Aniyah off at home. Aniyah knew what time to meet up over Daddy's house. Barbara had said that if Mama could act like she had some sense, that she was welcome to stop by and see Serena off. Barbara wasn't threatened by Tangie; she figured she had done the worse that she could do. But of course, Mama didn't know how to act, so she wouldn't be seeing Serena off for her birthday.

Aniyah was disappointed that Nathan couldn't come to Serena's party. She knew that the man had to work, but it was seriously interfering with her love life. Nathan had known how important it was for her that he be there. It had actually been a whole week since they'd had sex. She thought about Nathan and how much she enjoyed being intimate with him. She could have sex with him everyday, but she couldn't understand him. She didn't know how he could say that he loved her and share the same bed with her without him wanting to make love to her. It made her feel so unattractive.

She started to second-guess herself. Maybe she should have left the door open for Matthew. Maybe she had made a mistake.

"Hell yea, I'm upset Nathan. You knew how important this was to me."

"Baby, what am I supposed to do? I've got to work. I promise I'll make it up to you."

"How?"

"I don't know, I'll think of something."

"Whatever, Nathan," Aniyah said into the phone. She was so disappointed in Nathan; she couldn't believe him. She was tired of being understanding about cancelled dates. "Sorry you won't be able to make it." Aniyah said and then, hung up on him without saying good-bye.

Aniyah had mentioned it to Matthew, but she knew he wouldn't be there and she didn't want him to be. She didn't want Matthew and Nathan in the same room together; she didn't care how big the room was. But now that Nathan had officially cancelled, she was pissed. This hadn't been short notice; this event took an entire year to plan, and to think that Nathan wasn't going to be there was inexcusable, as far as Aniyah was concerned.

Mariah had breathed a long sigh of relief when she had seen Otis's face on that picture. She had had enough drama in one week, and she didn't need any more. She'd had a hard-enough time trying to stay stress free this week. She didn't need any more added surprises or disappointments.

Mariah and Carl had argued prior to the appointment with Dr. Muhammed. The whole Fatimah-and-Jason situation had really gotten to her. And it really had her wondering what she would do if she was in Fatimah's shoes. She didn't just have her five children to worry about, but she had the twins to worry about too. She wondered if she would let being a mother cloud her judgment about her marriage or would she do what she thought was right for her and the kids.

*　　*　　*

"Jason is a sorry sack of shit," Mariah had told her husband, as the children played in the basement. "He has been lying and cheating all these years, and it finally caught up wit his ass."

"Now, hold on. Fatimah knew what she was getting when she married him. You even said that. He was cheating on her way back in high school," Carl had said as he unloaded the dishwasher.

Mariah's back had been facing him, and she turned around and said, "So does that make it right?"

"No, baby, that's not what I'm saying. All I'm saying is that she knew what she was getting herself into. She didn't have to be married to Jason, she chose to be married to him."

"That makes no difference, Carl."

"That's your opinion, baby."

"What? Are you defending him now?"

"No, I'm just saying that a man's gonna do what a man's gonna do, and if you let him do it, then it's on you." Carl hadn't realized what he said, and he didn't realize what an affect it had on his wife.

"So you mean to tell me that it's okay for a man to cheat if his woman allows him to. Is that what I'm supposed to understand you to mean?"

"That is not what I said. A man or anybody else for that matter can only do what you allow them to do to you. You have the power to end any relationship that is not beneficial for you. No one is forced to deal with mistreatment. No one. Fatimah is a beautiful, intelligent, well-educated woman. There is no reason why she should have to stay with a man who repeatedly cheats on her. That's a choice. That is a conscious choice."

Mariah hadn't heard what he was saying; she was stuck on his previous statement, and what he had said made anger burn inside her, to the very pit of her stomach.

Carl had talked as he unloaded the dishes with his back turned to his wife, totally oblivious to the fact of how upset she was, not knowing that she had been staring at the back of his head so hard that she could have bored a whole through it with her heated gaze.

"Carl?" Mariah had said. She was angry, and he recognized it in her voice.

Carl turned around. Mariah was standing on the other side of the kitchen table with one hand on her hip and a dishcloth in her other hand; she had been cleaning splashes of spaghetti sauce from dinner, off the stove. "I need you to know this. I need you to know that these words are true. If you ever in life find yourself in another woman's bed or in our bed, for that matter with another woman, then I am gone. You hear me? Gone and not gone like Fatimah. I will leave and take my babies and start all over again. And I mean that. I will not accept a cheating husband 'cuz I don't hafto. I don't give a damn if I have a dozen babies."

Carl had sighed, turned around, and continued unloading the dishwasher. He knew his wife well, and every now and then, when someone else had problems, totally unrelated to her relationship with him, Mariah would sit around thinking too hard about how to help some other grown person solve their problems. She would step out of her relationship with Carl and put herself in their shoes and step back into her relationship with Carl without taking those shoes off. In times like these, she wouldn't listen to what Carl had said or even try to hear him out, because she was so focused on what she felt needed to be said and getting things off of her chest. So Carl didn't say anything, and he had patiently waited for Mariah to come back to reality and realize that she was talking to her loving husband and not someone else's unfaithful mate. But she hadn't, and instead of her realizing this, she had gone on until she had said something especially hurtful and then Carl felt that he had to address it.

Carl had turned to his wife and said sternly, "Stop threatening me, Mariah. Why do you think I stay in this marriage? Huh? Because you threaten me? I could walk right out of here today and find me another woman just like that," he said as he snapped his finger.

Mariah's mouth had dropped in shock. "I wouldn't be the first man to walk out on his wife and kids."

Mariah hadn't said a word; she couldn't believe what she was hearing.

"I'm here dammit because I love you and I love my kids. I'm here because I want to be here, not because I have to be." Mariah had closed her mouth; she threw down the dish rag, stormed out of the kitchen, and started up the stairs. She was crying.

Carl felt badly. He hadn't meant to hurt her. He loved his family with all of his heart, and he had what he had always wanted, a beautiful wife that loved him and children that he couldn't live without. He was wedded-bliss personified and he wanted his wife to know that, but he also wanted her to stop those inane threats, because he wasn't going anywhere. There wasn't another woman that he wanted and he'd never let anyone destroy his family and he wanted his wife to know that too.

Carl had grabbed Mariah and had stopped her from going up the stairs. She turned to him but couldn't look him in his face. He wrapped his arms around her and said, "I love you, baby. Look at me," Carl said. Mariah looked up at him, and he kissed her on her lips. "I love you more than you will ever know. There is absolutely no other place I'd rather be. This is the perfect life for me. I love waking up to you and my family every morning, and I love coming home to all of you every evening. You are the perfect woman for me. There ain't another woman out there that got anything on you. You have given me what I never had. A family and I thank God for you."

Mariah hugged him and apologized and promised never ever to do that again. Carl accepted her apology and kissed and embraced her.

"Carl, do you really mean all those things that you said about me?"

"You mean what I just said?"

"Yea." Mariah said.

"Hell yea! I love you and I love my kids. I aint goin' nowhere" Carl had said as he held his wife in his arms and kissed her on her forehead. She laid her head on his chest and pushed her full stomach against his. "Not to mention you give the bomb-ass head. Whoo!" Carl had whispered in her ear, as he laughed. Mariah pushed him away and smacked him on his arm.

"See, you play too much," Mariah had said with a smile; she'd taken that as a compliment too.

Fatimah was home, and all was right with the world. Everyone and everything miraculously fell in place. Jason and the kids too. It was as if she never even left, as if all was forgiven. Fatimah should have felt grateful; she should have felt blessed that her children weren't wearing the scars from the damage that she had done. She should have been appreciative of the fact that her husband accepted her lovingly, despite her recent admission of infidelity, not to mention the fact that she had walked out on him and her kids.

But Fatimah hadn't felt that way. She felt that the damage she had done wasn't really addressed. It would have been easier to face it and at least try and fix it if it was evident. But it wasn't. Everything had been smoothed over as if what had occurred was normal or natural. She knew her children were still hurting and afraid, and she knew that in order to address it, they'd have to confess it or else she'd have to dig it up, bring it to the surface, and then try to help them through it. That's where Dr. Muhammed would come in.

Fatimah was glad that Mama had left her and her sisters at the therapy session. Dr. Muhammed had a lot to say and even though Mama could have benefited greatly from hearing it, she wouldn't have given the doctor the opportunity to speak or complete a thought, and then no one would have benefited at all, so it was best that she'd left them right where they were. Plus, who really wanted to take that long ride home after what had just transpired in that session? Fatimah knew she didn't want to, and she doubted that her sisters did either.

Fatimah wanted to hug Nicole and sincerely apologize to her for all of the wrong she had done. She knew so much better than that. She was a Christian who struggled to live by the Word, every single day of her life, and even though she had been taught that this was true of every Christian, she had still convinced herself that this should not apply to her. Fatimah reviewed every scornful and hateful word that she'd hurled at her sister, and it embarrassed her that she could call herself a woman of God and be so mean and cruel to her own flesh and blood. She wanted to kiss Nicole and to try with all of her might to build a true sisterly relationship with her. But she knew that that wouldn't happen overnight and that she had time to make it right. Besides, she had so much to fix there in that house that she couldn't really focus on mending that fence with Nicole right now.

Fatimah wanted to thank Mariah for suggesting Dr. Muhammed. She really liked the smooth easiness of her conversation; she was calm, cool, and collected even though they'd brought The Jerry Springer show to her office.

*   *   *

"Ladies, I am very sorry that you all discovered something so very private and personal in such a public way. I am sure that your sister was not trying to intentionally hurt any of you. I am also quite sure that it was just as difficult for her to hold something so painful inside after all of these years. But I am glad to see that you sisters are consoling one another, and it seems to me that you all feel that your relationship with each other is very important."

Fatimah, Aniyah, and Mariah had moved their seats closer to Serena; she was crying uncontrollably, and they were comforting her as they cried as well.

"I really wish that your mother and your sister could have stayed for this, but I understand how overwhelmed your mother must have felt learning something so devastating and how very, very difficult it must have been for her daughter to reveal that. However, I'd like to focus on you ladies. Is that all right?" Dr. Muhammed had asked. The sisters nodded in agreement.

Dr. Muhammed had felt very badly that their session had taken a turn for the worse. But she'd chosen to abandon the crisis at hand. She had felt the need to redirect the session, back to its original purpose, and the ladies could discuss their feelings about what had just happened as the session moved along.

"First of all, I'd like to talk about relationships. Our relationships, whether they be casual, personal, or professional, really have a lasting impact on our lives. They affect who we are as people, as women. And the funny thing about it is that it doesn't matter how trivial or how long lasting that relationship is, it still affects us in ways we may not even notice. Would you ladies agree?" Serena hunched her shoulders as Mariah wrapped her arm around her, holding her close to her. Serena had thought that the session was over as far as she was concerned and she wasn't paying much attention to what Dr Muhammed was saying. The other elder sisters listened intently.

"We are all but stones making ripples in a large pond is what I'm trying to say. Perhaps you've heard that phrase before?" Dr. Muhammed had paused to see if it was all right to continue. "It is my philosophy that there are only two types of people in any relationship. Whether it be a family member, a friend, or a loved one. And these two types are what I call anchors and propellers." She went on. "Anchors are negative. They weigh you down and they prevent you from moving forward, and even if you have the strength to drag them along, they exhaust you under the weight of their negativity. They hold you down. They hold you back, and they have you spinning directionless and without a focus." Dr. Muhammed had paused as the ladies listened and asked themselves if they were an anchor as they mentally classified various other people in their lives. "Propellers on the other hand are positive, they push you forward toward your goals. They propel you toward something greater, and they push you toward your destiny." Dr. Muhammed paused again, allowing the women to think about what she'd just said.

"Any questions so far?" Dr. Muhammed had asked. "Any comments?"

There were no comments, until Serena said, "Mama is an anchor."

Fatimah had added, "Jason is an anchor."

"Nicole is a propeller," Aniyah had said. The other sisters had to agree, including Fatimah even as she waited for someone to announce that she was an anchor. But no one did. No one there, but her, would be that cruel.

"It's okay, ladies. I hadn't meant for you to say anything out loud. But I wanted you to think about that and ask that question about the people in your life. To evaluate your relationships," Dr. Muhammed had said with a nod and broad smile. She was glad that they had been listening and were participating. "I have resolved to only closely associate with those who are positive, uplifting, and encouraging. Those who are truly spiritual but not in the religious sense," Dr. Muhammed said, frowning and shaking her head, "but in the sense that they realize that we are all responsible for the upbuilding of each other, and not the tearing down of one another. Negativity is a true energy, many people don't realize that, and when it is released into the universe, it can do a world of damage." Fatimah had cried when the doctor had said that.

"Fatimah, why are you crying?" Mariah had asked.

"Because I am an anchor! I have always been an anchor. I am jealous-hearted, bitter, and vindictive," Fatimah said as she cried harder into her hands. "And I'm miserable." She had cried as her shoulders jerked and her voice sounded pained and broken. Her sisters gathered around her, hugging her.

"Fatimah, don't cry," Aniyah had said as she kissed her sister's wet cheek, "You're a bitch, but we love you." The sisters laughed. Fatimah did too.

"I don't know why I am the way I am, but I can't fight it. It's like when I see Nicole happy, something in me gets so angry and I have to try and do something to bring her down to size. And to think all these years she's thought that I hated her over something I don't even remember. I don't even remember what she's talking about. When we were kids, I was always telling Nicole that I saw what she did and I was gonna tell. I don't know, I guess that maybe she thought that I knew that something was going on, she just assumed that that was what I was talking about." Fatimah cried.

Fatimah had blown her nose, wiped her eyes, and tried to straighten up her face as best she could; then she said, "Dr. Muhammed, I am so unhappy. I do not want to stay married to my husband. I love my children, and I do want to go back to them. But I hate my life. Something has got to change. I just can't take it anymore. I feel like I'm on the verge of mental collapse. I had loved that man for so long."

"Well, Fatimah, you sound like you have some very important choices to make."

Fatimah had looked to the doctor and had thought to herself, "All that talking you just did and when I approach you directly, all you have to say is: I have some very important choices to make?"

"Fatimah, my goal in treatment is to provide you with a listening ear, to help you find a viable means of coping, and to assist you in developing constructive coping mechanisms. Numbness and denial are destructive, and they can often result in hurtful outbursts as you all have witnessed here tonight. I will tell you this, when being in love adversely affects your attitude toward your family, your children, your work, or any other activities of daily living, then you need to seriously ask yourself if love is really the emotion that you're feeling. It may be more like hurt, fear, or depression."

*   *   *

Fatimah was glad that she'd talked with Dr. Muhammed, and she was glad that her sisters were there too. But she hadn't needed to talk to her to know that her charade of a marriage was over; she didn't care how perfect and normal everything had seemed. Fatimah had decided that in order to put the broken pieces of her life back together again, she'd have to get rid of the 178-pound anchor that had kept her stale and stagnate all these years. So first thing Monday morning, she'd be headed to the divorce lawyer to end their marriage for good.

Nicole knew that Serena loved pictures, and she loved commemorating the different events in her life. Serena was very sentimental and nostalgic. So Nicole hired a camera crew for the entire evening to record the event. They would be there to see the expression on Serena's face when the limo drove up, and they would be inside the limo, with Serena and her friends. And they would be following Serena and her partygoers, documenting the event so that Serena could review it for many, many years to come.

Nicole had so many surprises in store for her sister, and she couldn't wait to see her reaction to them. Nicole was glad that no one had slipped up and told Serena anything, and she hoped that it would stay that way until tonight. She was so happy that Serena's close friends stayed away, rather than spill the beans to Serena even though it made them look bad.

As Nicole drove home alone, she realized that she had a lot to think about. Things that she had pushed so far back in her mind that it seemed as though they had never really happened, but just as soon as the memory of it was erased, the truth had a way of popping up and staring you right into your guilty face.

Nicole had so much to do, but she had plenty of time to get it done. She walked over to her tall wardrobe and opened its heavy oak doors. She looked in the bottom of the wardrobe and she reached way in the back and pulled out a red velvet bag. She walked over to her bed and sat down. She held the bag in her hand as her heart raced and pounded in her chest. She reached into the bag and pulled out an old, plain, white pillowcase. It was stained and it had yellowed over the years, but she'd kept it hidden deep within her massive wardrobe as if anyone who found it would ever know what it was.

*   *   *

Back when Daddy Ray was a hospice patient, not many people came to see him. Nicole's sisters were genuinely busy, and they'd stop in to visit him several times a week, to feed him or bring him something that they thought he would enjoy. They never stayed long though, mostly because they said they couldn't stand to see him like that. He didn't eat much, but he enjoyed having people read to him the most. Especially the Bible. Nicole didn't know why, but he seemed at peace as she read scriptures that she herself didn't understand the meaning to.

Eventually Daddy Ray, had gotten really bad. He couldn't keep much down and he was in a lot of pain. He was allowed twenty milligrams of liquid Morphine every hour if he needed it for severe pain and dyspnea, Ativan for his anxiety and a variety of other pain medications to keep him comfortable. Mama had only visited him once and that was the day before he died, and it seemed to Nicole that he appeared a little closer to death after her visit as if it were possible that there was something that she'd said or had done to quicken the dying process.

Nicole on the other hand visited him every day. She worked her visiting schedule into her daily routine, because she loved and pitied him and because he had no one else. Ray didn't keep friends because he wouldn't let them say anything negative about Tangie, and his family didn't want anything to do with him because of some undisclosed thing he'd done a long time ago.

On the day he had died, the hospice nurse had phoned Nicole at work informing her that he had taken a turn for the worse. Nicole was his power of attorney, and she headed there to see him right away. Ray's breathing was shallow and labored. He could speak clearly, but he was incoherent.

"Daddy? I'm here," Nicole had said to him as she sat down at his bedside. He had reached for her hand. A nursing assistant closed the door behind her to give Nicole some privacy. Ray's eyes were cloudy, but he turned in her direction when she whispered in his ear again, "Daddy, I'm here."

Ray pulled her close and said to her, just above a whisper, "I'm sorry 'bout what I done to you. You were a good girl. A good girl. Lord forgive me. Jesus please. Nicole, forgive me." Ray had struggled to apologize. Nicole had wondered if a dying man's apology was sincere.

Ray squeezed his eyes shut, and they began to water; then he'd said, "I don't wanna burn, I don't wanna burn, please forgive me. Say you forgive me." He opened his eyes and looked at Nicole. She wondered if he could really see her.

"I forgive you, Daddy," Nicole said and wondered to herself if she truly had.

Ray squeezed her hand as hard as he could. Then Ray uttered his last sentences, words that she would never forget, "Tell Fatimah and Tye to forgive me too. It wasn't my fault. Tell them to forgive me for what I done to them. Tell them I'm sorry. I'm so sorry."

Nicole had dropped his hand and stepped away. "What did you say?" Nicole had asked. Ray didn't answer; he was quickly approaching his time to die.

"What did you say, old man?" Nicole had asked. He wasn't old, really, but he was very sick and the cancer aged him as it ate away at his insides and withered away his once-healthy body.

"What did you say?"

"I'm sorry, tell them to forgive me."

Nicole cried and shook her head no. She'd held her hand over her mouth to muffle her cries.

"Please, no," she cried. "Had he done these things to them?" Nicole had wondered. She didn't want to even imagine that. "Oh god, oh god, oh god. Please no," Nicole had prayed, hoping that Ray hadn't said what she'd thought he said. She could count on one hand the times that Tye was in Ray's presence. She prayed that he hadn't done them any harm. Ray had stopped talking, his mouth was slightly parted, and his eyes had rolled to the back of his head. But he was still alive. He was still breathing, but his respirations couldn't have been anymore than ten breaths per minute. Without giving it so much as a thought, Nicole had picked up a pillow and pressed it against his face. He fought it a little at first as much as his weak body could. But then it had seemed as if he had surrendered. As if he preferred to go by her hands than to fade slowly and painfully into death as he had been for so many months. Nicole pressed and pressed until she thought every breath of air was out of his lungs, until he had no more life or breath in his body. Until his heart had stopped beating. Until he was dead.

When she had removed the pillow from his face and she had realized what she had done, she began to cry even harder. She looked at his lifeless body, the tip of his nose tilted to one side from the pressure of the pillow. Nicole blinked away tears and wiped his face with a damp cloth and tried as best she could to make his nose look as normal as possible. She stripped the pillowcase off of the pillow and stuffed it into her purse. It was wet with mucous and saliva from him struggling to breath. Nicole cried with her face on his chest.

"Why did you have to do that? Why did you have to tell me that? You should have taken that to your grave." Nicole cried so hard as she remembered the crotchless underwear that this man had "made" for her from her tiny panties when she was a little girl. The ones that he'd instructed her to wear on those nights that he wanted easy access to her. She had wondered had he made any for her younger sister too.

When the nurses came in, they tried to comfort what seemed to be a young woman who had lost her father to cancer. They were completely unaware that Nicole had beaten cancer to the punch and that her daddy had died by her own hands.

After arrangements were made and paperwork signed, Nicole left the facility, feeling like her whole world was crumbling around her. Her legs wobbled, and the nurses offered to call family members to come and drive her home. Orderlies had assisted her to her car; when they'd left, she sat there and cried.

Why had she done that? Why couldn't she control herself? Why was it so easy for her to take his life? She cried, knowing that he had passed on a burden to her that she'd now have to take with her to her grave. One of many.

* * *

Nicole looked down at the pillowcase and then stuffed it back into the red velvet bag. She had killed her father, for something that hadn't even happened. She thought that he had molested Tye and Fatimah too. She asked God to forgive her. But all she could hear ringing in her ears was Fatimah saying, "You reap what you sow." Nicole sighed, wiped her eyes, and slid down off the bed. Then she walked back over to her wardrobe to hide the one piece of evidence that proved she was truly a breathtaking beauty.

"Nicci, where are you? It's almost time." Aniyah said.

"Don't worry, I'm comin'." She wouldn't miss that for anything in the world.

"Well, hurry up, the limo will be here soon."

Nicole looked good. She wore the sexiest black halter dress; it hugged her coveted curves and accentuated her sexy legs. Everybody was meeting up at Daddy's house. Nicole's sisters and other family members had their cameras ready. Serena was dressed to kill. Nicole was proud of her; she had chosen well. She wore a sexy, hot pink, beaded minidress; it was backless, strapless, and she fit it like a glove. The dress sparkled like a jewel under the camera flashes and the lights, and Nicole thought that it was really going to look cute under the bright lights of Luscious in Velour. Serena wore high-heeled goddess shoes, which wrapped sensually up her calves. And she carried a small beaded clutch with a large pink, purple, and blue butterfly decorated in beads that sparkled like her dress.

The camera crew arrived a little while after Nicole. All of her sisters were there, and they all looked damn good. It was like prom night on Buckeye Road as everyone stopped and stared.

"What is going on?" Serena said, smiling.

"This is for you, baby doll," Nicole said.

Just then the Hummer limo came rolling down the street.

"Oh my god," Serena said as her face lit up like a Christmas tree.

Tye was there, and his eyes were as big and bright as Serena's. He was disappointed that he wouldn't be going, but he was so excited for her.

"That is niiiice," Tye said.

Serena and her friends giggled with delight as the Hummer parked in front of Daddy's house. Gretchen, Jada, Tootie, Meechie, Aishah, and Joy—those were six of Serena's closest friends. Serena had known them since grade school; these were her sisters, sisters hand picked by her. They screamed and giggled, as the limo's gull-wing doors opened up to reveal a lavish interior.

"Tye, look!" Serena squealed as she pulled her little brother by the arm and pushed him inside the Hummer.

The limo was luxurious: all-leather curved seats, strobe, fiber-optic lighting, and a full bar.

"Look at the flat screen!" Meechie said as she sunk into the plush seats. The camera rolled as they admired the upscale interior of the limo.

"This is so posh," Aishah said as she sat back and smoothed her hands across the leather.

"Hey, turn on the radio!" Joy yelled.

"Hey, it's time for us to go," Aniyah said, sticking her head into the Hummer. "Ooh this is nice," she said as she looked around.

Tye stepped out, and after all the picture taking had stopped, the Hummer pulled off with the ladies inside.

"Is the radio on? Turn it up," Tootie said.

"I can't believe you guys never—"

"Ssssh," everyone said to Serena."

Just then Mick Rock, a radio DJ from 107.9, said, "And I want to send a shout-out to Serena "Baby Doll" Turner. Happy twenty-first birthday, baby doll! From your family who loves you. Keep it hot, baby girl."

The girls screamed. Serena shook her head and started stomping and clapping.

"You almost missed it, Serena. With all that talking."

"What? I can't believe you guys kept this a secret," Serena said with a big ole grin on her face.

"Girl, puhleese! I didn't think I was gonna be able to hold it!" Aishah said as she laughed.

"I was so mad at y'all for not callin' or comin' to see me, and I couldn't reach y'all." The ladies all laughed. "This is gonna be so much fun! I love you, guys."

The ladies were having such a great time together, laughing and talking and catching up on old times.

"How is Eric?"

"Eric is history."

"Oh my god. Girl, what happened?"

"Tell ya later," Serena said as she winked at the camera man with a smile.

Serena's big night was going just as Nicole had planned. The family arrived shortly after Serena's limo arrived. Serena felt just like a movie star. As she entered the club, "Salute" by Fabolous and Lil Wayne blasted hard over the club's speakers. Serena could feel the bass pounding in her chest. The DJ announced: "Serena is in da building!" The crowd cheered. She was the center of attention, and she loved it.

Serena bounced and swayed her hips as she walked into the club. She bobbed her head and snapped her fingers. "Where's my sisters?" she said as she looked for them. The Turner sisters were in the building. They were some bad-ass sisters. Mariah was five months pregnant, and she was wearing a sexy electric blue tunic dress. Fatimah's dress was a simple red dress, but on Fatimah, it was on fire. Aniyah was still mad at Nathan, but she had every intention of going over Nathan's house to show him how sexy she looked in her sexy silver jeans and her black sequined blouse.

Nicole had arranged for a private buffet-style dinner for Serena's special guests. Drinks were on the house for those special guests also. Afterward, they headed downstairs and sang "Happy birthday to Serena." Around her favorite, a three tiered, strawberry cassata cake with whipped cream frosting.

Serena was having a great time. Nicole made sure of that, and one by one, her sisters left the club. Fatimah and Mariah went home to their families after giving Serena a kiss good-bye and wishing Serena one last happy birthday. Nicole left Serena and her friends and kissed her good-bye and wished her a happy birthday too. Serena hugged Nicole and wouldn't let go. She kissed her, thanked her, and told her that this was the best birthday she had ever had.

Aniyah couldn't believe it when she saw Matthew at the club. Nathan wasn't coming, but Matthew didn't know that. She was glad that Nathan hadn't shown up and she had hoped that if he had that Matthew would have stayed as far away from her as possible. But fortunately, Aniyah didn't have that to worry about.

"Hey, sexy." Matthew said as he walked up behind her and spoke directly into her ear. Aniyah recognized his voice immediately. Matthew smiled at her.

"What are you doing here?"

"I'm here with a few of my boys. I don't get out much, so I figured that this would be the perfect opportunity." Aniyah looked at Matthew.

He was smiling at her as if he hadn't done anything wrong, as if it was perfectly alright for him to show up at her baby sister's birthday party, unannounced, when he knew full well that Nathan was suppose to be there. "You wanna dance?" Matthew asked.

"No," she said as she shook her head "What are you doin' here?"

"I just told you."

"No, seriously Matthew. Why are you here? You knew that Nathan was suppose to be here." Aniyah said as she looked around nervously.

"Yea where is Nathan." Matthew asked looking around the club.

Aniyah sighed and looked at him

She watched him as he bit his bottom lip. She watched as his upper teeth combed through the soul patch below his bottom lip. He was so sexy that she couldn't look away.

"We've got to stop this?" Aniyah said, coming back to her senses. What if Nathan was here?"

"Yea, where is Nathan?" Matthew said pretending to look around for him. "Lemme guess, he's working."

"Yes, he is smart ass."

"Good man," Matthew said as he nodded, with a big sarcastic grin on his face. "So has anyone told you how sexy you look tonight?"

"As a matter of fact, yes."

"Hmmm." Mathew said as he rubbed his hands together. The club's overhead lights reflected off of the face of his watch making it shine. "Nathan has some competition on his hands."

"Believe me. Nathan has nothing to worry about."

"Says the woman who slept with me last Sunday." Matthew said, and smiled at Aniyah.

Aniyah stopped smiling and turned to walk away. Matthew grabbed her arm and apologized, "I'm sorry, Aniyah, I shouldn't have said that."

Matthew was so fine, and he could have had any woman that he wanted. She didn't know why he wouldn't just let this go.

"Matthew, I'm not talking to you anymore. I'm going to pretend that what happened between us never happened and go on with my life. I suggest you do the same."

Aniyah walked away and moved into the crowd. Matthew didn't follow her. She moved so far into the crowd of partygoers that she couldn't see Matthew at all.

Aniyah was the last of Serena's sisters to leave the club. She had kept an eye on Serena long enough. Nicole had arranged for the limo to pick Serena and her friends up after the party and drop them off at a nearby hotel downtown, a few blocks from the club. They'd stay there until one of the sisters picked them up Sunday afternoon.

Aniyah drove over to Nathan's house; she couldn't wait to see him. She was pretty upset with Nathan at first, but she was getting over it. Aniyah didn't bother to call Nathan first because she wanted to surprise him. She figured he would be excited to see her too.

Aniyah rang the doorbell. But Nathan didn't answer. Aniyah knocked on Nathan's door, and he seemed to take forever to answer the door.

"What's up? What took you so long?" Aniyah asked, when Nathan had opened up the door. Aniyah walked past him and into the house.

"I didn't even realize you were out here." Nathan said to Aniyah.

Aniyah looked up at Nathan and frowned as she walked in the doorway.

Aniyah turned to give Nathan a hug. But she didn't like the look on his face, he didn't look happy to see her.

"What's the matter with you?"

"What's the matter with you," Nathan said.

Aniyah moved a curl of red hair out of her face so that she could get a better look at Nathan. He wasn't smiling, and he looked more hurt than angry.

"What's going on?"

"Who's Matthew?"

"Are you still on that? I told you who Matthew was."

"Tell me the truth, Aniyah. Who is Matthew?"

"I told you Matthew was somebody I went to school with." Aniyah tried to act as if she was annoyed, but her mind was racing. Why was Nathan asking her this. Did he know anything?

Nathan sighed hard as if that was all that it took for him to keep his composure.

"Who was the dude I saw you with tonight?"

"What?" Aniyah asked. "When did you see me tonight? What are you talking about?"

"I went to the club tonight, and I saw you."

"Hold on a minute. What were you doing at the club tonight?"

"I wanted to surprise you."

"Why the would you have to surprise me? You've known about the party for a whole year. You were supposed to be there. I don't understand."

"Look, Aniyah, you know what I'm talkin' about."

"No. Really, I don't? My little sister had a surprise party that you have known about for a whole year. You were supposed to escort me to it. But you cancelled at the last minute. So what was the surprise supposed to be?"

"Aniyah, who was the man at the club?" Nathan asked again

"What man?"

"Aniyah, you know what man I'm talkin' about."

"Well, if you were there, then you should have come over and found out for yourself."

"Aniyah, get the fuck out of my house," Nathan said calmly.

"I'm not going anywhere," Aniyah said as she dropped her overnight bag on the floor and crossed her arms and stood her ground. Nathan had never put his hands on her before, and she didn't expect for him to do it tonight.

"Aniyah, I'm not playin' with you. I want you out."

"Nathan, are you breaking up with me?"

Nathan pressed his lips together tightly; his face was hot, and all he could see in front of him was Aniyah in the club with some dude all up in her face and grabbing her by the arm. He didn't know what they were talking about, but it looked heated from where he was standing. And he didn't look like just some casual acquaintance. Instinctively, he wanted to walk over to the two of them and bash that man's head in, but he'd said that he wouldn't allow a woman to cause him to lose his cool and as hard as it was for Nathan to keep that promise to himself, he was going to work hard to keep it.

"Nathan, are you breaking up with me?"

Nathan didn't answer. He was hurt and angry. He didn't even want an explanation. He just needed for Aniyah to get as far away from him as possible.

"It's cool. I've been through this shit before." Aniyah said to Nathan.

Nathan ignored Aniyah and opened his front door.

"Are you kicking me out?" Aniyah asked as she looked at Nathan daring him to say yes with her tone, but begging him to say no with her eyes.

"I want you out of my house." Nathan said calmly.

"So it's over?" Aniyah asked Nathan raising her voice.

"I need you to leave." Nathan answered as he smoothed his hand over his mouth, down his chin and over his goatee. He needed to keep his hand occupied. He wanted to hurt her. He wanted to put his hands on her.

"It's cool Nathan." Aniyah said and bit her bottom lip." I'll be broken hearted for a minute, but I'll get over it, and then I'll be with some other man doin' the same things I do to you." Why had she said that? As soon as those words had escaped her lips, she had wanted to take them back. She didn't know what had come over her. She couldn't explain it.

Nathan grabbed her bag with one hand and grabbed Aniyah by the arm with the other. He tossed her bag onto the front lawn, and it skidded along the grass. He dragged Aniyah down the first three steps as she fought to snatch her arm away, and then he flung her off the last two steps behind her bag. Aniyah landed on her knees and on the heels of her palms. Her palms were skinned and bleeding. Her jeans were intact, but her knees were sore and throbbing.

Aniyah cried out in pain. While still on her hands in knees, she turned and looked at Nathan as he stood in his doorway wearing his wife beater and his red boxers. Aniyah didn't say a word. They just looked at each other for a few seconds before he slammed the door. As Aniyah stood slowly, and dusted herself off, she wondered what in the world was she thinking, as guilty as she was. She wondered how different would the scenario have been if she'd told Nathan that it was Matthew that he'd seen her with at the club and that she had slept with him just one week ago. As she stood, she looked at Nathan's windows to see if he was looking out at her. He wasn't. She picked up her bag and walked to her car without even shedding a tear. She asked herself if she loved Nathan, and she had to answer "No," because if she had loved him, it wouldn't have been so easy to walk away.

Jermaine was so happy to be with Nicole. He had wondered if she'd ever see him again, and when she called him and invited him to her hotel room, he didn't know how to contain himself. She looked so good tonight, in that sexy black dress, the way her long dark curls fell on her shoulders as she moved her head. He couldn't wait for her to step out of that dress.

Nicole hadn't planned on inviting Jermaine up to her room, but she knew that somebody was coming, because she didn't want to sleep tonight. Jermaine just happened to be at the right place at the right time. Not to mention that he was looking so irresistibly good. So Nicole had agreed to spend the night with him and told him to meet her at her room.

As Nicole waited for Jermaine, she went over the highlights of the early morning in her mind. Nicole had looked into the envelopes of her youngest siblings. She knew who Serena's father was too, and it wasn't Otis or Ray; it was some white guy named Samson Xavier. Nicole could immediately see the resemblance. As much as she looked like her sisters, you could definitely tell that Serena was this man's child. There was something about the shape of Serena's face. She knew that Serena would be very disappointed. She was indeed the little Mulatto girl that everybody teased her about.

Mama had included pictures and a mini-bio on this man. Nicole shook her head at the sheer craziness of it all. Only their mama would do some silly shit like that. Nicole had to give her credit though. She was well informed about Serena's daddy. She knew what he did for a living, where he lived, where he worked, that he was married and had three children, and that Serena was his youngest. She even left a note for Serena, saying that she could contact him if she wanted and that she knew he'd like that. Nicole imagined how Serena would cry knowing that Otis wasn't her daddy. She knew that Serena would think that this disconnected her from her siblings somehow. Nicole would have to convince her that it didn't matter that she was 100 percent her sister, no matter who her daddy was.

Jermaine took Nicole's mind off the bizarre, craziness, that was, her life. She was going to let this young, dark, chocolate brotha with the clean bald head take her there again. He was happy to see her. And he intended to show her just how happy he was. Jermaine asked her to keep her heels on, and she did. She took her dress off herself; she didn't have time to see if he could work the ties and the straps. She let it slide to the floor as she looked Jermaine in the eyes.

Skin smooth like butter Dark and soft, Nicole stood in front of him. She had stood there posed sexily like a centerfold straight out of King magazine. "You are so beautiful." Jermaine said to Nicole. As sexy as she was he couldn't deny that she had such a pretty face. He stared into her large dark eyes. He watched as she seductively bit down on her bottom lip. Jermaine wanted to devour her. But he stood there drinking in her beauty, savoring it. He stared at her rounded, tear drop shaped breasts, nipples hard and protruding anticipating his hungry mouth, his wanting hands and the feel of skin against skin. Nicole smiled at him not a sweet smile, but the smile of a vixen or of a woman in heat.

"Mmmph. You look delicious," Jermaine said, as he licked his full and luscious lips. "Lie down and let me see if you taste as good as you look." He slid her thongs down with his teeth as she lifted her butt off the bed to help him. His lips tickled her skin as he used his teeth to gently slide her panties down on one side as he used his fingers on the other. He kissed and licked her inner thigh gently nibbling his way between her legs. He held her thick thighs in each of his hands and it looked as if he were eating watermelon. He massaged her butt in his hands as he stroked and licked and kissed her with his tongue. She threw her head back and closed her eyes. She liked the way he moaned as he licked her, and she liked how his hand moved up to her breasts as he feasted between her thighs. She liked how he teased her as she fought hard not to come. She watched him: his eyes open, his tongue in motion. She was soaked and throbbing, ready to receive him. He stuck two fingers inside her.

"Ooh," he said as he closed his eyes and let out a long sigh. "You're ready for me?" He made a come-hither motion with his finger while still inside her and played with her G-spot. Her body writhed with pleasure.

"Come on, baby," Nicole begged just above a whisper; he liked the way her lips moved when she said it. He liked the intoxicated look of ecstasy in her eyes.

But he said, "Not yet, baby."

He licked and sucked and stroked her, and her body shook and jerked multiple times. She cried out loud enough to make the walls tremble, but she didn't care; it felt so damn good. She didn't want this feeling to end; she wanted more. She had him stand in front of her with his hands behind his back as she put every inch of him in her mouth. She liked the way he threw his head back and closed his eyes as she caressed him with her mouth as if it was an oversized peppermint stick. "Ooh, Nicole you feel so damn good," Jermaine said. He was barely able to utter those words as he tried to fight the intense sensations that Nicole was sending through his body. She played with his manhood with her wet, warm mouth. Tongue teasing him and turning him on until he told her to stop. He lay on his back, and she mounted him like a Harley. She bucked and grinded on his erection as her sweet juices flowed down his shaft. He wasn't a lazy lover; he eased his pelvis up into her slowly, then faster, then harder. She bounced on him forcefully, gyrating and rotating her hips, holding her breasts in her hands as she looked at him and licked her sweet lips.

"Harder!" she said as their bodies collided together over and over again. They changed positions several times, because Jermaine wasn't ready for this night to end. When Jermaine finally came, he kicked and called out as if he was trying to fight the feeling. His body jerked and twitched against hers. He was right; he did make it worth her while. She enjoyed the show, and she smiled at him as she lay on her back and tried to let her heart rate slow down.

Jermaine plopped down on the bed next to her and said, "Did you come?"

Nicole said, "Nope. Wanna go again?"

Jermaine looked at her and smiled and said, "Give me a minute."

Nicole was exhausted, but she got up and went into the bathroom anyway. She washed herself up really good, brushed her teeth, and played with her hair. She was so tired, and she prayed that she'd be able to get some undisturbed, dreamless sleep tonight.

"Who is this?" Nicole said as she looked at the woman standing in her hotel room. She hadn't even noticed that Jermaine's hands were in the air.

"She's got a gun!" Jermaine said, motioning to the woman while his hands were still in the air.

"Huh?" Nicole said with a look of confusion on her face. This had to be some sort of a mistake, Nicole thought. This woman had entered the wrong room. "What's going on?"

"Put your hands up!" the woman said. She was noticeably nervous. Nicole could tell that she'd never done this before. "I said put your hands up!"

Nicole sighed; she didn't take this woman seriously. Jermaine was nervous as hell, and the fact that this woman may or may not have done this before didn't make him feel any better.

"Who are you? What do you want?" It was as if this woman was speaking to her in a foreign language, because Nicole acted as if she didn't know what put your hands up meant.

"Put your hands up, you whore! This will teach you to fuck with other women's husbands." Nicole listened to this woman's voice. Her words sounded as if they were rehearsed. She didn't sound as if she was comfortable using profanity either.

"Jermaine?"

"Don't look at me. She's not my wife." Jermaine said. He was unmarried. Not to mention that he didn't want any undue attention brought to him with this crazed woman waving a gun around.

"Who is your husband?" Nicole paid no mind to the woman, the gun, or her own nakedness. Clearly the woman had thought that she had or was having some sort of relationship with her husband and Nicole wanted to get to the bottom of it.

"Put your hands up! You, you, you, you bitch," she stammered, "I ask the questions here!"

Nicole didn't put her hands up. She was totally naked. And she had made no apologies for it. This woman had come into her hotel room in the wee hours of the morning.

"Who is your husband?" Nicole asked again sternly, pausing between each word as she directed the question to this stranger holding the gun.

"Put your hands up!"

"Who. Is. Your. Husband?" Nicole repeated.

"Put your hands up!"

"Why do you keep saying that?" Nicole asked; she was really becoming annoyed.

"Why? Because I want to see them."

"I'm naked, lady. What? Do you think I'm gonna pull a weapon out the crack of my ass? I'm naked."

Jermaine didn't say a word. He stayed out of it. He valued his life, and he didn't want to make the unstable woman angry.

Nicole yelled, "Who is your fuckin' husband?"

Nicole stood there in all of her naked glory, not a bit embarrassed, not a bit ashamed. But she was curious. She wanted to know whose wife this was standing in her hotel room wearing a light blue hoody and several layers of clothing. She wondered how in the world she was able to come to her hotel room unnoticed.

There was something very familiar about her though, something in her eyes.

"Do I know you?" Nicole asked as she tilted her head and looked at the woman.

"No," she answered, "but you know my husband."

Nicole stared at the woman with her eyes furrowed; she studied this woman's face, and then Nicole's eyes softened as she realized who this woman was.

"Kamar," Nicole called out as if she was calling out the answer during a board game, and as soon as this woman heard her son's name, she gasped. Nicole had said her baby's name. That piece-of-shit Darren had brought her son around his mistress, this whore, Nicole.

Nicole hadn't meant to say the little boy's name out loud. She knew it had struck a chord with this woman; she saw the change in her eyes.

"This is why I don't fuck with married men," Nicole said, as she looked over at Jermaine. It was as if she knew what was coming next.

The woman fired. The first bullet pierced Nicole chest, puncturing her lungs. Nicole's eyes widened, and she put her hand over the hole.

"Oh shit!" Jermaine cried out as he shook. He'd jumped as if he'd taken the bullet. Nicole's blood spattered on his bare chest and on his left arm. He was terrified. She'd shot her; she had really shot her.

Darren's wife closed her eyes and turned her head and squeezed off another shot. The second bullet dropped Nicole to her knees. Nicole couldn't breathe; her lungs had collapsed. She gasped for air as a pink frothy foam bubbled from her mouth. Blood poured out of her wounds, seeping through her clutched fingers, and formed an ever-widening ring on the beige carpet and around her naked body.

"Fuck, fuck, fuck!" Jermaine said as he looked over at Nicole's body, his hands still raised in the air. He wanted to help her, he wanted to kneel down beside her and help her, but he was too afraid to move. He looked over at the woman holding the gun as he shifted his wait nervously from foot to foot.

The pain was unbearable. Nicole didn't know whether to pray to live or pray to die. Her breathing was shallow; she looked and sounded as if she was drowning. The woman dropped the gun on the carpet and began to cry. It was bad, really bad. Jermaine didn't know what to do. He kneeled down at Nicole's side, trying to put his hands over her wounds, trying to stop the blood. But there was no use. She was dead. This stranger had killed her.

"She's dead."
"Who's dead?"
"Nicci Turner."
"Hell naw! You lyin.'"
"I'm serious, dude."
"How you know?"
"I've got my sources. But I'm only telling you. The family doesn't even know it yet."

"Aniyah?" Mariah said to her sister.
"Yea, it's me." Aniyah said, her voice dry and sleepy. "What is it?"
"Is Nathan with you?"
"No," Aniyah said as she was reminded that she and Nathan were through.
"Stay there, Carl and I will come and get you."
"I'm not at home." Aniyah answered. "Why? What's wrong?"
"We need you to—." Mariah stopped herself. She didn't want her sister to drive, especially not by herself. "Where are you, Aniyah?"
"I'm over a friend's house." Aniyah answered. She was still half asleep.
"Aniyah honey, I need you to wake up. Something has happened. Are you with someone who can bring you downtown."
"Why? What's goin' on?" Aniyah asked. Mariah could tell that she'd gotten her sister's attention. She can hear it in Aniyah's voice.
"I need you to have your friend bring you to Metro Hospital."
"What? Why?" Aniyah said. She sat up straight in the bed and rubbed her eyes.
"Can your friend bring you? Or do you need Carl and I to come and get you?" Mariah was calm. Aniyah was scared.
"Mariah what's going on?" Aniyah said. Mariah could hear the fear in Aniyah's voice.
"I'll tell you when you get here."

Mariah had the task of gathering the family together for the bad news. She'd also be the one to tell them of the death of her beloved sister Nicole. She wailed hysterically when the hospital called her to tell her the terrible news. She cried so loudly that it woke up her sleeping children, and they began to cry. It was surreal. She had just seen her sister; she had just talked to her and touched her. How could she be dead?

The good news was that the woman who killed Nicole was in police custody. She had tried to kill herself, but the gun jammed. And she couldn't bring herself to leave the hotel room. It turns out that Darren was so busy obsessing over Nicole, that he didn't even realize that some other woman that he had been seeing was obsessing over him. That was the woman who had been calling his home and harassing his wife. Not Nicole. But Nicole was the woman whose name she knew. Nicole was the woman he had been texting, e-mailing, and sending flowers to, and she was the woman fucking her husband on the many sex tapes that she'd found hidden within the confines of her family home.

One by one, family members piled into the small, cramped waiting area. Nicole was dead, but they didn't know it yet. Mariah would wait until everyone arrived. Twenty people were in that room, sleepy, scared, and confused. Each of them was asking what was going on.

"Is everybody here?" Aniyah asked; she was nervous, and the suspense was killing her.

"Where's Nicci?" Serena said.

Mariah looked at Serena as she held her lips tightly together, and she turned away from her because her eyes began to water.

"No!" Aniyah said as she shook her head and clasped her hand to her mouth.

"Where is she?" Serena cried.

"Mariah?" Fatimah said as she looked into her sister's eyes, hoping that what they all feared wasn't true. Mariah shook her head and looked down at her feet as her husband rubbed her back.

"Oh my god! Oh my god!" Tye screamed as he cried. His cries of mourning and disbelief sent chills right through their bodies.

Everyone screamed and cried and held on to each other.

Tangie fainted; she fell to the floor like a ton of bricks, hitting her head on the edge of the wooden arm of one of the couches in the waiting area. She was out cold. Some of the hospital staff rushed in to help her. The rest of their family was too engrossed in their own grief, to turn their attention to Tangie

"Darren killed her!" Serena cried. "Darren killed my sister!"

It was such an ugly Sunday. The sky was gloomy and gray, and the clouds were dark and menacing. It was as if the sky was in mourning too. Everyone stayed at Tangie's house. She was taking Nicole's death really hard. It was impossible for her to change or to erase all the pain and the hurt that she had caused. And it was so hard for Tangie to apologize, but to Nicole it would have made such a huge difference if she would have at least tried. But to apologize is to admit guilt and Tangie had never been one for taking responsibility for her actions. Otis was devastated. His firstborn daughter was gone. The girls had never seen him cry, and to see him breakdown that way was very hard to watch.

Granny tried to console Tye as much as she could, but she was overwhelmed with grief too. She couldn't believe the week that they were having. She'd thought to herself that if the Lord only allows you to go through that which you can bear, then she had to be a super strong woman to deal with this. Nicole had always told Mariah that she wanted a small private ceremony, with just family and a few close friends. Mariah would go to Charisse personally and give her the news. Carl had asked why her. Why did she have to have this responsibility?

Mariah had answered, "Because my sister wanted me to."

Even as the facts came to light, Serena and Tye had blamed Darren for Nicole's demise. Everbody did, really. They believed that Darren however indirectly, had contributed to Nicole's untimely death.

Nicole's death was a media spectacle especially because the circumstances surrounding her death was so scandalous. It had leaked that Nicole was gunned down stark naked, in a hotel room with her young lover, by the wife of her ex-lover. It was so degrading to her memory. Those strangers didn't know the type of person that Nicole was. So instead, she was portrayed as a dead whore who had gotten what she deserved.

No one knew that she never would have dated Darren if she had known that he was married. The media wasn't aware that Nicole had ended the relationship when she'd discovered that he was a married man. They didn't know that Nicole was a beautiful confident woman who didn't need another woman's husband to make her feel whole. All they knew was that she was a dead woman who's choices had led to her untimely death. So any other facts were irrelevant.

On Monday, Fatimah didn't go to a divorce lawyer as she had planned. Instead, she went with her sisters to make funeral arrangement for Nicole. Fatimah couldn't stop crying because of the guilt that ate away at her. The words, "You reap what you sow." And, "Maybe they should put that on your tombstone," echoed in her head. She had said those wicked words just a few short days ago. She hated herself for not taking the time to tell her sister that she loved her and that she was so, so sorry for being so cruel. Now it was too late. Nicole was gone forever.

Tangie wanted to die. Her firstborn was gone. It would have only taken a few seconds for her to tell her daughter how much she loved her and how sorry she was for all the lies and deceit and for the pain she had inflicted on her daughter. But now it was too late. Nicole had been taken from her, and she was gone forever.

There was no reading of the will. Nothing dramatic like you'd see in the movies. Nicole had left a copy of her will in a sealed envelope along with other important documents with Mariah. In addition to those papers, Nicole had left Mariah two videotapes. Nicole had told Mariah that she'd like for her immediate family to view them if ever something happened to her. Mariah had accepted these things without ever imagining that she would have to open them someday. Mariah invited Granny, Mama, and the rest of her siblings over her house to watch it. It was intended to give them comfort. But no one could stop the tears from flowing. They loved Nicole dearly, and they missed her already.

"Hi, guys!" Nicole said with a wave and a smile. "If you're watching this, then I must be dead."

Serena started crying even though Nicole was smiling and had said it in as comical a way as possible. Then Nicole pointed at the screen and said, "Stop crying, Serena." Nicole was about 25 five years old in this videotape, before Tamani, before Darren. A young woman with a seemingly full life ahead of her. Serena looked up at the screen and wiped her eyes with both of her hands. "I want to start off by saying that I love each and everyone of y'all. I don't have any money, but if I could, I'd leave Aniyah my confidence, Serena my maturity, Fatimah my heart, and Mariah, I'd give you my resilience. To my baby brother, I'd like to give my industriousness. I want you to be a strong, productive man, and I want you to stay out of those streets. You hear me?"

Tye answered, "Yes," Under his breath.

"To my mama," Nicole said with a sigh, "I leave my love and my forgiveness, something I couldn't give to you while I was alive." Mama cried. "Fatimah, I ain't mad at chu. Sisters fight, right? I still love you. Hopefully, we mended some fences and I died with a closer relationship with you." Nicole smiled into the camera and started talking to the person filming her off camera for a second. Nicole went on to leave a special message for her grandmother, and she reiterated how much she loved all of her family with all of her heart and despite all of their issues, she wouldn't have traded them for the world. Mariah had turned off the video when she started leaving messages to Daddy Otis. Mariah would take it by their house later. The family had agreed to look at the second video a little later on. It was too much for them to bear all at once.

Carl was concerned about Mariah. She didn't look good. She didn't feel good either, but she kept that to herself. Carl was already worried about her and all of the stress she had been under this week. It was true that this had been a week like no other week. That's why it should have been no surprise to Mariah when she'd discovered exactly how much money Nicole was worth. She'd almost fainted when she'd discovered how opulently endowed her sister was. Mariah had absolutely no idea. She wondered how shocked her family would be by all the wealth that Nicole had attained and who she'd left it to.

Nathan had called Aniyah and apologized about the way he had treated her. He gave his condolences to her and her family and told her that he wanted to stop by to be with her in her time of need. He told her that he still loved her and he wanted her back. Hakeem had called Serena several times to wish her a happy birthday, and he'd sent her a gift and a dozen roses to her mama's house. Serena continued to rebuff Eric's advances, and then Eric eventually stopped calling her.

Tye's phone rang, and he went into his sister's living room to answer it.

"Yea, wuz up?"

"Ready to do this shit, nigga?"

"Hell yea." Tye answered.

"Let's get dat mu'fucka."

Mariah's doorbell rang, and Jason came in with his newborn daughter in his arms and said to Fatimah, "We need to talk." Fatimah held her composure; apparently, Jason didn't know how ignorant he was.

So much had happened in that one week; they had learned, they had loved, and they had lost. The sisters had discovered things about themselves in this past week that most people don't learn about themselves in a lifetime. They discovered the woman that they really were inside when the pressure was on, and they had lost someone very special to them. Beautiful and tragically complexed Nicole, The Headturner . . .